BLUEBEARD'S BRIDE

BLUEBEARD'S BRIDE

ROBERTA COTTAM
KATHRYN COTTAM

Fox Tale
PRESS

Bluebeard's Bride

Story by: Roberta Cottam
Novel by: Roberta Cottam & Kathryn Cottam
Copyright © 2014

Cover illustration © 2014 by Roberta Cottam

Book design by Laura Wrubleski

Print Edition: September 2014
ISBN: 978-0-9921020-4-3

Ebook Edition: October 2014
ISBN: 978-0-9921020-3-6

Published: 2014

Published by: Fox Tale Press

Fox Tale
PRESS

www.thefoxtalepress.com

For our family,
with whom we share love
and blood.

1896

Dearest Reader,

I leave behind this simple epistle as a testimony that the extraordinary events I witnessed during the fading hours of this century were most certainly true. While there has been little mention of what occurred in North Yorkshire in the popular press, I wish to dispel any rumour mongering and transcribe a complete and accurate version of the events. This is my account.

Yours, Margaret

IT ALL BEGAN the day I received a letter from my sister's husband: brief and scrawled in haste, he described Helen's death as 'sudden and tragic'. His rough handwriting, smeared where my tears had bled into the ink, failed to explain how she had lost her life a mere five days ago, at twenty-eight years of age.

Enclosed within the envelope was a photograph of my niece, Lucille. I studied it as the train rattled towards North Yorkshire; although outdated — Lucy appearing no more than four, yet turning seven come winter — I was grateful. It was a touchstone of delight folded inside terrible tidings.

In Lucy's complexion, I saw little trace of her father's dark looks; Ford bore hair and a beard so black they shone nearly blue. But Lucy looked every bit a descendant of a Jaye, and I wondered if her freckled cheeks had now cleared to ivory, or if her strawberry locks had deepened to auburn like her mother's, or darkened to chestnut as had mine.

It was four years since I had last seen my niece. I recalled Christmas dinner at my sister's Syndenham townhouse in '92, where Lucy — then not yet two — toddled about in a miniature sailor dress trimmed with gold braid, an homage to her father's naval career. Other officers in epaulets with wives in glittering gowns, toasted Johnathan Ford, and Helen beamed with pride for her husband. Following upon the hard years since we'd lost our father, I had felt hope for the Jayes that Christmas. Our family, whittled to three orphaned girls, would now strengthen and grow.

While my younger sister, Rosie, and I sipped port and ate brandied cherries, we dreamed of future nieces and nephews. That December, lavishing Rosie and I with expensive gloves and linens, there was no indication that, only a few weeks into the new year, Ford would suddenly leave the fleet and sell his London estate. The following February he moved our sister and niece to a great house in North Yorkshire, taking with him that which was more precious to us than any brown paper package tied with a branch of holly.

I returned Lucy's photograph to its home, tucked between the pages of *Jane Eyre*, and slid the book into my carpet bag. I had received no photograph of Helen, and, with a bitter-sweet heart, ached to smell her scent in the house and touch the trinkets that she called her own.

Seated beside me, Rosie rested her head against the window as the train thundered north. She also had received a photograph of Lucy (along with an equally abruptly worded letter), which she had trimmed and set into our late mother's locket which hung about her neck. Fingering the silver locket now, she stared out at fields of meadow foxtail and spear thistle, the passing view blurred by the speed of the engine so that it looked like a bolt of green watered silk, the pigment marbled and bled dry in places. Tightening my travel cloak about my shoulders, I curled into Rosie's side and rested my cheek on the rough tweed of her jacket.

The train carried us closer to Blueford Manor.

I awoke.

Perhaps the train shifted or a gust of cold air caught my attention. Whatever it was, it caused me to awaken. It was now dusk outside and my neck was stiff from the awkward angle at which I had fallen asleep next to Rosie. I stretched my sore muscles and was startled to see a man was now seated opposite us in the compartment.

It was evident from the start that he was a local parson. He wore a simple thin black suit that was worn at the knees and elbows. There was a black hat upon his head that was frayed about the brim. His neck and hands and cheeks were tanned from the sun, as though he had spent a great deal of his forty or so years out of doors. His hair was dark and creases spider-webbed the corners of his eyes, revealing how many hours of his life he had given to reading. As he did now.

However, he must have felt my eyes upon him for he glanced up from his book and studied me for several seconds with dark brown eyes. I could feel myself flush under his appraisal and so I cleared my throat to relieve my discomfort.

"Good evening," I said.

He gave a subtle nod, then returned to his book. Somewhat surprisingly I found myself annoyed by the ease at which I had been dismissed.

"What are you reading?" I asked.

He didn't answer immediately; instead he placed his finger on the page as though to mark his place. Only then did he respond by holding aloft his book so that I might read the spine.

THE COLONISATION OF BATS AND OTHER NOCTURNAL CREATURES.

"Bats?" I inquired, "I shouldn't like to encounter such vermin."

"I assure you they are quite gentle," he said, settling the book once more in his lap. And then as if to reassure me further, "they're somewhat a hobby of mine."

"Is your parish in North Yorkshire?" I inquired. He raised an eyebrow and I gestured to the newspaper at his side which indicated its region of origin.

"Yes, Harrowgate," he stated.

"Why, that's where we are bound. Myself and Rosamund," I said, gesturing to the sleeping girl at my side. "Our sister lives there. Or rather, lived there." I felt the words wanting to catch in my throat and so I continued with haste, "You may have heard of her. Helen Ford of Blueford Manor?"

He thought for a moment and then shook his head.

"I have not met a woman by such a name, although I know Blueford Manor well. It is but a half hour walk from the church across the moors to that location."

I was disappointed that he had no knowledge of Helen, for I was thirsty for information of my sister and her final days.

"I'm Margaret," I said, holding out my gloved hand, "Meg to friends."

"Reverend Carlisle Farrow," he said, taking my hand in his warm grasp. I expected that the familiarity of names would open to more conversation. But it did not. Once he had released my fingers he reopened his book and returned to reading. I glanced over at Rosie to see that she was still asleep, and so opened my reticule and glanced at my pocket watch. We still had an hour before we were to arrive.

I leaned my head back against the cushions and closed my eyes. But I did not sleep.

Neither Rosie nor I had been invited to Blueford Manor, until now in the circumstance of our sister's death. The house which had once captivated me — causing me to daydream about the opulence that was Helen's life — now seemed insignificant in comparison to the mystery of her death. In the past few days I had found little comfort in sleep and rare solace in work; I only had an appetite for the truth behind the words that comprised Ford's letter.

The country manor came into view set against a series of low rolling hills furred with blue spruce. At the front of the house, the ridge fell away to an indigo river that sparkled like a string of cut-glass beads. A flock of swans speckled the water's surface, like bright sequins stitched to a swath of silk. Enormous stone bricks composed the house which, grey-blue in colour, added to the overall effect that Blueford Manor was cast in eternal twilight.

It was grand in its design — built as an homage to Art Nouveau with flowing lines and violent curves — consisting of two stories, one row of round windows on either side of the entrance and a row of six lined across the upper level.

Four thin chimneys sprouted at each of the roof's corners, like hat pins punched into a cushion. Each chimney pot was built in a spiral shape, and only upon close inspection could one see that they were constructed with a different number of bricks, making each unique in character. But the most remarkable aspect of the house was its glass cupola. The dome rose like a giant cage crinoline stacked upon the roof. It was fashioned out of latticed wrought iron and thousands of glass panes, save for one section where the glass was missing, leaving a dark hole. Despite its short life, it was apparent my sister's house was succumbing to disrepair.

Helen had written in one of her many letters that the manor's construction was begun by a Lord Benedict Blewe in '66, a successful tea merchant who never married and intended to live out his last days at the manor. Inspired by the Palm House of Kew Gardens in London, Blewe designed the glass dome to both reflect his modern tastes, and — quite practically — create a solarium where he could enjoy his favourite tropical plants, tea species included.

When Lord Blewe died before the house was even furnished, his heirs sold the manor to my sister's husband. It was at that time that Ford anglicised Blewe's name and added his own to create Blueford Manor. Helen and her husband's belongings from the London townhouse had barely filled Blueford's rooms. *Baby Lucy's cries echo in the empty chambers*, Helen had written, when telling us of her new home. It was the first indication that the luxurious life Helen had left behind in London might not be equaled at her new home in Yorkshire.

Though Ford was older than Helen, he was still very much in his prime. But having taken his leave of the fleet and finding no new occupation, I wondered if the current state of the manor's disrepair was a result of Ford's waning funds. Or simply, a lack of engagement with life — or even his wife.

In one letter to Rosie and I, Helen questioned Ford's choice of this home to raise their daughter. According to Helen, Ford had no interest in dressing the house with finery, or in hosting either seasonal parties or hunting weekends. Nor would he even consider inviting her sisters for Yuletide celebrations. Instead, he closeted himself in the parlour, converting it to a make-shift study, littering the chairs with naval charts when they should have instead sat guests.

As the carriage Ford hired to meet us at the station turned into the drive, a phalanx of orange and brown asters welcomed us to the manor. Hedgerows of oak and ash grew wild and unfettered. Helen had bemoaned on more than one occasion the meagrely maintained grounds. She was a passionate lover of wildflowers and a skilled water colourist, and she alone had taken on the task of planting bulbs and taming shrubs. But the extensive grounds proved too much for one woman's touch.

Over time, Helen's letters arrived with less frequency, which both Rosie and I took as a sign of her happiness. We had been warned by friends that with Helen's move the relationship between us sisters would change. And so, somehow Helen's faltering communication over the past years had simply led us to believe it was the distance that unravelled the closeness we three sisters had previously maintained. We imagined Helen at breakfasts in the garden, rowing on the river, at society dances under a dome through which starlight sparkled with more delicacy than a Venetian chandelier. We felt reassured by her silence and Rosie and I set about establishing our own lives in London.

But then a year had passed during which Rosie and I did not hear from our older sister. Our letters went unanswered. The occasional telegram was ignored.

Until last fall when a missive arrived in which Helen confided life at Blueford Manor was trying her nerves. Ford's habits remained unchanged, spending his days in solitude and his nights restless as he walked the moors. Helen's loneliness was near unbearable. And then Lucy fell ill with whooping cough.

By Helen's account, she begged Ford to return to London so their daughter would have access to the nation's best doctors. But Ford refused to leave Blueford Manor, insisting instead that Lucy recover at home. Helen assured me she would keep both Rosie and I abreast of our niece's condition. We both offered to go to Blueford and assist with Lucy, but Helen declined with vehemence, not wanting to risk contagion. That was six months ago, and the last I ever read in my sister's handwriting. Or indeed, the last I ever heard — in a manner — her voice. For the next communication from Blueford regarding my sister, was to announce her death.

Blueford Manor's carved wooden doors depicted two rearing bears with open jaws. After Rosie and I waited nearly ten minutes they were opened by a girl anything but blue; her auburn hair was tied under a brightly checked kerchief which matched the berry colour of her lips. A pink flush ruddied her snowy cheeks.

The girl greeted us with a smile and asked us to call her Edye; by her accent I judged her a southerner. She apologised for not greeting us in a more immediate fashion for she had been upstairs preparing our room. She reached for our cases but Rosie and I shooed away her offer, retrieving our own carpet bags, and followed her into the house.

Her forearms were strong and her frame stocky, a waist defined only by the sash of her apron. She was how I imagined Cinderella to be, on those nights my father — and later Rosie — had read me the tale. Exquisite in her features, but quite capable of cleaning a castle from top to bottom. Much to the annoyance of my older sister, I would question the illustrations in our book: if Cinderella were indeed as thin as a broomstick, how could she have possibly kept house? I decided the heroine depicted in my storybook was better suited to the pages of *Godey's Lady's Book*, and instead I imagined a Cinderella the likeness of some buxom beauty as the one who stood before me now.

The entrance hall was surprisingly dark, the natural light blotted out by heavy drapes over each window. I suppose I expected the elaborate glass dome to cast light here, but no. It obviously capped the ballroom and was hidden behind the set of closed double doors — also carved in the elaborate, flowing lines of Art Nouveau — that were directly ahead. Only here, stags with locked antlers echoed the posture of the bears found on the front doors.

Two free standing candelabras, six candles apiece, provided the only light in the hallway, illuminating the room's single furnishing, a marble-topped oval table in the centre of the parquet floor. Carved into the table's wooden pedestal were two swans, their necks intertwined so that their heads met beak to beak at the table's broad base. A chipped marble vase sat on the tabletop. Empty of flowers it looked more like an urn. Indeed, the entire room looked funereal. In mourning for Helen, black fabric covered two large wall-mounted mirrors.

Rosie and I fell into step behind Edye as she mounted the staircase to the right of the ballroom doors. It eventually terminated at the end of a long hallway that ran the length of the second floor, north to south.

The hallway was panelled in wood, and the closed doors that lined both sides were carved in the same manner of the walls, making them almost imperceptible. Each wall panel and door featured two carved hares sitting back to back, each looking over its shoulder at its mate, wild-eyed.

Had there been any sound from within the manor, it would have been dampened by the hallway's plush carpet, decorated with interlaced vines sprouting broad, veined leaves. But as it was, it was eerily quiet. Standing like a sentinel mid-hallway was a grandfather clock, but even its pendulum was stilled.

Everything was pristine — Edye's hand, no doubt — but

the polished wood panels and spongy carpet was barely worn. As though the house had sat unused over the past years rather than being home to a child about to turn seven. I wondered if Lucy's bedroom was on this floor. Or indeed if Lucy ever ran helter-skelter down this hallway, dandelion seeds caught in her petticoats and sprigs of grass tangled in her hair.

"Are Lucy's rooms on this floor?" I asked, startling Rosie who also must have noticed the unnatural silence.

"Yes, Miss Jaye, along with the master's rooms," she said, gesturing towards the south end of the hall. "As was the missus'," Edye said, crossing herself. "God bless her soul, though of course I didn't know her well."

I thought it an odd remark. As the sole servant in the house, surely she would have had a great deal of contact with my sister?

Edye stopped before a door on the right, or west side, of the hall and withdrew a heavy ring of keys from her apron pocket. I wondered why the room should be locked when our arrival was expected, and the house virtually empty of habitants and help.

But before I could ask, Edye pushed open the door and stepped back for us to enter. "Miss Jaye. Miss Jaye," she nodded as we entered.

Afternoon light flooded the room, pouring across a rug woven with lily pads. Once we were all inside, Edye pulled closed the door. She nodded towards some fresh water for washing and wood for the fire, although the sun had adequately warmed the room. She explained dinner would be served at seven.

Then she left as quick as we had entered, leaving Rosie to collapse onto the four poster bed, unlace her boots and drop them onto the carpet with a soft thud.

"It is too strange to be at this place without Helen," she sighed, and a tinge of sadness unraveled the edges of her words.

I shrugged off my cloak, unpinned my hat, and set them on a chair. Then I joined Rosie on the bed, laying my head upon her shoulder. Hot tears pricked the corners of my eyes.

"It is too difficult to believe she is gone," I said into Rosie's red hair. Despite the fact that we were both quite aware of our sister's passing, there was some small echo of hope in each of our hearts that upon arrival, this truth might prove to be false. The knowledge that Helen was gone — forever — renewed a terrible tightness in my chest.

When Helen wed, I was fourteen, and Rosie eleven. We were schooled at the Sisters of Mary, a private school in east London which was paid for with the dwindling funds left by our father's estate. When he died the year prior Helen's wedding, our sister took nothing, deeming Rosie's and my education the most prudent use of our father's earnings. For Rosie and I would still need to each find a career if we wanted to avoid one of London's many workhouses.

Upon our father's death, Helen became head of the family at the tender age of seventeen. She had searched for employment. What she found instead was Johnathan Ford, and was married within the year.

I had wondered at the time if she truly loved him, or if he were simply a harbour in a very difficult storm. He was twenty years her elder, though never before married, unless one considered the sea his bride. But clear from the onset was his depth of love for her. The wedding at St Paul's Cathedral was extravagant, flowers filling every spare recess. And of great delight to me, Helen wore an original creation hand-sewn by the *House of Callot Soeurs*, who were the height of fashion in Paris at the time. With childish enthusiasm I had begged my future brother-in-law to buy me one of their dresses as well. He had obliged, for in those days he would do anything to please his wife, especially if it involved her younger sisters.

For the occasion, I made my own hat. It was my first creation, clumsy in its design, the crown too tall and the brim too short to balance the height. I used straw instead of silk, and a dreadful combination of orange and yellow ribbons. But its construction was perfect for I had learned to sew before I had even learned to read. Our father worked in a garment factory, and was as quick with handwork as he was with the machines. In the evenings, he brought home piecework for me to earn a coin or two. And as the years went on, he taught me the craft so that he might instead rest his eyes by the fire and regale us with stories of adventure.

Those evenings were the favourite part of Rosie's childhood, feeding her love of literature.

The nuns at Sisters of Mary noted Rosie's natural affinity for reading, and encouraged her to pursue teaching. Rosie first helped the nuns, assisting the younger classes of students. Two years later, at sixteen and as headstrong as any of the Jayes, she secured work as governess to the Willis family, caring for the three children of a wealthy banker.

My aptitude for sewing developed into a love of fashion. I was inspired by the ladies' dresses I saw on the London streets surrounding our school, so lavish compared to the black habits of the schoolroom. I soon became interested in the styles of Paris and Milan. But I had no desire to become a factory worker like my father, for it had aged him well before his time. So instead, at fifteen, I sought out an apprenticeship in millinery. Though typically a man's trade, it did not take me long to earn a position at Hendry's Millinery, with the added bonus of a room overhead when I turned eighteen.

Two years later, my *damas dentelle* hats were in demand, bringing new business to Hendry's modest street corner shop. Frequently, my creations graced London high life, and were featured on pages of the *Lady's Quarterly* and the *London Woman's Herald*. Twice a year I was privileged to travel to Paris for supplies.

This attention to my career now seemed a very dear cost for losing Helen to the shadows of Blueford Manor.

"Margaret, Rosamund, welcome to Blueford Manor."

My sister's widower sat in a wingback chair at the head of the dining room table, his back to the fire. He wore no dinner jacket and his cravat was loosely tied at the open neck of his shirt collar. I had never seen him not in uniform; even on his wedding day he dressed in naval colours, his dinner jacket trimmed with braid. Now, he looked every bit the romantic poet, as though his days were spent chasing the muse with a feather quill. But a poet he was not — for there was no spark of inspiration in his eye, no lust for life. He wrestled only grief's stranglehold.

Ford half-rose as we entered, one large hand gripping the arm-rest. With the other hand, he gestured towards two place settings at either side of his. I pulled out the chair to his left and sat.

Despite the sudden loss of his wife, Ford looked to have hardly aged. If widowhood had twisted his heart till it were as taut as knotted twine, there was no trace of it in his face for he looked not a day older than he had that December in Syndenham. No grey dusted his jet black hair, nor his trimmed beard. His clean-shaven neck was that of a young man's, lean and well muscled. Few creases branched from the corners of his eyes as he watched me smooth my skirt and pull myself up to the table.

Rosie sat opposite. In the candlelight, her black dress and red hair, pulled tight in a bun, receded into the shadows, giving her pale face the appearance of a round moon hung in a midnight sky.

We dined in the macabre company of a flock of ravens: in each of the room's corners four rooks carved in cherry wood perched on fluted corbels, struggling to fly, their wooden wings forever rooting them in place. The ravens pointed their beaks to the panelled ceiling inlaid with a copper sunburst, which should have shed a warm glow, had the gas lamp at the centre of the ceiling been operational. Instead, in the low candlelight, the lamp appeared as though it were a sickly lily pad sunk in a stagnant pond.

"Will Lucy not be joining us?" Rosie asked, noticing no fourth setting. The table was sparsely set, and the room itself next to bare, but for its mahogany dining table and six mismatched chairs.

Ford sat back in his chair and regarded Rosie. "Edye will

bring her down shortly. I wanted to speak with you both first, privately." He paused to lean into the halo of candlelight and stare at my sister. "You are an uncanny echo of Helen."

Rosie blushed; it was true she had grown into Helen's charms, though I often failed to see her as anything but a child.

Ford broke his gaze on my sister by offering her wine, an inexpensive looking Madeira in a green bottle. Then he reached across the table to fill my glass. "You'll excuse my pedestrian service skills — Edye has just joined the household. You may ring her in the night if you need anything. She has a room at the back of the kitchen."

"My sister and I are more than accustomed to looking after ourselves," I smiled with politeness. "And we're here to look after whatever preparations need to be made for Helen." The memory of our father's funeral flipped through my mind; I saw the simple wooden casket on which Helen had painted flowers that would never fade, and inside, placed on his breastbone, Rosie's poem about our parents united in heaven's household. Pinned to the lapel of my father's jacket was a little fabric rose I'd sewn, so that he might be appropriately dressed to meet out mother. My throat tightened as I asked, "When is the service?"

Ford filled his own glass and set down the wine bottle before answering. "Helen's burial has already taken place."

There was a long moment of silence as though some creature hovering in the dark corners had swallowed all sound. And then Rosie spoke —

"What do you mean?" she cried, a deep frown puckering her brow as though a single thread were being pulled to gather her flesh together.

I found my voice as well, and it was laced suspicion: "Why so hasty?"

Ford's next words hung on the air as heavy as the damask curtains in our bedroom. "It was not a Christian burial." He paused as the truth of this weighed on Rosie and me. "Your sister took her own life."

2

"I DON'T BELIEVE YOU," I said, my voice brittle and unfamiliar. It was shock enough that my elder sister, so vital in my memory, was dead, let alone by her own hand. I pressed my fingertips into the wooden tabletop, slowing my heartbeat and drawing in strength. "I beg your pardon, Johnathan, but I cannot believe Helen took her own life."

"I saw her myself." His voice tumbled over the dinner table as thunder over a plain, his eyes fixed on the orb of candlelight. "A horror no husband should ever experience."

I glanced across at Rosie. Tears streaked across her cheeks like rain on a window pane. I wanted to say something to soothe her, but my thoughts were as scattered as a box of straight pins spilled on the floor. I wanted to challenge the words Ford spoke, but I stilled my tongue with a sip of wine.

"What happened?" Rosie asked at last, her voice giving no indication of the grief she was feeling.

"Last Friday night, Helen threw herself off the roof."

I coughed on the wine, spilling it down the front of my blouse. The dark red droplets disappeared into the black fabric as Rosie clasped a hand over her mouth, as though to prevent herself from speaking. Or screaming.

Ford continued his tale. When Helen hadn't appeared after the dinner bell, he had been angry. He had waited close to thirty minutes and then went looking. She was not in her room, nor in Lucy's. In fact, he had been unable to find her anywhere in the house.

But outside. That was where he had found her body. Sometime around sunset, a bag of shattered bones lying on the front steps.

As her body was too broken for viewing — and for their daughter's sake — he chose a swift and private burial. Helen was laid to rest on the estate, out behind the orchard. Ford felt it fitting for Helen had loved her gardens, especially the orchard in spring where she would sit for hours and paint apple and plum blossoms on stretched canvas.

"But why?" I finally asked, when Ford had stopped speaking. "Why would she do such a terrible deed?"

Ford swallowed a mouthful of wine. "Helen was unhappy. It grieved her to be away from London. Away from the two of you. But we could not return. Lucy's health requires we remain here."

As he fell silent once more, I was reminded of the bear carved in the front door that had silently roared our arrival. As in his letter announcing Helen's death, Ford spoke few words. Then, thankfully, he continued. "Leaving London caused her great sadness," he confided, "though she rarely expressed her true feelings regarding this matter."

"Surely it was an accident?" I said, "She may have misjudged the edge — "

"I assure you it was no accident," Ford interrupted, his voice hard. "She was very familiar with the layout. And besides, you forget that I was there."

I studied my hands. Helen had often expressed her frustration with living in such a remote location. But seldom sadness. Or at least if she had felt this way, she had told neither Rosie nor myself. In fact, she often wrote of the fun she and Lucy had despite their isolation. In her letters, she described picnicking by the river, crowns that could be made of daisies, the magnificent stars that couldn't be seen under the yellow street lamps of London.

If either Rosie or I had ever suspected Helen was capable of taking her own life, we would have been on the first train out of London. But if it was not sadness that claimed her life, the only alternative was murder and that was almost too chilling upon which to dwell…

"I should like to see Lucy now," Rosie said, in a hard voice, shaking me from my reverie.

Ford nodded. "I'll call Edye now." He pushed back his chair and crossed the room to the bell pull. He remained in the shadowed corner of the room as he waited for Edye, like a hovering raven. I met Rosie's eyes and gave her a sad smile. Her face betrayed the wound in her heart, newly reopened, but still she returned my gesture of affection. I took solace in my wine glass, setting it down when Edye arrived wheeling in the dinner cart, a cloud of delicious aroma accompanying her. It was hours since Rosie and I last ate, and I had forgotten my hunger. Now, my stomach growled in anticipation.

Ford crossed back to the table as Edye served Rosie chicken stew with potatoes, preserved beets and bread with butter.

"Without a full kitchen staff, we eat rather simply," Ford said.

I caught Edye's eye as she served me. "It smells delicious. Thank you, Edye."

"S'all right, miss," the girl smiled at me. Then to Ford she asked with a curtsy, "Anything else, Sir?"

Ford pulled the dish of stew close to his plate and spooned out a portion. "Yes, Edye, would you please bring Lucy to the table?"

Edye nodded and bustled from the room while Ford shovelled in a mouthful of food. I glanced at my sister, wondering if she would say grace. She met my look and, as conditioned by the Sisters of Mary, silently mouthed *Thanks be to God*. I mouthed *Amen* in return.

We three ate in silence as we waited for Lucy. I watched Ford, his head bent over his plate, long hair falling into his eyes. He used a slice of bread to soak up some gravy, then shoved the whole piece into his mouth and chewed.

I had looked so often upon the portrait Ford sent with the letter that I half expected Lucy to look as she did in the photograph: smiling and dressed in ribbons and lace with her hair artfully curled. As such, I was unprepared for her appearance when she entered the room with Edye.

Lucy was small for being nearly seven years of age for her stature was that of a child no more than four. Her gait was non-assured, of one who has only recently learned to walk. Her limbs, clad in a black pinafore and stockings, were as narrow as twigs. A broad brimmed hat, disproportionally large on her small frame, was pulled low over her brow and draped with an expansive layer of gauze which completely veiled her face. Covered head to toe in black, except for her two tiny hands, she looked no more than a thin shadow.

Hanging low about her neck were two mourning necklaces, one white and one red.

Rosie was out of her seat in an instant, kneeling beside our niece. "Hello, Lucy," she said, "I'm your Aunt Rosamund. You may not remember me as it's been four years since I last saw you. And this is your Aunt Margaret. We came from London to see you." Rosie pressed a hand to her heart. "We are terribly sorry about your mother."

It was impossible to see Lucy's expression through the veil but she released Edye's hand and mimicked Rosie's gesture, placing a small white hand over her chest. In her other hand, she hugged a well-loved doll. It was undressed, its soft body sewn out of cotton, and it was missing one arm. Its painted wooden head hung limp to the side, for most of the stitching that bound the head to the torso was undone.

Edye excused herself from the room, as Ford rose from the table. He led Lucy to the chair beside Rosie's, and set her doll on the table before helping her to climb onto the chair. On sitting, Lucy snatched back the doll and pulled it into her lap while Rosie took her own seat again.

"I like your hat," I said. Lucy's head swivelled towards me, and I smiled at the expanse of black veil, searching for her eyes, but failing; the material was far too impenetrable. "I'm a milliner."

"I know. Mother said. She talked of you both all the time." Lucy's words were clear and measured, sounding far older than her years. Perhaps Helen's death had forced a degree of maturity upon her. I remembered my own mother's death when I was five, but did not recall it a time of growing independent. Rather, I remembered how Rosie and I clung to our father, begging him not to leave the house, for fear of losing another parent.

"Remove your hat, Lucy," Ford directed, "you do not require it in the house."

"I will wear it whenever I like!" Lucy spat,. Then she coughed and began to cough, her slight frame shaking and the black veil shuddering as though it were a stream of ink tipped from its pot. Giving me a look of surprise — whether at Lucy's temper or violent coughing, I wasn't sure — Rosie leaned over and gently rubbed the little girl's back, only to have Lucy shake her off.

"Very well," Ford relented, "would you like to show your Aunts the ballroom?"

Lucy shook her head with vigour, a game perhaps, designed to make her veil dance side to side. She coughed again.

Ford pointed a finger in her direction. "There is no need to cough, young lady. You'll do injury to your windpipe. Come, remove your hat and have a swallow of stew. It will ease your throat. Rosamund, will you help Lucy with her veil?"

"I want to go outside and play!" Lucy barked, and slammed the wooden head of her doll against the hard edge of the table with a loud crack. Ford withdrew his pointed finger and ran a hand over his beard, as though losing patience with his daughter.

Rosie said, "Let me take you to your room, Lucy. You can show me where you put your baby to sleep."

"She's not a baby," Lucy sniped, sliding off the chair and wiggling her way out from behind the table. "She's six years old. Just like me." Lucy stomped towards the doorway, holding her doll by what remained of its hair.

"Very well," Rosie chirped, following the small black form. "Perhaps you would both like a bedtime story instead? A Florentine haunting or an Italian mystery?"

Rosie closed the door behind them and their footsteps died

away. At a loss for words, I shovelled a forkful of stew into my mouth. As I chewed, I snuck a glance at Ford. He sat in the wingback chair, head tipped back, as though gazing into an imaginary night sky. The candles had burned low, and now shed their light upon his face from below, casting deep shadows in the sockets of his eyes.

His youthful appearance was gone; now he looked instead like a man unraveled by grief.

Rosie had still not returned from Lucy's room by the time I tucked myself into bed and extinguished the lamp. Edye had kept the room warm by ensuring the fire remained lit while we were at supper.

The evening meal had ended quickly. No sooner had I taken my last bite, than Ford rose from the table and excused himself from the room, saying he had some business to which to attend.

Finding myself alone in the dining room, I removed myself from the table as well. I thought to try and find Lucy and Rosie, but given the girl's demeanour earlier in the evening, I knew Rosie had a better chance of calming her than I. As I made my way back to our room, I saw that each door I passed was closed tight, making the house feel very empty indeed. In fact, there was not a flicker of movement anywhere about me, save for my shadow, waving over the carpet like a feather caught in a draught.

I changed into my nightgown and climbed into bed, snuggling deep into the mattress. I thought of the reverend — Carlisle — who we had met on the train. As soon as we arrived in the station, he had risen from his seat, book and newspaper in hand, and departed the cabin without even offering to assist Rosie or me with our bags, or ensure that we had proper transportation to our destination.

This was a very unusual place, I thought as I drifted to sleep, and well matched by the oddness of those who chose to reside here.

I woke to my shoulder being shaken with some violence. A candle sat upon the bed stand and I squinted as my eyes adjusted to the warm light. Rosie stood above me. Whatever sleepiness I was feeling vanished as I took in her eyes, red with fatigue.

"Rosie, what is the matter?"

"I am sorry to awaken you so late. Or 'early' shall I say? It is half past two."

"Half past?" I rubbed my eyes. Rosie was still dressed, black as a crow. "Why haven't you come to bed?" I asked, pulling myself up to lean against the headboard.

Rosie motioned me towards the middle of the bed and climbed onto the edge of the mattress. "I am uncertain if everything is well. I'm worried about Lucy. She is very ill."

"Let me take a shift," I said, kicking back the covers and swinging my legs off the side of the bed. "Does she have a fever?"

Rosie grabbed my arm. "No, Meg, please stay in bed. I don't think you can do anything for her. I don't think I can either." Rosie rubbed her forehead. Strands of hair fell away from her bun and danced about her face. "She hasn't a fever, but her cough is severe."

"Then we shall call the doctor," I said, with a firm voice. "Surely if the child is ill, Ford has a doctor who has been appraised of her condition."

"No, no," Rosie said, shaking her head, "Sometime around midnight I went down to Ford to ask for medication. He said there is none, that the doctor has already seen to Lucy and she is quite well. He said the cough is a lingering tickle that Lucy tends to exaggerate for attention."

"And what do you think?" I asked Rosie.

She was quiet for a moment before speaking. "All signs point to her being ill. She is terribly pale and her hands and cheeks are as cold as ice. But if she is sick, it is the strangest illness I have ever encountered. I think the child simply needs rest, but she is as awake as an owl. I read to her — she has a collection of books Father would love! We played nursery games and sang songs. I can barely keep my eyes open. And still she is wide awake! So perhaps it is the cough that keeps her from sleep." Rosie unlaced her boots and kicked them from her feet, lifting her legs onto the bed. "She begged me to stay on at Blueford —"

Rosie must have seen how her words startled me, for she quickly added, "She's lonely, of course. For her mother." Rosie unpinned her bun and leaned against the headboard. Her hair fell about her shoulders, glowing copper in the candlelight, a hot fire of colour against the white bed linens.

"*I* am cold as ice," I smiled, trying to cheer my sister. "This house is as draughty as Scotland in the winter. Feel my hands." I reached out and squeezed Rosie's fingers. "She grieves Helen, cloistered under that ridiculous veil. No wonder she is restless and fussing for attention. You've done marvelously by her, Rosie, but I fear she may want to keep you up half the night for the fun of it."

"All the same." Rosie said, staring into the thick darkness beyond the halo of candlelight, "I think I should stay."

I pushed myself away from the headboard, "Stay at Blueford Manor?"

"Yes," Rosie said, not looking at me, as though she were afraid to see disappointment in my eyes. "At least until Lucy's cough clears. About two weeks."

From what I'd seen of Lucy's behaviour, I tended to agree with Ford that there was a degree of exaggeration to her ailments. For one, the mourning veil, which Lucy was clearly attached to, was unnecessary — an antiquated custom that could be a detriment to Lucy recovering from grief. "Do you think that necessary?" I asked. "Why don't we first spend tomorrow with Lucy? Take her for a row on the river. Some fresh air —"

"You haven't spent the last hours rocking her and rubbing her back, Meg," Rosie interrupted, folding her arms over her chest,

"She coughs incessantly. I don't care what Ford says about it being an affectation. Lucy's health is clearly not as it should be. I am hardly a physician, but I can tell when a child is in distress. Perhaps a second doctor's opinion is required."

I rested my head against the headboard once more and huddled under the covers. "True," I agreed, "You are the governess. But perhaps it's Ford's responsibility to help Lucy — not yours. After all, he is her father."

"We're family too, Meg!" Rosie snapped, as her eyes burned into mine. "Lucy is Helen's blood — *your* blood. How can you be so cold?"

I flushed with shame. While it was true I didn't have the same talent with children as did Rosie — and I tended to feel awkward in their presence — Lucy was my blood. Had I grown so far apart from Helen that I could not see her grieving child needed us? Needed me? How different would our lives have been, had we had a loving aunt — or two — when we lost our mother and father? Might our childhoods have been carefree? I confess I was scared to leave Rosie in this house where there were so many secrets, including the circumstances surrounding Helen's death, but was it really fair to use my own reservations as an excuse to keep Rosie from Lucy?

If anything befell Ford, Lucy's welfare would fall to Rosie and me. I had spent enough years separated from my niece; here was my opportunity to make it up to her. And to Helen. After all, it was only through Lucy that my sister would stay alive.

"We'll make plans in the morning for you to stay on," I said, and pulled back the coverlet for Rosie to climb underneath, still clad in her skirt and stockings. I smoothed the tangled hair away from her forehead. "But right now you need to sleep."

As dutifully as one of her wards, Rosie closed her eyes and relaxed into the pillow. "I shall miss the Willis children dreadfully," she sighed.

I continued to stroke her hair, and assured her not to worry about the Willises — their mother would find them a temporary Governess until she returned to London.

"Only two weeks," Rosie mumbled, half asleep already. I leaned over and blew out the candle. Only two weeks.

3

I ROSE EARLY. After my conversation with Rosie, I had not been able to sleep. I tossed and turned for an hour or two and when sleep finally came, my dreams were dark and turbulent, although I could not recall any of the specifics upon waking.

Not wanting to awake Rosie, I made the decision to rise. It was now cold in the room; Edye had not yet been in to light the fire. I gave myself a quick wash in the basin, using last night's water. When finished, I dressed in a fresh blouse and skirt and, still finding the air chilly, I donned my warm travel cloak as well.

I slipped from the room, closing the door behind me with great care so as not to disturb my sister. As usual, the house was somber and quiet, without a hint of its other occupants. I decided to find the kitchen so that I might make myself a cup of hot tea, but the doors to the ballroom caught my attention and before I realised it, I was standing before them, my hand on the smooth wooden back of one of the stags.

I was curious to see this room. Helen had spoken of it often and with great fondness — almost adoration. She had spent many hours within, painting with watercolours or playing with Lucy. And in truth, this, of all Blueford's rooms, intrigued me the most. I set my shoulder to the carved antlers and pushed.

I gasped. Here it was. Sunlight. So carefully shuttered out of the other rooms of the house. I walked to the very centre of the room and allowed it to wash over me in a warm waterfall. My eyes relaxed, no longer needing to strain as they did in Blueford's darkened corridors.

For the first time since I'd received news of Helen's death, I felt a sense of peace.

The glass dome made the room feel like a cathedral. Wrought iron struts, like flying buttresses, soared upwards thirty feet. If a church were a living thing, this would be its skeleton.

Beneath the dome was a honey coloured dance floor, shining as though recently waxed or —- perhaps more likely — barely touched since its construction. The walls were moulded with similar iron struts, snaking up the walls to meet in pointed archways. Between these were wood carved panels of frogs and foxes, wrens and wolves.

Set back against the walls were a dozen or more wicker chairs, sun-bleached and brittle. Scattered among them were wooden tables and empty plant pots. I imagined spiny palms or English ivy once filling the planters. I lowered myself into a cane-back chair, cautious that it might snap like a twig.

I needed to digest what I had learned since arriving here. I was still bewildered that Helen had taken her own life, and even more bewildered that I felt such little grief at the news. But how could I mourn my sister when I still felt so disconnected to her?

Why had Helen not written of her sadness? Why had she not troubled Rosie or me with her despair? Perhaps she had chosen to battle her melancholy alone. Since our father's death she had felt responsible for us, and perhaps she wished to save us the heartache. Stupidly, I had thought Helen was happy and diverted by life with her husband and daughter. I would never forgive myself for making this mistake.

Despite my travelling cloak, I shivered. My rooms in London were never this cold. Heated all day by the stove downstairs in Hendry's Millenary, the floorboards of my room stayed warm late into the night.

I looked up at the sky through the greenish-grey glass and noticed slight irregularities in the panes, hairline cracks and a scattering of bubbles. Had Helen felt like me, I wondered, shivering again in the morning solitude; a fish in winter trapped beneath the icy surface of the pond?

I found Edye in the dining hall pouring a strong cup of coffee for Rosie. The night's chill was still in the room, but perhaps a little lighter thanks to the pale fire in the grate. Smudges of charcoal blackened Edye's knuckles. A red kerchief knotted over her hair accentuated the ruddy bloom in her cheeks.

Edye chirped good morning and offered me coffee as well, but I declined, preferring tea. She filled my cup from the silver pot and I sat opposite my sister.

I was glad to see Rosie for breakfast. I had feared that I'd be dining alone with Ford. But there was no sign of him now and I wondered aloud where he and Lucy were.

"Mr Ford takes his breakfast in the parlour, and Miss Lucy in her room," Edye explained, serving me poached eggs, fried tomatoes and mushrooms, with two links of sausage. She then deposited upon the table a basket of soda bread with butter and jelly.

Rosie swallowed a mouthful of sausage. "They're not joining their guests this morning?" she asked. Her swollen eyes, pink not from tears but exhaustion, betrayed an impatience to speak with Ford about Lucy's health. Her black blouse was buttoned to the chin and her silver locket was displayed on her breast.

"No, Miss Rosamund. 'Tis their custom to dine alone except for the evening meal. If you've everything you need, I'll take my leave now. The Master will be expecting to eat, and I'm running late."

Rosie shifted in her chair. "Breakfast is lovely, Edye, and the only thing we require is our brother's company. We'd be most grateful if you'd ask him to join us when you take him his meal." It was not a request; although Rosie had spent most of her life as a paid governess, she easily exercised her influence now. I stirred my tea, watching Edye stiffen under Rosie's demand.

"I daren't think so, Miss Rosamund. Mr Ford follows a strict schedule, which he isn't likely to alter." Edye puckered her lips and a little crease formed between her eyes. "If I may be honest Miss, I prefer you don't ask me to do such a thing. Y'see, I would like a good reference from the Master, and I wouldn't like to set off his temper."

"Of course he has a strict schedule, Edye — what man doesn't? But it is hardly a typical day, our being here, is it? I'm sure he'll understand our wishing to see him." When children were at stake, Rosie could be as unbending as an oak. "*This morning*," she pressed.

Looking as though she were a fish trapped in a net, Edye's robust confidence dissipated and she was left standing before us, twisting her apron between her fingers. "Mr Ford does not like to be disturbed at breakfast, Miss. I always leave 'is food outside the parlour door." She paused to swallow hard. "But I suppose I could knock…"

"Let me knock on his door, Edye," Rosie said, interrupting the girl's misery, "In fact, Margaret and I will take him breakfast ourselves." Her eyes met mine over the rim of my tea cup as I drained the last swallow.

I returned the cup to its saucer and — whether for Edye's benefit or my sister's — I said with false brightness, "We certainly can."

⚷

While I held the breakfast tray, Rosie raised her fist and knocked on the parlour door.

There was no answer. Edye had told us it was her habit to call through the keyhole to Ford that breakfast was served. And so Rosie stooped to do so. "I feel like a child!" she whispered to me with almost a laugh. Then she called out, "It's me, Rosamund. And Margaret. We've brought breakfast."

Rosie had barely finished her words when the door flew open. Ford loomed above, staring down at her auburn bun, as though it too were a doorknob through which he might regain his privacy.

His eyes were black, his mouth set in a furious line. He wore no jacket over his shirt which was open at the neck. The sleeves were rolled to the elbow. He was ill prepared for guests.

More accustomed to holding a needle and thread than a full course breakfast, I adjusted the tray on my hip while Rosie recovered from her crouching position. Edye had laid out twice the bounty she'd served us. "It smells delicious," I said, "Might I bring it in for you?"

Ford said nothing, but stepped back allowing us into the parlour. Rosie led the way and I hurried behind her, feeling Ford's eyes upon me.

He made no move to take the tray, but instead said, "Set it there," and pointed to a large oak desk at the centre of the room. The furnishings formed an odd configuration, the desk positioned in the middle of the parlour. A chaise lounge was opposite, but the other settees were pushed back against the walls. Bookshelves, devoid of books, lined the walls. The bare wooden shelves looked like a series of ribs, as though we were in the belly of some great beast. The walls to the other side were covered with pins, and although I suspected they held some kind of meaning to Ford, I could find no sense of it.

My eyes followed the empty shelves up to the ceiling, where my gaze was snagged by a network of drawn lines. The ceiling, painted a pale gold, was penciled from corner to corner. Rules and arcs traced the coordinates of a night sky, each line intercepted regularly with the name of a star, or a full constellation, and notes regarding its position or orbit.

Additional lines, like latitude and longitude, divided the dome further. Degrees were marked and directions notated in pencil. It was not simply a mural, but a working map of the night sky, Ford's own hand present in each notation. A wooden A-frame ladder, twelve feet in height, stood behind the desk.

It was then that I realised the pins in the opposite wall also reflected the constellations. As I turned back to them, Ford snapped his fingers, drawing my attention. Then he cleared his throat and pointed at his desk. Cluttered with charts, I searched for a place to set the tray, but Ford swept his forearm across the surface, brushing aside a stack of charts. They clattered to the floor and I deposited the tray. As she waited for me, Rosie took a seat upon the cobalt blue velvet chaise. I joined her there as Ford selected a slice of soda bread from the tray and crushed it between his teeth.

"I do hope you won't mind if we chat over breakfast," Rosie said, as if we had been invited to partake in the fresh bread and jams. Ford chewed, watching my sister through narrow eyes. Rosie went on, "I — we — wish to talk to you about Lucy."

At this Ford's back stiffened and he dropped the remains of his toast upon the tray. "Go on," he said, his voice even.

Rosie leaned forward, hands folded neatly in her lap. "I stayed with Lucy quite late last night, as you know, but ——"

"She does not sleep well," Ford interjected. "She grieves her mother, and this exacbates her condition. I understand your concern, but I assure you it is nothing to fear." Ford leaned forward and poured a cup of coffee from the silver pot. Its warm aroma curled into my throat.

Rosie glanced at me, and went on, "I agree that Lucy will be quite all right in time, for it would appear that the worst of the whooping cough has subsided. But as some symptoms persist, I do recommend she receive further attention."

Ford leaned back in his chair once again, and fixed his gaze upon Rosie. He sipped the coffee, then curved his lips into a grin. "Helen never told me you are both a governess *and* a physician."

Rosie flushed, but pressed onward. "Working with the orphans at Sisters of Mary, I am very familiar with whooping cough." Rosie paused for a moment and then continued, "And with grief."

As Ford watched her and said nothing, Rosie relaxed, "I believe Lucy exaggerates her symptoms, perhaps even refuses to fully recover, because she is grieving. I have often seen children hang tight to an illness, desperate for the attention it affords them. In staying sick, perhaps Lucy feels she can remain a child, dependent on her father, instead of being the new mistress of the house."

Ford set down his cup and picked up a fork to stab a link of sausage. He gave Rosie a straight look, one eyebrow peaked: "Go on."

I exhaled a breath I hadn't realised I held in, and couldn't help but smile at my sister. I felt Ford notice, flicking his eyes over me.

"I predict that with a few weeks' care and attention, Lucy will be less attached to both her cough and her grief. I would be more than happy to be of assistance in helping her make this transition."

I could hear how difficult it was for Rosie to say the words. To replace our sister was something she could never do. But to nurture Lucy — in any small way — was within her ability. How often Rosie had played a mothering role to me, despite being the youngest sister. During our first year at Sisters of Mary, I crawled into Rosie's cot every night after dark. The school was cold, and we slept back to back, the soles of our feet pressed together. 'Sole sisters', she called us and we would giggle together, the experience bonding us in a way neither of us was able to do with Helen, who was by then engaged to Ford.

I wanted to stretch my leg and press the toe of my boot against Rosie's, but I kept still, hands clasped on my lap. Rosie sat perfectly upright, as straight and decorous as a governess ought to be. Her lack of sleep wasn't the least bit apparent, which is not what I could say for Ford.

He sipped his coffee noisily. "And how long do you intend to stay?"

Rosie glanced at me again, an excited smile lifting the corners of her mouth. "I will stay the week out, as Margaret and I thought we might be here for Helen's funeral. But now I will spend that time with Lucy instead. As well, I will remain an additional two weeks. I will write to my employers in London and let them know I shall be delayed. They'll understand; they know the circumstances of my visit here."

Ford grunted and turned his gaze upon me. "And what of

you, Margaret? Do you see it your duty, too, to stay on in my house?"

His question caught me off guard and I fumbled for words. I had not even considered the possibility of remaining with Rosie. I opened my mouth to speak, but Rosie answered for me.

"Not at all," she said. "Margaret must return to London. She has work commitments that are more pressing than my own."

"Are you certain?' I asked Rosie, "I will stay if you desire it of me."

"I am certain," she replied, reaching out to squeeze my folded hands. "There is no need for us both to remain behind."

Ford took another bite of sausage and chewed, watching Rosie and I all the while. I shifted uncomfortably, moving my eyes from the bare bookshelves to the pencilled ceiling tiles. Anywhere other than Ford's black eyes. Rosie, however, sat as still and poised as a dress-maker's form in a High Street shop window.

"Well," Ford said, setting down his fork at last, "It seems I am a very blessed man, having two caring sisters-in-law. One of whom chooses to take her sister's place … for a spell."

"For a spell," Rosie echoed, with a smile. But I could not match my sister's enthusiasm, for a knot had formed in my stomach and refused to let go.

The train was already pulling out of Harrowgate station as I made my way down the aisle with my carpet bag, finding my balance with every step.

I found my seat and noted a familiar face in the one next to mine.

"Miss Jaye!" Edye said, a wide smile upon her face. "Here, put your bag between our feet," she said, shuffling her legs closer to the window.

"It's fine," I said, settling my carpet bag on my lap. The bag was light, practically empty save a few items for my toilette and my copy of *Jane Eyre*. I had brought one change of clothes — the black blouse and skirt I'd sewn especially for Helen's memorial. I had left these behind with Rosie who had also only packed one outfit. For two weeks my sister would be dressed as black as one of the ravens in the dining room, blending into the shadowy corners of Blueford Hall.

I had no plans to continue wearing black upon my return to London; instead, I would grieve Helen internally, the pain in my chest having washed the walls of my heart in darkness. Fashion was bread and butter to me — both that which earned my keep and sustained my soul, giving purpose to my solitary life.

Edye untied the green cotton ribbon that kept her checked bonnet perched on her head, and set it upon her lap. She plumped her hair which had been squashed flat, and said, "You are leaving the manor house then?"

My own hat remained pinned to my head, but my kid gloves I tugged off and folded into my carpet bag. I replied that Rosie was staying on. A letter to the Willises explaining my sister's intentions was packed in my bag.

"They shan't miss me until a week Monday," Rosie had said, "so you needn't rush to deliver the letter."

"I shall deliver it the moment I'm away from the shop," I promised my sister, and tucked the letter between the pages of *Jane Eyre,* right next to the portrait of Lucy. As I'd packed to leave, I was disappointed to have seen my niece only the once, and veiled at that. But she had slept soundly all day because of her nighttime escapades. "Best leave her undisturbed," Rosie said, relieved that Lucy was finally resting peacefully. As I left Blueford to catch the evening train, I hoped Rosie might lay down for a rest of her own before the dinner hour was upon her.

When the hack departed the manor, I had no idea Edye was also leaving or I would have asked to travel with her. Ford had not even come bid me farewell. Only Rosie had waved to me from the front steps, as though she were the true mistress of the house.

"Are you going to London as well?" I asked Edye.

"No, I'll be changing trains at Hadley Wood," she said. "Going home to Potter's Bar. My pa and mam farm there, and my younger brothers and sisters. This was my first employment," she said with great pride, tilting her chin as though showing off a very fine hat.

"Congratulations," I said, recalling the first week I'd earned wages at Hendry's. "Is it a good post, working for Mr Ford?"

"Was good," Edye stated, matter-of-fact. "I'm no longer working there. I'm off home, and my mam and pa will be so pleased to have me. I can help with the little ones once I'm back, and I've a fair wage saved to contribute to the household." At this last statement, she grinned wide and the apples of her cheeks flushed deep pink, as though they were a pair of knuckles scrubbed clean by soap and hot water.

I, however, was somewhat perplexed, wondering why her employment had abruptly ceased. It seemed there was no emergency at home to tend to, and given how much Edye apparently enjoyed her income, unlikely she was leaving of her own accord. A first-time house-keeper was liable to a few mistakes, but had she done something recently that caused termination? A sudden thought came to me.

"I do hope you were not let go because you allowed Rosie and I — "

"Oh no, Miss," she said interrupting me. "I was employed for three months only. Yesterday was my last day."

Three months. I wondered at that. Surely Ford and Lucy would still require help? I frowned — would that role fall upon Rosie? And upon Rosie's departure, would Ford himself take over kitchen duties? I smiled at the thought.

Edye must have sensed confusion on my part for she spoke further. "The last girl was only hired for three months as well, Miss. She was my cousin and recommended my services to Mr and Mrs Ford." I wondered whose idea it was to employ a housekeeper for only a three month period. Ford or Helen's? Perhaps my sister didn't like the idea of another woman in the house. Although this possibility didn't strike me as a plausible; Helen was never one for jealousy.

The tea cart arrived and I purchased us both steeping cups of earl grey. At first Edye politely protested, but then relented, her hands eager for the hot drink. As she sipped her tea, she asked a multitude of questions about London — did I ever see the Queen; were the Houses of Parliament as magnificent as she had heard; and was I scared to be alone, given the tales of Jack the Ripper that had been reported upon in the press? No, I had never seen the Queen (much to Edye's disappointment); yes, Parliament was quite distinctive; and Jack the Ripper had only operated in Whitechapel, some distance from Hendry's. She continued asking questions for some time, ending with: where did I purchase my hat?

I explained I was a milliner, and satisfied her excited curiosity with tales of the wealthy women for whom I'd designed bonnets. I unfastened my own hat, withdrew it from my head and pointed out each step I'd taken in the process of creating it: from selecting the ribbon and trimming the brim to dyeing the pigeon wing that decorated the left side of the crown.

As Edye admired my creation, I was at last able to steer the conversation in a direction I preferred.

"Were you there when my sister fell?" I asked, eager to have more information about Helen's last days.

"No, Miss," she said, her fingers tightening on the brim of my hat. "Mr and Mrs Ford always gave me Sunday off so that I might attend church and have lunch with my mother's cousin in Harrowgate. I didn't arrive home until supper. After she...fell." Edye's eyes remained focused on my hat, her fingers stroking the pigeon wing as though for comfort. "I don't like to think on the events of that day, Miss. If I had been there, perhaps I could have prevented — "

She stopped, and I reached over to squeeze her hand in reassurance. It was not Edye's job to have prevented my sister's fate. It was her husband's. Or mine, I thought. It concerned me that Edye had been in town the day of my sister's death. But what bothered me more was that Ford had told me Helen was found at sunset. Yet according to Edye's tale, this could simply not be true.

The girl continued, "I never really knew her, Miss, but she were a good lady when she would speak with me. Though she stayed in her room all the long day, wanting her privacy, not wanting to leave. And Mr Ford, Miss! Why he would remain in the parlour, without even visiting his wife? And little Lucy all alone in her room. It was a very quiet house. Even a little strange." Here she leaned towards me, and lowered her voice, "Begging your pardon, Miss, but I am relieved my employment was only three months. Coming from a family of ten, I don't understand the quiet so well."

I nodded, as I too found the house as sombre and still as a mausoleum, and — by Edye's account — it had been this way long before Helen's death. I held back the tears that prickled like pins at the back of my eyes, imagining the life my sister had endured at Blueford. Edye had been the brightest, friendliest presence there, and now she was leaving. I shivered at the thought of Rosie waiting on new help; how soon 'til Ford rehired? Had I known Edye was leaving, I would not have been so quick to return to London.

The last moments of my stay had reunited the three Jaye sisters; Ford explained how to find our way to Helen's grave-site, through the flower gardens and beyond to the path that wove along the south side of the house, behind the hedgerow. We'd come across a small courtyard — now overgrown — its concrete benches upholstered in moss. As we walked, our boot heels clicked across the flagstones, but soon we found ourselves on a dirt path that led through a bower of elder and elm trees. Beyond was the orchard, terribly overgrown, the trees unpruned for years. Rosie and I ducked under the twisted branches and made our way to the far side of the orchard, where we climbed a grassy southwestern slope to Helen's grave. It seemed a poor site to bury our sister, for it was exposed to the elements. What would prevent the rain from sweeping down hill and washing away whatever wildflowers might mark her grave?

Wind whipped at our skirts as we knelt before the small grey stone. The ground looked undisturbed around the headstone and I wondered if Ford or Lucy ever visited this spot. The headstone was simple and Rosie ran her fingers over the plain, engraved lettering:

HELEN. WORTHY OF REMEMBRANCE.

For a man of great wealth, the stone seemed a meagre gesture towards his wife and our sister. I lifted my eyes to the sky, and prayed for Helen. Prayed that, in escaping the darkness of Blueford and the starkness of this sapphire hillside, she might find beauty and comfort with our parents in Heaven. We wept then, Rosie and myself, allowing ourselves to feel the full import of our sister's death. Arms around one another for solace, our salty tears seeping into one another's dresses until we had no more to cry.

Then, using the scissors that hung from my châtelaine, I snipped the threads that fastened one of the pigeon wings to my hat. I tugged it free, and laid it in a small well I dug in the earth. Rosie added a token as well: a poem in memory of Helen that she'd penned the night before we left London. Then, we spread the dirt over our small *memento mori.*

Finally I turned my face towards the north, and saw for the first time why Helen was buried here. Ford had done well by her after all. True, the hill was washed and plain, but the view was breathtaking.

From here, Rosie and I had not only a clear view of the house, but also one of the surrounding hills, thickly covered with spruce, brilliantly blue. I turned my head the other direction, and spied the river beyond the ridge; it snaked in a lazy manner towards the south. I saw no swans, but was certain that on most days, Helen's spirit would be able to watch them.

She loved those birds, once writing to me about them in great detail as she recalled the times she and Rosie, as children, had teased me of being an ugly duckling. It was only a game, but it ceased when our mother died as I was the daughter that looked most like her, having the same chestnut hair and long thin nose. I knew our father saw this in me as I grew, and my looks became sacred in our family. Something no longer to be teased, rather something that allowed my red-haired sisters and father to remember the woman we all loved. Even I was sometimes startled by my mother's likeness in the looking glass. From then on, I was no longer an ugly duckling but 'Magpie', an avian twist upon my name — given to me by Rosie — in tribute to my love of the glittering beads with which I dressed my hats.

What is awkward on a child — sheer cheekbones or a long nose — becomes attractive on a woman. Now, I was used to highlighting my features with extravagant hats, using long plumes to accentuate my neck and angular features. Each time I designed for myself, I imagined that I designed for my mother. Often I wished my father were still alive, that he might see me as a woman, grown into my mother's beauty.

Edye began to hand back my hat back so she could don her own bonnet and I realised that our conversation had carried us all the way to Hadley Wood. I shook my head.

"No, please keep it," I said.

"Oh, Miss!" She gasped, "I couldn't possibly."

"Of course you can," I said, rising to take the hat from her hands and place it upon her own head. I used pins from her hair to secure it in place, then stepped back and admired the effect.

"You look very beautiful," I said. And indeed she did, her red hair looking like fire against the forest green velvet.

"I shall never forget you," she said, throwing propriety aside and embracing me in thanks. I returned the gesture, grateful for her touch, pushing aside the loneliness I knew I would soon feel for Rosie.

Hendry's Millinery was organised like a sweets shop: a long wooden counter ran the entire length of the shop-front. Light from the windows fell onto it, making it an ideal work surface. And indeed, this is where Hendry and I spread our materials and together worked millinery magic. Because we were not cloistered in the back, we drew interested shoppers to our window everyday, many who paused for several minutes to watch as I arranged a splendorous array of birds on all manner of hat.

Along the shop's back wall climbed a checkerboard of cupboards and drawers filled with a rainbow of delight: ribbon, buttons, beads, feathers and their kin. When laid across my counter, their display of colour would shame Kew Gardens.

Hendry emerged from the back room where he preferred to sit, making the moulds for which he'd earned his fame. Here, we also conducted fabric dying and machine sewing. "I took the liberty of ordering the skin while you were away," he said, as we discussed Lady Saxonhurst's newest commission.

Lady Saxonhurst was Hendry's best customer. In the London socialite scene, she held position as one of the most stylish women in London. Never to be seen in the same hat twice, she ensured each creation matched one of her many custom made gowns. Typically, Lady Saxonhurst commissioned hats from Edith's or La Mademoiselle on High Street, where shop prices were in line with the street of their residence, and the labels were the envy of all.

But while I was away, Lady Saxonhurst had arrived at Hendry's to express that my Bird of Paradise hats were exceptional and when would the designer be returning to London? Until that day, neither Hendry nor I had known she was the client for whom we designed; her measurements had arrived by telegram and payment was delivered to us when her coachman arrived to pick up the hat. Then, Hendry and I would scour the papers trying to decipher which of the hats described in the social column was the one we had created. But invariably the descriptions were erroneous and led to much discussion as to whether the client was ours or not.

Hendry slid a box from the plumassier's across the workbench towards me. "She's going to the opening night of Mr Wilde's *An Ideal Husband* at the Saint James Theatre. She's wearing forest green taffeta — " and here Hendry produced a swatch of fabric from the dressmaker "— and a choker and earring set of emeralds and obsidian."

The materials were dark and in the dim theatre may not be noticeable. And that would not do. Not for Lady Saxonhurst. As always, her hat would have to be a show-stopper for at intermission, Lady Saxonhurst's hat must trump all other conversation topics.

"She is seated in the dress circle?" I confirmed.

Hendry's eyes twinkled behind round spectacles, "Naturally."

A seat in the dress circle presented me with two unique challenges. First, the hat would have to be truly exceptional, for when the house lights were lit, it would be clearly visible from all seats in the theatre. Everyone always wanted to know what Lady Saxonhurst was wearing, as she appeared with great frequency on the social pages of London's many magazines. I suggested a crow, and that we use dephlogisticated marine acid to transform the tips of the wings and tail white for a dramatic ombré effect. The stark white would catch the eye and throw the bird's body into sharp relief against the hat's dark green form.

Second, the hat's silhouette, despite its black and white wings spread in full flight (my signature look), had to be low profile. It would be in the poorest of manners for Lady Saxonhurst's hat to obscure the view of other patrons.

Hendry and I continued to discuss the design; and found that if I perched the crow carefully on the crown, the bird could easily span the hat's brim, allowing for a reasonably modest profile. But not too modest — my design aesthetic demanded attention, and was the reason Lady Saxonhurst had commissioned me in the first place.

From the drawers, I selected two emerald glass beads for the rook's eyes and drew up my stool to work.

Hendry had taught me the craft of millinery after my father died: how to build the wire form, rush the fabrics, drape the ribbons and gauze, and so forth. In the art of mounting feathers and bird skins I was self-taught. During my apprenticeship, Hendry had noticed my keen eye for setting a feather. And as a result he began stocking ostrich plumes, remarking that I managed to place each feather for maximum lift, so that as the hat was worn, the feathers moved in such a way as to accentuate the rhythm of the woman's gait, catching the eyes of passers-by, who might just happen to stop and ask where she had found so lovely a hat.

When the annual plumassier shows were held in Trafalgar Square, the cobblestones of which were obscured by crate upon rack of imported feathers and skins — egret, parakeet, hummingbird, all glowing iridescent in the sun — Hendry suggested I attend. He handed me ten pounds, which seemed an exorbitant sum, but the freedom to spend the money as I saw fit allowed me to buy a few quetzal and some wings from an egret, which I later dyed with cryptothecia rubrocincta to achieve a vivid crimson hue.

With a desire to explore the craft, I worked long hours with the feathers in a way few other milliners did. Instead of nesting the birds in demure postures of sleep, I spread their wings, snapping the bones to reset them in dramatic poses of flight. Animating them with rhinestone and pearl eyes that, although less than realistic, were far more interesting than applying the typical glass options. These were now the signature elements of Hendry's Millinery that had caught Lady Saxonhurst's eye.

The days after returning from Blueford provided sufficient distraction from Helen's death. But at night, I fretted in bed, missing Rosie desperately. Unwilling to repeat the mistake I had made with Helen, I wrote to Rosie daily and was pleased when I received her missives in return. I had never lived alone in London; these past years with Helen at Blueford, Rosie and I had one another for comfort. Now that Rosie's three weeks were drawing to a close, I discovered I was far more desperate for her to return than I had at first realised.

4

"HERE IT IS, PAGE SIX!" Mrs Millicent Willis exclaimed, as I was shown into the drawing room. She still wore a house-dress and morning cap, though it was now after five in the afternoon. "But there's no mention of you, my dear Margaret." Mrs Willis lifted her pince-nez and peered at the black ink. She read, "Lady Saxonhurst dressed in emeralds by Chantelle of Paris, and a hat bedecked with a raven from Lady Elaine's Plumassierie. Why does the damn feather monger get all the credit?" she fumed, dropping her pince-nez and rattling the paper. "It is absurd they never mention Hendry's Hat Shop, let alone you, my pet!"

I smiled and walked over to where she reclined on the sofa, leaning in to kiss both cheeks, pink from a nip of gin. "Her paycheque is acknowledgment enough," I said.

Mrs Willis sniffed, tossing aside the paper, her fingers reaching to play with the ropes of white pearls she wore about her neck. "Well, when I wear a Margaret Jaye original, you know I sing your praises better than any canary," she winked.

I laughed and sat opposite her on a French settee draped in Indian paisley. The room was decorated with many *objets d'art* from the East — cloisonné vases and monumental lions. My favourite was a round jade Buddha with a wide smile upon his face. I leaned forward and handed her a small paper parcel. "Before I forget."

Mrs Willis' eyes lit up like a child given a new doll. "Oh, delicious!" she cried, tearing open the paper and extracting two wings, one from a dove, the other a budgie. On occasion, we received skins or plumage that were unsuitable for use due to water damage or some other form of disrepair. These I passed onto Mrs Willis, who loved to dabble in black magic.

Neither Rosie nor I believed in the dark arts but it pleased Mrs Willis to receive the animal parts, and as she had always been most gracious to my sister — and a faithful patron of Hendry's — I obliged her. Rosie always dined with the Willis family on the weekend, even though she was not required to work. And at least twice a month the invitation was extended to me. Mrs Willis may have had strange taste in elixirs and potions, but she governed an exceptional kitchen, and I enjoyed elaborate dinners I would never otherwise prepare for myself.

Tonight was one such occasion, though it would not be the same with Rosie still in the north. I remarked that her children must be missing my sister dearly.

"Indeed!" Mrs Willis agreed. "But not as much as I or Mr Willis. We're terribly disappointed that she has given notice. Whoever shall we find to replace her?"

I was taken aback. Surely Mrs Willis had read the letter I delivered to her upon my return to London, explaining Rosie's intention to stay for two additional weeks only.

"I beg your pardon, Millicent, I think you misunderstand. My sister will return to London in two days."

Mrs Willis reached towards the small table beside her sofa and held out a letter. In a cool voice she said, "Read it, dear Margaret."

Immediately I could tell that it was written in Ford's hand as it resembled the same writing that had announced the news of Helen's death.

It said:

Miss Rosamund Jaye has agreed to serve as governess to her niece, Miss Lucille Ford at my home in Harrowgate and will therefore not return to your employ. I include in this letter a cheque equivalent to one month's wages for Miss Jaye, that you may apply these funds to finding a suitable replacement. Miss Jaye apologies that she is unable to send word herself, but I am sure you can understand the urgency of the situation as my daughter has recently lost her mother.

Yours, Captain J. Ford

I stared at the letter in disbelief; it couldn't possibly be true.

My face must have betrayed my distress as Mrs Willis' voice softened considerably, "Obviously, my dear, your sister has changed her mind about returning." A frown knotted her brow. "Although, it is most unfortunate to not hear from her directly."

I could feel tears form in my eyes. "It is terribly unlike her not to write of such news herself," I said, my voice shaking with bewilderment. "I shall write to her immediately and rectify the situation."

I looked up at Mrs Willis to see her watching me with quiet concern. It was too much. In a burst of emotion, I cried: "It cannot be! She must return. She loves your children, Mrs Willis. She loves London!" It was only in my head that I wondered if her delayed return was determined by someone other than Rosie herself.

⚷

I arrived home in an anxious state. I had begged off dinner with the Willis family, confessing to a sudden headache. Mrs Willis said she understood and offered to have her man drive me home in their carriage. I declined, desiring cold air in my lungs, hoping a brisk walk would clear my head. Besides, I intended to go the Post Office and send Rosie a telegram.

I advised my sister I would be on the morning train to Harrowgate the day after tomorrow. I didn't want to leave immediately for it would be unfair of me to depart Hendry's without a word. But more than that, tomorrow was the day Rosie was scheduled to return. What if Ford's letter had been a mean spirited trick upon my sister? Perhaps she had annoyed him in some manner and so out of spite he cost Rosie her employment with the Willis family. What if Rosie arrived in London tomorrow after all and I was not there to greet her? I was confused, my mind wanting to both catch the first train to Harrowgate and remain in London to see if Rosie returned.

My humble room which used to feel safe and comfortable now seemed small and claustrophobic. I examined the space, suddenly comparing it to the vast expanse of Blueford Manor — the modest wardrobe which overflowed with hats and dresses, the fragile wooden table with a single chair, its white paint cracked and peeling, the small iron stove now cold to the touch.

I climbed onto the thin single mattress and crawled under the quilt I had made using the leftover scraps of expensive hat fabric. I closed my eyes, clasped my hands together and prayed for Rosie, for Lucy's recovery, and for Edye. But mostly I prayed for my sister, pleading to whoever listened that I would see her beautiful face tomorrow at the train station.

I awoke to a great pounding.

At first I was uncertain as to my whereabouts; was I not still at Blueford? But no, I'd only dreamt of Ford. Watching my brother-in-law burst into Mrs Willis' parlour where Rosie reclined on the settee, a waterfall of pearls about her neck. With which Ford had been strangling her. I shuddered and the pounding sounded once more. There was someone at my door.

I climbed out from beneath the covers and crossed to the door, still dressed from the previous evening. My gown was creased but presentable. A telegram boy stood on the stoop.

"Miss," he said, holding out two telegrams. I took them from him and found a few pennies in my reticule for a tip. He dipped his head with thanks and was on his way.

I looked at the letter's origin: North Yorkshire. My hands trembled as I sat in the chair by the window. If these were from Rosie, it meant that she would not be on the train today. Perhaps, as long as I didn't read them, all would be as planned. I'm not certain how long I sat there but when I heard noises from downstairs it meant that Hendry had arrived and was opening the shop and I could delay no longer.

The first one read as follows:

```
EVERYTHING FINE
STAYING ON AT HARROWGATE
DO NOT WORRY, MAGPIE
LOVE ROSIE
```

I blinked. Whether to bring the words into sharper focus or hold back tears I did not know. This couldn't be from Rosie. Could it? Perhaps Ford had sent it. Just like he had sent the letter to the Willis family. But that was impossible; he couldn't have known about my pet name. There would be no reason for Rosie to tell him.

I read the second telegram:

```
COME TO BLUEFORD ON THE FIFTEENTH
WEAR BLUE OSTRICH HAT
LOVE ROSIE
```

I laughed, although it was more a cry in sound. The telegrams *were* from Rosie! Ford could not have known about that hat. Even Helen had never seen it. Only Rosie. And it was her favourite of all my creations.

The fifteenth. By the time that day arrived, it would be the longest I had ever spent away from Rosie. If I threw myself into my work, the time would pass quickly. Three weeks, I told myself crossing over to the basin to wash my face and set my hair. Only three weeks until I packed my bags, and saw Rosie again.

The wind rattled the wooden shutters on the storefront window and kicked up the skirts of passers-by; herringbone, jacquard and plaid pinwheels revealed a buffet of cotton underskirts and ankle boots. Hats, too, suffered the wind. Ribbons frayed, fronds escaped their feathery spines. It would be a long day of repairs, for the first winds of fall tested the integrity of these hats worn through the calm of summer.

It was the start of September. Despite the weather, I had a smile on my face for it was only one more week until I would see Rosie again.

Hendry was out, visiting a new hat shop that had opened up down the street from us, scouting the competing styles on offer While he was gone, I hand-ruched a modest wedding bonnet in a light blue velvet. As I sewed, I though of Rosie and Lucy. Were they taking advantage of the wind, drifting along the river in a row boat, fingers trailing in the water as they floated on the wake of swans? Or did they turn their backs to the gusts, giggling as they ran inside, smoothing their hair as they settled into the brittle chairs of the sunny ballroom? Did they —

A loud thud on the window pane broke my reverie. I set aside the bonnet and stepped outside into the blustery day to see the source of the noise. Sometimes newspaper boys done for the day came down our street, throwing apple cores at the shop fronts as they passed, but seldom had their missiles struck with such force. However, there were no boys in sight, and where a smear of apple might have been, I saw blood.

The bright red trickle led my eye downward to a small form on the pavement.

The side of the bird's head was crushed, feathers matted with blood that obscured its eye. One wing lay twisted as though still in full flight, while the other was folded under its little body. A passing gentleman paused, offering a hand to help me rise. Had

I dropped a glove or perchance a piece of jewellery, he inquired. I shook my head and when he saw the sparrow, he offered me a handkerchief. I accepted, but not for my tears.

I lifted the bird into the white cotton. Its body was warm, but the limp head told me it was already dead. I caught my reflection in the shop window: clad in a grey woollen winter dress and skin pale from working inside all summer, I looked as ashen as a ghost. In my hands, the white handkerchief looked like an envelope sent from heaven. Surely, the bird had seen its reflection as it spiralled into the window? But then I realised that from a higher vantage point, the bird would have seen nothing but a reflection of blue skies, the wind having blown away the clouds.

Inside the shop, I set the bird's corpse on the workbench. I placed a finger where the pulse might be, but discerned no movement. The wing felt broken at the shoulder joint. I pulled at it tentatively. Indeed, the tendons had snapped, and the wing operated in my hands as an independent unit. My fingers traced back up the wing and gingerly felt the bird's head. By now, it had cooled significantly. The bird's left eye had been crushed in the impact, the skull partly caved in. Its beak, too, was slightly bent. I turned the bird over to hide its injuries from my view.

In this new position, the sparrow looked as though it were simply asleep.

"Good God, is that blood?" Hendry's voice startled me. I had been so engrossed in the bird, I did not realise he had entered the shop. I hid my hands which were smeared with blood, thin red lines of it threaded between the folds of my skin at the base of my thumbs and across my palms. But Hendry was not looking at me. He stood in the doorway, one foot propping open the door, his head cocked around the frame to survey the window pane.

I hid the sparrow under the handkerchief.

"A bird struck the window this morning."

Hendry frowned. "A bad omen, I say. Fetch a rag and some hot water, Margaret. I'll get the ladder."

"Yes, Hendry," I said, and went into the back to boil some

water on the stove.

Minutes later Hendry was up the ladder as I raised a steaming bucket of water, my arm shaking with the effort. I blinked into the sun as Hendry wiped away the scarlet smear. The words he had spoken in the shop resonated in my head: *bad omen*. Not that I believed in such silly things. Birds fly into windows every day, do they not? Despite being enveloped in a cloud of warm steam, I felt chilled to the bone.

⚷

"Destiny brought you to us today, pet," Millicent Willis crooned, leading me into the dining room where five other women sat at a round table. "My dear sisters," Mrs Willis said in a low voice as she gestured for me to occupy one of the two empty chairs, cascades of jet black beads clattering about her neck, "this is Meg."

Mrs Willis seated me between Mrs Taylor and Lady Hull. Our hostess completed introductions around the table: Mrs Crane, whose name I had heard before as she was wed to the notable politician, Mrs Gainsborough who looked rather like a younger Lady Saxonhurst, and Miss Montgomery who wasn't a day over sixteen. Including our hostess, we numbered seven which —— according to Millicent —— was preferable to the devil's six when conducting a séance. It was fate, she said, that had brought me to the table to replace Mrs Colborne who had taken ill.

I had not intended to participate in any such enterprise as this when I had stopped to see if Millicent might spare a moment or two to speak of what she knew of omens, in the form of dead birds. Yet now I found myself seated at a séance.

Mrs Willis took a deep breath, "Not long ago, Margaret's eldest sister, Helen, took her own life." Soft exhortations erupted from about the table. Beside me, Mrs Crane harrumphed indecorously and refrained from meeting my eye.

I shifted in the chair, annoyed that such a personal topic

would be raised before complete strangers. The chair was hard-backed, with no upholstery, and the two arm-rests were carved with half-clad creatures that were part human, part animal twisting one over the other. I tentatively placed my hands over their rather grotesque bodies. I had yet to touch such portions of a man's anatomy in this lifetime; the creatures' anatomy jutted uncomfortably against my palms and I released my hands. Sweat beaded my temples.

"God has brought Miss Jaye to us today, that we might commune with her good sister Helen." Mrs Willis' voice trailed off in a dramatic fashion and the others waited, breath frozen, for her to continue. The smoke from incense hung as heavy as a curtain, casting everything — and everyone — in a bluish haze. A fire, more appropriate for winter than a warm September, roared in the marble fireplace.

Mrs Willis' words crawled into my ears like a curious spider. "Millicent — " I said, apprehension drifting over my skin like a falling spider's web.

She waved her hand at me with a shush. However, the look of concern on my face must have given her pause for she reached over to squeeze my fingers. "Trust me," she whispered. "This will only serve to bring Helen peace. There is nothing to fear."

I had never before attended a séance, let alone imagined what occurred at one. Many times I had gifted Mrs Willis feathers and skins to use as she pleased, but had not given much thought as to what they would be used for. Now, as I sat stiff and upright, my clammy hands working over the writhing wooden forms carved into the chair, I felt frightened. In the heat of the room and the fog of the incense, I felt transported and unsure of where this journey would take me.

As I waited for the séance to unfold, I cannot say if I expected to commune with Helen. I cannot say if I even believed that communion was possible. I became distracted by the magic of it all — the way Mrs Willis rolled her eyes, fluttered her hands high above the table, and hummed unevenly, like a bumblebee negotiating its way to the centre of a lily.

Moments later, Mrs Willis' hum reached an even tone. At this, the women around the table linked hands. I happily accepted Mrs Gainsborough's and Miss Montgomery's in place of the chair's hideous arm-rests. My companions' palms felt cool and dry, and I was embarrassed at the dampness of my own.

The other women joined in the hum; I tried to match the tone, but my voice bumped over the notes, out of tune. Mrs Gainsborough squeezed my hand and gently shook her head. And so I ceased, and she favoured me with a slight smile and a wink.

Soon, the women hummed in perfect unison, the constant drone of a hive. The sound expanded, reverberating in the room. Goose flesh rose on the back of my neck and despite the fire, the room's temperature seemed to drop.

Mrs Willis quieted and the group followed. Her eyes were now shut, lids fluttering. The women breathed deep in silence, their eyes closed as well. But mine would not comply. No, my gaze was transfixed on Mrs Willis. Her breath escaped as though a mist, mingling with the smoke of the incense.

"I see...I see..." Mrs Willis moaned, near inaudible. Miss Montgomery gripped my hand tightly and I returned her grasp with increased might.

"I see a small woman. She is not from here, she is from another place...black. She is a black girl, from...the Orient, perhaps? No, not black. Wearing all black. Like a ghost. No, not a ghost— a shadow. A mystery." Mrs Willis coughed, but her eyes remained shut. When she spoke again, her voice was dry and coarse. "Who are you? Helen, is it you?"

I held my breath, as if frozen. And when I exhaled, my breath, too, escaped in a chilly mist.

Mrs Willis continued, "She's — I cannot see —- she...she has no face." And then she coughed again. And I realised her cough sounded exactly like —

"Lucy!" I cried. "But it is not possible. Lucy is not dead!"

Lady Crane shushed me but I did not care.

Mrs Willis, however, continued as if there was no interruption, "Are you Lucy?"

There was a sudden bang, something heavy had fallen. All but Mrs Willis jumped, but none lost their concentration. I looked around the room with wild eyes. On the hearth, silhouetted against the fire, I saw that one of the elephant statues had fallen over.

Mrs Willis smiled and tipped her chin higher. Her voice flowed from her throat like chiffon, "Welcome, Lucy."

I had to quell the panic rising inside of me. Had something happened to Lucy? To Rosie? A lump gathered in my throat and I feared I would scream. But then Miss Montgomery sneezed and it was enough to break the spell. I took a deep breath. Of course it wasn't Lucy. At least not Helen's Lucy. Séances communed with the dead and I knew in my bones that Lucy was full of vim, as she always had been. My body relaxed and my fear subsided. The hoax was revealed.

Mrs Willis was using the tragedy of Helen's death as entertainment for her friends. That was all. I felt affronted, as though what was occurring before me was a play, and I had been unknowingly lured into the starring role. I decided to leave but as I was about to break hands, Millicent Willis cried out:

"I am the question!"

Her voice was strange, high-pitched like a bird. Her eyelids fluttered open, and even though the room was darkened, her pupils had contracted to the size of a pin-head. She stared into nothingness.

"I am the question," she repeated, in child-like tones.

Across the table, Lady Crane addressed Mrs Willis. "Welcome, dear Lucy. What is your message?"

Mrs Willis repeated, "I am the question. She is the answer. *I am the question. She is the answer!*" And then she pointed at me, which is when the second elephant fell on the hearth. Lady Crane uttered a cry and jumped in her seat, her eyes snapping open.

Mrs Willis exhaled loudly. "She is gone," she said, in a manner without any of the drama it had carried moments before. "She is gone. But she has left a message for Margaret." She turned to look at me, "There is another who is…veiled. But you cannot see her."

My eyes were pinned to Mrs Willis and I would not have been able to look away, had I even tried.

"There is an answer. It is in the wardrobe." The words made no sense to me. With the same speed I had lost faith in the ritual, its magic settled over me once again. There is another who is veiled. Who, Rosie? And what was the significance of the wardrobe? And whose wardrobe? I had hundreds of questions to ask and opened my mouth to do so.

But Mrs Willis forestalled me with sad eyes. "I am sorry Margaret, I have no answers for you. The connection is gone."

5

THIS TIME I DID NOT DECLINE Mrs Willis' offer of a ride home. The other women chose to stay for tea and chatter. But I had appetite for neither food nor talk. Although the séance had lasted only an hour, I was exhausted. The sight of Hendry's filled me with comfort as I stepped from the carriage upon arrival home.

I had just enough energy for the stairs to my room, and longed for the rest a good night's sleep would bring. Inside, Hendry had kindly lit the stove and the room's cozy warmth welcomed my weary bones. As I removed my coat, I noticed a letter on the table.

It must have arrived by evening post. I saw at once that it was from Rosie and was filled with delight. Impatient to hear her voice, I neglected the letter opener, using my forefinger instead. Her words, however, startled my heart; I felt as if a flock of pigeons roosting in my ribcage had suddenly taken flight, their wings hammering at my chest for release.

Yes, the handwriting was Rosie's, the loop "R" of her signature was the evidence. But the penmanship was that of a woman three times her age, as though her hands were crippled and her eyesight poor. Stranger still was the letter's lack of sentiment. The words were ever so brief — so unfeeling — that I wondered if Ford had dictated it, for my sister rarely wrote with such economy:

Dear Meg,

Johnathan and I are to be wed. Please send my belongings for I shall not return to London.

Yours, Rosie

I might have considered Ford the author himself, except for the postscript faintly scrawled in pencil on the back.

Please come at once to sew my wedding gown.

'At once' was underlined with a shaky streak of graphite. And the edges of the paper were dusted with even more. Or was it charcoal?

I sunk to my bed in disbelief. Rosie and Ford to be married? It hardly seemed possible. Why, Helen had not yet been in her grave for long at all. Had their relationship progressed so far in the scant weeks I had been absent? Had Rosie always been in love with Ford, yet given no indication to either Helen or I? I set that thought aside at once; Rosie had only recently blossomed into womanhood. So then why the urgency?

Truly, Ford was a lonely widower. And given the account Edye had described of the household leading up to Helen's death, not a very happy husband. And Rosie was so lovely, what man in his circumstances *wouldn't* fall in love with her?

But how could Rosie fall in love with *him*? We both carried an uneasy suspicion of Ford somehow being involved in Helen's death. Was this some kind of ploy on my sister's part to draw closer to him and discover the truth?

My brain reeled. And then I was moving, fetching my carpet bag from the wardrobe, and gathering my clothes and toilette. This time, I resolved, I would not leave Blueford Manor without my sister. Wedding or no wedding.

As I packed my bag, I recalled the words Mrs Willis had uttered at the séance. "There is another who is veiled." Could she have meant Rosie on her wedding day?

⚷

Despite the lateness of the hour, my mind would not quiet, nor could I sleep. I could not shake off the growing fear that Rosie was in danger and I must go to her at once. Hendry had made me some warm milk before leaving for the day, but it did little to comfort me. After tossing and turning for several hours, I rose from bed. In the past when I could not sleep, I would often sew, taking comfort in a ritual I found calming. Remembering the bird that had died earlier in the day, I retrieved its body from a wooden hat pin box on my book shelf. I had tucked it away, thinking I would give the bird a burial in the little garden behind the shop-front. But first, I intended to restore it to its former glory. I was, after all, a master of making birds even more resplendent in death than in life.

I lit a lantern and unwrapped the creature from its white shroud. The handkerchief offered by the gentleman on the street bore an embroidered monogram, a navy blue 'F' which reminded me of the Reverend Farrow whom I had met on the train. What prayer might he recite over a dead sparrow? Perhaps, like Rosie, he was a bit of a poet. I imagined his blessing as lyrical as birdsong, lean brown hand placed gently over the creature.

With my own light touch, I laid the bird bare of its dressings upon the tabletop. In the shadows of my room, the sparrow's former glory seemed faded. I selected a needle and thread from my sewing basket. Earlier in the day I had chosen a brilliant blue glass eye to replace the one that had been damaged in the crash. A few quick stitches and it was in place. Then I set about examining the broken wing. With strong twine, I secured the wing in place. Finally, I added extra feathers in the area where the skull had been crushed to disguise the injury.

If not for the fact that the bird had no soul, it might have been mistook as alive.

I set the sparrow back in the hat pin box and went to wash my hands. Then I tucked away my scissors and thread. In the morning I would bury the tiny corpse. But now, my head was heavy. The sewing had done its trick to relax me. I crawled into my bed and slept.

Once again, I found myself awoken to someone knocking on my door. Only this time it was Hendry. "Carriage is here to take you to the train, Margaret."

"Thank you," I said, stumbling from the bed half asleep, startled that I had overslept. I yanked off my nightgown, and stepped with haste into my stockings. My fingers shook as I dealt with my corset and I feared it would delay me. But then I was in my dress, with my hair bound. I threw my travel cloak over my arm and grabbed my carpet bag. I spied the wooden hat pin box on the table: the dead bird. I had hoped to have time to bury it this morning. I would have to ask Hendry to do so for me.

I reached for the pin box, and stared at it in disbelief. It was empty. How could that be? I had placed the bird there myself last night. Had someone else been in my room? Impossible, the door was still locked. Perhaps, in my exhaustion, I *thought* I had placed the bird in the box, but had, in fact, laid it elsewhere. I did a quick search of my room — under the table, in the wardrobe, on top of the stove.

No bird.

There was a tin of fabric swatches on the shelf next to the window. I spread it out on the table. I spied a small patch of brown velveteen, which, for a brief moment, I mistook for the bird. There was another basket of larger scraps next to my bed. I spread these out upon the table as well. But no, nothing but fabric.

I stared at the pin box in confusion. In the bottom was the folded handkerchief which I intended to lay over the bird once I placed it in the ground. The monogrammed initial, still stained with sparrow's blood, taunted me. 'F' for *forgetful. Foolish.* I rubbed my forehead in frustration. Where had the bird gone?

Hendry knocked on the door again. "Margaret!" he called.

"I'm here," I answered. I looked about my room one last time, but still couldn't see where I had mislaid the creature, but I had no more time to search. Not if I wanted to make the train to Harrowgate. The mystery would have to wait until I returned.

The coach arrived at the train station in good time, and my earlier nerves waned. I might even have time to read a little of my newest Brontë novel. And so, I purchased a cup of tea and sat outside on one of the many patios that surrounded Victoria Station. I thought how different this trip to Blueford Manor was, compared to the last. I held the steaming cup in my hands and enjoyed the autumn morning. The winds had calmed and the skies were dyed a brilliant blue. Yes, the air was cool but it wasn't cold. Soon I would see Rosie, and all would be well. My anxiety floated into the atmosphere along with the steam from my cup.

I breathed slow and deep, relaxing my shoulders which were so often tense from hunching over my handiwork. I closed my eyes, listening to the birds sing. No, not *birds*. *One bird*. It was very nearby. Its song pure and clear, as though it were the happiest creature in existence. A song so full of joy that I smiled. It had been a long while since I felt true happiness. Even the days I spent in blissful work at Hendry's were always tinged with sadness, reminding me of my father's death. Or my mother's. And now Helen's came most quick to mind.

The song grew louder and I suspected, should I open my eyes, I would find the bird very near at hand. I did so with great caution, not wanting to disturb the creature's melody. And there it was, standing on the table beside my tea cup, its beak parted, notes spilling forth. Then my very breath caught in my throat. This was no ordinary bird, for I recognized its one blue eye in an instant. This was the sparrow that I'd laid to rest in the pin box. This was the sparrow that I had sewn with my own fingers. This was the sparrow that had been dead.

It hopped closer, out of the shadow of the building and into the sun, where its brilliant glass eye caught the light and it flashed like a gemstone.

It couldn't possibly be real, I thought. Perhaps I am still at home in bed and this is a mere dream. But then the waiter arrived to remove my empty tea cup and the little bird flew up to perch upon my shoulder.

"You seem to have found a friend," the man said, before departing with his tray.

How was it possible that this little creature's heart beat once more in its chest? How was I so mistaken in thinking it deceased? I cupped my hand and held it out. The sparrow accepted the invitation and hopped down my arm towards it, wings spread. It tipped its head, examining me as much as I examined it. I gently touched its smooth feathered head with my small finger, stroking the feathers I had attached there only the prior evening.

The clock chimed and I saw that I did not have much time before the train departed. I opened my carpet bag and deposited the little sparrow inside. I closed it once again with great caution so as not to harm the bird, and made my way over to a woman selling seed to feed the pigeons. I purchased a packet, then inquired if she might know someone who sold birdcages, but she was hard of hearing and shook her head, smiling, while pointing to her ear. I bought a second bag of bird seed, and returned to the tea shop. Here, I requested a tea canister and parted with several pennies to purchase one. Though emptied of its leaves, the tin cylinder retained a Darjeeling fragrance. Two embossed elephants charged one another on the tin's exterior. The Indian beasts brought to mind Mrs Willis' séance, when their ceramic kin had toppled from the mantle, as if Lucy's mischievous hand were at play. Mrs Willis believed spirits had expressed their presence in her dining room — how would she explain this mysterious bird?

I opened the satchel containing sewing supplies which I had belted to the side of my carpet bag. I selected a pencil the approximate length of the tea tin's diameter, snapped off its tip and wedged it inside for a perch. I tore a page from my sketchbook to line the tin and catch droppings. Then I transferred the sparrow to the tin and covered the canister with a strip of gauze torn from yardage I'd packed for Rosie's wedding gown. I'd chosen white for her dress. (Since Queen Victoria's bridal gown, the trend to wear white was growing in popularity.) Then I snipped a length of cream coloured soutache and lashed the ribbon around the top of the tea canister to secure the swatch of gauze.

The train whistled its pending departure and I made my way into the station.

In the familiar gloom of Blueford's entry hall, I introduced myself to the new housekeeper, whose wet blond fringe clung to her forehead as though she'd been dredged from the bottom of a pond. With the back of her red-knuckled hand, she wiped away the steam — or sweat — on her brow and curtsied.

She said her name was Hester and I thought her the antithesis of Edye. She stood tall and reedy — like a broomstick — and her hair was the colour and texture of a straw whisk. Her frame was fragile, skin translucent and lips wan. I wondered if she were physically capable to be cook, cleaner and doorman of Blueford Manor.

But perhaps her performance was of secondary concern; her sedate demeanour seemed perfectly suited to the position. If Edye and her tales could be described as diverting as a storybook, this girl was a page from the King James Bible. The Book of Hester; an epitome of obedience and contrition. A thimble-sized cross carved in wood hung about her neck.

She apologised for the delay in answering the door — she'd been in the kitchen and dinner would be served, as soon as I washed. I nodded, a little uncertainly, looking about for Rosie but I heard no approaching movement. Surely my sister would have heard our voices by now, echoing through the sparsely furnished house. But there was no evidence Rosie intended to meet me at the door. My heart fell. I was sure — when she did not greet me at the railway station as I had hoped— that her open arms would embrace me at once behind the heavy, bear-engraved doors of the Manor.

While I carried the sparrow in the tea canister, Hester lugged my carpet bag, bracing it against her narrow hip with two hands as she led me upstairs. Now that I had arrived, I found I was ready to be rid of the exhausting days I'd spent without Rosie. In fact, I was excited to be here. Excited to see my sister and to put my mind at rest. On my first visit, Blueford Manor had been a dark omen of Helen's death. This time, the house did not intimidate me. Instead, I felt its decorated walls opening to greet me. As we entered the upstairs hallway, I imagined the carved wooden rabbits turning their heads in greeting as I passed.

At the top of the stairs, a door at the opposite end of the hallway opened to release a small bounding figure.

"Aunt Margaret!" Lucy called, running down the corridor. Again, she was clad in black, the veil hung over her face. She flung her arms around my legs and squeezed tight. I bent down and kissed the top of her wide-brimmed hat, the closest I could come to her face.

After she had released me, she tilted her head and asked, "Have you come to live here as well?" I could just make out her lips moving behind the veil.

"Not forever," I said, "but I shall certainly be here for a while." Or at least until Rosie's wedding day. If that should be what Rosie wanted.

Lucy spun on the spot, giggling as her skirt and veil swirled about her. She only stopped when she broke into a violent fit of coughing that caused her to crouch upon the carpet and catch her breath, her tiny hands splayed on the floor to steady herself. I dropped beside her and rubbed her shoulders.

My spirits fell. So Lucy had still not fully recovered. I resolved to ask Rosie about my niece's condition as soon as possible.

Though the coughing fit sounded dreadful, Lucy displayed sprightly energy in every other aspect. Having recovered her breath she popped back onto her feet and began to chatter about the wonderful stories Rosie told and the games they invented together. In her excitement, she stumbled over her words making it difficult for me to understand the detail. But I understood the impact my sister had made in Lucy's life by staying on at Blueford and I silently thanked Rosie for her choice to stay, for it had certainly been the correct one.

From her apron pocket Hester withdrew the heavy key ring I'd seen Edye wield so easily, to unlock the same door to the room which Rosie and I had occupied on my previous trip.

At that time Edye had prepared the room to be welcoming, the window dressings drawn and some wildflowers occupying a vase. But this time, the room felt as if it had been entombed. It was cold and damp for no fire was lit. A thin layer of dust lay on the mantle and furnishings, and it was obvious Hester had done little to ready the room for my arrival. Clearly, Rosie had not been staying in this room — and would not be my bedfellow these next nights. I wondered where she slept in the house.

Hester excused herself as Lucy followed me into the room, enthralled by what I carried.

"Is that a sarcophagus?" she asked, breathless in her excitement, poking at the white gauze stretched across the mouth of the tea tin. "Aunt Rosamund told me all about Egyptians wrapped in linen and stuffed inside painted boxes!"

I set the tin canister onto the table beside the curtained window, and untied the ribbon securing the gauze. "This," I said, with the dramatic flair of a ringmaster, "is Soutache!"

Lucy jumped with anticipation as I lifted away the gauze and held out my index finger. Accepting the cue, my feathered companion alighted onto my finger and cocked his head to survey the new surroundings.

"Can I pet him?" Lucy asked, fingers curled in delight.

"Not today," I replied. "He is quite nervous, having taken such a lengthy train ride. In a day or two, perhaps he'll be more settled, and you may hold him then. For now, though, you may simply look."

Lucy thrust her veiled face close to my hand. Soutache was

undisturbed by the wall of black fabric and let out a cheerful chirrup. When Lucy responded with a clap of her hands, the noise startled Soutache, who retreated to the pencil perch inside the tea tin.

I could hear the frown in Lucy's voice, "What is wrong with his eye?"

"It was damaged," I told her, "And I mended it best I could." I did not tell her that I believed Soutache dead. I was still coming to terms with the fact myself. "Would you be so good as to fetch some water for him?" I asked Lucy. "I am certain he is thirsty." I thought she might protest, but she ran to the bureau where Hester had deposited a pitcher and eagerly set to the task.

Doing so gave me a moment to examine Soutache. He looked strong and sturdy perched atop the stick of graphite. I had tried to leave him in peace on the train, but I'd found myself untying and retying the ribbon to reassure myself the bird was still alive. Yesterday, I had been so convinced he was dead, for he had not twitched even once while I stitched him back together.

But I had been wrong. I stroked Soutache's feathered head with my small finger and he whistled with pleasure at my touch.

Lucy returned to my side holding a wavering tea cup saucer filled with water. Her fingers were wet from her efforts.

I took the saucer and set it in the base of the tin. Soutache hopped down from the pencil and perched on the edge of the saucer to drink. Although Lucy was hidden by the veil, I could tell that her eyes were focused on the bird.

I shook some of the seed out of the packet beside the saucer.

"May I have him in my room one night?" Lucy asked.

"We shall see," I said. "We must give him time to heal from his wounds."

Lucy began to protest, but I interrupted with the suggestion that we go to dinner. "Soutache needs to rest," I explained.

But really, I could not wait a moment longer to see my sister.

But wait I would.

"She's gone to Moorwood. It's a half day by carriage. She shall stay the night — there's a reputable hotel — and be back tomorrow." The shadows cast by the chair's wings coloured Ford's complexion a dark blue.

"Did she not know I was arriving today?" I pressed, feeling hurt that Rosie did not seem to be as eager to see me as I was her.

"Perhaps, but if so, she did not tell me," Ford grumbled.

"Or me!" Lucy exclaimed through a mouthful of food. My niece had agreed to fold back the veil on her hat for supper, and it was the first time I had seen Lucy's face in years, save the portrait I still kept pressed inside the leaves of *Jane Eyre*. Her features had changed little. Indeed, her nose was turned up sweetly in much the manner of a younger child, and her lips formed a natural pout, as one might see on a baby. Her blond locks curled in robust ringlets, their flaxen colour mingling with the auburn mourning necklace made in Helen's honour. My eyes darted to Ford, curious as to who had braided it. Ford with his knowledge of sailor knots, or Edye perhaps?

"I didn't know you were coming, Aunt Margaret, until I heard the buggy on the drive! Did I Father?" And here she stopped, and her face gathered together in an expression of thoughtfulness, "Although, I did not hear Aunt Rosamund *leave* by buggy — "

"Do not speak with a full mouth," Ford growled. And so Lucy closed her lips over her food and chewed silently, eyes wide and watching her father. Her cheeks bulged with food as she stuffed even more into her mouth as though in an effort to antagonise him. I noticed how pale her face was, practically white. She had obviously not spent any time out of doors over the summer.

"But if she knew," I said, "Why would she go away on the date of my arrival? It makes no sense."

"Well," Ford said, "She does have a wedding to prepare. And there are far finer shops in Moorwood than in Harrowgate. We expect her return tomorrow, though I'm sure you understand how indecisive a bride can be."

I smiled, although there was no joy behind it, "Indeed, I have made many a bride's hat and veil."

"A veil like mine?" Lucy piped. She waved her fork through the air, a piece of potato threatening to fall. Ford cast her a warning look.

"Of course," I said. "But always in white."

"Oh," Lucy scowled. "I shouldn't like that at all." Her voice broke off into a ragged cough.

Ford's gaze flickered over his daughter, but he made no comment regarding the cough. Instead, he barked, "Remove your hat. As we discussed, you shall not wear it at the table."

Lucy obeyed, lifting her tiny arms to struggle with the unwieldy creation. I rose to assist her, but Ford scowled at me and ordered: "Sit down." And like Lucy, I too obeyed, resuming my seat to study the meat pie on my plate.

Lucy stuffed the veil into the bowl of the hat, and balanced it on its crown beside her plate. Ford frowned at it, but said nothing.

So Ford had no idea Rosie had invited me to Blueford Manor. Why had Rosie invited me in secret? Was there some suspicion she had that I was unwelcome, or did I misjudge the situation? Ford was clearly a private man — I knew as much from his marriage to Helen. There was no reason he ought to change his habits in marrying a second Jaye daughter. As private as Helen's burial was, so he might wish his wedding. It was, after all, a hasty ceremony, Helen dead only a very short time. Church and Crown would surely frown upon such a thing.

I gathered my knife and fork and cut into the meat pie. "How disappointing for me," I remarked coolly, steering the conversation back to Rosie's absence. "Since I travelled with haste. However," I continued with false brightness, "I look forward to seeing her tomorrow."

"Yes, well — " Ford mumbled into his fork.

"Well, what?" I asked.

But neither he nor his daughter answered, both attending to their food with great interest as though dire secrets were buried deep within the pie. Not wanting to make the meal any more uncomfortable than it already was, I bowed my head over my plate and, my appetite lost, picked at the meat pie.

6

THE NEXT MORNING IT RAINED. Not a downpour, such that soaks the hem of your skirt and seeps through the seams of your boots, but a mist-like rain that coats your skin like cobwebs, leaving your dress damp in all places. But that did not stop me from rising early, feeding and watering Soutache, and making my way up the hill to Helen's grave. I sunk to my knees and dug my fingers into the loose soil, bringing the dirt to my face to inhale its fragrance. How many times had Helen worked the gardens at Blueford Manor with trowel in hand and a smile on her face?

What I could not imagine was Helen buried beneath me. I restored the dirt to the earth, wiped my fingers on my skirts and clasped my hands in prayer, conjuring thoughts of Helen at rest. But in my mind's eye, I saw Helen alive and healthy, her red hair scattered by the wind, standing beside me with her paintbox and sketchbook. Her presence felt so near, so real, that my eyes flew open and I half expected to see her there. But she was not. I dropped my hands into my lap and looked out over the view with a sigh.

Below on the river the paper-white swans had returned; there were at least a dozen today. But one in the flock was black. I decided to take a closer look. I rose, making my way down the hill and onto the path through the orchard.

Here again a single track had been cut into the tall grass, brown from the fading summer sun. I walked towards the blue spruce that lined the cliff edge which gave way to the river below.

Last night, I had been frightened by a terrible nightmare. I dreamt that there was someone in the chimney of the bedroom, but all that was visible was a pair of shoes hanging down in the fireplace, just inches from the flames. When I awoke, there was no fire — it had gone out again — and, of course, no shoes. I had hopped from bed and dressed in my woollen suit, shivering all the while. Because I had not eaten much the night before, I had been ravenous. But my early morning appearance in the kitchen flustered Hester.

"Please, I don't wish to trouble you." I said, "I am quite happy to fix my own breakfast."

"Yes, Miss," Hester said. She wore a yellowed kerchief over her hair which heightened her pale appearance. "The kettle's just on to boil."

"And please call me Margaret," I said, as I helped myself to bread and butter. I cut an extra slice to break apart for Soutache later and wrapped it in a linen serviette.

"You needn't trouble yourself with my breakfast on any of the days I am here," I insisted, "You have much to do at Blueford Manor as it is."

Hester smiled, the first time I had seen her do so. "Aye, Miss Margaret. It ain't easy being the only help around a house this size." She banged a heavy skillet onto the stove-top. "Though I don't mean to say I'm not up to the job — I most certainly am — it's just it do tire me out."

I took a seat at the table, enjoying the warmth of the kitchen.

Hester dropped a spoonful of fat onto the skillet. "I'm making the master's eggs, and some for Miss Lucy. I'll scramble one for you if you like." She rummaged in a drawer for a whisk. "I swear, I'll finally remember where everything goes, and it'll be time for me to leave!"

Surprised at the statement, I asked Hester if she'd found another posting. She replied, "No", scratching at her kerchief. But she was hopeful the Master would write a letter of reference. Given my experience with Ford's epistles, I was doubtful.

Why, after Edye's recent departure, was Hester already moving on? In Hester's words, 'It were preordained.' The kettle began to scream. Over its cry, I asked, "What are the terms of your contract?"

"To stay three months, Miss Margaret. T'is all." Hester poured the tea. "Sugar, Miss?"

I declined, taking the cup from her and sipping at the hot beverage.

"Delicious," I sighed, and was rewarded with another smile on Hester's face. "How is Rosie?" I asked, eager for news. If Ford were not forthcoming, perhaps Hester would be.

"I ain't seen Miss Rosamund in some time, Miss. The Master says she is sick. Needs rest."

Rosie hadn't said anything in her letter about being ill. Nor had Ford mentioned it last night, for that matter. Had she caught Lucy's whooping cough? And if indeed she was sick, why was she in Moorwood and not in bed? I wanted to ask more of Hester; but these were questions that needed to be addressed to Ford. And so I finished off my tea, bade Hester good morning and made my way outside.

The rush of the river grew louder and soon I pushed through the low hanging spruce to gaze at the river, its surface ruffled by the wind. The water — so deep in hue —- appeared as purple as wine. Downstream, the river looked like a tabletop set for tea; white swans bobbing on the current, each bird's neck curved as though it were the handle on a china teacup.

I glanced across the riverbank and saw a familiar figure watching me. It had been over a month since Rosie and I had met the reverend Farrow on the train to Harrowgate, but I recognised his tall, black-clad form immediately. I raised my hand and waved, but he did not respond. Perhaps he did not recognise me, I thought. And so I called out a greeting, and my name.

But instead of answering, the reverend turned his back and made his way up the well-worn path to the top of the hill. After a moment, he disappeared from my view. I remained still, watching the spot long after he had vanished. Perhaps he neither recognised me nor heard me call out, I considered. Or perhaps he did, but was intent on his study of bat-life and did not want to be disturbed. Although, I thought, glancing up at the overcast sky, it was morning and surely the creatures were roosting in whichever dark corners they called home.

A noise from the trees startled me and drew my attention from the riverbank, now bereft of the reverend's silhouette. I turned, peering into the shadows, barely discerning a small form.

"Lucy! Is that you?"

A moment later, my niece untangled herself from the branches and picked her way through the bracken to where I stood on the river bank. Her veiled hat was askew, spruce needles littering its brim. There was a tear in the left leg of her black stocking.

She folded her hands and stood still as a statue before me, displaying none of the verve I had witnessed last night.

"Are you quite all right, Lucy?"

"Yes, Aunt Margaret," she said, with a curtsy.

"Are you playing here, all by yourself?"

"You won't tell father, will you?" she demanded, in an authoritative voice.

"Not if you don't wish me to," I said.

"Besides, I wasn't playing." Lucy countered, her hands still neatly folded before her.

"Well, I shouldn't mind if you were," I said, trying to lighten the mood, "After all, ladies must get their hands dirty once in a while, mustn't they?" I wondered what rules Ford had enforced for Lucy's behaviour. I recalled his stern remarks regarding Lucy's table manners, while he himself demonstrated little restraint of his own when dining.

"I ought to be in my room," she coughed.

Considering her lungs, I found no fault in Ford keeping Lucy indoors. "We can walk back together," I said, "And I won't say a word. But before we go, would you like to see the swans?"

"Swans!" Lucy yelped, coming to life. "I love them! That's

why I came! I came to look at the swans." She turned her head wildly, left and then right, the crooked brim of her hat flopping over her eyes.

"Down there," I said, pointing. The birds had travelled a ways and were now almost disappearing into the shadows of the little bridge which joined the two river banks.

"I don't see them!" Lucy wailed, stamping a foot.

"I should imagine it's difficult to see at all through that veil. Here," I said reaching out, "let us remove it."

The moment I touched my niece, she hissed, "No!" and slashed the back of my hand with her nails. I cried out, startled by her reaction and the sudden pain. Her fingernails were deceptively sharp; it only took seconds for four tracks of blood to well up upon my skin. I stared in horror at the wounds while Lucy stood frozen beside me, her veiled head bent over my hand.

I raised my hand to examine the wounds closer, but Lucy grabbed for me again. Her hands fastened around my forearm, yanking me forward with great might.

"Stop, Lucy! Enough!" I shouted, and wrenched my arm free. I held my arm tight against my chest, my heart hammering. I wanted to ask her why she had reacted in such a manner, but I could not find the words. And then it was too late, for Lucy had turned and ran in the direction of Blueford Manor. I stood for a moment, my hands still clasped to my chest, trying to calm my nerves. I prayed that Rosie had not been thus treated by our niece. After I stooped beside the river to cleanse my hand, I cupped my palms and scooped some cooling water, drinking it as though it were a calming elixir. Droplets cascaded down my chin and dampened the front of my dress where it was already stained with blood from my hand. What a mess I am, I thought. As much as the river water improved my spirits, my hand — and dress — required hot water and soap, and I a cup of tea.

I stood, brushed the grass and moss from my skirt and followed Lucy's tracks up the river bank towards the house. When

I reached the top of the embankment, I paused for one last look at the swans. They were gone. But high on the other riverbank, where I had last seen the reverend, stood a solitary, dark figure watching me.

Once I'd washed my hand, ensuring the deep scratches were clear of any dirt or debris, I wrapped my hand in a strip of linen I trimmed from one of my many bolts of fabric. As Rosie had not yet returned from Moorwood, I lay upon the bed to rest. Soutache settled beside my ear on the pillow and sang me to sleep.

I had thought to sleep for twenty minutes, but when I woke the sky outside was dark. Soutache had returned to the tea tin to peck at the seed on its bottom and I heard the dinner gong reverberate throughout the house. My stomach growled in response. I had slept through the lunch hour, tea, and perhaps even Rosie's return. Though I would have expected to have awoken to the sound of carriage wheels on the gravel drive outside.

I checked my hand which, although still red and throbbing, no longer bled. Then I washed my face and tidied my hair. My dress was dreadfully creased, but I had not packed many —favouring the trunk's space for fabrics and notions for Rosie's gown — and so it would have to do until I could launder it in the morning. Ford never dressed for dinner anyway, and Rosie wouldn't care. With haste, I went down to the dining room, eager to greet my sister.

But dinner was yet another disappointment. Only three place settings adorned the table. At the head of the table sat my dour host. Thankfully, the bowl of stew welcoming my arrival offered more charm than he. I desultorily took my place opposite my niece.

Ford's voice rumbled in the shadow of his wingback chair. "Rosamund is tired from her journey; she took dinner in her room."

"Did she not ask to see me?" I asked archly.

"She did," Ford stated, much to my surprise, "but Hester told her you were at rest, and Rosamund had no desire to disturb you."

I glanced over at Lucy. For the first time, she was no longer dressed in black, but a light blue frock which did little to warm her complexion. Gone was the veil and hat. She refused to even look at me. "Which room?" I asked.

Ford lifted an eyebrow at me.

"Which room is Rosie in? I will visit her after supper."

"I can assure you, Margaret, she is most tired. Morning will be time aplenty for your visit." My eyes darted to the light at the centre of the room. It was still empty of its bulb, a cavernous gaping mouth, and above it, the inlaid ceiling. Above which upon the hardwood floor, Rosie's slippered feet would be padding about. It took all my strength to keep my own feet planted beneath my chair.

I wanted to challenge Ford, but it was possible he was speaking the truth. Rosie had spent the night away from her home. She could indeed be tired. I decided to let Ford win this round, and gave him a smile, "Well, I will be glad to see her in the morning." I made silent grace and picked up my fork to eat.

"Mind her wishes, Margaret," Ford said, his voice bearing an edge of reprimand.

"I beg your pardon?" I asked, the fork poised to enter my mouth, my eyes on Ford.

He shrugged. "You may call upon her if you will, but if she is fatigued, I ask that you honour her desire to rest. I understand you are quite an adventurer."

An adventurer? I thought. How absurd. If only I led such a diverting life. As it was, I was desperate for occupation in this sombre household, since I had been so far bereft of my sister's company. Why should he say such a thing, and as though he read my thoughts he said:

"I saw you walking along the river this morning." So the Reverend Farrow was not the only man watching my explorations.

"After visiting Helen's grave," I said levelly. But my words, designed to cut, appeared to have no impact upon Ford. And so I continued, "Hester says that Rosie is ill. Is this true?"

Ford selected his wine glass and took a long swallow, his eyes not leaving mine.

"Not at all," he said, "she is merely tired from her preparations for the wedding."

I nodded, wondering why Hester would say such a thing. She did not seem the type to lie. Which meant that my brother-in-law had indeed told Hester that Rosie was sick. Why? I could feel a headache starting behind my eyes, matching the pulse in my wounded hand. Despite my long nap, I still felt tired and restless.

Ford distracted me from my thoughts with an offer of wine. I settled my fork on the plate and held out my glass. Ford eyed the wrappings on my hand, glanced at Lucy, then turned back to me. "Explain your injury."

I looked over at Lucy who was staring at me with pleading eyes. I had promised I would not mention I had found her at the river. And, I did not want to break my word, as much as I felt I ought to tell her father about the scratches. Perhaps Lucy had not trusted me when I touched her this morning and if this were so, it would not do to weaken her confidence in me further by breaking my promise.

"Brambles," I lied.

Ford cocked his head towards my hand. "Did you do this to Margaret?" he asked his daughter. Lucy scowled at her father in silence. Finally, Ford broke the impasse. "Lucille," he said evenly, "go to your room."

"Johnathan—" I said, but he cut me off.

"Now!" Ford demanded and Lucy slammed her fork onto the table. "Or you shall never see that damned hat of yours again, or go down to the river. Do you understand?"

Lucy kicked the table leg as she slid off her chair, then stooped to pick up her one-armed doll which had lain hiding in the shadows, and stomped out of the room. I sat in silence until she left, then turned to my brother-in-law to defend my niece. She had not confessed, nor had I condemned her. And yet he punished her all the same.

But as I surveyed him, I saw that he was not angry. No, another emotion flickered across his face. Fear. I saw that he did not punish her without cause. Indeed, he knew the truth that Lucy was at fault. Had Lucy scratched Rosie? Or ever been violent towards Helen?

Ford took a slug of wine and dragged his chair close to mine. In soft tones he uttered, "Unwrap your hand."

I looked at him in surprise. "It's quite fine, I assure you. I don't feel any pain."

"Nor does the mutineer on the gang plank, though his fate is determined."

"Mere scratches. Really, I— "

"Damn it, Margaret!" Ford bellowed, and snatched my hand, knocking over my wine glass, and pulling me forward off the chair onto my knees. I bumped my chin against the table's edge as he stretched my arm upon it, elbowing aside his dinner bowl, sending it smashing to the floor. He pinned my arm in place with his left hand and with his right, tore away the bandage.

In the dim light, he brought his face close to my wrist to examine the skin. His cool finger traced a path over each of the four scratches, his nostrils flaring as he spied the dry blood.

He lifted his face to me, his expression dark and unreadable. "My daughter scratched you?"

Frozen in his grasp, I nodded.

His face relaxed and his hands released mine. I drew it back immediately as I resumed my feet. My wrist throbbed where he had gripped it, and I expected it would be bruised come morning. It was only then I noticed the wine stains upon my dress from my overturned glass.

"You are wet," he said, "Here," and he passed me his serviette. "Pardon my impatience." He leaned back in the wingback chair and rubbed a hand over his face. "Sometimes I have a century of patience, other times not." He smiled partially, one side of his mouth turning up.

I said nothing, unsure of what to say. My mind was reeling as I seated myself once again, dabbing at the wine with the serviette. When I finished, I righted the wineglass with a shaking hand, wishing it once again contained wine, or something stronger. He must have seen the tremor in my hand for he reached out and gripped my shoulder with one hand.

"My God, I am sorry, Margaret," he said, "I am a foul beast sometimes." His other hand he laid over his breast. "I promise you, I am not unkind to Rosamund. I am never rough with her. I was only concerned your wound was worse. That Lucy may have bit you."

I shrugged. "Children do bite, sometimes," I said, thinking of the times Rosie had laughed off the Willis children's cruel administrations.

He grunted. "Rosamund said as much when I warned her. She said children act out in many ways when they lose a parent. But Lucy is different. She is strong willed, always has been, even before Helen —— "

His voice faltered as he suddenly noticed the mess —— the table awash with wine, his dinner plate shattered and its contents flung across the floor, the blood stained bandage trailing from my hand. I would have to rewash the wound and cut a clean strip of linen to bind it for the night.

"If you will pardon me, I am rather tired..." My voice tumbled from my mouth as feebly as my legs moved as I pushed myself from the table and rose to leave.

"Of course," he said, waving his hand as though I was now no more than an errant thought. Feeling as though I had been dismissed, I left the room without another word.

"Heavens above, Miss! Are you quite all right?"

Hester's face froze at the sight of the skirt in my hands.

"Wine stains," I assured her. Although indeed, the dark red patches did look very much like the dried blood on the bodice. However, I made no mention that those smears were caused by my own sanguine fluids. I waggled the fingers of my bandaged hand. "And this is only a scratch."

In fact, the bruises I'd received at Ford's hand would likely linger longer than Lucy's tracks. Thankfully, the purple coloured fingerprints were hidden beneath the sleeve of my warm woollen travel jacket.

I asked after chalk for the stains.

Hester wasn't sure about chalk, but her mother swore that milk ought to do as much good for them. I thanked her, and found a basin in which to soak my garment. It would be prudent to soak the skirt overnight.

"Let me take care of that, Miss. No need for you to get your bandage wet."

"Would you, Hester? Thank you. But only if I might give you a hand elsewhere."

"Nonsense, Miss," she chided, "T'is my job."

"You do far more than your share as it is, Hester. And you must call me Margaret."

"When I'm finished, I'll hang it to dry by the fire in your room," she said, as she poured milk onto my garments. "There's a nice shirt tree there to help it hold its shape."

"I think it best to dry it by the kitchen fire, if it won't be in your way," I said, "For there's no fire in my room."

"D'you need more coals, Miss?"

"No," I said, shaking my head, "You've well stocked the hearth, Hester. It's only that the fire you light each night goes out by morning."

Hester face took on a puzzled look. "That's odd, Miss. My mother taught me to build a fire at age four, and I've not had more than three fires that have died on me since." She wrung the skirt, her slight hands surprisingly strong. "In fact, I'm quite proud of my skills at the hearth."

I smiled. A proper Cinderella, after all. "I've no doubt you build a good fire, Hester, but every night it dies. Might it be the chimney's doing?"

"All the chimneys look clean to me," she pondered. "I put a lantern up each morning when I sweep the ash, just to see if any of them bats are in there."

"Bats?" I asked.

"Yes, the Master says they like the chimneys. Dark and protected. Why, I shook five or six of the creatures out of Lucy's chimney last week." I shivered at the thought of bats roosting in the chimney while I slumbered in my room.

"Still, would you be so good as to ask the Master when they were last swept?"

"Ask the Master?" Hester's hands twisted the skirt again, though it had been wrung dry. "I — he doesn't much like to be asked questions, Miss," she said, shaking out the fabric and draping it over the back of a chair by the stove. "Besides, I hate to disturb his mood, if you know what I'm saying, Miss." She dropped her voice to a whisper. "It were a terrible mess, in there this evening."

Of course Hester must think him a brute, I thought, coming upon the dinner dishes strewn across the dining room. "Never mind," I said with a smile, "I'll ask him myself when I see him." She gave me a little bow and I could see the immediate relief upon her face.

<hr />

After Hester had hung my dress, the two of us returned to my rooms. Me to feed Soutache, Hester to tend the fire. Hester had given me a plate of millet grains she found in the dry pantry and I held out a palm's worth to coax the little bird out of the tin. As though happy to see me, he hopped onto my unharmed hand with a chirp.

"There, that's a right good fire," Hester said, rising from her knees to admire her work. "It'll take the chill off in not ten minutes."

She beamed bright as a lighthouse, and I hadn't the heart to tell her that the fire was liable to smoulder before long. When we had passed Ford in the hallway, he had grumpily explained that the flues were clear, regularly swept, the last time not six weeks ago. The only explanation was the fuel itself. As a child, I remembered one winter when father had bought a shipment of coal that had not been properly dried. We'd suffered a week without a fire for cooking or heat for sleeping until father had been able to afford another bucket of the stuff. But Hester was determined to prove Ford wrong, informing me the coal was just as it should be.

Hester let herself out while Soutache and I drew close to the fire, enjoying its innocent heat as it struggled to work its way into a rage.

But not ten minutes had passed before Hester knocked again. "Come in!" I said, but my words were met with a second knock, louder, startling Soutache. It sounded like the toe of a boot kicking the door. I set Soutache on the mantelpiece, crossed the room and opened the door.

To my surprise, Ford stood there, a large copper basin in his hands. He blinked at the dull light coming through the windows, and pulled back into the shadows. "Would you draw the curtains please?"

I wanted to ask why, but instead, crossed to the drapes, and drew them closed. It was only then he came into the room and set the basin on the floorboards. As he bent down, a crucifix strung upon a chain swung out from the open neck of his shirt, and clattered against the edge of the basin.

"I've brought you a tub. To bathe. It will help to warm you." It was the same tub in which Hester had washed my skirt.

"Thank you," I said, startled by the gesture.

"Forgive me if the house is chilled, I do not notice the

temperature. I've asked Hester to heat some water. Ah, here she comes now."

In each hand, Hester carried a large bucket of steaming water, her cheeks red from the exertion of delivering them upstairs. Ford met her at the door to take the buckets, then poured the steaming water from each into the basin.

I was eager to get in the bath, but even more eager for privacy. There were altogether too many bodies in my room, and none of them Rosie. I felt my heart tighten, the smile peeling from my face like old wallpaper. Soutache chirped for the fire was now fully ablaze. To Ford and Hester, I expressed my gratitude for the bath.

"But it's not full, Miss."

"Hester will fetch more water," Ford directed.

"No," I said quickly. "No, thank you. I don't need a full tub. This will be more than adequate to dispel any chill."

Hester looked sidelong at Ford, not sure whose instruction to follow.

"Very well," Ford said, motioning for Hester to leave. She did as instructed, and carted away the two empty pails. As Ford turned to leave, a song emanated from Soutache's throat and he twitched his small tail from side to side.

Ford paused and nodded towards the mantelpiece where Soutache perched.

"What do you have there? Did you find him in the orchard?" he asked.

Soutache chose that moment to flit from the fireplace to my index finger.

"London," I said.

Ford considered the bird's unblinking glass eye. "And what would explain this curiosity?"

I hesitated at first. How to explain I had thought the bird dead, and attempted to repair him for burial? Only to discover the creature yet lived.

"He was injured and I mended him," I said. Ford's eyes rested upon me, but he did not speak. And so I continued: "His wing is weak, so I do not trust him to the wild. But there is nothing wrong with his voice. That can soar well enough." In the shadow of the room, I saw a flash of Ford's smile. "Here, hold him," I offered.

Ford stiffened and made a move to step back, but I reached out and stilled his arm, bringing my hand to his and nudging Soutache onto Ford's. The bird's slender toes looked like fragile branches curled about Ford's thick finger.

Ford examined the bird, twisting his hand this way and that, while Soutache adjusted his posture as his perch shifted. "It is a wonder, Margaret," Ford mused, "that you should perform such a trick."

"Trick?" I said, "In healing, there is no trickery. Only compassion. And patience."

Ford grunted, raising Soutache to his face and sniffing. "If you call such a craft 'healing'." He brought his hand back to mine whereupon Soutache immediately jumped to my wrist. "This creature astounds me," he murmured, with little intention that I should hear. And then he looked up at me with his dark eyes. "As do you," he said.

I took a step back, too aware that we were alone in the room.

"I'll bid you goodnight," he said, and crossed the room and pulled the door closed behind him.

I blew out a sigh, set Soutache aside and quickly undressed by the fire. As I was pulling my shirt-dress over my head I spied a small white square of paper on the corner of the mantle, held in place with a small piece of coal. How curious. Soutache had been perched on the mantle not ten minutes prior, and yet I did not recall seeing the note then. Had Hester placed it there? I sighed, so many things in this house were unexpected. As I slid aside the piece of coal I instantly recognised the author of the spidery writing which spelled out my name. It was from Rosie! Had Ford left it on my sister's behalf?

I tore open the folded paper, which had been sealed with a messy drop of red wax, and dropped to my knees to read by the light of the fire. Rosie's handwriting was, once again, awkward and deliberate. It was hers, to be sure, but written in a hesitating style, as if unsure of which words to employ. In many places the ink was pooled where the pen had stood too long at the end of a letter.

Meg,

Forgive me in not personally welcoming you to Blueford Manor. As it is my new home, I ought to be its mistress. But I am not myself of late. I assure you I shall be much recovered once I am wed. I know that you will want to talk me out of this decision and ask me to return with you to London. But you must trust that this is what I want. Nothing you can say will convince me otherwise. Please respect my wishes and be happy for me.

I ask that you begin sewing my wedding dress at once. Only when the gown is ready, will I be well enough to see you.

Your sister, forever.
Rosie

I did not understand the meaning of Rosie's request. In what manner was she not herself? Ford had assured me that she was not ill. So it couldn't possibly be that. Was it her grief over Helen? Had it debilitated her in some manner?

I rose to my feet but was overcome with vertigo. I gripped the edge of the wash basin for balance, and as I did so I dropped the letter. The thin paper fluttered like a dying leaf into the tub. When it settled on the water, the ink bloomed into black violet and bled into the bath, until it resembled one of Helen's dark watercolours. When we were children, Father could not afford watercolours. And so, Helen would sneak a thimble's worth of ink from our Father's desk, mix it with water and paint in washes of black.

The water grew tepid as I hunched naked by the tub, the coal burning at my back.

As was becoming habit, the fire died once more in the night. On all fours I peered into the fireplace to feel for a draught. There was none, but I could see a great deal of soot had fallen on the coals. I blew upon them and a grey swirl of cinders swirled in the air, like some dark spirit.

I'd had the same nightmare again, the one with the shoes in the chimney. Only this time, it had been accompanied by a scraping noise which awakened me. I had sat up in my bed, peering into the dark, wondering if perhaps it was Soutache who caused the sound. But no, I had closed him into his tin before retiring and the noise definitely came from the direction of the chimney. I was certain it was not my imagination for despite the late (or rather early) hour of the morning, it had been as clear as St Paul's bells on Sunday. I cocked my head towards the hearth, straining to hear. It wasn't possible it was a mouse — something larger was causing the sound. A rat? I shivered. I would take the reverend's beloved bats over four-legged vermin. Perhaps I had not dreamed at all, and mistaken a pair of bat wings for the illusion of two patent leather boots.

I'd remained awake for several hours, my eyes staring into the dark, my ears straining to discern the origin of each creak and groan of the Manor. As much as I wanted to knock on every door until I found Rosie (a fool's task given all the doors were kept locked), and demand we depart at once to London, I knew that I couldn't disappoint my sister in such a manner. Rosie had made it very plain in her message that she wished to become Ford's wife. I suspected she had made this decision more for Lucy than for herself but it was hard to say. I'd fallen asleep at last, but my rest did not endure. Soutache awakened me soon after, chirping a melodious note of good morning.

As my dress was still drying by the extinguished fire, I donned my travelling clothes, the cool morning air coaxing goose flesh along my limbs. When I finished, I drew the drapes and was pleased to see wind had chased away the grey clouds of North Yorkshire and a brilliant blue sky was visible as far as the eye could see. I pulled the fabric cover from Soutache's home and bade him good morning in return. I refreshed the saucer of water with a few frigid drops from the pitcher, spread seed across the mantelpiece and left him free of his tea-tin home to explore the room.

As I made the bedding, I found the crumpled note from Rosie. I had taken it to bed with me last night, holding it against my breast for comfort as though it were her own hand. Although the slip of paper was crushed and torn, I smoothed it out upon the mattress, then refolded it with care and placed it in the pocket of my wool skirt.

I made my way downstairs to breakfast with Hester and paused before the ballroom. I had previously only seen the room in dull light. But now like a siren it called to me. I dismissed the notion that I would be trespassing upon the space. This house was now home to more than one of my sisters. I stepped over to the massive wooden doors and entered.

The interior was lit like the sun itself blazed from within the centre of this room. Light sparkled and danced as it made its way through the glass domed ceiling. The air, in contrast to the rest of the house, was warm and welcoming. It reminded me of the lazy summer days of early childhood.

When my eyes had become accustomed to the light, I noticed the bleached and brittle chairs were now neatly arranged in a group, facing one another, as if placed for friendly conversation.

All of the dead leaves were gone, the floor cleanly swept and — on closer inspection — recently scrubbed. To my right, at the far end, was a chest of drawers with a mound of burlap sacks resting beside it. I had not noticed them the last time I had been in this room. Now, they caught my eye, as a stack of plant pots sat towering there.

In one of the burlap sacks was rich black soil which gave off a delicious, damp aroma. The second held flower bulbs, full of mystery. Tulip or hyacinth? Crocus or bluebell? This was my sister's work, to be sure, and I smiled to myself.

At last a thumbprint of Rosie was evident at Blueford Manor. Rosie.

How the words in my sister's letter had disturbed me last night. I pulled the letter once again from my pocket wishing I could discern some hidden meaning from the mess of black ink. But there was nothing. *When the gown is ready*, my sister had written, *I will be well enough to see you.* Although the words were no longer readable, having blossomed into black smears, they were seared into my consciousness. I did not believe my sister was ill. Nor apparently did Ford, although he did defend her need for rest, saying she was tired from planning the wedding. Yet I had seen little evidence of their upcoming nuptials so why travel to Moorwood to shop? Moreover, my sister was not the sort to fuss over grosgrain or sateen for a wedding bonnet. No, she were more likely — if so in love and longing to be wed — to curl up by a fire and pen lengthy and loquacious love poems. Where was my sister, the poet? Where, indeed, was my sister?

When the gown is ready…

Rosie had not given me a date to finish the dress. She had simply said that when the dress is ready she would see me. *Well then*, I determined, straightening my back as though to welcome an invisible dance partner, *I would travel to Harrowgate this very morning and purchase the necessary fabric.* The sooner I completed her wedding dress, the sooner I would be reunited with one of the last remaining Jayes.

I folded the letter back into my skirts and, with a heart much lightened by my plan, went to prepare for the journey.

Given that the train station for Harrowgate was located on the outskirts of the town itself, this was the first time I had walked the town's cobblestone streets. The bracing country air and cheerfully painted shop fronts were a welcome sight when compared to the dourness of Blueford Manor. After breakfast, I had knocked on Ford's door to inform him of my plan, only to find him seated behind his desk, head lowered, eyes fixed to his charts, with little patience for my intrusion. However, when I announced my intention to visit Harrowgate to find materials for Rosie's wedding dress, he straightened at once and declared it a "splendid idea." I felt his enthusiasm had less to do with his confidence in my skills as a seamstress and more to do with the fact that sewing the dress would certainly keep me occupied and out of his way. He offered to fetch a carriage, but I informed him I had already asked Hester to make the arrangements. When I asked if Rosie had selected any fabrics from her recent trip to Moorwood he simply stared at me, a blank expression on his face, as though he had forgotten her recent journey. I said I did not wish to purchase supplies if she had already done so, but Ford merely grunted before unlocking a desk drawer from which he withdrew a sizable handful of pound notes, saying to buy whatever was necessary.

I protested at the amount Ford offered, but he merely threw the notes upon his desk and told me that Rosie's happiness was worth more than he could ever hope to spend upon her. As his head turned back to his papers, I recognised I had been dismissed. I claimed the money from his desk and left at once.

Upon arriving in sunny Harrowgate, I immediately spied a shop that sold birdcages. I found one that particularly entranced me, its wires bent to form the minarets of a maharajah's palace. It reminded me of the many curiosities in the Willis home, and so suited my own feathered curiosity very well indeed. I paid the shopkeeper, reminding myself to reimburse Ford for this purchase, and continued onward to the main street of the town.

The selection and quality of fabrics and notions available in Harrowgate was certainly not as extensive as I was accustomed to in London. True, I had travelled north with a reasonable selection of my own favourite fabrics, but I could not commit to one until I had seen all that was available to me. In Harrowgate, there was one shopkeeper in particular, one Mrs Soapwith, who carried a beautiful array of silk, gabardine and chiffon. My indecision grew as each bolt of fabric was placed upon the counter before me. I fingered each weave, but could not focus on one design concept. How could I, when the words of Rosie's letter, and the echo of that dreadful séance, replayed in my mind? In the end, and with Mrs Soapwith's excellent guidance, I chose enough silk and lace for two wedding gowns. Although I was still unclear of the design, I knew Rosie would love whichever I chose, for she habitually dressed modest and plain, and was always delighted to don one of my creations. Then, having shown Mrs Soapwith the selection of ribbons and gauze I had brought with me by way of inspiration for the veil, she displayed her own selection of materials suited to the task.

On Rosie's veil, I spent extravagantly. I bought several more yards of soutache ribbon straight from Paris, as well as dove feathers, silk roses and glass beads. Mrs Soapwith pursed her lips and commented that the veil might look a tad lavish. It was the fashion for country girls to wear a simple crown of flowers and only one layer of veiling. I brushed aside her doubts; Rosie's bridal headpiece was my opportunity to make her wedding day a truly splendid affair. And while I was a most accomplished seamstress, it was my millinery work that was truly outstanding. Let Rosie be the most lavish bride from Harrowgate to Moorwood! I cared not about local opinion.

Mrs Soapwith's reservations about my taste ended when she saw I was quite serious about outfitting Lucy and myself in equally exquisite styles. In addition to the muslin and fine fabrics I chose for Rosie's wedding gown, I also purchased several yards of blue silk for my own dress and one for Lucy to match. As well, I chose a varying selection of printed georgettes to make some bonnets. I thought it would tickle Lucy's fancy to choose a colour and print for herself. Mrs Soapwith was in quite a flutter as she made a tower of brown paper packages and tallied the bill. And in the end, I spent only half of what Ford had given me.

Taking up my packages, I thanked Mrs Soapwith, and stepped outside the shop. I made my way down the street to a simple tea shop that I had spied earlier. I found an empty table in a little nook beside the front window and settled myself there, placing my many packages and Soutache's cage on the floor beside me. The sun streamed in through the glass, warming my face. I delighted at the feel of it upon my skin.

The general chatter in the tea shop had quietened upon my arrival and, glancing around, I saw that I had garnered quite a bit of attention. Perhaps it was the exotic birdcage. Or perhaps it was my ostrich feather hat — which, the rage in London, suddenly seemed frivolous and vain among the plain dress of the townsfolk. I could hear the fervent whispers of the shop's clientele which made me feel rather like a stage performer amidst a pious congregation. Well, I thought, sitting straighter in my chair, perhaps it was high time I take a page from Lady Saxonhurst's book, and accept that I was the subject of gossip.

On the other hand, Mrs Willis often said it behooved a woman to fit in with the natives, wherever she went. India or no, I decided to shush the tongues around me by removing my hat, which I tucked inside the birdcage before pushing both beneath the long hanging folds of the tablecloth.

When my tea arrived, I drank it with haste, scalding my

tongue. But I did not wish to remain longer than necessary under the watchful eyes of Harrowgate's villagers. Finished, I left enough coin on the table to meet the cost of the tea, and departed with my wrapped packages and Soutache's new cage.

I would have to catch a carriage back to Blueford on the edge of town. But I had not anticipated the weight of the fabric and my arms grew weak under the strain of so many yards. Additionally, the cage was awkward and banged against my knees making it difficult to walk.

I had set the cage down to rest when a cart and horse came rolling up beside me. I looked up to see a familiar face.

"'Evening," the Reverend Carlisle Farrow said, tipping his black hat.

"Good evening," I said, flexing my gloved hand, trying to restore its circulation.

"You have returned to us in Harrowgate, Miss Jaye," he said, drawing the horse to a stop.

"For a short time," I admitted. "My sister is to be wed to my brother-in-law."

"My congratulations," he said affably, though his eyes narrowed, looking none too pleased at the fact. I nodded, also displaying false delight in the news.

Then, alighting from the carriage, he said, "You look as though you could use some assistance."

"I don't wish to inconvenience you," I said.

"Nonsense," he advised, claiming Soutache's new cage from where it rested at my feet. He lifted the contraption into the back of the empty cart, then took the packages of fabric from my tired arms and placed them there as well. He climbed aboard and held out his hand to assist me. I accepted, hiding a wince as his strong fingers curled around the bandage — hidden beneath my glove — and pulled me onto the seat. He offered a rug for my knees and then the horse was on its way.

"I thought I saw you the other day, Reverend," I said conversationally, "down by the riverbank. Near Blueford."

He shook his head, "It wasn't me. And please. It's Carlisle."

"Then it seems you have a twin, Carlisle," I said, casting him a sidelong glance. "Whoever it was watched me for quite some time."

"A lovely young lady draws curious eyes I suppose," the reverend — Carlisle — said, not taking his own eyes from the road.

"Yes, I suppose so," I said, turning away as if to admire the pastoral scenery, though in truth it was to hide the flush in my cheeks. "Have you been asked to officiate?" I asked, turning the subject back to Rosie and Ford. I had learned no other details regarding their wedding plans, so perhaps they were already arranged.

Not so, for Carlisle shook his head. "I have had no such request from Blueford Manor. And even if I did —"

But whatever thought would have finished his sentence was discarded and not to be retrieved for he touched the crop to the horse to speed him along the road. Again I was struck by the secrecy that shrouded my brother-in-law. Was I always to be the outsider? Was it to remain the same when he was married to my second sister? Would I lose Rosie, the same as I lost Helen?

Ford might be enigmatic, cranky and short tempered, but he had never mistreated me. Nor Helen or Rosie, as far as I could tell from their letters. My suspicions that Ford was hiding something in regards to Helen's death were only that — suspicions. And it wasn't Ford who was keeping Rosie from me. That was Rosie herself, as detailed in her letter.

We continued to sit in silence as we left Harrowgate behind us. When we reached the sweeping hills a few miles from Blueford, Carlisle stopped the cart.

"Look," he said, pointing into the sky. At first I could not see what he was trying to show me. The sky and air and trees all seemed painted in the same dusky tones. But then I saw a darker form darting through the gloaming.

"A bat," I breathed. I had never before seen one in flight.

"More than one," he said.

And there were. At least a dozen. No, perhaps more. It was difficult to discern in the fading light. They were swift of motion, their pointed wings a blur on the horizon. They flew with such speed my eyes could almost not follow. We remained there for an endless amount of time, the horse content to attend to a clump of long grasses. We watched the bats dance overhead as the day's shadows disappeared into the dark of the night sky and the sun tipped over the horizon to give reign to the stars and their light. We watched and watched until the evening chill came upon us and I found myself shivering.

"You are cold," Carlisle said, drawing the rug tighter against my thighs. I slid a little closer to him on the carriage seat — to warm myself, I thought, though mostly I enjoyed the feeling of his shoulder pressed against my upper arm. Then, he tugged at the reins for the horse to move.

"The bats are magical," I said, disappointed to leave behind such a sight. I decided I would no longer be afraid of these creatures, should they take up residence in Blueford's chimneys.

Carlisle smiled as though he possessed a secret. "I am glad you are fond of them."

It seemed mere moments later that Carlisle stopped the cart at the front doors of Blueford Manor and helped me to alight. Hester must have heard the cart for she was there to welcome me, opening the doors wide for the light to escape from within and illuminate the drive. She claimed the parcels from Carlisle and advised she would take them to my room. That left me with only Soutache's cage to carry.

"Thank you," I said to Carlisle, giving him my hand. "Would you like to come in? You must warm yourself by the fire before you continue your journey."

He took my gloved hand and pressed it to his lips, then released me.

"Not tonight," he said, "perhaps another time."

My heart fell, for there was an easiness about the reverend that I would have found most welcome at the dinner table. Indeed, no reverend had ever made me feel so couched in comfort before. His company had lifted my spirits, while Ford's poor manners tired me.

But he had said *another time* and the thought pleased me. I went to turn towards the front door, but Carlisle stopped me. He reached out a hand and pressed his thumb against the pulse in my neck. Then, his broad fingers closed over my neck, almost like a choker but incredibly gentle. His hand was cold, but where his fingers laced around my throat, I felt my skin heat. He rubbed his thumb back and forth, pressing against my vein. His dark eyes were transfixed, as though lost in memory, or thought. I froze, unsure of his intentions. Unsure of what to do.

I dropped the birdcage.

At that Carlisle released his hold and took a step away from me. "I beg your pardon, Margaret," he said, "please forgive me." Then, he leapt into to the cart, grabbed the reins and circled the horse about to head back down the drive from whence we came.

I was still standing in the expanse of light that spilled out from the open door when Hester returned, startling me.

"Who was that, Miss?" Hester asked.

"Reverend Farrow," I said.

"Reverend?" She said with a furrow in her brow, "Which parish, Miss?"

"Harrowgate," I said, shivering again in the night air, "I believe his church is not very far from the manor." I gathered my cloak about me, retrieved Soutache's cage, and entered the house. "I shall take supper in my room, Hester. Please tell the Master that I am tired by my outing and gone early to bed." As I climbed the stairs, I realised Hester was still standing on the front steps, watching after Carlisle, a look of confusion upon her face.

"Hester," I said, an idea taking form in my brain, "Would you have a set of keys I can use? I would like to find the perfect room in which to sew Rosie's wedding dress. The light is of utmost importance." It was true that I would need a proper workspace, but that could wait until morning. In whichever room Rosie had cloistered herself, I would find her. Tonight.

"I believe there is a spare set in the kitchen, Miss," Hester replied, my words breaking whatever spell that reverend had cast. "I'll fetch it for you right away."

8

I STOOD IN THE DOORWAY OF MY ROOM, enjoying the full weight of the key ring in my hand. Like the one Hester had in her possession, it was heavily strung with keys to all the rooms in Blueford Manor. Flakes of rust crumbled from the old, bent ring like dried blood from a wound.

"I believe it's a full set," Hester had said before departing.

I felt somewhat silly that I had not thought to request a set of keys prior to this. I shivered in the dark air despite my grey wool dress and had braided my hair back so that it would not impede my quest.

The enormous key ring would not fit in my pocket, and if I carried it in my hand, the keys jangled with every movement. Hester carried hers in an apron pocket, but a white apron would make me easily visible, and questions may arise if Ford happened upon me. So I placed the key ring in my travel bonnet, tucking some fabric over and around them. Should I encounter Ford, I could merely say I couldn't sleep, and was looking for a quiet place with enough light to work. The hat might raise suspicion. But then maybe not. After all, I was a milliner.

It was midnight; the time to take chances. I stepped into the quiet of the corridor, and closed the bedroom door behind me. Soutache was settled into his new cage, which seemed to delight him to no end. By now he was asleep under the paisley scarf I had also bought for a cover. I hoped the rest of the household was also asleep.

The first stitch begins at the edge of the fabric. So, I would start with the room directly beside my own, work my way down the hallway, and return on the other side of the corridor. There were ten rooms total upstairs, not counting mine or Lucy's, and of course Ford's suite which took up the entire north end of the house. I found ten keys similar in size and shape threaded one next to the other on the key ring. Surely these were the keys to the bedchambers. I located mine, and tried the one next to it. It was not a fit, but the one on the opposite side of my room's key slid in the lock perfectly.

With my heart racing, I pushed open the door. The interior was dark, but I dared not carry a candle. I made my way blindly across the room, arms outstretched to feel for furnishings, shuffling my feet so as not to stumble. I drew back the curtains and surveyed the room by the half-moon's light.

The room was a naked version of mine, except that here, there were no furnishings and dust coated the windowsills and mantelpiece. The fireplace looked like a black maw of a mouth cut into the wall, stretched open in a silent roar. There was no ash in the grate, but some soot had fallen over the hearth.

Tracks where I'd crossed the room marked my path on the dusty floor. The room had obviously not been opened recently and there was no sign that Rosie had ever been sequestered here.

Each key on the ring was in order of the rooms upstairs. This made my search easier and efficient, and alleviated some of the dread I had of being caught in the hallway fussing with keys. I silently thanked Edye or Hester or one of their predecessors who had the sense to order the keys on the ring. Each time I entered a room, my heart would seize, expecting to see Rosie. And each time the room would be empty and my heart would relax. But it relaxed not with relief — but rather, disappointment.

Though none of the rooms held Rosie, I sensed a presence of another kind. Upon entering each room, I heard a ubiquitous sound in each chimney. A faint shuffling, like taffeta, and with it, the sense of being watched.

Bats, I deduced. Thinking of the creatures reminded me of watching them with Carlisle in the carriage under the stars. And then of that strange moment at the front door when he placed his hand on my neck. I could still feel the warmth of his fingers as they settled there.

The bats were either following me from one chimney to the next (a fanciful notion indeed) or they were more prevalent than Ford realised. They had, no doubt, resided undisturbed in these dusty rooms until my midnight sojourn. And now — in addition to it being nightfall — they were sensing my intrusion, coming awake, flapping their wings against the brick. It surprised me so many should still be housed within the chimneys when they ought to be out hunting.

As I worked my way through the rooms, their similarities were clear: curtains drawn, sparsely furnished, dusty and unused. Yes, the house was shrouded, due in part to Helen's passing, but it seemed as though it had been this way for years. Had my sister and her husband never entertained? Had these rooms never housed guests? They hadn't even appeared to have been cleaned on a regular basis.

Each successive room was more tomb-like than the last, and my fears for Rosie began to mount. There didn't seem to be a trace of my sister anywhere at Blueford Manor. I steadied my nerves. I had only a few more rooms to go. The only ones I would not be able to search, of course, would be Lucy's and her father's. Dare I search Ford's by day? It was worth pondering the question, at any rate.

I slid the key into the lock of the last room, which was located to the left of my own. I pushed open the door and my breath caught in my throat. In this room moonlight illuminated the space with an ethereal quality.

Hundreds of watercolour paintings papered the walls. I found a lantern and matches on the dusty mantelpiece and soon had light. Each painting depicted a flower, and each painting was signed in Helen's soft hand.

The sunny ballroom may have fallen into disuse and the grounds overgrown without care. But here, at last, I had found Blueford's true garden, alive with colourful blooms. Alive by the grace of Helen's touch. Locked behind a door that, all along, was only paces from where I slumbered.

All four walls were covered with Helen's botanical studies, starting with Asters to the left of the door, and working around the room clockwise to Zinnia, interrupted only by the windows looking down over the front drive of the house; Helen would have needed as much natural light as possible by which to paint. Across the room, twine was strung and pegged with paintings hung to dry long ago. Now, covered in dust and curled at the edges, the still-lifes had faded where the sun had beat upon them. Brushes stood like forgotten soldiers in jars of tepid water, their wooden handles sodden and misshapen from having been long abandoned. I imagined my sister moving through the space, choosing a brush, selecting a pigment, mixing a colour. The contents of the room were trapped in time, like a fly in a web.

What caused the room to be so hastily closed? It could not have been Helen's death; for upon close examination, the most recent painting was dated last spring, one year ago.

Drops of paint stained the floorboards in a delightful kaleidoscope of colour. I collected the sketchbooks that were scattered across three wooden tables arranged in the shape of an H.

Her work was prolific indeed. I estimated at least three hundred paintings on the walls, and dozens more in her portfolios. How quiet her days at Blueford must have been, this her only distraction aside from mothering. How often did Lucy nap here or play with her doll while Helen lifted a brush to paper? The colours were accurate to each flower, and painted with such verisimilitude that I could almost imagine their scent. What a talent had blossomed in my sister.

Instantly, my heart yearned to show this discovery to Rosie. Or perhaps she had found it already. I shivered in the cold moonlight, the candle's flame doing little to cast warmth in the expansive room. I stared down at the key ring in my hand. There were still a few keys that had not yet been used. They would be for the rooms downstairs. As much as I hesitated to leave, I now felt hope. I had not found Rosie, but I had once again connected with Helen and her presence in this room gave me the faith to continue my search.

Moreover, I would not be able to sleep. I felt emboldened by the ring of keys and the ease by which I'd searched the upstairs rooms. I left Helen's studio, closing the door behind me, and went downstairs. I stood a long moment before Ford's private room. I pressed my ear against the wooden door, but could hear nothing from within. Did I dare knock? I tapped lightly and held my breath. No resounding bellow came from within.

I slid a key into the lock and turned. The sound of a click rewarded my ears. I pushed open the door and slipped into the parlour. I relit the candle I had used in Helen's studio and had light. Upon seeing the room again, I held a new appreciation for its contents — the naval charts that were hung on the walls, the star charts that drifted over the furniture like paper dress patterns, the scopes and sextants and compasses and astrolabes, all scattered about as though they had washed ashore from some ship wrecked long-ago at sea.

I sifted through the star charts littering the blue velvet chairs, each one peppered with smudges of ink and a hasty notation. *Venus trine* or *sextile, Mars ascendant at twenty-eight degrees.* Sometimes there was a sketch, a perfect pencil arc drawn with a steady hand, and stars placed alongside its axis in coloured chalk.

Ford was indeed an artist of the skies and seas, and how it must pain him to live a life on land. I dug into my memory, remembering the last time I saw he and Helen in London, hoping for a glimmer of understanding as to why they had moved inland with such haste. But I could come up with no reason, aside from the ones they gave at the time.

On Ford's desk was the largest diagram of all; a circular map of the sky. I peered at it, the constellations drawn repeatedly, and beside them, the month, as though Ford were tracking their movements. But it was not a full hemisphere. I recalled the nuns showing us northern and southern hemispheres; the tropics of Cancer and Capricorn. But this was a narrower view, a section of sky seen through a telescope, perhaps. I picked up the chart, at least three feet across and held it at arm's length. If an Italian lacemaker followed its pattern, it would make a remarkable —

"If Father finds you here, you'll get a whipping!"

I jumped at the sound of her voice, nearly dropping the chart.

She ought to have been in bed, or at the very least dressed for sleep. But no, Lucy stood in the dark shadow of the doorway in her grey pinafore, the dilapidated doll wedged under one of her arms. The hat and veil was gone and her hair was carefully curled, unmussed by sleep.

"Goodness, Lucy, you startled me!" I said, returning the map to the desk. "I did not mean to pry," I found myself apologising, and scrambled for a lie. "I could not sleep and was looking for a book to read." I claimed my hat, hiding the key ring, and hoped Lucy would not question me.

"If it's a book you're looking for, you won't find one here," Lucy pouted, watching me approach.

"Rosie likes to read, doesn't she?" I encouraged, hoping to extract information from my niece as I extinguished the candle to follow Lucy out of the room. As I closed the door behind me, I noted to myself I would have to return later without Lucy in order to lock it. I did not want her to know I had unlocked it to gain entry. "Do you share your books with her?"

"More like she steals them!" Lucy sulked. I surveyed my niece, trying to grab hold of the thread of questions unravelling in my head. What was she doing awake and dressed? Surely it was well past the hour of two by now. And why call Rosie a thief?

"Well, where is Rosie now," I pondered, "with all these books? We must go and ask her for one."

"I don't know!" Lucy huffed. "But the minute I'm not in my room, she swipes another!"

"How very rude of her!" I commiserated, screwing up my face much to Lucy's delight.

"She's very sneaky," Lucy affirmed.

"Well, why don't we find Rosie and then we shall ask her to return your books at once?"

"Please, let's!" Lucy said, clapping her hands.

"Where shall we look first?" I asked.

"Let's try the ballroom," Lucy said, eyes wide as coat buttons.

"What a splendid idea," I agreed, trying to ignore the creeping terror that even my niece seemed not to have seen my sister of late. Especially as she was the very reason Rosie had remained at Blueford in the first place.

Of course I did not expect to find Rosie in the ballroom at this late hour, but I humoured my niece and hoped the adventure would tire her. Our footsteps echoed as we crossed the parquet floor en route to the ballroom. As usual, it did not require a key and thus I didn't need to explain to Lucy why I was carrying a full set in my hat. We entered together, Lucy visibly expectant, but, of course, there was no Rosie. At the centre of the room, below the grand glass cupola, a pool of moonlight shone bright. Overhead, the chandelier sparkled like ice, and beyond, through the giant glass eye surveying the stars, the night sky winked. I shivered in the cold room. There was no hearth in here, only sunlight to warm it by day.

Lucy reached out and took my hand, her fingers like icicles. "I like it here at night," she said. "It's like an angel's house!"

I squeezed her hand, comforted by the fact that she now appeared to trust me.

"Is there dancing in an angel's house?" I asked.

Lucy looked thoughtful. "Not that I've seen. But mother used to dance here, and she is just like an angel. Sometimes," she said, her voice dropping to a whisper, "you can't tell the difference between an angel and a lady!"

I laughed and squeezed her hand. Helen had taught both Rosie and me to dance. But the only dancing we'd ever done was in nightgown and slippers, around the parlour as father sang us a folk song. Or later when he put us to bed — the door shut and lamp snuffed — Helen would lead Rosie and I in a dance around the room, holding our hands and silently giggling until we finally fell into our beds half asleep from the exertion.

"Let's dance, Lucy!" I said, setting my hat aside. Infused with a sudden happiness, I longed to give Helen's daughter as sweet a memory as my sister had given me.

Lucy dropped her doll and locked her hands in mine. Together we spun like dandelion puffs caught on a draught, around and around, our shoes skating over the carved floorboards and our skirts slapping against our legs. My cool breath hung between us, a visible veil of white in front of our faces. We turned and spun and laughed until Lucy broke out in a fit of coughing.

"Too much," I scolded myself, and pulled my niece into my arms. "Dearest Lucy, hold on."

She curled her fists into the fabric of my coat and when her convulsion subsided, nestled her face into my neck. I kissed her cheek, smoothed her hair and said it was time we went upstairs.

Lucy's bedroom was, by far, the most lavishly furnished room in the house. There was an aquamarine velveteen settee with silk pillows. A low ornate cupboard which looked as though it may have at one time held books. And along the back wall was a mural of a ship at sea in tropical climes. I imagined that Helen had painted it. The swift strokes that brought the palm trees to life on one of the distant islands certainly had my sister's hand about it. I studied the small, dark, figures aboard the vessel but was unable to discern if one was Ford. I helped Lucy change into her nightgown, washed her face using the freezing water we found in an ewer on the nightstand and drew back the covers of the bed when it was time for her to climb in. I pulled the red coverlet up to Lucy's chin and tugged closed the brocade curtains that hung on the four poster bed, enclosing us in a soft, warm tent.

Hugging her doll to her chest, Lucy dropped her head onto the pillow and observed me with wide eyes, as though everything I did were of a great curiosity to her. I brushed away some hair from her face. How many nights had both my sisters sat here, at her side, trying to ease the pain of her illness?

"I saw you go into all the rooms, Aunt Margaret."

My hand paused as I smoothed her hair. "I'm sorry I disturbed you," I said. It would not do for her to mention my trespasses to Ford. But I could not ask a child to hold a secret for me. I decided upon a change of subject instead. "Did you notice the bats too?"

"Bats?" Lucy said, frowning. She sat up in bed. "I've never seen bats, but I should like to. Are they like swans?"

"They fly, but they are not birds."

Lucy thought about this for a moment. "Tomorrow I should like to see a bat. Will you show me?"

"I do not think they would like to be disturbed. When I meet one that doesn't fly away, I'll be sure to introduce you."

"What do bats eat?"

"Flies," I answered. I felt capable of answering her questions as I had discovered that Carlisle had either mislaid a book on the subject within the stack of my packages. Earlier that evening, I had curled up next to the fire reading it, grateful it had helped to pass the time prior my search.

"Swans eat fish and tadpoles. Raw," Lucy said, clearly impressed by a swan's diet. "And flies that swim."

I nodded, encouraging Lucy's spirit of exploration. It was no wonder she was fascinated by the natural world, given she lived in a house where every square foot was carved with wooden flora and fauna.

"I shouldn't like to eat a fly, but Aunt Rosamund once ate a spider."

"Lucy," I chastised.

"It's true!" she exclaimed, "When you see her you can ask."

"I will," I said, tucking the blanket under her chin once again.

"Do you see Rosie every day?" I asked.

Lucy looked at the ceiling of her room and sighed. "No. Aunt Rosamund says she's too sad to play now, but sometimes she comes by to wish me sweet dreams. She lies in my bed and rubs my back. I like those mornings best of all."

Her words, exhaled with the innocent longing only a child can express, set my mind racing. So Rosie was here after all, and still tending to Lucy, though not on a regular basis. But if she was well enough to move about the house, where did she bide most of her time? And if not well enough to roam, where did she take rest? Clearly with Lucy at times. But why not visit me? And why was she sad? She had expressed none of this emotion to me in her letter.

Was this a sadness that came on because of her grief for Helen or a sadness that settled sometime after she waved good-bye to me on the front steps of Blueford? Was Rosie's sadness alleviated by her engagement to Ford, or intensified? And if sad, why marry Ford at all? Why say that this was what she wanted?

That Rosie was here at Blueford, however, was now confirmed. But where was she? The only other place in the house I had not searched was Ford's bedroom. My cheeks suddenly coloured. Was Rosie with him? Before wedlock? It seemed unlike my sister, but Ford could be demanding. Helen used to remark that she found him magnetic and impossible to refuse, something neither Rosie nor I understood in our girlhood.

I pressed Lucy for more information — did she recall seeing Rosamund yesterday, or the day before? How about the day of my arrival? It seemed not a day went by that my sister and niece did not spend some time together. But as for Rosie going to Moorwood? That had never happened, Lucy said. It was just a game, Lucy had recounted, that her father suggested be played with Aunt Margaret.

My blood filled with anger at Ford for lying. Although, Lucy confirmed Rosie was still at Blueford, I was now entirely convinced that it was Ford who was keeping her from me.

Well, if games were to be played, I would strategize in kind. I bade good night to Lucy, kissed her cheek and reclaimed my hat before exiting the room. In the hallway I felt for the key ring and closed my hand around it reassuringly. I counted the keys assigned to each of the manor's rooms — the bedchambers upstairs (including Ford's apartment, yet to be inspected) and the living quarters downstairs. So why was there still one key, crudely cut and slightly rusted, left unaccounted for? Was that where my sister was? If I were Ford, holding a young woman captive, where would I put her? Rosie had a strong spirit, strong voice, and even stronger figure for her young years. She lifted hefty five year olds in the throes of a tantrum without batting an eye. Perhaps Ford needed a more isolated prison? But the fact that Lucy saw Rosie regularly indicated she was no prisoner. Unless my niece were lying. Was it possible Ford had told her to tell me what I wanted to hear?

My head ached from thinking. I made my way downstairs and relocked the parlour. And then? Well, dawn was not far off — it was time to rest.

I lay on my bed, playing with Soutache, watching the little bird hop from one finger to the next. Though I had slept only a few hours, as the sun came up a lively energy coursed through my veins. I had yet to search Ford's room, and by the hands on the mantle clock, I could see that it was nearly ten. Usually by this time, Ford had breakfasted and would be ensconced in his study. I realised I could delay no longer if I wanted to ensure I would not be caught.

I rose and restored Soutache to his cage, leaving the door open so that he might sit on the window sill if he so chose. I then made my way downstairs and once again found myself at the door to Ford's study. I could hear rustling from within and the sound of footsteps. Good. I hoped that he would remain occupied at least long enough for me to take a quick peek in his room.

I slipped back upstairs and down the hall to Ford's bedchamber. I tiptoed past Lucy's room, thankful for the plush carpet. It would not do to notify my curious niece that I was about to enter her father's rooms. I prayed that she was either still asleep or taking this opportunity to spy upon Hester. I no longer carried the full key ring. Instead I detached the two remaining keys I'd yet to use and carried them in my pocket.

The lock to Ford's room gave as easily as the others and I was inside before I dared exhale my breath.

The room was as black and as dark as a chimney flue. I could see nothing. I opened the door again, by a crack, allowing a sliver of light to enter so that my eyes might adjust.

The chamber was easily twice the size of mine, but aside from a plain wooden wardrobe, there was only the bed. But what a bed it was! The bed posts soared at least ten feet tall, practically scraping the ceiling. They were as thick as tree trunks and carved with vines. The drapes revealed themselves velvet to the touch and dark in colour and I guessed them to be blue. I pulled one back.

A dark form slumbered in the bed, covered in blankets, unmoving.

My pulse quickened. "Rosie?" I whispered.

There was no reply.

I reached out my hand to touch the sleeper, and immediately knew my mistake. The form was too large for Rosie, but it was too late. Ford rolled over, grabbing my hand in a firm grip. I squawked in surprise.

"Rosamund!" he barked, yanking my arm forward, causing me to fall face first onto the mattress. I scrambled to an upright position before he could touch me further.

"No, it's — it's Margaret!"

"What the damnation are you doing in my bed?" he bellowed, releasing my hand.

"I'm sorry," I said, scrambling away from him.

I could hear him sigh in the darkness, "Good God, Margaret, you're the only woman I've ever known who has the power to send me to my grave. *With fright,*" he added acerbically.

He rummaged in the dark for a match and lit up a candlestick on the bed stand. In the warm yellow glow he looked youthful, his inky beard smooth over his jaw, his chest a burnished tan against the white of the bed sheets. Candlelight winked on the pendant strung about his neck. My eyes darted away, I felt claustrophobic with the curtains draped around us — as though I were in a fabric tomb.

Did no one but Hester keep ordinary hours? Myself included, I thought, thinking of my midnight prowl through the house last night.

"Well?" he demanded. "What are you doing here?" He repeated the question as I stammered for an explanation. And yet he seemed neither angry nor displeased to be woken from his slumber.

I had no choice but to confess the truth. "I was looking for Rosie. I know she's here. *At Blueford.* I thought perhaps she might be in your chamber. I — I'm very sorry to disturb you."

Ford looked momentarily frustrated. "Of course she's here at Blueford. I have told you as much. But, as you can see, your sister is *not* in my bed."

My cheeks flushed and as much as I wanted to run from the shrouded walls of his bed, I made no motion to move. "Then if not here, where is her room? Where does she sleep?"

He pushed himself up against the headboard, the bed sheets falling away from his shoulders and bare chest. "I assure you, her virtue is quite intact." He drew a finger over his heart, as a sailor might make a promise, and as he did so, it caught on the chain he wore about his neck and the pendant flipped over. Only, it was not a crucifix as I had previously thought, but a key. I felt the blood in my veins begin to race.

Was it the key to another room or secret chamber? It hardly seemed possible, as it was a small key, such as one might use to lock a writing desk or a sea chest. Or perhaps a padlock. I searched my memory but could not recall seeing such a lock anywhere in the manor. Still, the key opened *something*, and led to another secret. I had to get the key that hung on Ford's neck. How I would go about that seemed an insurmountable obstacle. Over six feet, Ford towered over me. His hands were twice the size of mine, his chest a wall of muscle. There was no way I could overtake him. Even if I were to enlist Hester's help, her slight frame would lend me little strength. No, brute force would not be on my side. If I could not take the key by surprise, I would have to take it by trust. Either way, I would have to remain close to Ford to take full advantage of any opportunity.

"Margaret?" The usual gruff edge returned to his voice. My eyes jerked away from his chest and met his once again.

"I'm sorry," I said, sliding from the bed and stepping away, "I shall leave you to your rest. Of course Rosie is not here. I—I should have known better." I pushed through the heavy curtains and made my way back towards the door. Rosie was not here. But she was somewhere that would only be revealed when the mystery of the key around Ford's neck was solved.

Ford's voice, muffled by the velvet curtains, stopped my exit. "I know it pains you, Margaret, not to see Rosamund. Please believe me when I say that your sister misses you very much. She is as tortured with longing for the moment of reunion as I can see you are. But she will not come out until our wedding day."

I swallowed hard, not answering. How could a man who lied so adeptly, also speak the truth so plainly?

9

THERE WAS ONE ENTRANCE TO THE CELLAR, and that was only accessible by a set of crumbling stone stairs outside the hall, to the right of Blueford's rear kitchen door. For a house this young, the disrepair of the steps could only be explained by disuse. Lichen and moss upholstered the risers and drifts of leaves gathered in the corner of each stair, clearly undisturbed of late.

"When I go down for the coal, all's I see is bat droppings," Hester had said when I'd asked her if she had any knowledge about the remaining unused key. Her nose had wrinkled up like an old orchard apple. "I don't like it down there, Miss. It's rank, and frightens me."

The door hinges protested in anger as they swung open and pale light filtered inside from a hole set in the wall. I imagined its purpose was to release the gases from the house, had gas ever been piped to the lamps and appliances. In fact, there were about a dozen such holes set in the cellar walls roughly six feet above ground, and covered with decorative grates. Now, light threaded its way through these holes and cast a pale latticework on the dirty floor.

The floor was, as Hester described, covered with droppings and the air smelled strongly animalistic. Beside the door was an overturned wine crate, and on it an old brass candlestick and a scattering of candle stubs. I fit one into the candlestick and lit it. Holding it out before me, I slowly waded into the cavernous darkness, the cellar door swinging shut behind me.

"Rosie?" I called out, "Rosie?"

There was no reply, except a slight stirring above my head. I held high the candle. The rafters were strung with sleeping bats, their wings neatly wrapped about them as they hung in rows like slippers at a shoemaker's. I paused, my heart beating so loud I was sure it would awaken them. But no, they continued their sleep undisturbed by my presence.

To my left was the pile of coal used to heat a house which had not yet joined this decade by installing gas. The air was damp here, which might explain why the coal burned so poorly. There was a large fireplace at one end that appeared to lead to the other flues in the house. And within its mouth was a collection of books, ready to be burned. I selected one. It was a book of children's nursery rhymes. Were these the books Lucy had been talking about? Had Rosie brought them here to be burned, and whatever for? I found a bible as well, its pages dog-eared and marked with bits of string. Wax drippings had turned the pages translucent, suggesting someone had read the Lord's word by candlelight rather than a lamp. Rosie had never been overly devout although the nuns had tried to encourage her. And yet several passages were underlined, including Ephesians 6, 12:

For we do not wrestle against flesh and blood, but against principalities, against powers, against the rulers of the darkness of this age, against spiritual hosts of wickedness in the heavenly places.

I wondered what occurrence resulted in such a sentence being underlined. Perhaps Ford had felt that evil spirits had taken his wife, Helen. I returned the bible to the grate within the fireplace and surveyed my surroundings. There was a stack of old furniture along the back wall: Ford's old sea chests, a wardrobe in pieces, chairs in need of repair, a desk with only three legs. Along the wall to my right, dusty crates of wine casks longed to be uncorked under the ballroom stars.

I'd reached the far side of the cellar, disappointed to have come up empty once more when I spied something of interest in the near darkness. I lifted the candlestick to see the surface texture changed mid-way along the stone block wall.

A small wooden door, not quite full height, was set into the brickwork. I couldn't imagine its purpose. Surely the door sat against the earth? Perhaps a small space had been cut behind it? What was its intention? And who built it? The door was padlocked but I yanked on the handle all the same. Rosie's name tore from my throat as I pulled on the lock, trying to free it. But the lock did not give. And Rosie did not answer my pleas. Not a sound echoed from within.

Still, this closet was the one place in the house to which I had no access, and so it seemed more than plausible that Rosie was hidden — or hiding — here. The key was most likely the one strung about Ford's neck. I released the lock from my grasp and with my back to the wall, sunk to the floor. I sat in the dust, head on my knees, tears falling, feeling like a lost child.

After a few minutes, I wiped my eyes clear of the tears and there on the ground next to me, I made a sad discovery. Laying in the dust was a tiny bat with no life in it. I picked up the little creature's body which had stiffened in death.

Here was a bat that did not fly upon introduction.

The next morning, Hester and I cleaned and organised Helen's former studio. I eradicated every last cobweb and dust ball while Hester scrubbed the floors and windows until they shone. However, we removed not one painting from the walls or lines strung across the room. Despite the fact that Helen would no longer occupy this space, I could not bring myself to take down her work. A modest fire tickled the hearth.

"Refreshments!" I exclaimed, as Hester returned to the room with a tray of tea and iced cakes to celebrate our efforts. Like Hester, my shirtsleeves were rolled up to my elbows and a kerchief covered my hair.

"S'good place to work, Miss," she said, setting the tray on the table. "If I were a seamstress, I'd like to sit just by that window and look out at them swans." The freshly washed panes gave a perfect view of the river. "Anything we missed, Miss?"

"Not a thing, Hester. And I have taken you long enough from your daily duties. Please have a cake and feel free to be on your way." She selected a sizable pastry with a wide smile and left, closing the door behind her.

I poured a cup of steaming tea and gazed out the window. Perfect inspiration for a wedding gown, I thought, catching sight of a swan's arched back and elegant white plumes. Though dark doubts prickled at my mind regarding Rosie's whereabouts, I could not help but feel excited to begin my task. Despite the strange circumstance of designing a dress for a missing bride, it was always a comfort to have needle and thread between my fingers.

As I could not draw encumbered, I unwound the bandage on my right hand. I examined the scratches which were very nearly healed and realised I could discard the wrappings.

I took the little brown bat from my pocket and deposited it in an empty pin box found among a meagre assortment of sewing supplies that Hester had discovered in the pantry. Whether the basket, notions and scraps of brightly coloured fabric belonged to Edye or a former house-keeper, she did not know. Then I tucked the diminutive coffin and its occupant back into my jacket for safe-keeping. It would not do for Hester to discover my little keep-sake. Rummaging again in the sewing tools, I fished out a pencil, sharpened it with a pen knife and bent over my sketchbook.

All great gowns begin with the ghost of an idea. I breathed deeply and turned my thoughts, once again, to Rosie. But this time, with delight. I pictured her a beautiful bride — and though difficult as it was to imagine her on the arm of Helen's husband — I could envision her, as elegant as a swan, sailing down the aisle of a quaint country cathedral. I sketched until the afternoon light faded, the tea grew cold and my eyes protested the meagre efforts of the lamp light.

Closing my sketchbook, I glanced over at the stacks of Helen's paintings that Hester had organised into baskets under one of the room's worktables. I found the most recent portfolio, marked Autumn '95 in Helen's neat handwriting, and untied its string.

Expecting studies of the orchard's apples and plums, I was surprised by the loose pages that drifted onto my lap. Each one was a single wash of black paint, pricked with dozens of pin holes. I rapidly flipped through the portfolio — every piece of paper was the same; as black as soot as though rubbed against the bricks of a flue and pierced multiple times with a pin. I ran my fingertips over the underside of a single sheet, feeling the pattern of holes raised in the paper. I imagined Helen crouched at the work table, thrusting a hat pin repeatedly into page after page. Had she been enraged, a moment of intense anger driving her to rupture these papers? Or perhaps she had succumbed to madness? And if so, then it may have been possible she *had* taken her own life. When Ford first spoke those words, I had refused entirely to believe them. Now, however, the portfolio I held shone a different light on my sister's mental state. Surely she was feeling some sort of darkness in order to create such macabre curiosities?

I retied the portfolio and placed it at the bottom of a basket, heaping Helen's cheerier accomplishments on top. Night had settled over Blueford Manor and the aroma of Hester's wholesome cooking curled under the door, tempting my stomach to growl in response. Dinner would be soon and I would have to present myself with an open and honest face. Ford must never see that my softening was only so that I might access the key at his neck. The one that surely held an answer to the mysteries that — unless revealed soon — would drive me to madness as well.

⚷

The following morning, I was setting aside my sketchbook

and pencils when I saw the door to the studio creep open inch by inch.

"Is that you, Lucy?" I called out. The door stopped, and started to close. "Rosie?" I said, standing in such an abrupt manner that the chair upon which I was sitting tipped over. Whether the falling chair or the crack in my voice demanded response, Lucy appeared to mollify me. Her hair was dishevelled, her cheeks smudged with dirt and her dress hanging loose upon her limbs, as though it were meant for a child twice her size. In her left hand she clutched the decaying doll that accompanied her everywhere.

"Please don't tell father," she begged, clutching the door handle as though for reassurance. "He said I mustn't interrupt you when you're working."

"You are always welcome, Lucy," I said with a smile. "Please, come in." It was all she needed. Within seconds she was running to my side.

"What's this," she asked, pointing at my sketchbook.

"My drawings," I said, flipping open to the pages where I had sketched Rosie's wedding dress.

"Oh," she breathed with delight.

"Do you like it?"

"Is that for Aunt Rosamund? It's very fancy." She ran her hand across the surface of the paper as though it were the fabric of the dress itself.

"One day you will have a dress like that," I said.

"I think not," Lucy said, without a trace of resentment. "You see, Father says I shall always wear dresses like this." She frowned at the rather plain and shapeless garment she wore. Then she turned a page and her fingers seized mine in a tight grasp. "What is *that*?" she demanded.

It was a page of sketches I'd drawn for Hendry — illustrating the trends and styles we would be creating for the upcoming season.

"My hats," I replied.

"You made these?" she asked, staring at me as though seeing

me for the very first time.

"I will," I said, "when I return to London."

She dropped her doll on the floor so that she could use both hands to run her fingers over the drawings.

"Do you like them?" I asked, inspired by her enthusiasm for my work.

Her finger jabbed one drawing in particular, "I'm very keen on this hat," she said. "Red is the most delicious colour."

"And how little of it there is here at Blueford Manor," I said, thinking of the cool tones that made up the house's rooms. "It is one of the loveliest colours for a flower." I thought of Rosie on Helen's wedding day — how beautiful her red hair had looked in a blue velvet hat trimmed with red roses.

Lucy turned a page and squealed in delight at a sketch for a wool bonnet. "What's this one?" she demanded, rubbing a finger over the checked pattern.

"Tartan," I replied. How sheltered Lucy was! How often did she go into town, let alone play with other children or even see other people? Even life at the austere Sisters of Mary had been more diverting than passing one's days at Blueford Manor. Well, if Lucy could not go to the city, I would bring it to her, I decided.

Turning to another page, Lucy sighed, "Oh, I should like a hat like that!"

"Then you shall," I said, reaching for a measuring tape.

"What in hell's damnation is that on your head?" Ford growled as Lucy and I took our places for supper. He cast a dark look at me and scolded, "And not a word out of you until Lucy answers."

I smiled my best impersonation of the Cheshire cat and unfurled a serviette on my lap as Hester came in with supper on a tray, remarking, "Oh, Miss Lucille, you do look fine!"

Lucy craned her neck to show off the new hat, a replica of the red bonnet she'd admired in my sketchbook. "This is what all the ladies in London wear," she declared.

"Is it indeed?" Ford mused, a smile pricking at the corners of his mouth. "Well, I think it outlandish, this new fashion. But I am an old sea dog, and what do I know?" He bent over his dish as Hester scooped into it a healthy portion of stewed lamb.

As Hester moved to Lucy's place, the girl slammed her palms over her dish. "No, Hester. I don't want any."

"Remove your hands at once, Lucy," Ford ordered.

Lucy's hands remained over the dish, and Hester stood by, still as a street post with her eyes on the ladle. "You always make me eat, Father, but I shan't! I'm not hungry. *Ever!*"

Ford's voice dropped in tone and speed. "You will do as I say now, Lucille. Sit up straight, tuck in your lip and eat your supper." Then, with a glance at me, he added, "Besides, all the ladies in London eat lamb stew."

Lucy cast me a doubtful look, but I licked my lips in agreement. Defeated, Lucy slumped in her chair and sourly watched Hester spoon a small portion of stew onto her plate. When Hester served me, I thanked her warmly and complimented the meal. *What a trial to feed the Fords*, I thought! Had Lucy spent a fortnight with the Sisters of Mary, she'd certainly appreciate that there was more than salted turnip in her stew.

I ate in silence and Ford made no further comment on the hat I'd made Lucy. I knew he despised the fact that she wore hats to the table, but I didn't dare dash Lucy's excitement when I'd presented her the gift. She wanted to show her father, and — since she was seemingly starved for his attention — how could I argue? After a day puzzling over dress design, I'd been grateful to dive into the making of a hat — far more familiar territory than a wedding gown.

There was only one difference between the hat I made Lucy, and the hat in my sketchbook. I'd added a veil in sheer crimson crepe, which Lucy now lowered, drawing a wall between the cooling stew and the scowl on her face.

Ford's eyes snapped to his daughter. "Right then, off to your room."

Lately, Lucy never made it more than ten minutes into the evening meal before being sent to her room. I wondered when Ford would relax his expectations. Or Lucy learn her manners. I made to rise from my seat, with every intention to escape his presence and spend the evening at Lucy's bedside so that I might question her more about Rosie.

But Ford stilled me, his hand shooting out and encircling my wrist. His eyes stayed on his daughter. "You'll go alone, Lucille. Shoo!"

Lucy slid from her chair and bounded from the room, the red veil fluttering as she went.

I seated myself once again and when Ford removed his grip — seconds longer than was comfortable for me — I retrieved my spoon and occupied myself with the stew.

"Sitting with Lucy in her room would belie the punishment," he said in an even tone.

Keeping my eyes fixed on the candelabra in the centre of the table, I ventured, "Perhaps Lucy would benefit from more of your time and attention, and less from being isolated in her room."

Ford's utensil dropped to the table as he leaned back in the chair. Cool eyes studied me. "Like Rosamund, you grow more opinionated of my parenting each day. But you are neither of your sisters, neither mother nor governess to Lucille. You are here at Rosamund's bequest, not mine. You would do well to remember your place as a guest in my house." The last word dripped with icy disdain.

"I am more than a guest," I parried, throwing down my serviette, "I am blood — Lucy's *aunt!* Helen and Rosamund's *sister.* Whether or not you care for me, you cannot change that fact. You cannot marry my sisters and keep them from me," I spat.

"I am doing no such thing — " he said, but I interrupted any further words.

"In binding yourself first to Helen and now Rosie," I continued, "you bind yourself to me! My opinions of Lucy are my entitlement, not mere meddling. They are born for Lucy's benefit!"

"Let me tell you about Lucille's benefit," Ford hissed, leaning forward. "My daughter's misbehaviour is more than grief for her mother. She is willful and spiteful by nature. And dangerous at times." His eyes flicked to my right hand, no longer bandaged, and their grey depths seemed to warm in noticing the healed scratches. "As in her Aunts, these attributes can be attractive… but I would be remiss to raise my daughter without the ways of a lady."

"You expect too much for a child so young!" I protested. "And ill! Be gentle with her — for God's sake — while she recovers!"

"You will not accuse me of neglecting my child's needs!" he countered, in a voice as hard as iron. "You forget she knows better. She is six — merely small for her age." I understood his frustration towards a sickly child who turned up her nose at nourishment, night after night.

"All of this I explained to Rosamund," he growled, bringing his hands down swiftly on the armrests of my chair and dragging it — along with me — away from the table. I gripped the sides of the chair, watching him. "I do not enjoy defending myself to a *third* Jaye sister."

The key around his neck swung free of his shirt, glinting gold in the firelight only inches from my nose. But I could not lift my fingers, frozen with fear. Ford continued, "When Rosamund and I are married, she will resume care of Lucy and you will be on the road to London where you belong."

His face was inches from mine. I swallowed hard and turned my head aside, but he snatched my jaw and forced me to look at him. "This situation is not what I desired," he snarled. "I wanted to be left in peace to mourn my wife." His voice cracked with emotion. "But you and Rosamund came and interfered. And Rosamund, she — she looks so like Helen…in moonlight."

Barely breathing for fear I might miss a single word he spoke, my jaw remained locked in his grip, his voice merely a whisper. "I lost my head. I came through the orchard, and there she was, softly crying at Helen's gravestone. The wind had tugged her auburn hair loose, and it looked as though she were Helen herself come to life. I lost my mind! I —" He released my jaw and dropped to his knees at my feet, fisting his hands in my skirts.

"What did you do to Rosie? What did you do to my sister?" I felt like I was screaming, although I knew my voice was no louder than a whisper. I lifted a trembling hand to rub my aching jaw.

"Forgive me, Margaret," he begged, burying his face in my skirts, "I...was overcome with passion. Overcome by memory. I knew not what I did."

"Where is Rosie?" My closed fists beat his shoulders, "Bring her to me at once! Release her from this engagement! Let her come home with me. We shan't bother you — or Lucy — ever again. *Please*," I begged, my fear disintegrating into grief.

He laughed, a hard snap like wind filling a sail, and batted away my fists. "Oh, Margaret. You're like that little bird you keep, so stupid in the ways of the world. It isn't *I* who asked for Rosie's hand in marriage." His face relaxed into an expression of defeat as he looked me directly in the eyes. "It was *she* who begged *me*."

I made my way upstairs, as though in a trance, confused by everything Ford had just said. I wanted to believe his words were nothing more than lies, but another part of me saw him still haunted by widowhood, and unable to speak anything but truth. I had never felt more lost. And now a new series of emotions simmered in me. Anger at Rosie. How dare she abandon me in this situation? Was her lack of communication deliberately designed to make me mad? If so, she was surely succeeding.

I paused as I neared my room for the door was ajar, and lamplight spilled out into the corridor. I heard Soutache squeak and with haste I pushed open the door.

Lucy stood beside Soutache's cage, one hand firmly gripping the bird, raising him to her open mouth, teeth bared as though ready to bite.

"What are you doing?" I shouted, stepping into the room.

Lucy whirled about, dropping Soutache. He hit the table with a thud for his mended wing did not allow him easy flight. I crossed the room and gathered him into my hands; his heart beat wildly, his pulse hammering against mine as I clutched him to my breast.

"Get out!" I choked.

"I'm sorry, Aunt Margaret," she began. But I could not bear the sight of her. What had she intended to do? Kill him?

"Get out!" I shouted again, turning my back upon my niece. I pressed my lips to Soutache's small head and waited until I heard Lucy close the door behind her. When she was gone, I returned Soutache to his cage, hopeful that the familiar surroundings would calm him. I spoke soft words to him and when I saw him finally relax, I refreshed his water and food, gave him a pat and then lowered the paisley cover on the cage to allow him further recovery. I had not thought to keep the key to my room when I returned the ring to Hester, but I did keep the one for Helen's studio. Ensuring Lucy was not lingering in the corridor, I exited my room, unlocked the door to Helen's workroom, and entered with Soutache's cage. I placed it in a recess near the window where he would not easily be discovered.

I checked on him once again, pet his soft cap of feathers, waited for his soft chirp and only then locked the door and returned to my room to retrieve my cloak, bonnet and gloves. I needed fresh air. Hopeful that a brisk walk would calm my nerves, I made my way downstairs, grabbing Hester's lantern from where it sat on a table at the bottom of the stairs. With trembling hands, I lit the candle. Then I stepped out through the wide main doors.

It was dark for the skies were filled with heavy cloud cover. Perhaps a sojourn along the river would return me to my senses.

I found the bridge that traversed the river and made my way across. The water was like a length of black velvet ribbon, threading its way through the darkness. The night was very silent and not even the wings of bats disturbed the air. I took deep breaths until my heart was calm, but despite the lateness of the hour, I had no desire to return to the house.

What was Lucy thinking? Had not Helen — or Rosie — taught my young niece to respect even the smallest and weakest of God's creatures? It disturbed me that Lucy was permitted to act thus, but given Ford's severe words this evening, there was no one with whom I could discuss her behaviour.

I walked along the edge of the river until I found a path that cut through the gorse and scrub and made its way up the rolling hill. Drawn into the darkness, I followed. As long as Blueford Manor was at my back, I couldn't get lost. Strangely, it felt safe out here in the blackness, like I was cocooned in some great cape. The air was cool upon my face, but my cloak and gloves were warm. I climbed the stone path to the top of the rise, to where I had seen the figure watching me some days past. Down below, on the other side, I could see a little stone house set against the hillside. There was a light on in the window and smoke dancing from the chimney. Supper was cooking and the smell of savoury stew reminded me that I had taken very few bites before Ford, in his rage, had dragged me away from the dinner table.

Raindrops began to fall but I did not move. Instead, I wondered about the occupants of the house. What family lived there, in such a cozy manner? It reminded me of life before Helen's death, before Ford, before being orphaned. How delighted we three girls had been as children with a father who loved us. We could never have imagined the grief that would come to us later in life. I said a prayer for the family that resided there, feeling bound to them by my thoughts, and dashed away the tears that had found their way to my eyes. I did not wish to leave my place of vigil. But the rain had increased in tempo and my coat was now quite wet. I shivered, reluctant to return, but

I had no choice if I did not wish to catch a chill. I turned.

A figure, dressed in black, stood directly behind me. I cried out in alarm and stepped back only to twist my foot beneath me. I fell, tumbling down the path, sliding against the wet, grassy embankment, and landing in a heap at the bottom of the hill.

The figure ran after me until he was above me and crouched down.

"Miss Jaye?" came the voice, and I recognised it as belonging to Carlisle. His hands fastened onto my arms, helping me to my feet. "My abject apologies. I did not intend to frighten you."

I nodded my head, as I did not trust myself to speak quite yet. My hands stung from where I had tried to break my slide, and my legs and arms felt bruised and battered. I was now thoroughly soaked and trembling from the cold.

"This way," Carlisle said, leading me towards the lighted cottage I had pondered only moments ago.

10

I WAS STILL CHILLED, but having divested myself of my wet dress was an immediate improvement. I wrapped the wool blanket Carlisle had given me around my bare shoulders and stepped out from behind the oriental screen.

He had hung my dress next to the fire to dry. I was not sure that I would be able to get the mud out of the skirts, but perhaps with Hester's help, it would be possible. I sat on a chair next to the fireplace, its fabric faded and frayed from years of use. A small pot resided within the flames, the source of the heady aroma I had smelled upon the hill.

Unlike the fire in my room at Blueford, this one gave off a reassuring heat as I surveyed the small cottage. It was really just one room, with a little pantry off to the side. A screen with enamelled elephants, tigers and pythons separated a narrow bed from the rest of the room's furnishings: a table, covered with dozens of handwritten pages (Carlisle's sermons, I wondered, or a new volume on bat life?) and an overstuffed bookshelf containing only half of the man's literary collection. Stacks around the room revealed that most of the books appeared to be natural history guides on bats and other nocturnal creatures. It struck me as somewhat odd that there did not appear to be a bible amongst them.

The door to the cottage opened, and Carlisle appeared with a stack of wood for the fireplace. He tossed a few onto the flames, although the fire did not appear to require tending, and set the wood on the hearth. *A much better fuel than the damp coal of Blueford*, I surmised, appreciating the crackling fire. How odd I had found not one piece of kindling in the manor.

Carlisle disappeared into the pantry and I heard him wash his hands in the basin before returning with a dish and spoon. He crouched before the fire again, this time lifting the lid of the pot to scoop out several spoonfuls of stew into the empty dish.

"It'll warm your bones," he said, passing me the steaming bowl. As I reached out for it, he snagged my wrist with his hand. Unlike Ford, however, his touch was light and gentle. He examined the bruises there, then ran a thumb over the scratches on the back of my hand, but said nothing. His face hardened as he met my eyes and I felt a chill down my spine. It was not the first time he had examined my person with strange, scientific observation, and I was equally spooked. Perhaps I was most unnerved by his apparent lack of compassion, expressing curiosity instead.

As much as the reverend puzzled me, I was grateful for his hospitality. The stew was as hot and as thick as I imagined it would be. Carlisle sat in the chair opposite mine and lit a pipe. As he smoked, I devoured the meal. Within minutes I was finished. He retrieved my empty bowl and returned it to the kitchen. When he reappeared, he held a large mug of cider.

"Drink," he instructed, and I did. The golden liquid was warm and the alcohol burned my throat as I swallowed. When I finished the mug I drew my legs into the chair and rested my head on my knees. The cider had made me sleepy, and the heat from the fire had now cleared any chill from my bones.

"Why the bruises?" he asked.

I turned my head so that I could see him. His face was partly in shadow, partly illuminated by the fire. He looked more like a spectre than he did a person.

"It was nothing," I shrugged. "A disagreement."

"About your sister?"

I nodded, wishing that I could see his eyes and read what he was thinking.

"Does he touch you often?" He asked, his voice rough and dark.

"No," I said, my cheeks colouring. "The scratches were from Lucy, not Ford."

That was the last question for a while. We both sat in silence and watched the flames dance in the fire. But then an ember popped, breaking whatever spell we had been under.

"I thought Ford had done something to Rosie," I said at last, and Carlisle turned his head back to me. "I accused him of harming her, but — " and I clutched the wool blanket tighter around my shoulders, "now I am not so sure. It appears Rosie was the one who proposed marriage to Ford. If only she would talk to me." I could feel the tears in my eyes and throat, "why won't she visit me? Have I wronged her in some manner?"

"Margaret — "

"I want to see my sister," I said, wiping my eyes, "Is that too much to expect?"

"Not at all," Carlisle said, leaning forward to squeeze my fingers. His hand was warm around mine, and I felt safe and protected for the first time since arriving at Blueford.

"Then why won't she see me?"

"Perhaps," he said, and took a long breath, "she would see me, instead?"

I raised my head to look at him. The flames created a halo of light behind his head, making him appear as though he was on fire.

"Would you try?" I asked, and I grasped his hand in both of mine as though in supplication. Though Rosie respected the nuns for their love of children (certainly more than for their love of God), someone had dog-eared that bible in the cellar. Perhaps the reverend's confidence would be just what my sister needed. "I would be ever so grateful."

"We'll discuss it in the morning," he said. In the morning, I thought. That seemed so very far away. And I needed to rest my eyes for a moment. They were so terribly heavy.

"In the morning," I nodded, leaning my head back against the chair and closing my eyes. I felt the wool blanket slip from my shoulders, but I was too tired to move. Within moments, however, I felt Carlisle tuck the wool blanket about me once again.

And then I slept.

The next morning, it was no longer raining. I held Carlisle's arm as we walked along the path that led up the hill to Blueford Manor. My dress had dried, although it was still quite stained with streaks of mud.

Carlisle had offered to cook me porridge, but I declined; Hester, having become my daily breakfast companion, would notice my absence.

"I didn't realise you lived so close to Blueford," I said, as we climbed the hill, "Is the cottage located on the estate?"

"Yes," he said, steering me around a large boulder, "Ford lets it to me for a modest sum." He glanced at me, then continued. "I knew him as a boy in London. Then he went to sea, and I to sand. South Africa, to be precise. I returned for a family — ", he paused, considering his words, " — crisis, during which he offered me the use of the cottage."

"Will you go abroad again?" I asked.

"It will depend upon my brother," he answered, "for his health remains somewhat fragile."

"I'm terribly sorry," I said, "I know the heartache of losing a sibling." He glanced down at me and squeezed my fingers in gratitude. It didn't take us long to make our way down the hill and across the bridge at the river. As the sun climbed over the blue hills set behind the hall, it bleached out the shadows among the apple and plum trees.

In the orchard, dew steamed from the grass in the day's first heat. As Carlisle and I neared the house, I saw that between the rows of tree trunks, a figure moved towards us. In a long cape and wide-brimmed hat, more like pirate than captain, I did not at first recognise Ford.

I almost turned and ran as he closed the distance quickly, but Carlisle placed his hand on my arm as though to prevent flight. After last night's admission that Ford had in all probability molested Rosie, it frightened me to be alone with my brother-in-law.

But Carlisle was here, I reassured myself. In his presence, no harm would come to me.

As Ford drew nearer, I saw he was dressed in more layers than I, as though, like me, he had been out walking in the dead of night instead of dawn's first hour.

"You're out early, Meg," said Ford evenly, his tone neither welcoming nor inquisitive, examining Carlisle as he approached. I was so surprised by his use of the diminutive of my name that I stumbled for an explanation. My cheeks coloured and I forced a smile, mumbling, "Likewise."

However, I knew full well it was my behaviour — coming towards the house on the arm of Ford's tenant before breakfast — that was worthy of comment. Moreover, it was hardly my place to question the Master of Blueford Manor's unusual meanderings.

"Carlisle," Ford said, dipping the brow of his hat. It shaded his face, tinging his cheekbones a shadowy blue.

Carlisle merely grunted, a rather shocking response for a man who — not very long ago — had sounded genuinely appreciative of his landlord's grace. A moment of awkward silence followed, until I felt moved to alleviate the tension.

"Do you go to visit Helen?" I asked.

"Never. Not since — " his eyes flashed to Carlisle, and back to me but his voice trailed away and he licked his lips. Carlisle watched him closely, and Ford cleared his throat under the stare. "I walk the grounds of Blueford every day before dawn. But never again to Helen's headstone. There is no meaning in it for me. And nor should there be for you, Meg. Why torture yourself so?"

My tongue replied sharply. "It is no torture to remember my sister."

The sun rose higher, drying the dew in the orchard, and yet Ford appeared colder by the moment; lowering his hat on his brow and burying his leather-clad fists in his cape.

Though Ford's face was hidden beneath the brim of his hat, I heard a thousand emotions in his voice. "*Remember* her, yes — I do everyday. But not at her epitaph, Meg." He bowed his shoulders against the brightening sky, turned towards the house and began to walk away. "She is not there."

"What do you mean?" I asked, releasing Carlisle's arm and grabbing hold of Ford. He stopped and shook off my touch, glancing over at Carlisle.

"Dearest Meg, I only mean her soul is not to be found buried under rocks and dirt." Then he snapped his head around to Carlisle and hissed, "Correct, Father?"

Carlisle paused to study Ford's cloaked figure before he answered, "As you say." I suddenly saw how similar the two men appeared, comparable in height and clad entirely in black. Once again Ford turned towards the house. I thought it strange he did not invite us to walk with him. Carlisle held his arm out for me to take and I fell into step. Then Carlisle shouted out to Ford, "Miss Jaye requests that I speak with her sister."

Ford stopped ahead on the path, but kept his back to us. I held my breath. How would Ford sidestep Carlisle's challenge? If Ford would not allow his bride's only surviving sister to meet with her, it was not likely he'd acquiesce to the local reverend's request.

How wrong I was.

"Of course," Ford said, the words flung over his shoulder like a cape on a windy day. With an edge to his voice he said, "This way, reverend."

⚷

I paced the entryway between the front door and the ballroom. The two men had gone upstairs which had confused me, as my search had proven that Rosie was not to be found anywhere on the

125

upper floor. I had, of course, tried to follow, but Ford, sounding rather like a naval captain addressing his crew, had instructed that unless I were to wait downstairs, he would not permit Carlisle to see Rosie. And so here I remained, feeling as though time stood still.

Hester had offered to fetch me tea or a clean gown, but I declined both requests, unable to be distracted from this terrible purgatory of waiting.

At last, I heard a door open above me, and the low murmur of male voices. I crossed over to the steps and stood with my hand clutching the smooth oak railing that led upstairs. I had to wait several more minutes, however, before Carlisle finally appeared on the steps without Ford.

"Did you see her?" I implored as he approached.

"I did," he said in his usual calm manner. He took my arm and led me into the ballroom where we could talk freely.

"Did you tell her I wish to see her?" I asked, twisting my hands together. "May I go to her now?"

He placed a hand on each of my shoulders, as though to hold me in place. "She repeats that she will not see you, Meg. At least not until the dress is ready."

My hands dropped to my sides, and hot tears filled my eyes. I felt like a child, one that has been told she cannot have the toy she desires the most. "Why ever not?" I demanded. "Have I done something to offend her?"

"She spoke of her wedding only," he said.

"Tell me what she said. Her words, precisely," I begged.

He met my eye: " *'They shall be as white as snow; though they are red like crimson, they shall become like wool.' *"

I looked confused.

"Isaiah," Carlisle clarified. "Chapter one, verse eighteen. About sins." For Rosie to quote the Bible puzzled me. "Rosamund was — Rosamund confessed her sins to me. Something she wished to do prior to her wedding. She is very devout, your sister." His fingertips brushed my forehead, signing the cross. A look of relief seemed to pass over his face as he completed the motion.

But I was not convinced he had spoken to my sister. Rosie needing to confess sins? Certainly she'd done nothing more grievous than allow the Willis children a few extra caramels at bedtime? And devout? Refusing my company? This was not a sister I recognised. Was Carlisle playing games with me, like Ford? Were he and Ford playing the same game?

"Are you certain it was Rosie you spoke to?" I asked.

"Long red hair, pale skin, blue eyes?" he queried.

I bit my lip. Yes, that was my sister. I looked up to the glass dome overhead and blew out a sigh of frustration. My sister was so close, and still I could not see her. Could I trust Carlisle? What did I know of him anyway?

I surveyed him carefully. Though he was a peculiar man indeed, he did not seem dishonest. Secretive, perhaps. Mysterious, most certainly. But what did I know of men who travelled to the wilds of South Africa? If Millicent Willis were here, she would laugh off my suspicion. *Trust him*, she'd say, *for life is an adventure, and all the grander given the right company*. Besides, through Carlisle's word, I might learn Rosie's. "What else did she say?"

Carlisle stepped closer, his eyes upon me, dark and thoughtful. Pipe smoke perfumed his wool coat. The dark shadow of a beard dusted his lean neck and much to my surprise (for I knew not from what the thought arose) I longed to touch my fingertips to its coarse texture.

In a soft voice he recited,

"Poor ugly duckling, so lost and far from grace;
Do you not know a swan when you look upon its face?"

I had heard the couplet before. Seen it written on a dozen birthday notes over the years. Been reminded of it every time I looked in the mirror, remembering the words Rosie had cooed to me when I struggled to sleep at Sisters of Mary.

And so it would seem he had spoken to my sister after all.

"Very well," I said, wiping away tears. "I will do as she asks."

He squeezed my shoulders, then removed one hand, using a

127

gentle thumb to wipe a tear from my cheek, whereupon he licked the salted tear from his finger. The simple action shook me to my core. The room seemed to shrink in size until it contained only the two of us and nothing more.

But we were not alone.

"Luncheon is ready, Miss — " but Hester stopped short in the doorway as cool air rushed into the room. Her cheeks pinked to have walked in upon us, the reverend's lips only inches from my own.

"Thank you," I said as Hester retreated, my own complexion matching hers and deepening a shade.

"I'll be off," Carlisle said brusquely, and whatever spell had been created was now pulled apart like a spiderweb battered by the wind.

I thanked him for seeing Rosie, and for relaying her message and he nodded, giving me a shallow bow. I watched him disappear through the door and was still standing there ten minutes later, my fingers on the exact spot he had brushed my cheek, when it occurred to me that it was Sunday morning. And yet, Carlisle hadn't mentioned at all whether I had kept him from the pulpit.

A pall hung in the air of Helen's studio as Hester had not yet lit the upstairs fires. I stood in the window feeling as starved for sunlight as one of Helen's paintings, each of her floral subjects and eater of sunshine itself. But Soutache, who now knew the room to be his new home (safe behind a locked door when I was not with him), never minded the weather, cheerily singing as he flitted between the lines of hanging paintings.

I worked quickly, measuring lengths of white muslin, to avoid my fingers stiffening in the room's chilly air. Although I smelled the fresh, yeasty evidence of Hester's ministrations in the kitchen, the house was otherwise as still as a catacomb and I felt eerily alone. However, as the afternoon wore on, I sensed that someone was watching me, almost as though, if I turned my head quickly, I would see a face just behind me, over my shoulder, monitoring my progress.

But when I put this thought into action, there was — of course — no one there. The room contained no closets or cupboards and the door never opened. An uninvited guest would be impossible. But my unease passed to Soutache, who clung to my shoulder, talons digging through the fabric of my sleeve and into my flesh, like an epaulet stitched through to my skin. Then— rather suddenly — he alighted, flying in an awkward manner to land in a flutter of feathers upon the mantle.

He sat there and sang as I began to cut the pattern pieces, but every few minutes he fell silent, as though interrupted. Each time he grew silent, I quieted my scissors, for I too heard what disturbed him: rustling in the chimney.

I laid aside my scissors and pattern pieces and crossed to the fireplace where I dropped to my knees on the hearth, the chill of the flagstones seeping through my skirts. I ducked my head into the flue and looked up, searching for a glimpse of the bats, but I could see nothing in the blackness. Perhaps the sound was merely old soot flaking off the bricks and sifting down into the fireplace. But when I rubbed my fingers against the interior of the chimney, it came away somewhat clean and only a light dusting of ash remained from yesterday's fire. Yet one thing was out of place; in the back corner against the brick, a small object glinted, round and reflective like Soutache's eye.

I reached into the fireplace and picked up the item: it was a small glass button. I recognised it immediately as belonging to my black mourning blouse. I had left it for Rosie before returning to London. It was clean of soot, and untouched by fire. Last night Hester swept out the ash, and it was unlikely that she would have missed the button with her whisk. Rosie must have leaned into the fireplace, like me, to listen for the same strange scratching. Which meant that my sister had been in this room sometime in the last twelve hours.

This thought emboldened my heart.

Perhaps Rosie had not distanced herself from me in quite the way that I thought. I felt as close to her in that moment as I had when I'd read her note. I rubbed the button between my fingers, then pressed it to my lips. Sweet evidence! I threaded a needle and stitched the button to the inside hem of my left sleeve. The cool button pressed against the pulsing vein of my wrist, an ever-present reminder that Rosie was nearby.

With Soutache installed in the workroom, and an entirely different creature in my hand, I rapped lightly on Lucy's door. I had hoped to see her at luncheon, but neither she nor Ford materialised, and so as usual, I'd eaten alone under the watchful gaze of the carved ravens. When Lucy did not respond to my knock, I tried once more. Still Lucy did not answer, but I heard coughing from within. I pushed open the door and called out her name.

Though it was early afternoon, the room was pitch black. Again, no response came from my niece but for her persistent cough. Perhaps she could not speak for the discomfort in her chest. Though I did not wish to disturb her nap, she sounded in need of water. I stepped into the room and closed the door behind me. "It's me, Aunt Margaret."

Having seldom visited Lucy in her room, I did not know my way in the darkness and was liable to knock over the washstand before I even located it. I required light and so I shuffled over to the windows and pulled back the heavy drapes.

In the centre of the room, the curtains around the four poster bed were drawn tight. I deposited the bat in its box on the bed stand and peeked between the hanging damask. Lucy lay peacefully, clearly asleep. Every few breaths she coughed. How could Ford possibly say her cough was an affectation, a mannerism? Something she ought to quell? Clearly, it plagued her even in sleep. I let the curtain fall closed and checked the room for a chest rub or liniment. There was nothing. Water, at least, filled a pitcher on the wash stand. I fetched a glassful and placed it next to the pin box.

Since she had confided that her favourite moments with Rosie were when they lay together and cuddled, I decided to do the same. I slipped off my boots, unbuttoned my jacket, and drew open one of the canopy panels.

As light fell upon Lucy, she woke and scrambled out from under the covers, diving through the curtains on the opposite side of the bed and climbing the bed post.

"Lucy!" I cried, as she shimmied up the back of the bed. "Come down at once! What are you doing?"

I ran around to the other side of the bed where I found my niece clinging to the canopy rail, her thighs tightened about the post.

"I don't like the sun!" she spat at me. "It hurts my heart!"

I hastened to the window, stockinged toes tripping on my skirts, and yanked shut the drapes. I moved away from the curtains, and called out to Lucy, hanging precariously, tangled in the damask panels. "There, it's done. Come down now, Lucy. Please."

Lucy crept down the post and slithered back onto the bed. Her wild eyes — as large and black and round as the button stitched to my sleeve — studied me.

I stepped towards the bed. "I meant no harm," I said tenderly, lighting a candle and lowering myself onto the foot of the bed, as far from where she was huddled on the pillows as I could sit. Lucy continued to stare at me. "Would you like some water?" I offered.

She shook her head, her eyes still focused on me as though I were something that had just stepped out of a nightmare.

Perhaps distraction would lighten her mood. I reached for the pin box I had brought and snapped open the lid. Inside, the expired bat was wrapped in white muslin like a little bride.

I pulled back the fabric and set the box on the mattress between us.

"This little lady doesn't like sunlight, either," I said. "She only comes out at night, and sleeps in the day." Lucy's eyes drifted towards the bat, and her shoulders relaxed. I plucked the creature out of its dressing and held it out. It struck me as a macabre gesture, passing a dead animal to my niece, but the sight of it seemed to interest her.

With gentle fingers she took hold of the creature. Her care impressed me considering her recent handling of Soutache. She stroked the bat's downy fur with a small finger, holding it only inches from the tip of her nose.

"She's very pretty," Lucy stated.

I agreed. "Bats are similar to birds," I added, knowing how much Lucy adored the swans on the river, "since they fly. But they are mammals, like you and me."

"What's a mammal?"

"Mammals have hair instead of feathers and give live birth instead of laying eggs. And are warm blooded."

Lucy looked up at me, as I edged closer to her on the bed. "Like mother. I remember her warm blood."

I imagined Lucy wrapped in Helen's warm embrace. I longed to do the same, but feared breaking the fragile trust between the two of us. Lucy was like a bat herself, I thought — skittish and liable to take flight at the smallest fright. I nodded with understanding and stayed where I was at the foot of the bed.

She had lost so much. First her mother, and then her health. And now, for both her wellness and safety, Ford kept her indoors, and her freedom was slipping away too.

"Mother and I watched the swans every day. Sometimes we picnicked and threw seed to them. But that was...before I was ill." So Lucy's illness was *prior* to Helen's death, not since. Ford was right; the cough was long-standing.

"I like birds, too. Soutache especially," I said, hoping Lucy might regard my pet with the same affection as she did the swans.

"Wings," Lucy exclaimed, "are very delicious!" and sunk her

teeth into the bat.

"No!" I cried, and threw myself across the bed, wrestling the bat from her mouth. Startled by my response, Lucy pulled back her head sharply, teeth firmly set, tearing the bat's wing from its body.

Shocked, my hands fell away. Lucy spat out the shredded wing and it fluttered to the bedspread.

"Oh, dear," she said, blinking at me.

I could find nothing to say, horrified as I was.

"Now it looks like Mother," Lucy remarked, staring at the wingless corpse splayed in her palm. "Only one arm."

A shiver needled my spine. "One arm?"

Lucy explained, rather matter-of-fact, "When mother fell from the rooftop, she broke into pieces. I saw her arm come off, and her head too. At the neck."

My stomach surged, threatening to spill. I struggled to find the words. "Did you see your mother jump, Lucy?"

Lucy frowned and curled her lip, her teeth pale points in the darkness. "No."

"But you said — "

"I saw her fall and smash upon the stones." Lucy said, picking up the bat's wing and waving it like an autumn leaf. "But she was already dead."

Ford was welcome to rage at the workroom door (it was locked) when Hester delivered the message that neither Lucy nor I were coming to supper. But he never appeared, only Hester, accompanied by a tray of pork pie and preserved apple which I dug into hungrily but which Lucy never touched.

I could not face Ford tonight. Lucy's words had led me back to the place where I wondered if my brother-in-law had caused Helen's death in the first place. Until I could investigate further, I counted Ford a murderer who had sought to hide his dark deed by creating the illusion of another.

Is that why Ford never told us that Lucy had witnessed Helen's fall from the roof? Yes, Lucy seemed to take all manner of nightmares in stride, but that she had seen such a sight gave me pause. A dark little angel was my niece. I wasn't sure if I'd brought Lucy into Helen's studio for her own protection, or if I considered her as a sort of chaperone of my own safety. I had pressed further in an attempt to glean more information — had her father been on the roof as well? How had her mother died if not from the fall? But Lucy had simply blinked at me and stated, "Father will be quite cross if he hears me talking about mother with you." And no matter how much I prodded, her lips remained quite sealed.

And so, I turned to Rosie's wedding dress, while Lucy sat perched on the worktable in her new red bonnet with a blanket wrapped about her nightclothes. She watched as I cut the last pieces of muslin. She'd refused to accompany me to the airy, bright workroom without hat and veil and I did not argue. Instead, I suggested a blanket over her shoulders and stockings on her feet might add to her comfort, though unlike myself, she never seemed to notice the cold. On the way out of her bed chamber, Lucy snatched a pair of gloves and donned those as well.

Now, she played with the dead bat, fanning its one intact wing, happily occupied with her new treasure. Hester had long ago lit a fire, and the room was comfortably cozy, reminding me of Carlisle's cottage. I wished I could confide to him my new concerns, and be safe in his company.

But I shook off the thought. I could not let the promise of a blossoming friendship distract me from the danger at hand. At Blueford I would remain, for Lucy's and Rosie's sake. I had lost one sister, and I would not lose another.

I kept my head lowered and worked, one eye on Lucy, one ear listening for footsteps along the corridor. As the afternoon waned, my eyes grew weary of the reams of white fabric. I stood and stretched, moving about the room to light the dozen or so candlesticks that lined the mantle and windowsills.

It was then that I noticed a watercolour was missing from the collage on the wall. I drew close to the empty space, reading the titles at left and right to determine which one was now absent. Rest-harrow, then rosemary.

"Lucy," I said, "Did you move the painting of the rose?"

"Hm?" Lucy murmured, engrossed with the bat. She turned to face me, but her expression was hidden beneath the scarlet veil.

"Right here was a painting of a rose. A red rose, like the velvet one on your bonnet. And now it is missing."

"Perhaps Hester took it," she said. "Or Aunt Rosamund."

The veil frustrated me; there was no way I could look into her eyes to see if she was speaking the truth. Even if I could, though, it was unlikely I'd catch her in a lie. My niece was, I feared, as adept a storyteller as her father. Since my time at Blueford, more strange utterances had escaped Lucy's lips than during the entire séance at Millicent Willis'.

"Well, that *is* strange," I said briskly, although hesitant to shrug off yet another mystery. Lucy paid no mind to my bewilderment. She hummed softly as she toyed with the bat. I came back to the workbench and fell heavily onto my chair.

"Aunt Margaret, please mend the bat's wing," Lucy said and glanced over at Soutache's cage. "Like you mended Soutache." The little bird perched inside, watching our movements with clever twists of his head.

"I'm not sure I can," I said thoughtfully, taking the torn wing from my niece's outstretched hand to examine it. Lucy's teeth had damaged it beyond repair. "I think we would need to fashion a new one, like Soutache has a new eye. Perhaps we could find a scrap of leather?"

"How about this?" Lucy asked, holding up a gloved hand, fingers spread. She tugged off the patent leather glove and passed it to me. Diminutive to fit Lucy's small hand, it was the perfect size for the bat. I threaded a long, sharp needle with tough silk thread. Then I pushed a thimble onto my finger and set to work.

First, I stitched together the fingers. Lucy approved, clapping her hands, for this would make the little leather glove appear more like a wing in form. Then I neatly stitched the gauntlet to the bat. I knotted and snapped the thread, and welcomed Lucy to take the creature.

"Now she can fly!" Lucy exclaimed. "Look!" and she flung out her arm, tossing the bat into the air.

Her sudden movement surprised me, and I jumped out of my chair, reaching to catch the bat as it fell.

But it did not.

The creature tumbled through the air, and somewhere between leaving Lucy's fist and reaching the zenith of its path, a life force tore through its body, twisting it wildly until its mismatched wings beat violently, and struck a path towards the ceiling.

I ducked beneath the bat's wild flight path, overcome with astonishment. As the bat passed overhead, Lucy tilted her head back and roared with delight in a manner that reminded me of her father. The creature circled the room several times straightening its route with each lap as it learned how to fly with its new wing.

I was as enraptured as Lucy, but not with the bat's ability to fly with a glove for a wing — rather, that it should fly at all. *Breathe* at all. I'd come to doubt my assessment of Soutache's demise, but there was no doubt that this bat had been dead. It had been cold and stiff for at least two days in my possession, and how much longer in the cellar?

What kind of dark magic did Lucy possess to animate the creature? My eyes strayed to her as she giggled and clapped her bare hand against the one that was still gloved. But then my heart paused for a beat as I recalled Ford's words when he beheld my darling Soutache.

What trickery? he'd asked. He inquired not after Lucy's dark magic, but my own. Was this magic the same that had restored Soutache? I looked down at my hands, then at the needle I'd thrust into the pin cushion. Enchanted tools? Or enchanted fingers? I rubbed my hands together, then pressed them over my eyes, willing away the roar that grew in my ears. Blood pounded against my temples as I recalled the infinite number of birds over the years that I had dyed, stuffed and picked apart to be stitched into hats.

How little thought I'd given to the feathers I'd plucked from their skins. How little thought I'd given to the bones I'd tossed aside. How many lives might I have reinvigorated, instead of repurposing? Overcome by these thoughts, I dropped into my chair, my hands to my face and cried. I did not open my eyes even when I felt Lucy's hands upon me. But then she was climbing into my lap, her slight arms slipping around my neck and holding me tight while I wept.

I awoke in the night with the sensation of being watched. But the dim silhouette of the chair against the doorknob reminded me it wasn't possible that my sister, niece, or brother-in-law could have breached the room. Nonetheless, I could not return to sleep and so I lit a candle and rose, wrapping myself in my travel cloak for warmth.

I set aside the chair and opened the door, peering out into the hallway. It was empty. I returned to my chamber, dressed in my travelling clothes and took hold of the candle I had lit. Then I made my way into the hallway and stepped downstairs, careful to ensure I made no noise as I opened the front door.

The night air was damp, and my cloak did little to prevent the chill from setting into my bones. Using the directions Lucy had given me earlier that night, I found the stairway to the roof with relative ease. It was a steep climb, each step a single brick of the same blue-grey stone with which the house's exterior walls were built. A thin iron railing set into a low wall on the outer edge of the staircase was all that would break a fall two stories to the ground. Were a child to loose her footing, she could surely slip through the opening between the banister and the top of the wall. I wondered at the whereabouts of Lucy's vantage point when she'd seen Helen fall from the roof.

I rolled the waistband of my skirt three times to lift the hem for I did not intend for Blueford Manor to claim the life of another Jaye sister, albeit accidental. As I climbed, slate coloured lichen, lacing the edge of each riser, broke away under my boot heels and drifted to the stones below like rice thrown at a wedding.

Arriving at the summit of Blueford Hall, I felt like Alice shrunken in a wonderland tea party; the glass cupola rose at the centre of the flat rooftop like an overturned glass bowl. Surrounding the dome, chimney tops jutted from the roof tiles as though they were candles thrust into a cake. Beyond the rows of chimneys a substantial parapet outlined the roof.

And beyond the parapet, a breath-taking view; my eyes traversed the blue spruced hills behind the house, giving way to oak and willow as the land sloped down to the inky river sparkling in the moonlight, and then up again into the sloping hill to the cottage where Carlisle lived. I wondered if he were awake, and out of doors, pursuing the bats he loved so much? Or deep asleep, entwined in his bedsheets. My cheeks warmed and I drew a deep breath, and was strengthened by the crisp air.

A strong wind whipped my clothes and blew out the flame on the candle. But a full moon shone bright, providing enough light so that I could see my surroundings. My skirt flapped about my calves like a victory flag planted on a mountaintop. Feeling courageous, I edged closer to the parapet and took a dizzying look forty feet down to the paving stones where Helen had been found.

But from where had she fallen? Or been tossed, if I were to believe Lucy. Here, at the front of the house, where anyone might see? Or around back, where only the housekeeper might? Thank goodness Edye had not witnessed the tragedy, I thought. My eyes studied the roof and I saw that the surface was slick with green moss, except in one spot. I went over and dropped to one knee. My fingers touched the tiles where the moss had been scraped away — possibly by footprints? I identified the shape of a woman's boot heel, then another, and another. Helen had walked here. Of that I was certain. So perhaps Helen had not already been dead when she fell? I rubbed my upper arms to fend off the icy rooftop wind.

Stepping back from the boot heels, I located a second set of footsteps — these ones obviously male — and following Helen's. Where the two sets of prints intersected was a flurry of scuff marks, the moss completely scraped away and the remnants scattered about like discarded scraps of fabric.

The length of the scuff marks indicated shoes sliding in haste. Had Ford run at Helen, and pushed her over the edge unawares?

I shuddered at the thought and crept once more to the edge of the roof. I leaned over the parapet and envisioned Helen's body on the paving stones below. The ground tilted violently and I hauled myself backwards, sitting against a chimney stack to catch my breath.

Were the footprints evidence enough that a murderer lived in this house? Would the police be able to cast a net based solely on suspicion? What about Lucy's testimony? If it were even reliable. Lucy had said Helen was already dead when she fell from the roof. But if that were the case, I would have seen only one set of footprints, those of Ford carrying a body.

Or did the woman's prints belong to someone else? Perhaps to Rosie? Would she have come up here, as did I, wanting to know more about our sister's death? Had Ford stopped her? Or did something else occur? And why even allow me to stay at the house? Why not send me back to London? Elope with Rosie and ship Lucy to boarding school? Were there not a hundred measures he could take to retain privacy? After all, he limited his housekeepers to three month's employment. Surely that condition was to protect some piece of information he dared not share. How hard would it be to limit my residency, as well?

And then it occurred to me. He allowed me to stay because Rosie demanded it. My presence here was because my sister, his bride to be, insisted I be allowed to stay. It had been she who called me to come. And surely she who demanded I stay. Ford had no choice, no say in the matter. And for the first time in days a smile touched my lips.

Only Rosie could illuminate the mystery of Blueford Manor. I needed to finish the dress, if that was to be the ransom required to see my sister.

⚷

By afternoon of the next day, the muslin of Rosie's dress was complete; a cotton blueprint for the finer version yet to come.

I admired it at arm's length, the lightweight fabric grazing the floor boards like the tail of an albino peacock.

The gown embodied the modern trends of the day and was very much the style of what a woman in the west end of London would wear to wed at St Martin in the Fields; a minimal bustle, with the focus on a delicate waist and soft bust line. The design retained the continent's influence: celebrating a woman's natural shape, the graceful S-curve of bust, waist and hips.

It pleased me to have created this, for it reminded me that I lived in modern times, not some Gothic novel. And *I* was a modern woman, with a diverting career. Being able to replicate what I had seen in contemporary fashion papers indicated that I was a talented seamstress, and had the capacity to grow beyond millinery. I did adore hats, but knew I could never again surrender a bird's wing to fashion.

With no dressmaker's form — and no Rosie — I would have to fit the dress using myself as the model. Although I was taller, Rosie and I were of similar stature. I would fit the bodice and skirt to my weight, and mark the hem once the dress was upon my sister.

I peeled off my clothes beside the fire and shimmied into the muslin. The wedding gown fit generously, blousing too much at the bust, and the puffed sleeves — extravagantly constructed — nearly touched my jawline. But such was the fashion, and I knew the dress would look stunning on my sister. The bodice I would take in, but to pin the seams symmetrically, I required a looking glass. Conveniently, two mirrors — shrouded in black morning cloth — hung in the entrance hall.

I padded downstairs in the muslin, a pin cushion secured to my wrist, looking more like a ghost than a flesh and blood woman, and stood before the mirror on the southerly wall. I yanked away its heavy black damask cover, but beneath the cloth the frame was empty of glass. I peeked behind a large sea chest pushed against the wall, should the glass be propped behind. But it was not.

On the opposite wall, the glass was also missing from its

frame. I puzzled as to the meaning — if one troubled to remove the glass altogether, why bother to dress the frames in mourning? I thought to ask Hester, but remembered the shrouds had been in place prior to her arrival. It was Edye who was here when the house had first been dressed in black.

No matter, there had to be mirrors aplenty upstairs. I fetched the key ring from Hester, but my search was fruitless. Even in the locked, unoccupied rooms, black fabric hung over empty frames. Frustrated, I rubbed my head and blew out a loud sigh.

Though I doubted that Hester knew the whereabouts of the missing mirrors, I returned to the kitchen and told her about my quest. Her puzzled frown reflected mine, "It don't make sense, Miss. I've no idea where they might be."

"No matter," I shrugged. I would pin the dress as best I could, then remeasure my edits by laying the dress flat.

"And if you don't mind me saying so, Miss, that's a very fine dress. I think your sister will wear it proud. I surely would!"

I thanked her and turned to go, then remembered another missing article.

"Hester — would you happen to know — well, there's a painting missing upstairs from Helen's studio and —"

"Oh, Miss, I am sorry!" Hester burst out, slapping flour-dusted hands to her cheeks. "I didn't think you'd notice, but I swear I'm no thief! I never stole before in my life, I am as honest a housekeeper as any! Please don't tell the Master…I'll get it straight away!"

I was shocked by the confession. I'd not suspected she'd taken it — only that she might have seen it, waylaid somewhere by Lucy. Before I had a chance to respond, she darted around the corner and I heard her open the door to the pantry. She returned a moment later, holding the painting between two fingers wrapped in the clean corners of her apron. She blew away a puff of flour from the page, her face red as a radish, and offered it to me.

I thanked her, but flipping it over I was confused. "But, Hester, this isn't the rose painting."

"Rose painting?" she echoed. "No, Miss." Her eyes darted wildly and she licked her lips. "'Tis Clover, Miss."

I studied Helen's painting, a delicate green three-leaf clover, with more in bloom in the background and a single bee in the upper right. "It's lovely," I remarked. "But I was looking for a painting of red roses. Never mind." I passed the painting back to her. "Keep it, if you admire it so."

"R-really, Miss?"

"Of course. Tell me, does clover hold special meaning to you?" I smiled, hoping to set her at ease.

She studied the watercolour, as if for the first time, and her cheeks pinked. "The holy trinity, Miss. A leaf each for the Father, the Son and the Holy Ghost." She touched the cross at her neck and glanced up at me. "Miss, you must believe me I ain't no thief. I wouldn't dream of taking anything of value. I mean, Mistress Helen's paintings — God bless her soul — are very valuable to you. And to the Master, I'm sure, but I thought you wouldn't miss this one. It weren't on the wall, just in one of them baskets under the table, and there were so many, and it being so lovely, I— "

I reached out and gripped her shoulders. "Hester, I won't tell the Master. I want you to have the painting, if it brings you comfort. Helen would have liked that."

"Oh, it do Miss! It brings me comfort and peace. Comfort and peace." She nodded vigourously to herself and I left her in the kitchen, staring down at the clover with a smile, the smell of fresh dough lingering in the air.

Since I had eaten all of my meals alone, it had been some days since I'd last seen Ford in the orchard with Carlisle. And so, tonight when I arrived in the dining hall, I was very much surprised to see Lucy and Ford already seated.

"Margaret," Ford said, as I joined them and I nodded my head in greeting. My heart skipped with excitement, for the game was on; though I'd appreciated the reprieve from Ford's stormy disposition, I'd not had an opportunity to obtain the key that hung around his neck. Perhaps tonight would prove lucky.

He poured a glass of wine for himself and looked at me with appraising eyes. "You look as though you spent the day ferreting out our secrets."

"Not at all," I said with false confidence, and held out my glass for wine; I would need courage to see me through the next hour. I hoped that neither Ford nor Lucy had seen me on the roof last night. And I especially did not want my brother-in-law to realise that I had grown suspicious of him yet again.

Much to my relief, Hester arrived with the dinner cart, drawing Ford's attention. When she saw me, she blushed and ducked her head, still clearly embarrassed by our earlier conversation. As well, perhaps she harboured concern that I may have told Ford about her indiscretion in taking the painting.

I tried to catch her eye that I might reassure her, but Hester quickly served the meal (rabbit with dumplings), behaving not unlike a rabbit herself. Then she moved on to Lucy. Usually Ford was served first and so he watched her curiously with half-lidded eyes. By the time she came to the head of the table, her hands were visibly shaking. As she passed him his dinner, the plate slipped and careened to the table. Ford's hand shot out to save the dish from skidding over the edge and a shank of rabbit spun onto the cuff of his shirt. Without a word, he picked it off and tossed it back onto the plate, gravy splattering over the front of his shirt. Lucy laughed uproariously.

"I'm so sorry, Sir," Hester choked, looking like she was about to be condemned.

Ford interrupted her. "Your apron, Hester."

"Sir?" she croaked, her face draining of blood.

"Your apron, please, Hester. I'm covered in goddamned gravy."

She hastened to untie it and all but threw it at Ford. He grunted his thanks and used the white cotton to mop his sleeve and scrub at the gravy spray. When finished, he tossed it back to her and she stood holding it between her fingers as though it were a dead rabbit itself.

"Very well," Ford said, lifting his brows and waving his hand. "You may go."

Hester scurried from the dining room and Ford looked at me questioningly. "What the devil has gotten into her?"

I looked at my rabbit with intent, and busied myself with knife and fork. "Perhaps Hester is overworked," I said.

"Overworked?" Ford scoffed. It was plain that his tastes were simple and his house modestly kept. "How do you arrive at that conclusion?"

"Only that now she cooks for four instead of two," I said, although I wondered just how much appetite Lucy and Rosie displayed. "And extra laundry and fires to tend, now that I am staying — "

"So you think yourself a burden?"

Taken aback, I set aside my fork and took a swallow of wine. "That's hardly what I meant, only that — "

"Only that the increase of her workload is entirely due to you. No, no, don't argue. I fully see your point, Margaret. A day off would be good for her, don't you agree?"

I met his eye. "That would be very fair," I said. "And most generous."

Ford grinned. "I am glad you concur. Now, tell me about the increase in *your* workload. Are you not tasked to sew a wedding dress?"

I responded in the affirmative and took another bite of food, uneasy about where Ford's line of questioning would lead.

"Well, then," he continued, his eyes narrowing, "is it now also your place to exhume the dead on my property?"

So Ford knew about the bat. Or, as Lucy referred to it, her pet 'Flue'.

"Because she sleeps in the chimney in my room," Lucy explained. "I shan't light a fire in my room ever again!"

I smiled warmly at Lucy's delight but inside I felt frigid.

I dearly wished Ford would change the subject. I did not care to be questioned about the bat's new-found life.

But Ford persisted. "You puzzle us, Margaret. You and your remarkable ways." He leaned close to me, as if sniffing out a rat. "My daughter showed me your latest creation. A bat that came to life, along with a bird that sees out of a marble eye." Ford's eyes remained locked on my face. "What else yields under your hand? Locked doors and mossy rooftops?"

My eyes darted to the key chained around his neck, then refocused on his face. I opened my mouth to speak, but before I could utter a word, Ford slammed his palm upon the table top. "Thank God for you, Magpie," he practically shouted. His voice dropped to a whisper. "You have successfully entertained my daughter with your magic. Well done."

Lucy shrieked with excitement. "Oh, Father, *do* entertain me! Might we have a ball? I would love to dance in my delicious red bonnet!" Lucy had obediently cleared her plate, for once having had no argument over her serving, and jauntily tossed her utensils aside.

Through a mouthful of meat, Ford mumbled, "A ball?"

"Oh, yes please, Father! I think Aunt Margaret would like one, too!"

Ford raised an eyebrow at me. "Indeed?"

I shook my head as though to disagree, but Lucy continued in a lofty voice, "Aunt Margaret danced with me in the ballroom the other night."

Ford dropped his knife and fork, and sat back to study me. "Do tell! Dancing, in my ballroom? That *is* a feat of magic, Lucille, considering the ballroom is off limits to you."

"But it was night-time..." Lucy explained, as though the admission would mollify her father. Then she widened her eyes at me, making a funny shape with her mouth as she realised I too fell under Ford's reprimand.

"Let me explain — " I began, not knowing how in the world I would.

But Ford did not wait for whatever lie would pass my lips;

instead he banged his fists on the tabletop, causing the cutlery to jump. "A ball it is, Lucy!" He pushed back his chair and held out his hand to his daughter. Lucy jumped with glee, clapping her hands, then locked one together with her father's.

Ford held out his other arm in an expansive gesture. "Shall we, Margaret? Ah, and here comes Hester now!"

Upon hearing her name, Hester paused as she entered. She looked at me with alarm, and I gave her a small smile of reassurance.

"Devout little Hester," Ford said, "we ask so much of you! I wish you to take the day off. Or rather, Margaret wishes you to take the day off. Tomorrow."

Hester flushed and managed a small curtsy. "Thank-you, Sir, Miss. That's — that's very kind. Might I — might I go to Moorwood?"

Ford put his hand to my back and began to lead me towards the door. "A splendid idea! In fact, I'll make arrangements for Carlisle to take you. I think he might like you very well, Hester." Ford looked sidelong at me and moved his hand up to touch the back of my neck. "Very well, indeed."

His fingers were like ice and caused me to shiver, whereupon he released me immediately. Then he held out his hand to the housemaid. "The key to the pantry, please, Hester."

Hester suddenly looked as though she were a rabbit about to be dressed and stewed, and curiously reluctant, she fished in her dress pocket to withdraw a small key. Ford took it and pressed it into my palm. "For you, Margaret. In Hester's stead, you shall run the household, starting at dawn and ending at dusk. You shall be most occupied, I think, with very little time to sew. Or explore." He grinned and held out his arm, implying that I should take it. "Shall we?"

Without knowing what to say, I pocketed the key and took Ford's arm. As we passed Hester in the doorway, my eyes locked with hers, but I could think of nothing to say.

12

THE BALLROOM, BY NIGHT, was a cavernous tomb. With neither fire nor chandelier lit, Ford led Lucy and me through the dark to the centre of the room to stand beneath the dome. As our eyes adjusted to the low light, the vast expanse of the room fell into shadow beyond the circumference of where we stood. Lucy broke away from Ford at once and tore into the shadows, laughing and coughing in the dark, footsteps echoing like knuckles rapping on a door.

Cool moonlight, filtering through the intricate iron struts of the cupola, threw lace-like shadows over my skirt, our hands, his cheekbones. The moonlight flattered Ford's pale skin; how youthful he looked with scant creases webbing his eyes and his beard silky as a new colt's coat. Eyes calm as the sea at low tide searched mine as he struck a dancer's pose. I slipped my hand into his and felt his other arm curl around my shoulder blades. For the first time I saw the man with whom each of my sisters had fallen in love.

"Make her dance!" Lucy chimed, emerging from the shadows, as though I were a puppet on strings. In the dim light, her red hat was as dark as blood.

"It would be my pleasure," Ford said, and he moved forward over the floor. I was unpracticed, but he was patient as I tripped over my skirts, struggling to match his steps.

"Not her!" Lucy barked, "Dolly!" and she waved her doll by its arm, its head swinging at a macabre angle. Lucy's words echoed in my mind: *I saw her arm come off, and her head mostly hanging off too, at the neck.* I shivered and Ford tightened his hold, but his touch did nothing to warm me.

"I want you to make her dance, Aunt Margaret. Mend her like Flue — I want her alive, too!"

Extracting myself from Ford, I bent to Lucy's height. "I'm so sorry, Lucy, but I cannot. Dolly's not — nor was she ever — alive."

"Of course she is alive," Lucy argued, stamping her foot.

It broke my heart to dash Lucy's hopes, but I had no choice. I took her hand in mine and said, "If I could I would, dear Lucy. I am truly sorry."

Lucy yanked her fingers from my grasp, and hurled Dolly across the parquet floor. The doll skidded into the shadows and we heard a thump as it hit the wall.

"A song perhaps," Ford suggested, suddenly at my shoulder. I felt his hand on my elbow as he pulled me to my feet. "Lucy, you choose. What shall we sing?"

"I don't care!" she sulked, crossing her arms over her chest.

"Hm," Ford mused, curling me into his arms once again. "That *is* a good one. Let me remember how it goes..." He fell into step, gliding me across the floor. Then, pulling me closer, he began to sing, his voice warm and low, carrying past my ear and over my shoulder. His words drifted through the air, finding their way to Lucy.

> *"How much heartache can one man take,*
> *When he's terrified his ship may break?*
> *Upon still waters, the night full of dread*
> *This watery grave, our final bed.*
> *But I don't care, we'll sail away,*
> *And pray the wind will come to stay."*

My breath caught in my throat — the beauty of his voice! — but Lucy protested. "Not that one, Father. My favourite! Sing my favourite!" Lucy broke into pirouettes around us, her huge red hat wobbling wildly on her head.

And so he began, "*Shake and rattle! cry the men, Bloody roses all about* —" but the tune was not as melodic as the last. Instead, a pulsing chant. His chest heaved with each syllable, pumping like bellows against my breast.

Lucy joined in, "*The flaming sails hang still at noon, Bloody roses all about!*" Her frail voice carried the high notes, and it bounced against the hard bare surfaces of the room.

Then they sang in unison and Ford swept me into a dip. It startled me and laughter bubbled up in my throat.

"Ah — there she is," he whispered, before righting me again and hammering into the second verse.

"*We'll die of thirst this awful morn, Bloody roses all about!*"

As he sang of sailors' plight, I lowered my eyes to his neck, only inches from my nose. In usual uniform, he wore no dinner jacket. His collar was unbuttoned and a loosely tied cravat did its best to hold his neckline closed. The key glittered like quicksilver beneath his open shirt collar, tempting me to touch it. But my hand was firmly held in his, the other clinging to his shoulder as I was spun beyond my senses. I imagined using my mouth instead, burrowing my lips into the folds of his shirt, fishing out the key with my teeth and yanking as hard as I might. Just as Lucy had torn the wing from the bat.

Ford's voice floated on, "*Just one more heave—*"

And then, transfixed by the key and forgetting to follow the rhythm, I caught a heel in my skirt and stumbled into Ford. The cold metal key slapped my cheek as my nose banged into his shoulder.

"I beg your pardon," I mumbled, breaking free of his hold.

"Do I sing that poorly?" he teased, as Lucy continued to carry the tune and skip around us in circles.

"I fear that I dance poorly," I stammered. The chain encircling his neck had caught on an edge of his collar, the key now laying exposed against his white shirt, taunting me. It reminded me of another key I now held in my possession, that to the pantry. "I best be to bed, as morning will come soon enough and I've breakfast to make." I didn't hold back the bitter tone in my voice. Of course I appreciated his kindness to Hester, but I begrudged him denying me my progress on Rosie's dress.

He grunted in agreement. "But before you go," he stopped me, "what would you like to ask?"

"Ask?"

"You've not accosted me with a barrage of questions since I found you in the reverend's company." His eyes flashed in the moonlight, "I must admit, I have quite missed your accusations and suspicions."

Lucy stopped dancing, and stared up at me, my cheeks reddening.

"I've finished the muslin of Rosie's dress," I replied. "I've only to finish fitting it to myself before I put together the final version. Then I will need to fit it to Rosie. Would you...would you tell her?"

A strange expression — fear? — flashed across his face, but he quickly recovered. Lucy looked at her father, reading his change of mood, and then back at me, curious.

His captain's confidence recovered, he said, "Of course. I shall her let her know to come for a fitting the day after tomorrow. I am...*pleased*...that the dress is nearly complete." His voice trailed away, clearly thinking of the wedding suddenly upon us. The event would change everything.

"Thank you," I said, and turned to go.

"Margaret!" he said with great authority.

I stopped and turned. Now I was completely in shadow, no longer under the cupola. Moonlight fell over Ford as though through the boughs of a forest.

"Soon the dress will be complete and...well, is there anything you need?" And then his voice softened to a tone that was almost lost to the dusk. "Anything at all?"

How could he ask such a thing? How many times had I asked him for answers? What I needed was the truth, but doubted this was what he had in mind. Or did he simply mean comforts in my room — a bath, a fire? But why would he care about that — he'd dismissed Hester fully accepting that I would not only look after myself, but he and Lucy as well. Or was he hinting at something else, altogether? Some kind of relief for my lonely stay in the house, desperate and separated from my sister? As I considered companionship, my mind conjured an image of Carlisle.

I cleared my throat. "Do you mean —"

His face restored itself to its usual cold demeanour, "Do you require anything to complete the dress?"

My breath deflated. What had I expected him to say? I squared my shoulders. "A looking glass," I replied, watching his features for a reaction.

He stiffened. "A looking glass?" His eyes darted to Lucy. "There is one in the house..." He drew a hand across his bearded chin, thoughtfully, then dropped it to his breast where he clawed for the key. "The looking glass was Helen's. Here." He snapped the chain from his neck and extended it towards me, the key hanging seductively, like lost treasure found at last.

I walked back into the light beneath the dome and held out a trembling hand. He dropped the key on its chain into my palm. Though it had hung next to his heart, it was as cold as ice.

"You have wanted this key, yes?" he said, his dark eyes glittering as they searched mine.

"Thank you," I said, closing my fingers around the key. Yes, at last I had what I wanted. But he had given the key so freely, dare I hope it reveal anything more than old dust and grief?

Or *had* he given it freely? Did he feel cornered by my request, a position he so frequently enforced upon me but which was uncustomary for him? His eyes, so light and warm only minutes ago, had hardened to coal. Lines creased his forehead and his jaw was set. If some terrible secret was ensconced in this room, what had moved him to grant my request?

He went on, "There is a closet in the cellar — you know it, I think — where I have stored Helen's belongings. You will find what you need there."

I was speechless, almost unable to believe that the last locked door of Blueford Manor was about to share its secrets.

"I have only one request, Margaret," he continued. Lucy moved to her father's side and hung on his arm, looking up at me wide-eyed.

"Do not ask for my help to carry the looking glass. I do not wish to see her things." He gathered Lucy up into his arms, and roughly kissed her cheek. "Or anything that reminds me of her, any more than I am already reminded."

"I want to see mother's looking glass!" Lucy whined, squirming in Ford's arms.

"Not yet," he growled, burying his face in his daughter's ringlets. And then he turned and carried her out of the room, resuming his song, leaving me with the key. I stood alone in the dark room while his words brushed over my skin, *Bloody roses all about*.

How could I sleep when I had Ford's key in my hand?

The cellar was dark, but I came prepared with a candlestick and matches. As I lit the candle and opened the door, I was immediately assaulted by the odour of mildew. I held my hand over my nose and mouth as I made my way through the cellar. I glanced at the ceiling and the bats were gone. It was near midnight; they were most certainly hunting. I was thankful for I did not fancy startling them at this hour.

And then there I was — at the locked door. The lock yielded smoothly to the turn of the key and I opened the door wide, holding the candle high. It was a small room — indeed, barely more than a closet — and densely packed with Helen's belongings. My eyes grew accustomed to the dark as they scanned the spidery shadows thrown by old chairs and stacks of trunks.

Dust covered everything, and there was no indication that

Rosie had ever been to examine Helen's things. I stepped inside, propping the door open so that I could not be trapped within. It was a tightly arranged space; there was barely enough room to turn around. Setting the candlestick on a central tower of steam trunks, I had just enough light to pick through the contents of the room. Behind the door leaning against the wall, I found what I was seeking: a looking glass draped in an old linen. But that could wait. There was much more than that to explore.

I opened the steam trunk closest to me. Inside, I discovered a treasure of memories. Fingering the delicate dresses and nightgowns, fragranced with lavender and rose water, I caught the scent of Helen. I tumbled into the deep tunnel of my past. Most of the garments were pink, my sister's favourite colour. As I child I'd pleaded for her to wear green, for it flattered her red hair. But Helen had resisted, teasing my critical eye. From her I had learned that it did not matter how a woman *looked* in a colour, it only mattered how she *felt*.

Next I found a trunk of old gardening tools and packets of seeds. In another, editions of botanical illustrations, gardening almanacs and personal journals about the orchard at Blueford Manor. With my little finger, I traced her hand written notations about the apple and plum harvests. I guessed that the books had been stored longer than the weeks since her death as already they'd mildewed. Shame.

Her belongings had once graced the rooms of the house; now they were vanquished to this closet, like forgotten memories. Yes, Helen was gone, but did all trace of her need to be erased from the house? For Lucy's sake, why not exhume some of her mother's treasures?

Hours passed as I pored over Helen's belongings, and the sister from whom I'd grown apart began to feel much closer. Though I had seen little of her in the past few years, I knew she was still the Helen of my childhood — light at heart, a lover of flowers, herself as fragrant and beautiful as one of her cultivations. How difficult it must have been to live here, at the isolated manor in the cloudy climes of North Yorkshire.

I wondered if Ford ever came here, seeking comfort in the scent of her clothes, the touch of her belongings. Was it frequent visits to this closet that kept the key close to his heart? But no, he said he did not wish to be reminded of his wife. I was offended by the comment, for I very much wished to feel connected to both Helen and Rosie.

But even if Ford could not bear the painful loss, was it fair for Lucy to live as though her mother never existed in the first place? If Ford and Lucy truly missed Helen, why not hang her paintings in the parlour? And why did Lucy not inherit Helen's fine hairbrush and hand mirror, or music box and brooches, as a loving reminder of her mother? Why bury them in this dark recess of the house?

I wondered again if there was something here that Ford wished to hide. From me, from Lucy, or even from his own memory. I scanned the room and started opening each drawer in each of the three armoires. Empty. Everything had been neatly packed away into the trunks. The work of Edye?

A hope chest revealed a single spider scurrying for cover, an old hair comb, broken and forgotten, and a shard of blue glass. Lastly, I tried the wardrobe doors.

To my surprise they resisted. Not that it should surprise me that something else at Blueford Manor was kept under lock and key. I jimmied the door but it did not budge. The lock was tiny but strong; where in this house would I find the right key? It had been trial enough to secure the key to this closet.

The wardrobe was short, not fully five feet. Its small scale lent itself more to a child's room, than an adult's. I knocked on the doors, listening for the tell-tale rustling of mice nesting in fabric, but there was only silence.

I felt along the top of the wardrobe for a key, then underneath. My fingers found nothing but dust. To find a key among the dozen or so packed trunks would be akin to searching for a pin among the fallen spruce needles that littered the grounds of Blueford Manor.

I sighed and brushed off my hands. The candlestick had burnt to a stub. I took one last look around the room, knowing I would return to the closet tomorrow to collect the mirror. Then I locked the door behind me.

I made my way back inside Blueford Manor, taking care my movements would not awaken the other occupants of the house. But I needn't have worried. As I made my way past Ford's study, on my way to the staircase, I saw a sliver of light shining from beneath the door. There were shuffling sound from within and the low murmur of Ford's voice. I wondered if Rosie were in there with him. I pressed my ear to the door and strained my ears, hoping to hear the sound of her voice.

Which is when the door suddenly flew open and I spilled into the room, landing with a sprawling thud on the floor. Ford jumped back with a shout, obviously startled to see me.

"What in damnation are you doing, woman?" he roared, standing above me and staring down. I wished he wouldn't yell, given the proximity of Hester's quarters. I quickly righted myself, found my feet and wondered how I could explain the fact that I was listening at his door.

"I'm sorry," I said, peering into the room to determine who he had been speaking to, but Ford was alone. Coming up with the only excuse I could muster, I stammered, "I wanted to return this." I held out the key he had given me earlier.

"Hmph," he said, taking it from my fingers and tossing it aside. It skidded across the desk where it landed and fell to the floor. Then he made his way over to the fireplace, leaning his hands against the carved mantelpiece, staring straight ahead at the plaster overmantel. I approached slowly and, as his back was turned, reclaimed the key from the floor and hid it in my skirts.

I turned to make my escape. "I'll be away. I did not mean to interrupt."

"I've lost the key," he said.

The word '*key*' stopped me and I turned. How many other mysterious keys were there at Blueford Manor? Ford looked over at me, a scowl upon his face.

"Do you have it, Margaret?" he asked, appraising me with dark eyes.

I shook my head, wondering as to which key he referred. "I have no keys," I lied. He approached and I retreated, but he was instantly between me and the door. The wall was at my back and I was pinned in place like a butterfly mounted inside a shadow box.

He stood directly in front of me, lowering his face so that we were nose to nose. His eyes were dark and his fingers came up to brush my collarbone.

"I wonder..." he said at last.

"Please, do not hurt me," I begged, my heart beating fast. I trembled at the touch of his hand, the hand that may have harmed Helen.

He blinked, and took a step back.

"Hurt you?" he said. "Why ever would I hurt you?" His hand dropped away. "You distrust me, still."

I bit my lip, wanting to apologise, but feeling uncertain as to what to say.

"I want to show you something," he said, dislodging me from my thoughts. "Here," and he clamped a strong hand about my arm, leading me to the desk. "Sit," he ordered, pushing me into the chair he normally occupied. With a sweep of his arm he cleared the naval charts, scattering them over the rug. He pounded a fist against one of the drawers which, like the others, contained a small keyhole.

"I put the key somewhere safe, so Lucy could not get into the drawer. And damn it, if I haven't forgotten where."

He looked at me as though I might know the location, but I could only shake my head.

"Never mind," he said, making his way over to the fire and grabbing the poker. I recoiled into the back of the chair as he jimmied the tip of the poker into the space at the top of the drawer. He heaved on the poker and the tiny contraption gave way. He yanked the drawer so vigourously it tumbled onto the heap of charts on the floor.

Inside the drawer was a slew of sketchbooks. Ford grabbed a handful and dumped them into my lap.

"Look at them," he ordered. I selected a sketchbook, flipped open the cover and gasped in amazement. It was a portrait of Lucy as a newborn. And on the next page another of my niece as a infant, this time being held by her father. Page after page. All painted or drawn by Helen.

"They are remarkable, are they not?" Ford asked, leaning over my shoulder.

I nodded, continuing to turn the pages, admiring portrait upon portrait of Lucy throughout the stages of babyhood. Another sketchbook was devoted to Ford. And yet another to Helen herself, or at least parts of her: a drawing of her left hand, sometimes a foot. Tears welled in my eyes. On the page, Helen was alive to me once more. I wanted her to step out from the paper and lead me away from here, back to our past. I felt Ford's hand on my back; it was warm and reassuring.

He slipped the sketchbook from my fingers and handed me another. This one was full of flowers, full of roses. The last few pages were a marked contrast to the early drawings, as the only flowers pictured here were dead and dying.

"And this," Ford said, holding up a painting of himself. "This was my favourite. She painted this in '94, that last winter we were in London. Once she came here, she never painted me again. She grew to hate me, you know."

His words caught me off guard. Ford had been careful not to share the details of his and Helen's marriage. And now, here he was, baring his heart. It made me feel awkward, as though I were a bird on a lamp-post, eavesdropping on lovers.

"I'm sure she didn't," I said, honouring my sister's memory.

"Oh, Margaret," he said, holding the sketchbook to his chest for a moment before dropping it into the broken drawer. "You do want to think the best of people."

If only he could read my mind, I contemplated, for I had certainly not thought the best of Ford.

"She still painted Lucy," he said, showing me a more recent sketchbook filled with portraits of my niece. "But stopped when our dear daughter fell ill. Then, only flowers. Goddamned flowers day in and day out. Crying all the time. For you, for Rosamund, for London."

I was silent. If Helen had missed us so much, why had she never written? Did Ford prevent her from doing so?

"Nothing I did could stop her tears. She cried an ocean of them everyday. Had I not suffered losses, too?" He seethed, and I saw the resentment he held for my dead sister and it shocked me. Did her depression drive him to kill?

I held my breath, wondering if he was going to confess further. But instead he started gathering the sketchbooks together and stuffing them into the yawning hole in the desk where the drawer ought to have been.

"You're very different than Helen, Margaret. You have a loyalty that does not wane. Loyalty to your sisters. A loyalty that one day you will give to a man. And he will be a very lucky man indeed."

His dark eyes were on my face, and I could feel my cheeks warm. I did not want to talk of a future I could not see and so I turned away from his gaze. At the bottom of the drawer I spied some loose sheets of black paper. I leaned over the arm of the chair and plucked out a black painting with pinholes, similar to the ones I had found in the studio.

"Was Helen sad when she made this?" I asked.

His expression softened as he took the page, and a smile twitched at the corner of his mouth. "She painted these when she could no longer paint flowers by the light of the day. Here," he said claiming the candle from the desktop, "hold it up to the light."

As I lifted the painting, he moved the candlestick closer. The paper was opaque, thanks to the black pigment, but light shone through each of the pin pricks.

"Constellations!" I cried, delighted by the spectacle, unable to resist the breeze of joy that inflated my heart like a sail.

Ford smiled and it softened the hard planes of his face.

"We made hundreds of these," he said, placing his face next to mine so that he too could see the stars. "On warm nights we would climb to the roof and count the stars. On cold nights we would drag a mattress into the ballroom and sleep under the moon's light. Helen became obsessed with painting these. And each corresponds to my master map." He looked up.

Of course. The map on the ceiling. The narrow circular view which I thought to be a telescope was rather the glass of the domed roof of the ballroom. Ford never intended that room for flowers as I'd assumed, but for stargazing. The ocean might be a sea captain's livelihood, but the night sky was his lifeline. I wanted to see each of Helen's star maps, and Ford obliged, holding up one after another for me to examine. Each pattern of starts had a name, many of them animals. My constellation, he informed, was Taurus.

"I found more of these," I told him. "In Helen's studio. A whole set, from Autumn '93."

Ford then returned the candlestick to the desk, but the constellations he did not return to the drawer, instead stacking them neatly and hugging them to his chest as though they were a map to the shores of Heaven. Regarding the most recent portraits of Lucy he said, "Those I won't have. Take them to London. Or burn them, if you would."

"Why ever would I?" I gasped. "Surely, if you don't want them, they should belong to Lucy?"

"Helen created those while I was away on my last voyage. I do not wish to be reminded of those months."

"It was a difficult voyage?" I questioned.

"In a manner. I fell ill on that voyage and have been land-locked ever since." He then set aside the star maps, took my arm, lifted me from the chair and steered me towards the door.

"I am quite tired," he said, although he looked nothing of the sort.

I paused at the door before he could shove me through.

"Thank you," I said. And I meant it. In showing me the artwork, Ford had given Helen back to me. I don't know if that was his intention, or if in trying to remember his wife, he had simply allowed me to remember my sister. But whichever the reason, my heart felt lighter than it had in days.

I stepped forward and embraced his wide shoulders. It took him a moment to respond, but then his arms were strong about me and I did not want to ever let go.

But his hoarse voice broke my comfort: "On your way."

I released my embrace and as I turned towards the stairs I heard his voice in the darkness. "I did not give up my profession willingly, Margaret."

I waited for further explanation, but nothing came. I turned and mounted the stairs. I longed to wake Soutache and hear his song, but it was late. Indeed, dawn was breaking. It had been a long night, a night in which I'd felt Helen come alive. I went to my bed and crawled under the covers. When I closed my eyes, I did not see darkness. All I could see was the stars.

13

GIVEN THE LATENESS OF THE HOUR upon which I had retired, I was only able to gain a few hours of sleep before I had to rise and begin my household duties. It had been my intention to assemble Rosie's dress today so that it would be ready for a fitting tomorrow. But Ford, intentionally or otherwise, had foiled my plan. I cursed under my breath as I descended to the kitchen, shivering in the frigid air of Blueford Manor.

Once in the kitchen, I shoved handfuls of straw and coal into the range and lit a match with a satisfying hiss. Once the fire caught, I filled the kettle to boil, and decided I myself would be happy with bread and jam for breakfast, while Ford and Lucy could have eggs and toast. They need not complain of the simplicity of the meal, for Hester would be back in the kitchen tomorrow.

As the kettle began a melancholy whistle, I mulled over my own frustrations. Without the looking glass, I could not effectively make alterations to the pattern. And if I couldn't do that, I couldn't confidently cut into the expensive silk I'd purchased for Rosie's dress. If I cut incorrectly, I would have to return to Harrowgate to repurchase the materials, and there was no guarantee Mrs Soapwith would have the same fabric stock.

To avoid a grave mistake in the construction of Rosie's dress, I would wait to continue until the looking glass was installed in the studio. But without Hester to assist me, I could not carry it upstairs. Given its size and weight, it was definitely a chore for two. Ford was unwilling to lend his strength, but he was not the only man about the estate. And then I remembered — Carlisle had taken Hester to Harrowgate. His muscle was not available either. I thought about the two of them, their devotion in common, and wondered how different my day would be if it were me instead of Hester in that carriage. Feeling rather out of sorts, I prepared three pots of tea.

Luncheon was no issue; every day Hester left bread, cured meat and preserves on the countertop for us all to help ourselves. Although, it seemed I was the only one who ever did, taking my cold plate of delicacies into the dining room. Supper, however, was another matter. Once breakfast was sorted, I would give some thought to the last meal of the day, then follow up with building fires.

Thus the shape of the day was set; and so today the studio would stay closed. I would perform my kitchen duties, and when that was done, catch some sleep in my room with Soutache. How delicious rest would be on the heels of such a long night. Fatigue pressed at my temples, weighing down my eyelids.

The kettle's scream snapped me awake. I steeped Lucy's tea first, being the weakest, and two strong pots for Ford and myself, the first sip of which burned my tongue. Then, Hester's key to the pantry in hand, I went in search of preserves. What I found inside startled me beyond words.

The store pantry and cold room, usually kept spotlessly clean and tight as a crypt in order to keep out the mice, had been transformed into what looked like a chapel. A series of shelves on the left had been emptied of preserves, and instead displayed small objects of personal religious value.

Among the collection were several tattered cards depicting Catholic Saints which leaned against silver salt shakers. Helen's painting of the three-leaf clover held centre position, surrounded with saucers of water. Water? I queried, and then surmised it was likely blessed. A pocket version of the King James Bible stuffed with bookmarks sat beside a candle meant to be used for reading. Kindling of various sizes was crudely lashed together to form crosses so that the entire shelf resembled a miniature graveyard. Wreaths of dried garlic bulbs hung from the ceiling. A single rosary of deep burgundy beads glowed with an inner fire and lay the entire length of one of the shelves. I fingered the glass beads and wondered why Hester had arranged these items here and not in her room.

Perhaps Hester was more devout that I had realised and chose to pray throughout the day instead of waiting until she returned to her room at the back of the house. But was it devotion only that had built this sanctuary? Bible verses scrawled on scraps of paper were littered among the wooden crucifixes and suggested another motive:

Ephesians 6:10—12, Finally, my brethren, be strong in the Lord, and in the power of his might. Put on the whole armour of God, that ye may be able to stand against the wiles of the devil. For we wrestle not against flesh and blood, but against principalities, against powers, against the rulers of the darkness of this world, against spiritual wickedness in high places.

1 John 3:8 He that committeth sin is of the devil, for the devil sinneth from the beginning. For this purpose the Son of God was manifested, that He might destroy the works of the devil.

Psalm 91:3-9 For He will deliver you from the snare of the fowler and from the deadly pestilence. You shall not be afraid of the terror of the night, Nor of the pestilence that stalks in darkness, nor of the destruction and sudden death that surprise and lay waste at noonday. A thousand may fall at your side, and ten thousand at your right hand, but it shall not come near you.

This was no chapel for worship, but a shrine for protection. I sent a silent prayer skyward, and for a fleeting moment was relieved of the fear I felt on a daily basis at Blueford Manor. I could count on both hands the things that frightened me — from the possibility of Helen being murdered to the dubious whereabouts of Rosie. But Hester seemed shielded from all of this, so what frightened her so?

I examined one of the wooden crosses, tightly lashed at its intersection with a bit of red yarn. Perhaps Hester was wiser than me. Given that I questioned the safety of both my sisters, and — at times — that of my niece, was I a fool to not be more vigilant of my own safety? How careless had I been to explore the cellar in the middle of the night, let alone the roof?

I returned the crucifix to its company, determined to hide in my room, a blazing fire to dispel the gloom, a heavy chair against the door. And damn the chores; Ford and Lucy never seemed to mind the cold, let alone the dust and drifts of dried leaves. Let Blueford shiver for a day without fires. I would be toasty in my quarters, and wile away the hours until Hester's return. Weeks had passed since I'd last cracked the spine of a novel.

And for the first time since arriving, I didn't even care if today was one more day that I did not see Rosie. Today would be a day for regaining fortitude. I smiled at Hester's altar; it had given me strength. Now, to keep my strength with food. What to prepare for tonight's meal?

There weren't many stores; on the shelves along the back wall were canned preserves — stewed plums and apple sauce and berry jams. On the right, two shelves of fresh eggs, cheese, grains and vegetables. I gathered what I needed to prepare breakfast. A cured ham, the one Hester sliced for sandwiches at yesterday's luncheon, gave off a salty aroma. It would do for dinner.

Having deposited two breakfast trays — one outside Ford's room and one at Lucy's door — I stopped by the studio to collect Soutache, and then slipped into my room. Then I turned the lock and pushed a chair against the door.

Soft morning light trickled in through the window. It was a fine day, blue skies with only a dusting of clouds. I envied Hester and her day in the village with Carlisle and entertained thoughts of the Willis family enjoying Hyde Park and Hendry selling the newest trends of the fall season. I set to building a fire in the hearth, stacking the coal to allow adequate air flow. Despite her practice, Hester had not been able to build a lasting fire in this room, and with my lack of skill, I feared an even poorer outcome.

Before striking the match, I peeked up the chimney to ensure the flue was clear of bats.

About two feet up, just where the light was eaten by darkness, a pale grey square was visible on the back wall of the chimney. Curious, I stretched forward, bracing myself against the brick with my left hand, and reached into the chimney with my right arm. Soutache warbled nervously as my head disappeared from view. My fingertips strained, grasping for the edge of the object — paper! — and I finally snagged it, tearing it away from the bricks. Once in hand, I withdrew from the chimney shaft and stared at the sheet with wonder.

Helen's painting of the rose. It had been subjected to fire for the paper was grey with soot and the corners were dry and brittle. Sooty fingerprints peppered the singed edges. I spread my own fingers over the marks: a near perfect fit.

A tear fell from my eye to see Helen's painting mistreated so, and where it landed it washed away a spot of ash, revealing the bright red pigment of the rose petal beneath, looking ever so much like a single drop of blood.

I propped the battered painting on the mantle and cleaned my blackened hands in the frigid wash basin water. As I washed, questions swirled in my mind. How did the paper come to be up the chimney? Caught on an updraft? Placed there deliberately? By who? And why would they wish to burn it?

Hester hardly seemed a suspect, odd as her habits may be. Her private altar only solidified my belief that she was God-fearing and good. Besides, she was not an accomplished liar; a thorough flush to the cheek gave away her every secret.

Lucy's culpability I could imagine: stripping the page from the studio wall, trespassing in my room, tossing it into the flames for a lark. But the fingerprints could not possibly be hers — Lucy's fingers were no larger than a four-year-old's. And Ford's fingers were twice the thickness of mine. There was only one person who had handled the painting with sooty fingertips.

Rosie.

I slept, but not for long. As Soutache woke me with fervent song, I groaned and stretched. After finding the painting I had curled up on the bed, trying to decipher when Rosie could have placed it in the chimney. Or even why. But fatigue won me over, and I had fallen asleep.

I blinked in the afternoon light and tried to focus on Soutache's dizzying flight path. I had forgotten to light the fire, and now Soutache zipped in and out of the chimney, wildly wheeling due to his one weak wing. I whistled to catch his attention and after a few moments he came to rest atop my pillow. He regarded me with his one working eye, an annoyed expression upon his tiny face.

The room was ice-cold. Dampness pricked my joints and my breath hung in white clouds, like a veil shadowing my face. I crawled out from under the covers and went to light the coal I had prepared earlier, but now it was collapsed, some pieces falling from the hearth onto the floor.

"Soutache, how naughty!" I scolded. He gave a sharp tweet as though to reprimand me as well and perched in the window. I restacked the coal and stood to fetch the matches from the mantle. My hand froze as I touched the matchbox, my nose level with the mantelpiece.

Where was the rose painting? I glanced around the floor, thinking a draft from the chimney — or Soutache's flight — may have caused it to drift away. But nothing. I checked the door, but the heavy chair was still in place preventing entry or exit, and moreover, the door remained locked. I returned to the fireplace and ducked my head up the chimney to see if the picture was back inside the flue. Still nothing.

I began to doubt that I had ever found it in the first place. But no, the sooty water in the basin was evidence that the picture existed.

I shivered, and lit the fire. A moment later a warm blaze pushed back the chill. I could not have slept more than a couple of hours, and though I'd been up through the night, sleep was now the last thing on my mind.

If Rosie had returned for the painting, how did she gain access to the room? The window was closed, so she had not entered that way. Besides, I was on the second floor and a ladder would be required, and I had yet to see one of those in all my explorations of Blueford. Perhaps there was a hidden entrance.

I started examining the walls, searching for any crack that might suggest a hidden doorway. But nothing. I also checked the floor. But each and every floorboard was nailed in place. Could it be possible that Rosie had already been in the room? Indeed, how many times in the house had I felt watched when I was sure I was alone? A chill crept up my spine and I turned my head to assess the room. Could she have been behind the drapes? Impossible — I'd pulled them open myself. Under the bed? I dropped to my knees and looked under the bedskirt, feeling like a child afraid to discover a monster. Nothing but dust and not much of that either, thanks to Hester.

The wardrobe was small and held my few meagre dresses. Which left only a table, two chairs and chest of drawers. None of which could serve as a hiding spot. And even if she had been there, how could she have left without disturbing the chair at the door? I went to the window and stared out at the drive below, tapping the glass with my fingernails. As I puzzled, Soutache flew up to my shoulder with a merry chirrup.

There simply was no rational explanation for the fact that the picture had disappeared. I dared not let my mind entertain more irrational thoughts, for it was not as though my sister could walk through walls. No, that was not something Rosie could do. I was determined to believe she still consisted of flesh and blood.

And anyway, I told myself, you don't believe in ghosts; the nuns had long since chased those ideas out of every naive head at Sisters of Mary. Besides, apparitions did not leave hand written messages, steal paintings, or shed their buttons.

Frustrated, I picked at the button I'd sewn to my sleeve. I cursed Rosie and her mischievous doings. *What are you trying to tell me, dear sister?* I silently begged.

Perhaps the window would solve the mystery after all. I returned to it and examined the sash and shutters. A movement outside caught my eye and I saw a figure emerge from the house. Dressed all in black, it was Carlisle. What was he doing here? Had Hester changed her plans and he'd returned her early? But there was no sign of the carriage. No, he'd come by foot, just as he was leaving.

It occurred to me then that perhaps he had come to see me, but Ford had turned him away. I banged on the glass to catch his attention, but he either did not hear me or chose to ignore the sound. I tried to raise the glass, but it was stuck fast, and by the time I had wrenched it open, Carlisle had disappeared across the driveway, heading for the path that led through the orchard and down to the river.

I dragged the chair from the door of my room and ran down the hall to the stairs. I pushed open the door and followed Carlisle's path, cutting through the orchard, expecting to see him by the river. But he was not there.

"Carlisle?" I called.

There was no answer. I crossed to the bridge and stood at is centre, as it allowed a vantage point of the surrounding area. But aside from the sparkle of sun on the water, the drift of the swans, and the shadow of Blueford Manor, I was alone. Like Helen's painting, Carlisle too, had disappeared.

I turned and made my way back through the orchard, into the house, and up the stairs. I stopped at Helen's studio to gather some supplies and the remaining crimson gauze I had used to construct Lucy's hat. Then I returned to my room where I curled up on the floor beside the crackling fire and began to sew, my bird singing all the while.

Neither Ford nor Lucy had eaten anything I had prepared for breakfast, and so I did not expect Ford to answer the door when I knocked to announce the arrival of his dinner tray. But he did, catching me mid-bend, lowering the tray to the carpet.

"I was dressing to come down," he said, running a hand through dishevelled hair and wearing nothing but a night shirt which hung about him like a sail slack upon its mast.

Pinning my eyes to the plate of cold ham with mustard and hard boiled eggs, I straightened my posture. I'd heaped his plate generously, hoping he'd share the repast with Rosie. "I brought dinner."

Ford frowned at the tray. "Or breakfast."

"I never boasted I was a cook," I replied stiffly, pushing the tray towards him.

He took the tray and peered down the hall to see the tray sitting outside his daughter's door. "I see Lucy's been served. Your work is done for the evening. Won't you join me?"

I shook my head. "I ate in the kitchen."

"Then stay while I eat. Besides, I have something to show you." He turned and disappeared into the room where I heard him set down the tray. I stayed planted in the corridor, but leaned my head in to see what he intended to show me. I quickly pulled back when I saw him tugging on a pair of trousers.

Sloppily tucking in his nightshirt, he popped his head around the door and motioned for me to sit in one of the chairs facing the window, though the curtains were drawn.

"Is it dark yet?" He asked, clasping his belt buckle.

"Yes," I answered, crossing to the chairs, thankful to turn my back to his state of dishevelment.

"Go on," he urged, "let's see if any stars have made an appearance." I rose and opened the drapes to an indigo sky freckled with white light.

"That—" he said, coming up behind me and pointing past my cheekbone, "is Venus. Goddess of Love. The ruler of your sign." I followed the line of his finger to a point low on the horizon, just above the fur of spruce on a hilltop. "The brightest, most beautiful heavenly body, one might say." He smelled of candle smoke and sandalwood. Then his hand dropped and tugged at the shawl on my shoulders. "What's this?"

"A shawl," I said, "I made it for Hester." I'd not expected him to see it. Made of leftover gauze from Lucy's veil, it was scarlet red, and — of translucent material — not at all practical. But it was not intended for warmth. It was intended for prayer. And protection, of a divine kind. I'd finished the edges with black lace and embroidered a crucifix at its centre. Underneath the cross, in tiny stitches, I'd stitched one of Hester's verses: *Put on the whole armour of God, that ye may be able to stand against the wiles of the devil…*

He glanced at the script with a bemused expression on his face. "I wonder which devil you feel you need to arm yourself against tonight?" he laughed.

My face turned the colour of the shawl and I repeated that I had made it for Hester.

He winked, then crossed to the bureau and pulled the cork of a crystal carafe. "Scotch? Or is that against your faith?" He didn't await my answer, pouring two drafts and passing me a tumbler. I took a seat in the chair by the window and sniffed the amber liquid.

"Drink up, Margaret. We'll call it communion." He threw back his whiskey and exhaled loudly. Though I had no taste for spirits, I took a tentative sip and promptly coughed.

Ford guffawed, "Nothing like a double distilled to shrug off a day's work, yes?" Snidely, I wondered what work filled his days, but before I could comment he asked, "Did you enjoy your day playing housekeeper?"

I blinked and straightened my back, "It is more important, I think, that Hester enjoyed her day."

"Ah yes, God-fearing Margaret always thinking of others," he snorted. I straightened my back at his criticism and then to prove I was as tough as a wooden hat block — or at least as stubborn headed as he — threw back the whiskey in the manner in which he had just done. I succumbed to a coughing fit severe enough to rival Lucy's. This was nothing like the drink Carlisle had given me the other night.

Grinning, Ford poured himself another finger of scotch. He passed the bottle to me, but I shook my head. Through the window, the purple sky was now stained black as India ink.

Having regained my breath I said, "I hope you won't mind, but I've given Hester one of Helen's paintings. Of clover."

"I wonder if you ever tire of being so thoughtful," he mused. There was a long moment of silence, in which his dark eyes studied mine.

"May I go now?"

Ford looked defeated. "If you wish. I half hoped you might appreciate Venus as much as I do."

I cringed at my own insensitivity. What sewing was to me, star-gazing was to Ford. He had invited me into his room and shared a drink with me. And I had counted the seconds until I could escape.

"I do appreciate Venus, Ford," I said sincerely. I gazed at the planet again, "She makes for a lovely view."

Ford looked to the sky again. "You may think it nothing, just a speck in the sky, but it is a lighthouse." He reached over and tugged the shawl on my shoulders. "For some, a verse of scripture lights their way. For you, Margaret, it is something else that shows you the way home—"

"— my sisters," I breathed before I knew I had spoke.

He nodded and his voice dropped to a whisper. "Yes, your sisters. And for me, my lighthouse is the heavenly bodies. Polaris. Venus. Mars. There were times at sea, many years ago, that the stars alone kept me alive." And then he laughed, as if it were a funny thing to be alive.

He recovered himself with a sigh and began to pick at the ham on the tray as though it were an insect, and I felt I had been dismissed.

I stood and bid him *bon appetit*. But before I left I asked, "Was Carlisle here to see me?"

"Carlisle? When?" he asked.

"Around mid-day."

He watched me a moment with eyes I could not read. "Carlisle didn't come for you."

"I saw him leaving the house."

Ford shook his head, "You forget Carlisle drove Hester to town."

My jaw tightened as I felt the trust I had been building with Ford over the past few days disintegrate. Why lie about something so menial? I turned to leave his room when Ford spoke my name.

I paused, turning to look at him.

"Be careful of Carlisle. He isn't who you think he is."

"And neither are you," I said with deliberate shortness. Then I took a breath and closed the door behind me. As I retraced my steps down the hall, I noticed that Lucy's tray was no longer outside her door.

The next morning, the smell of sausage beckoned me downstairs; I smiled to know Hester had returned, and had found the pantry key I'd left for her in the lock. I was possibly more excited to see Hester cooking at the range than if Soutache himself had delivered me breakfast in bed, for with her return I could finish the wedding gown, bringing my reunion with Rosie all the closer. I entered the kitchen to bid Hester a cheerful good morning, but she forestalled any such greeting with a sudden outburst.

"Miss! Thank you ever so much for the prayer shawl!" The gift I'd left on a shelf in the pantry was now wrapped around her shoulders and tucked into the neckline of her apron. Its scarlet hue brought out a rosiness in her lips I had not noticed before, and I noted that Hester was rather attractive, but for her features twisted into an expression of shame. "You must think me such a terrible sinner, taking hold of the pantry and having — well, taken the painting. I'm a good worker and a good girl!" She collapsed into tears. "Please don't send me away again."

My mouth fell open. I had not thought that in having a day away from Blueford, Hester would think the decision was based upon poor work or a desire to be relieved of her position. By all counts, her day in Moorwood had been a reward and it was I who'd been punished by the switch. I stepped across the kitchen and gathered her in my arms.

"Oh, Hester," I said, "I'm so sorry. I missed you terribly."

"You did?" she asked, blinking through her tears.

I nodded, then regaled her of my failed attempts to boil an egg exactly to my liking, least of all to Ford's. I'd ruined at least four in the attempt and went on to explain my mishaps in trying to open a jar of preserves. Her laughter disintegrated into joyful tears. By that time, the water in the kettle had boiled and I offered to fix us both a cup of tea, but she ordered me to take a seat lest I fail miserably at that task, too.

"I'm so pleased you like the shawl," I said, taking a sip of tea, while Hester returned her attention to breakfast preparations. "But I didn't give it to you because I think you a sinner, Hester. I am aggrieved that something here has frightened you, and do not wish for you to be afraid."

"Oh, Miss, I can't hide it anymore, can I?" Hester used a fork to turn the sausages so that they would not burn.

I was almost afraid to ask. "Hide what?" What other dreadful secret was I about to learn?

Tears streamed from her eyes again, but not from laughter. "I think terrible thoughts, Miss. I think — I think — " Her voice trailed off into sobs. I returned to her side and took her hand in my own.

"We all have terrible thoughts, from time to time, Hester.

Sometimes I think Lucy is a bit of demon," I confessed with a smile, "but I love her still."

Instead of laughing, Hester moaned, "Oh, a demon!"

"What is it, Hester?" I asked, gripping her firmly. "You must tell me."

She sniffed and took a swallow of tea. "I think…"

There was a long moment of silence.

"Do you think the manor is haunted?" I offered, casting my mind back to my own misgivings, when I'd imagined Rosie passing through walls.

"It's not the hall, Miss. I like the house just fine." She smiled and relaxed. "I like the carvings of them rabbits. They remind me of home. No, Blueford Manor is just fine. When I'm by myself in a room, I feel quite happy, scrubbing and polishing like I been hired to do." She sat straighter and beamed with professional pride.

I reflected her smile and prodded, "Then?"

And here she leaned her head towards mine.

"I think maybe the family is cursed," she whispered.

I moved my ear closer. "What do you mean?"

"I mean, I feel frightened by the master and his daughter. Like they isn't real people. And I never see Miss Rosamund anymore. I know she's sick as a cock on Sunday, but oughtn't the master call for the doctor?" Hester shivered and tugged the red shawl tightly about her neck. "Don't you think them strange, Miss?"

Of course I thought them strange, but revealing my suspicions about Helen's death and Rosie's disappearance would do nothing to inspire Hester's confidence. In some respects I was grateful Hester was as aware of the odd events at Blueford as I was. But I didn't want her to leave Blueford. Leave me. Whatever I felt, I must keep a brave face.

And so I said, with a sense of terrible guilt, "I couldn't say, Hester. They're my family, after all."

"Oh, I'm terribly sorry, Miss! T'is terrible to speak ill of your kin and I didn't mean to offend. You see? Terrible thoughts, they is! You've been so good to me — doing my duties yesterday, and giving me that painting. Oh, and this shawl! Such a lovely prayer shawl — how can I repay you?"

I smiled and clapped my hands together as though to dispel the gloom. "There is one thing with which I need your help…"

✦━ⅱ

"Oh, Miss! It's divine!" Hester exclaimed, from the doorway, head tilted to one side as she gazed at the full skirt and graceful train of Rosie's wedding dress, fashioned in silk.

I blushed, realising I held a pose any bride would, with my shoulders back and my hands held low against my abdomen as though I clutched a bouquet. I dropped my hands and smoothed the silk skirt in need of a pressing. Reflected in the mirror, the finished gown took on the pale blue hue of the late afternoon light.

It hadn't been an easy task, the two of us carting the mirror up two flights of stairs; encased as it was in a heavy cherry wood frame. It weighed at least seventy pounds. There were many times, much to Hester's shock and delight, that I had audibly cursed Ford for claiming he could not assist.

No more pleasant was the task of sweeping up the scattering of dead bats upon the floor, lest we trod on their diminutive bodies as we dragged the mirror through the cellar. The sight had been a sorry one; at least half a dozen of Flue's kin were deceased. Would Carlisle have had an explanation? I didn't pause to wonder; few macabre things surprised me anymore at Blueford, least of all dead bats. And I was in a sour mood as we muscled the heavy looking glass. Let Carlisle's precious bats die off. What did I care?

That I was annoyed with the reverend was quite unfair. But when Hester told me that although Carlisle had only driven her to Moorwood, and had not remained, I realised it could very well have been him who had stopped by the manor yesterday, despite Ford's opinion. Well, if he hadn't come to see me, perhaps it was Rosie he had intended to visit. For all I knew, Rosie herself could had asked for his company. Perhaps they were planning the wedding ceremony. But if so, why would Ford so adamantly deny Carlisle's presence? And why would Carlisle not ask to see me while on the premises, given we were friends? Or were we? Wasn't it true that the only time I had spent in Carlisle's presence was when I was in need of aid? Was he simply being a gentleman? I blushed when I remembered the scene in the ballroom, wondering if his lips so close to mine were indeed what a gentleman would do. I blew out an exasperated breathe. Enough. I had work to do. I thanked Hester for the compliment and said, "I couldn't have finished the gown today if you hadn't helped carry this bloody looking glass this morning."

"You're very welcome, Miss," Hester smiled, ducking her head. "Supper is served. 'Tis a bit early but I brought the chicken fresh from the village yesterday and it roasted up in no time."

I surveyed the dress in the looking glass, making notes as to what required finishing: lace trim along the train and embroidery on the bust — pale blue roses, I decided.

"Would you be so good as to bring me up a plate, Hester?" I asked. "I would like to work through the evening, for I mean to finish the gown by morning."

Hester nodded, "Will do, Miss," and left.

I stripped free of the gown and threw on my own dress. I couldn't wait for Rosie to see what I had made for her! At that very moment, I wondered where she was. Lucy had spent some time with me this afternoon, playing with Flue and Soutache under my supervision, and mucking about with my pencils and sketchbook. I wondered if she'd report my progress to Rosie tonight?

I had just finished tacking the lace to the gown when supper arrived, announced by a sharp rap on the door and a succulent aroma.

"Enter," I called.

"I return the favour: supper in your room. Or Helen's room, rather," Ford said, shouldering open the door, a laden tray in his hands, and peering into the studio. "Though I see you've much taken over. Ah, the looking glass." He raised his eyebrows for me to take the tray, lingering in the doorway.

"Thank you," I said, draping the wedding gown over the mirror so that it would not drag on the floor. It was the only place in the room to hang the garment. I retrieved the tray from his hands and carried roast chicken, gravy and pudding to the workbench.

Ford followed me into the room with tentative steps, as if Helen were about to appear from thin air. "How nice that this studio be in use again." Aside from Hester's pantry, this was the one room in Blueford that looked lived in, enlivened with the detritus of creativity. Fabric scraps and loose threads littered the floor. Paper pattern pieces were pinned to the line that strung the room, interspersed between Helen's watercolours.

From within my scattered drawings and pattern calculations, Ford picked up a child's drawing of a bat with scarlet wings. He pinned Lucy's sketch in the gap on the wall where the red roses had once hung. "I see what good you've done for Lucy, Margaret." He paused, pondering the picture. "This workroom is more yours than Helen's now. *'Margaret's Annex'* we'll call it."

Except I would abandon the room, and be far from Blueford, the moment I knew Rosie was safe. Though perhaps Rosie herself might find inspiration here one day too, lining the walls with rows of books and penning sonnets from a seat on the windowsill.

Ford walked over to Rosie's gown and peered at the fine silk.

"Feel free to lift it," I said, taking a seat at the supper tray, famished from the day's work. "It's finished." The words hung in the air without ceremony. How long I had laboured to complete the gown, how many hopes had been hinged on its creation. And now it was done. And my announcement received as little fanfare as the drop of a pin.

But Ford did not pick it up, though he reached out a hand, and — as though it were covered in thorns — gingerly fingered the seams, tracing the shape of the woman he would wed in only a matter of days.

"You'll let Rosie know?" I urged, searching his face. "That I need her...for a fitting. Tomorrow."

"If she's prepared," he said, turning away from the dress.

I set aside my fork and met his eyes.

"*Prepared?*" I challenged. "You promised."

"I did nothing of the sort," he replied.

I stood abruptly, bumping the tray which spilled the gravy. My hands clenched at my side as I steadied my angry nerves. I opened my mouth to speak, but his words were quicker than mine.

"Let me remind you that it was your sister who promised." And swift as a bat, he departed the room. I glanced down at the tray. The chicken looked like a slip of human skin and the gravy had started to congeal. Whatever appetite I once had was now gone.

14

Patience is one of an artist's greatest virtues. It is as necessary as the making of art itself. As necessary as skill and proficiency. A water colourist waits for one wash to dry before applying another. A poet sleeps on a sonnet, allowing its rhythm to settle into her breath so that it might flow as smoothly as speech on the morrow. A designer stands by to button her muse, for she who inspires a gown is she who will wear the gown.

Patience was not my strong suit. How many times did I meet a deadline for one of Hendry's patrons, only to have the client not attend on Friday as promised, but instead — the gala having passed — appear sometime in the next fortnight, dropping coins on the counter and banishing the hat to a box? Every time it happened, I felt intense disappointment; the hat's would-be debut on the social scene was the culmination of my craft and creativity I craved. I never grew accustomed to my client's apathy, never grew accustomed to the wait.

But wait I did for Rosie. The wedding dress was pressed and laid out on the worktable, the train dipping towards the floor but inches shy of skimming the boards. I made the veil, something I had planned to do with Rosie's input, but my hands burned for occupation. When it was complete, I turned the remnants into a tutu for Lucy's doll.

Of course, I could have started constructing dresses for Lucy and myself, but I was far too distracted to draft patterns. Mathematics were more than my impatient mind could focus upon. By mid afternoon, my fingers were picking apart scraps of lace. As pieces fluttered to the floor like desiccated moth wings, I could sit still no longer.

"Is Master Ford in the parlour?" I asked Hester who was chopping vegetables in the kitchen.

"Think so, Miss. He took his breakfast there, and I haven't seen him come out since. Are you well, Miss?"

"Pardon? Oh, yes, Hester. I'm fine," I said, despite having not eaten all day, being too anxious to leave the studio. 'Margaret's Annex'. Hardly! What a fool I felt, sitting there all day as limp as Lucy's doll. It was merely a cage to match Soutache's. I would not be belittled so! Had Ford even delivered my message to Rosie? In spite of their engagement, she seemed miles from his mind.

I left the kitchen and went in search of my brother-in-law.

"Where is she?" I demanded, bursting into the parlour.

Sprawled in one of the blue velvet chairs, Ford slumbered by the heat of the fire. Fallen charts were scattered across the floor, curled around his boot ankles. He stirred and grumbled, "You've forgotten how to knock?"

"You've forgotten to how to talk?" I countered. "Did you tell Rosie the dress was ready? And if not, haven't you the decency to tell *me*? I stayed in that room all day!" I could feel tears beginning to flood my eyes and I blinked rapidly to dispel them.

Ford looked at me with half-lidded eyes. "Toasty by the fire, were you? Sun on your shoulder? All the pretty flowers around you? Can't have been that bad."

"What are you talking about?" I snapped, confused by his words. When he didn't respond, I continued, "I need Rosie to fit the dress. Without the dress, there's no wedding. Damn it, without *Rosie* there's no wedding! Where is my sister?"

In two strides Ford was up from his chair and inches from my face. "What does it matter when the wedding is?"

"Because I can't stay here forever!"

"Then go!"

"Don't be absurd. You know I won't leave until I see Rosie.

And Rosie won't see me until you marry her."

He drew back, a quizzical expression upon his face. "Who told you that?"

"Rosie. In a note. She sounded urgent. About the wedding, that is."

Ford turned his back to me and walked over to the fireplace. He pressed a hand against the mantle, then ran it up the carved plaster of the flue. "Rosie didn't come today because I didn't tell her to."

"What?" I stepped over to him, grabbed his arm and pulled him around to face me. "Why not?" I demanded.

"Don't hang about me, woman," he barked, shaking me off. "I was frightened for you, Margaret." Then he brushed past me and retreated through the door.

"Wait," I called, running after him. But he had already crossed the entryway and mounted the staircase. I clung to the banister. "What do you mean you were frightened for me?"

He ignored my cries, his feet flying over the steps while I struggled to keep up, my skirts twisting against my calves. I chased him into the studio where he marched past the gown and veil without notice and proceeded to kick out the fire, rolling hot coals onto the hearth and grinding embers under his boot heel.

"What in God's name is wrong with you?" I cried, tears streaking down my cheeks, certain he had gone mad.

He rounded, gripping me by the shoulders and shaking me with some violence. "Do you want to take your last voyage?"

When I started to choke on my tears, he pulled me against his torso, pressing my head to his chest with one hand and stroking my hair with the other. He rocked me then until my coughing and crying subsided. Then, resting his bearded jaw against my temple, he spoke soft and low.

"Rosamund is ill, Margaret. As am I. As is Lucy. I would not have you be next. I fear that if you meet with your sister, you too will contract our sickness."

I tilted my head back until my chin touched his chest and my eyes found his. "But you've not made me sick. Nor has Lucy.

How many times has she coughed into my hair or on my hands? I believe I'm immune."

He laughed, a hard and bitter sound, and smoothed the hair that clung to my forehead, damp with tears. "You are not immune, Meg, not for a dream. Nor I immune to you, God help me," he said, and kissed my forehead. His lips were as cool and dry as his voice. "And God help me, I'll give you what you ask."

He released me then and led me to the door, his hand gripping the base of my neck. "Come away now, it's getting dark. Take Lucy to the kitchen and eat with Hester there. I'll speak with your sister tonight. In the morning, you will be reunited with your dear sister Rosie — your heavenly Rosamund, or better known as Rosie from h—." But his final word was drowned out as he suddenly leaned in and brushed his lips across my mouth. When he pulled away, I was left alone standing in the corridor, my pulse beating a heavy rhythm.

All that night I did not sleep. I left my bedroom door ajar so that if Rosie wished to come at night, she would feel welcome. Every rustle and creak in the night had me peering through the darkness to see if my sister had materialised in the room. Come morning, I was exhausted from lack of sleep.

I did not breakfast right away, but instead went directly to Helen's studio to attend Soutache. I removed the paisley cover on his cage and whistled good morning with false cheerfulness. I did not hear the door open or close behind me, and so I was startled to hear the rustle of fabric very close to my shoulder.

I spun around.

My sister stood mere inches from my face.

If Rosie had been named for the warm glow in her cheek, there was no sign of it now. Against her red hair, haphazardly pinned, and her black dress, her skin was a pale white and showed the blue of her veins.

183

I uttered her name, though the word sounded like no more than a sharp intake of breath. And then without pause, I dragged her into my arms. She brought her arms snug about my neck and leaned into my breastbone, cutting off my breath as I cried.

She clung to me like old ivy to a chimney. We remained as thus for several long minutes until finally I pried myself away so that I might look at her. Dark circles outlined blue eyes, which — once as bright as cornflowers — had faded to the dull hue of a rained-out sky. She said nothing, but stared at me as though I were not myself, but a mere reflection of her.

"Do not be frightened," she finally whispered.

"I am not," I said, though in truth the pallor of her appearance did cause me worry. I took her hand and led her towards the workbench. Helen's studio — usually so inviting — felt grim and unwelcoming. No fire burned in the grate. Someone had turned the looking glass to face the wall. A single lit candle on the mantle threw off a weak glow in the gloomy morning light.

"Sit," I said, assisting her onto the stool. "I will light a fire."

"No, no fire! But…" She shuddered and glanced at the fireplace, as if someone watched from its shadowy depths, then threw a look over her shoulder towards the door.

I went to the door and turned its key in the lock. "We won't be disturbed," I assured, returning to her side and collapsing onto the stool next to her. "Oh, Rosie! I have been so afraid for you." I dropped my head in her lap, suddenly weary of the worrisome days and nights. The fabric of her skirt was cool and damp and she smelled of soot. Her hand passed lightly over my hair. "Where have you been?" I asked.

"Here," she replied. "Always here. Within the walls of this house."

"But why would you not come to see me? I longed for you so!"

"I know," Rosie said, as she stroked my hair. "I watched over you every night. Saw that you were safe. Saw that Ford treated you well."

I raised my head to look at her. "You watched me? You know that I looked for you? I thought Ford had locked you away! Or done you some terrible harm!"

She nodded, her face solemn, "Forgive me for watching in silence, Meg. You are so much stronger than I — despite being alone. Look at all you've done for Lucy! And for me! What a beautiful dress!"

"You've seen the wedding dress?"

"I've seen it from pattern to finish. I've seen Lucy's hat, from your hands to her head. And what you did for the bat. For Flue." She smiled tightly, as though her lips were a knot that she struggled to loosen. "I know how hard you searched for me but you were safe, and that is all that mattered. You have never been in any danger, Meg. He treats you —" she paused to choose her word, "— kindly."

I sat up then and clasped both her hands in mine. "No, Rosie. You're wrong. There is grave danger in this house! At his hand. Something is terribly wrong for you to hide from me so long! But it's over now, Rosie. We will leave tonight."

Rosie laughed and the sound was bitter and cold. She gazed at the coal strewn hearth. "I am not going anywhere, Meg."

"But, Rosie —"

"No one can save me but God," she said in a sharp voice. "I have counted the days until the wedding, when I might set foot outside of this house and at last enter a church."

"Why say such a thing?" I asked. "There is nothing God would forgive of you that I would not." I bit my lip, "Ford told me that he attacked you. The fault lies with him."

Rosie shook her head with vigour, red tresses tumbling loose onto her shoulders. "I am cursed, Meg. God has cursed me for my actions, and only God can lift my punishment!" She covered her face with her hands and whispered through the cage of her fingers, "I am so ashamed, Magpie! So ashamed."

I wrapped my arms around her shoulders and held her close.

"I will not believe it, Rosie. You are a rose. Pure and perfect."

She was and always had been my touchstone, through the deaths of my mother and father, through all those years at the Sisters of

Mary, through the loss of Helen. "Tell me everything for I will not judge you."

Rosie lifted her face and fixed cold eyes on me. "Then I shall, for your forgiveness means more to me than God's."

We sat on the floor; I with my back against the low wall beneath the window, spine cushioned by the drapes that covered the window casing. Rosie lay curled as though she were a cat, her head in my lap with my arm wrapped snug about her shoulders. And at last the veil was lifted:

"It was not long after you'd left for London," she said "that — like you — I found myself lonely at Blueford Manor. Lucy and Ford kept odd hours. They seemed to be awake all through the night and wanting to sleep only by day. I found my own sleep patterns disrupted as I began to match theirs. Then one night, I sought solace at Helen's grave.

"The moon was full, casting bright light on our sister's headstone, and in this glow I sat, my cloak over my white nightgown. I did not hear Ford behind me until I was in his arms.

"He called me 'Helen'," she said, her hand tightening in mine. "And in truth, Meg, I did not correct him. Did not want to correct him. I was lonely, too, and missing our sister. There were tears upon his face and so I gave in. I gave in to his embrace and allowed him to kiss me.

"Oh, Meg," she sighed, "his touch was unlike anything I had ever experienced. He tore my hair from its bun and it fell over my face, hiding my features. And when our lips were not together, he called me by Helen's name, over and over and over. I know not what possessed us! We were wild, like wolves — clawing and biting one another. "

My cheeks were warm and my hands tight in her grasp.

"We desecrated her grave with our unnatural behaviour," she moaned, closing her eyes. "And for a brief amount of time I was

186

in Paradise. But from that moment on, I was cursed. Guilt kept me awake each and every night, which was just as well for sunlight stung my eyes. I felt cold all the time as though I were preparing to join Helen in death. My fingernails stopped growing, and became brittle and pale. I am , it seems, frozen in time," she cried. "God wants me dead. I ought to be … to atone for my actions. But I cannot die, as much as I wish. For my heart is still very much alive," she said. "It grows in love for Lucy, aches with longing for you and bleeds with pity for Ford, who mourns our sister so deeply."

"Rosie, you must forgive yourself," I said, wiping away her tears with my skirt. "You and Ford were raw with the loss of Helen, stricken with grief. You cannot be faulted for falling into his arms, confused by your emotions." I said, thinking of how I'd felt in Ford's arms on more than one occasion. Then I asked softly, "Do you love him?"

Rosie laughed, and it was a harsh sound. "How can I? I know so little of him and have hid as much from him as from you. But marry him I must! Such unbridled passion may be forgiven only within the holy rites of matrimony. Everyday I pray, but everyday the curse rages inside me. I cannot tell you what terrible things I do, what terrible cravings I have! The only way to banish such evil from my thoughts — my actions — is to do what is right."

My heart longed to lift her pain. And I could. The wedding dress was ready, Rosie was only steps away from the ceremony. "Come," I said, helping her to her feet, and leading her towards the dress, "let us set things right."

Now that Rosie was clad in matrimonial white, she looked even more deathly pale than she had been when she was dressed in black. If I'd ever entertained thoughts that Rosie was a ghost, she certainly fit the part now. I asked her to turn away so that I might fit the back of the bodice and dropped to my knees, pins in my mouth, and fit the waistband against her rib cage.

Though Rosie was convinced her salvation lay in marriage to Ford, I feared it was the doorway to her death, for Ford was not be trusted. I knew I had to stop Rosie from marrying him, but I didn't know how to accomplish such a feat. My sister was set in her purpose, convinced that atonement was required for desecrating Helen's memory. Perhaps I merely had to state my fears aloud.

Through teeth clamped down on the pins, I said, "I believe Ford is responsible for Helen's death."

I heard a sickening snap, and Rosie's voice — steeped in disbelief — was eerily close to my ear. "You think he killed her?"

Pins fell from my lips in horror catching in the front of my dress: Rosie's head was turned completely backward on her long neck, pale eyes staring at me in shock at what I'd said. But my shock was greater.

I screamed.

At the piercing sound of my voice, Rosie's hands flew to ears. Quick as a bird, her head spun back around like an owl's. She ran to the hearth, plunged into the fireplace, and scrambled up into the chimney. I heard the tell-tale scratch of her fingernails as she clambered over the bricks inside, a sound I had heard so many times before and mistaken for bats.

I clasped my hands over my mouth, cutting off my scream, not wanting to alert Ford or Lucy or Hester. When I was quite confident I could control my voice, I removed my hands and crawled over to the fireplace. Hanging low from the chimney were my sisters booted feet.

"Rosie…" I called, in no more than a whisper, "Please…please come down from there."

Her feet disappeared and I heard a rustling within the chimney. Then her upside down head slowly lowered into the fireplace. Her red hair dragged over the coal grate like limp flames of fire. This way, her face looked as I remembered it in London, the muscles of her cheeks falling with gravity and filling out the bags under her eyes.

I smiled, drawing closer. "So this is how you kept vigil."

Rosie nodded, her pale face all I could see of her body in the dark space of the fireplace, bobbing back and forth like an apple on a branch. She cried, "What kind of creature am I?"

I reached into the fireplace and touched my fingertip to a tear tracing down her forehead. "You, dear one, are my sister."

⚷

Rosie and I passed the day in the workroom. Only once did I leave to fetch bread and cheese which I desperately needed for sustenance, and was thankful to return to Rosie having encountered no one on my way to the kitchen or back. I offered some to Rosie, but she declined, declaring she was not hungry. Instead, she sagged in a chair at the worktable, still in the wedding gown, which was now stained with soot. As I ate she described the past month to me — roaming the rooms of Blueford Manor via the network of chimneys, too ashamed to face Ford though he often called out for her, or me for that matter. On the first floor, the large chimneys of the parlour and dining room split into four apiece; one stack at the north end of the house, the other at the south, diverging into individual stacks that fed air to the smaller fireplaces in each of the second floor's rooms.

Before I had arrived, she'd spent her days in our niece's room, sleeping in the chimney by day and playing with or reading to Lucy at night. Come my arrival, however, her habits shifted, favouring my room, where she dampened the fire with ashes in order to watch over me while I slept.

I did not tell Rosie that her watchful presence, the noises emanating from the chimney and the fire that would not stay lit, frightened me. What did it matter? To hear about her loyal vigil was a comfort to me now.

I confess a part of me had at times believed Rosie's presence either a manifestation of Lucy's imagination or a lie of Ford's making. Though I had always clung to hope that my sister lived

— the note, the button, the stolen watercolour — part of me had thought her dead. But now that Rosie sat beside me, the weight of worry on my heart had been lifted. Ford no longer held power over me. Whatever had happened to Helen, Rosie and I would discover together. There was no way he could hide anything from me — *from us* — now.

When she finished speaking, I tried to lighten the mood.

"You spooked me dreadfully taking the rose painting!" I teased, "I thought you a ghost, capable of walking through walls!"

Rosie laughed, but her eyes remained sad. "It brought me a glimmer of joy to behold. I spent so many hours in the chimney of your room that to have the painting there — well, both my sisters were in one place. United!"

Just then, someone rapped on the door. Rosie froze and I kissed her cheek reassuringly. "It is only Hester, I'm sure. With dinner."

My guess was confirmed when I opened the door a crack and slipped out into the hall, closing it behind me. The sweet aroma of supper assaulted me and my gut growled in response. I'd not noticed how quickly the day had passed in Rosie's company.

"Just came to call you and Miss Lucy to supper, Miss. It's a quarter of six and only the Master come down."

"Oh, Hester, I completely forgot!" I said, "I shan't come this evening, thank you. There are things I must…attend to. But Lucy is not with me."

Hester frowned. "No, Miss? But I heard you laughing together."

I squeezed her arm excitedly. "The laughter is Rosamund's!"

"Indeed?" Hester said, her face paling. "Is she well?"

I pursed my lips. "She is not fully recovered and so I should like to stay with her. But it is so good to see her! I think she will be well soon, now that I can nurse her."

Hester nodded, the creases on her brow softening. "I'll bring up some soup, then, Miss. For both you and Miss Rosamund."

The wedding veil covered Rosie's face, making her appear as much a ghost as she ever would.

"I always thought I'd wear Helen's veil..." she said dreamily.

"You can if you wish," I said, closing the studio door behind me once Hester had departed. Though I knew Hester would return any moment with the soup, I turned the lock in the door. I was not prepared for Lucy to burst in and find us together. I wished Rosie only for myself tonight.

"I was only too happy to do this small thing for you," I said, referring to her wedding ensemble, "when I felt I could do so little." I tugged at the soiled skirt of her gown. "But it is rather the worse for wear now, wouldn't you say?" I laughed. "Shall we look for Helen's wedding dress instead?"

Rosie pushed back the delicate veil from her face where it framed her red hair like a halo. "What if she's buried in it? And what did you mean when you said you thought Ford killed her?"

"I have no proof," I conceded, "only my own suspicious. But I do not think Helen was alone when she jumped from the roof. In fact, I am not sure she jumped at all." I repeated what Lucy had told me of witnessing her mother's fall. Rosie listened in silence. "And how can we believe what Ford says, especially after he lied about your trip to Moorwood?" I continued, "He is so secretive. He has hidden both your presence and your condition. He did not even explain in what way you were ill, and I did not know whether to believe you dead or alive!"

"I hardly know myself," Rosie replied in a hollow voice.

"And I cannot help but think there is some clue in the cellar. Why keep Helen's belongings locked away unless there is something he did not want revealed? There is a small wine closet there where Helen's things are stored. But Ford keeps the room locked — or did, until he gave me the key."

"If he gave you the key, then surely there is no mystery," she reasoned.

"I am not sure," I confessed. "He kept the key around his neck, and when he gave it to me, he — well, he did not seem reluctant, but perhaps...defeated. And there is a wardrobe in the room that is also locked. Why? If it is no longer of use, and contains nothing valuable, why lock it?"

"Perhaps Lucy knows what's inside?"

I shook my head. "No, I don't think she's familiar with the room, let alone the wardrobe." I suddenly shivered as I remembered the séance. Oh, that windy day in London — how long ago it seemed! "I did not tell you," I said with hesitation, fear prickling at my neck, "that Mrs Willis held a séance to communicate with Helen."

"With Helen?" Rosie laughed, and for once I heard genuine joy in her voice, "Bless her heart!"

"You are sorely missed by the Willis family, Rosie. Millicent would rehire you in a heartbeat, even if you were to hang about like a bat in their rafters!"

My sister swatted my arm and then said, "Tell me about the séance."

"Millicent swears that Lucy delivered a message: *The answer is in the wardrobe.*"

"You believed this?" Rosie asked, raising her brow. "You are an unlikely mystic, Meg!"

I smiled grimly, thinking about my mystical pet Soutache. "Unearthly message or not, I think it worthwhile to break into the wardrobe. Every other lock in this house has yielded to an interesting discovery. If nothing more, we may find Helen's wedding dress."

If only I had known then the state in which we would find that gown.

15

Impatient, I stamped my feet and tucked my fists under my arms to keep warm. In the cover of darkness, the cellar was bitterly cold. It was a clear night and could possibly frost. Rosie was not bothered; she explored Helen's belongings with delight, exclaiming with joy when she recognised a familiar trinket or possession that recalled a happy memory. Although I was uncomfortably chilled, I did not wish to break the spell by encouraging my sister to hasten her search — Rosie had not looked this happy since before Helen's death.

But as we had entered into the cellar, Rosie was shocked to see the pile of dead bats Hester and I had swept up. For these, she cried out, she was responsible. Before my arrival, few fires were ever lit in the house and the bats, like Rosie, roosted in the chimneys. Some nights, when she hardly knew herself, she was overcome with the desire to drink to their blood and so she bit tiny neck after tiny neck and drank.

But the instant their juice touched her tongue, she was brought to her senses. As each one fluttered away, screeching for freedom, she'd pray they would recover. She did not know they had returned to the cellar to die. She picked up one of the poor creatures, found the tell-tale bite mark buried in the downy fur of its neck, and showed it to me.

I wanted to shy away. Of everything I had seen of Rosie that day, this alone horrified me. But she was my sister, and as such I loved her. If she believed she was beyond God's love, it was doubly important she knew the value of mine.

When we reached the wardrobe I selected from my châtelaine a pair of thread scissors: the blades were made of strong steel. Rosie held the candlestick close while I jammed the scissor blades into the lock. I wrapped a scrap of muslin around the handle twice for a better grip.

The lock was no match for our determination. Once the two of us applied our hands to the task, it snapped with a satisfying crack. Why had I not done this sooner? I exhaled, restored the scissors to my châtelaine and looked at my sister. Rosie nodded and, each of us grasping a door handle, we opened the wardrobe together.

🗝

Rosie's scream reverberated in the wine closet. Ford and Lucy and Hester must surely have heard. I clamped my hand across Rosie's mouth, shutting off the sound, as she turned and cowered against the opposite wall.

"Hush," I admonished. She nodded, her eyes large and fearful. I waited a moment, then removed my hand from her lips. I confess I was a little frightened she might bite me as she had the bats.

"God help us, Magpie," she whispered.

"I know," I said, stepping towards the wardrobe and pushing the doors closed to hide the grizzly sight from view. The contents of my stomach threatened to rise and I could hear Rosie vomiting to my side. I stumbled over to Rosie, the skirt of her wedding gown now soiled black and spattered with red spray.

I placed a hand on her shoulder, "Come, Rosie — we must leave at once." We would depart now under the cover of darkness. On foot, I estimated we would reach Harrowgate in just under three hours. Rosie opened her mouth to speak, but made no sound. I fumbled for her hands, closed mine around her cold fingers, and pulled her upright. She sagged against me and I hauled her out of the closet and into the main room of the cellar.

Rosie screamed a second time when I pulled open the cellar door: time had passed without our notice and dawn had broke. She retreated into the darkness beyond the slatted light of the gas vents.

"Ssh!" I hissed. "What is wrong? We must leave now."

"I cannot, I cannot," Rosie panted from the shadows. "I shall burn alive."

I closed the door, shutting us once more in darkness. "We can't stay here," I said, walking into the darkness and bumping up against her trembling form. "We must get away from the house!"

"What about Lucy?" Rosie asked.

I shook my head, no. "Ford will not harm her. She is everything to him. Besides, the journey is too far for her legs. We will return with the Constable. " And then I thought of the other occupant of the house. We could not leave Hester here.

"I will fetch Hester," I said. "She is not safe."

"And the light is not safe for me," Rosie sobbed.

"I will find a way," I said, gripping her shoulders and kissing her clammy cheek. Then I fled the bowels of the cellar up the steps into Blueford Manor.

I ran to the kitchen and found it as still as a tomb but for a kettle boiling on the stove-top. I shouted for Hester and she emerged from the pantry, prayer shawl shrouding her hair. When she saw me, she drew it back from her forehead, allowing it to fall to her shoulders.

"Hester, you must come at once!" I exclaimed.

"Oh, Miss!" She removed the kettle from the stove and turned to follow me. "Thank goodness, you've found him."

"Found who?" I asked, thrown from my quest.

"I'm so dreadfully sorry about it, Miss, I looked everywhere, I did! And Miss Lucy, too. The Master made her comb the house top to bottom." She clasped her hands as if in prayer.

"What do you mean? What's happened? Who's missing?" I asked, her words finally sinking into my brain.

The blank expression on my face must have alerted her to the fact that we were having two different conversations. "You did not know?" she asked, with a slight expression of fear upon her face. "It's Soutache, Miss."

"Soutache!" I cried in alarm. "What has happened to him?"

"I went into the studio last night to close the curtains as I always do. The little fowl was gone, Miss. The door to the room and the door to his cage were both open wide as paddock gates on butchering day."

"Has he — did he…come to harm?"

Hester wrung her hands. "I don't know, Miss. All's Miss Lucy said is she set him free to fly with Flue, and then up they went into a chimney and neither's been seen since."

I collapsed into a chair and stared at the steam rising from the kettle. Lost in time with Rosie, I'd neglected my faithful feathered companion. If he found his way outside, any sort of danger may have befallen him. Rendered nearly defenseless with only one eye and an imperfect wing, he may as well have been stuffed and mounted on a hat for all the chances he had.

But then again, a cat or an owl may have been the least of his foes. Did Lucy tell the truth, or had she caused him harm herself? As much as it pained me, I could not search for him now. There was a greater danger at our backs.

"Hester, you must listen to me. It is not safe for us to stay here. We must leave at once. I am afraid — "

"Afraid?" came a voice from behind me. I stiffened as his boot steps approached. Hester lifted her gaze from me and stared at Ford over my head. First his voice settled on the back of my neck. "What frightens the hens in the coop?"

Then his two hands slid over my shoulders and settled upon

my flesh, his thumbs kneading the knotted muscles at the top of my spine, his fingers only inches from encircling my throat.

I stared at Hester and mouthed the word: *Go.*

Colour rose in her neck and cheeks as she stammered, "I'm just off to…" and turned towards the pantry. In that moment, Ford removed his hands from my neck and in a single stride was at Hester's elbow. He pulled the string of her apron, spun her out of it and yanked the prayer shawl from her shoulders.

"Very good, Hester. I'm much obliged." He pushed her into the pantry and slammed the door. From her apron, he withdrew the key and locked her in.

I bolted towards the kitchen door, but he was fast.

"Stay where you are, Margaret!" he roared, lunging to catch me in his grip and dragging me against his chest. I fought fiercely, but he deftly wrapped Hester's prayer shawl around my torso, binding my arms against my ribs. "You leave me no choice!" he snarled in my ear.

"Miss!" Hester's voice called to me from behind the pantry door as her hands pounded on the wood, but she was powerless to help me.

I spit in Ford's face, "You killed my sister!"

"I beg you, a little decorum, Margaret," he seethed.

"And you've shown yourself to have the manners of a king?" I cried, fighting to free my arms.

"Make this easy on yourself, Margaret." He pushed me ahead of him, out of the kitchen towards the rear entrance of the manor.

"Where are you taking me?" I demanded, kicking at him with my boots, refusing to walk. But I was like a bird ensnared in a net, unable to extricate myself.

"You can join your sister," he snapped, wrapping his arms around me and hoisting me over his shoulder. "I need to think things through. In the meantime, I need to protect Lucy from you." Before opening the back door, he yanked off my jacket, popping several buttons as he did, and threw it over his head like a highwayman. Then he carried me out of the house. My screams echoed in the empty landscape.

I dropped the scissors, my fingers and hands exhausted. I had forever mangled the blades and they would never again trim stray threads. But no matter how I manipulated the scissors, they could not pry the pins free of the rusted hinges on the cellar door. Nor was I able to free the cellar door lock. It was too large and heavy to be unlocked by any of the instruments on my châtelaine.

"Is there no hope?" Rosie wailed, crawling out of the shadows. She crouched inches from the dimly cast light seeping through the gas grill in the cellar wall. Already the day was fading. How many hours since Ford had locked us in?

"I may never be able to sew again," I grumbled, assessing my battered hands. Rust stained my fingers, dirt outlined my fingernails, blood crusted over the cuts I'd received when the scissors slipped from their hold more than once. I flexed my fingers, coaxing blood into fingers that were stiff from exertion and chilled by the damp basement air.

Rosie's eye tracked the blood on my moving knuckles and the tip of her tongue passed over her lower lip. As I hid my hands from her view in my skirts, she tilted her head back, nostrils flaring as she sniffed out something on the air.

"They're awake!" she hissed.

And within seconds I heard it as well, the stirring of hundreds of wings, and a dark cloud of bats emerged from the cellar shadows. The flock rushed at the gas grills and one by one pushed through the slats, finding their way into the night.

"Quickly! Before they're all gone!" Rosie shrieked and lunged into the air. She caught one in her teeth, the way I'd seen Lucy bite into Flue's wing. It squealed and flapped in her jaw until she crunched down on its tiny skull, a spray of blood squirting across my skirt.

I whirled away from her and gagged, staggering over to the wall and leaned my head against it for support. All the while,

I could hear Rosie sucking on the bat.

"Help me catch them!" she cried as I heard her jump again. But I could not. Instead, I clasped my hands over my ears so I did not have to listen to the crunch of bones in her teeth.

Several minutes passed before I felt the touch of her stone-cold hand on my arm. It took me a moment, but eventually I turned to see what had become of my sister. Blood stained her lips and cheeks like cheap rouge. An exsanguinated bat hung in her fingers. She looked at me, childlike. "I cannot help myself, Meg."

"I know," I said, though I did not understand her urges in the least. But the nightmare of our situation somehow seemed less grizzly if we were united.

"I've killed so many," she continued, her voice constricted with pain. "I pray for forgiveness each time, but the desire still haunts me." I drew her head against my shoulder as she crumbled into tears. "Fix me," she cried.

I had never felt more helpless. But then an idea began to take form in my mind. If I could not fix Rosie, there was perhaps something else I could do for her.

One by one they came to life.

Limping at first, then taking flight, circling on unsteady wings as they bumped into the rafters. I snapped a fresh length of thread from the sewing kit I'd found in Helen's affects and knotted it through a needle. Rosie passed me another bat carcass. So far we'd rejuvenated half a dozen in all.

It was possible that she was even more joyful than Lucy as she flung each resurrected bat into the air, clapping her hands with delight.

"Not this one, Rosie," I said, as she handed me the skeleton of a bat long since dead of more natural causes.

"Please," she begged, and I relented. I had only so much strength left to fight, and it was not Rosie against whom I wished to be pitted. The bat's bones were like matchsticks in my palm. I lashed them together with thread, tying knots that would make a sailor wince. Moments later the bat hopped from my hands and into Rosie's lap.

"He cannot fly," I remarked. The flesh between the bat's digits had rotted, leaving nothing of its wings but long pale bones.

Rosie smiled. "Then he shall be mine." She placed the skeletal bat on her head where it nestled into her ragged chignon, hanging upside down from bony feet. Against her red locks, the bat's rib cage shone pale like a delicate hair comb.

"No more," I told Rosie, as she reached for another. I was exhausted. My world upended. I needed rest. I rose to return the needle and thread to the sewing box in Helen's closet. As I stood before the room, I stared at the wardrobe containing the greatest horror of all. As I contemplated what I had accomplished with the bats, a new thought took shape in my mind. If I could revive a bat that had been dead for weeks — or more — what else could I grant life?

Much nourished by the bat's blood, Rosie helped me haul Helen's trunks out of the closet and into the main area of the cellar, clearing a space for me to work in front of the wardrobe. Her eyes functioned much better in the dark than mine, and I took to holding her hand as we moved between the cellar and closet. I'd stumbled several times before pausing to stab my sewing scissors through the bottom inches of my skirt and tearing away the hem. Now, my blood-splattered skirt would not impede my progress.

"And candles," I said. "I need candles."

Rosie found a trunk of mementos from Lucy's birth — a lock of hair, an inked footprint and a baptismal candle. Rosie reached for it, and instantly dropped it with a yelp. I examined her hand and saw that the skin had blistered as though hot to touch. And yet the wax candle was like ice in my hand. I struck a match to it, thankful for the box I had left by the door when Hester and I had returned to fetch the mirror.

In the light of the flickering flame, I spread out my instruments — scissors (badly bent), thread of more than one colour, needles, a thimble and measuring tape. I looked to Rosie for courage, took a deep breath and opened the wardrobe.

Helen was as we'd found her: her frame clad in her wedding gown, her spine curled to fit into the corner of the cupboard, her legs folded in front of her, knees touching her chin. Or would have been, were it not for the fact that her head lolled unnaturally over her right shoulder as it had been almost torn completely free of her neck. Her right arm was pulled clean away from her shoulder socket, and — bent at the elbow — hooked over a clothes hanger.

Trembling, I reached in and unwound her arm from the hanger. It was stiff and surprisingly heavy. I threaded my fingers through Helen's and folded my hand about hers. It had been years since I had felt her touch. I called for Rosie's help. She crept over to join me, averting her eyes, and helped me to shift Helen's body onto the floor.

I worked with great care, reinforcing each stitch as I sewed. Rosie hovered behind me and whispered encouragement. The flesh at Helen's right shoulder was black with rot. I hacked it away with the scissors and trimmed up the edges. Next, I bent to the task of repairing her neck. The muscles and veins had torn down the left side. A half dozen vessels protruded from the opening at her neck, empty as reeds, the blood having long since flowed away. The left side of her face was slightly crushed, the edge of the eye socket bloody and chipped. I imagined the force of her fall, her cheekbone shattering against the pavement as she landed. I rotated her head, squaring it back on her shoulder, and asked Rosie to hold it in place. She shuddered, but did as I requested. Helen's neck was torn almost clear all the way around; I sewed a double row, for good measure.

Rosie sat in quiet vigil as I worked, only occasionally

instructing me as to which tendons to connect, sounding ever so the governess she'd been to the Willis children. Neither of us dared express hope. And as I came to the last stitches that would set Helen's neck, my hands began to shake. I knotted and snapped the thread in my teeth, and our sister's eyes flew open.

Startled, I launched myself backwards, kicking my heels against the dirt floor. Rosie caught me in her arms, wrapping them about my chest and pressing her cheek against mine as we stared at our sister. Helen's wide silver eyes fixed on Rosie and me. Then her lips began to move. And the fingers of her mended arm. She bent her knees, pulling them closer to her chest as she lay crumpled on the floor. Next, she tested her neck, rolling her head from side to side, and flexing her jaw muscle.

Rosie and I separated then, creeping forward, helping Helen as she struggled to sit. We grasped her arms and helped her upright. Then we pushed shut the wardrobe doors and propped her against them. Once again, she opened her lips but no sound came out. She tried a third time, frustration creasing her brow. I panicked. Perhaps I had not repaired her trachea correctly. Then, in an instant, Helen lunged for me, clamping her teeth around my arm.

"No!" Rosie yelled, wrestling my arm free of Helen's mouth, and plunging her own wrist between Helen's jaw. Helen's eyes fell closed as her teeth sunk into Rosie's arm, and blood leaked from the seal of Helen's mouth.

"She's empty," Rosie murmured, as Helen drank. Although I watched in horror, Rosie sat calmly, watching Helen with a calm patience and stroking her head. I stayed where I was, an arm's distance away, hugging myself. The candle flame flickered, threatening to gutter.

At last Helen broke away and sighed. She opened her eyes, and fixed them on me. This time, when she opened her mouth, she managed to speak: "Margaret, you did this." Her hoarse voice was unrecognisable as her own, as thin and sharp as the whistle of a broken flute. She stared at me. "You stitched me together."

I nodded, and glanced at Rosie for reassurance, unable to reconcile *this* Helen with my sister. But Rosie smiled down at her with affection, brushing a stray hair from Helen's face.

"Yes," I croaked, and moved a little closer. "I mended you." I leaned into the candlelight that Helen might see me better, but I was at a loss for words. I had not prepared a greeting should my plan have worked. And it had.

For here she was, my eldest sister, long dead — alive and fevered looking — taking in the towers of trunks surrounding her. "I'm still at Blueford Manor?"

"Yes," I said. "We are trapped here, but we will get out. I promise."

"Trapped?" Helen hissed, her broken voice rising in pitch, as she leaned into my face. "I'd escaped this curse, you strumpet!"

Helen spat in my face, and I scrambled away. Rosie grabbed her by the shoulders, pinning her to the wardrobe as Helen's fingers clawed the air, trying to grab me. "I jumped into Heaven — a delicious three-second flight!" she shrieked. "And now you've dragged me back into Hell!"

"So I am once more what I once was," Helen seethed, resting upright against the closed wardrobe doors. Her head lolled forward on her neck as she stared at me through crumbling eyelashes. She looked like a doll without stuffing, unable to support her head, stitches where a toymaker had mended the seams. "Still a creature of the night. And you —" Helen swung her head towards Rosie. "It has happened to you, too."

"A creature of the night?" Rosie echoed, bewildered. She sat on her knees, hunched before Helen, gripping her hands. I stayed where I was, my back pressed against the far wall, by the door. I was exhausted, having had no water or food in nearly two days, but fear of Helen kept me alert.

"Certainly," Helen hissed, a smile playing at her lips. "Your blood is old and dead. It's sickening to taste."

"Don't say such horrid things!" I cried. "Rosie is unwell enough, without such fiendish notions filling her head." My well-read sister had surely cracked the spines of *Frankenstein* and *Varney the Vampire*.

"You'll believe it well enough when you're one of us!" Helen threatened. "Do you think you stand a chance, locked down here with Rosamund? And now me? Your clever little needle just reduced your chances of surviving this night." Helen lunged for me once again, but Rosie's arms shot out and pinned her against the wardrobe. Helen's head snapped backward and banged against the wooden door.

"Stop, Helen," Rosie pleaded. "Let us feast on bats. Listen!"

Dawn was returning and with it, the cellar residents. The sound of their wings was like the rush of a cold spring.

"Come now," Rosie cried, springing to her feet and pulling on Helen's newly repaired arm. "Let us feed!"

Helen rose to her feet, supported by Rosie, and stood for the first time since her death. Then she took tentative steps, like a toy come to life.

I stayed where I was, my back to the wall, and watched as my two pale sisters drifted past me, ghost-like, and disappeared into the cellar's darkness. The baptismal candle had long since burned out, and there was no other source of light. Without my sisters' luminous eyes or their white gowns, I had become blind once again.

I ventured from the closet and into the cellar, hugging the far wall as I inched towards the door where morning's first light slanted through the gas grates. I stumbled into a rectangle of sunshine and sank to the dirt floor, resting my forehead against the cool wall. Bats screeched as they were torn limb from limb. The wet sound of my sisters' feeding flooded my ears and I clapped my hands over my head. To drown out the screams, I hummed a melody Soutache used to sing.

I must have fainted. Whether from exhaustion or thirst, I know not.

My eye lids fluttered open with the shaking of my shoulder. Rosie crouched above me, a shaft of light streaming across her skirt which was now striated with bat blood. Her lips were almost black from the feast.

"There's not one left," she said, hollowly.

I struggled to an upright position, pressing a hand to my pounding head. I was dizzy for lack of water.

"Mend them, Magpie," she pleaded, and looked over her shoulder at Helen. In the dim light, Helen glowed pale like Rosie's shadow in a photographic negative. Her chin glistened red from the feed, a trail of blood threading along the stitches in her neck, flowing down her décolletage and disappearing into the crevice between her breasts. At her feet, a mound of bat corpses stood a foot deep. Not one bat remained to cling to the rafters or flit through the air.

"No," I cried, my lips cracking as I spoke, the sharp taste of blood flooding across my tongue. Rosie's pupils widened and I quickly staunched the blood by sucking my lip.

"I won't. I can't. I need —" I sagged against the wall, unable to complete my sentence. They were refreshed by bat blood, yet I continued to suffer without water. For two days I'd been held prisoner here, without food or light. I was a cut rose, wilting in its vase. In my head, I suddenly heard Ford's voice erupt in verse: *Bloody roses all about.*

Rosie fell to her knees, careful to stay out of the light, and pulled me onto her lap, cradling my head. Behind us, Helen drifted into the recesses of the basement, returning to the wine closet. I heaved a sigh of relief and relaxed into Rosie's skirt which smelled of blood and bat guano. Ford's words repeated in my mind. My eyes closed once again and another voice joined the first as Rosie began to sing:

"Springtime is come and the daffodils say,
Welcome fair ladies to the merry month of May;
Hey bonny lass, your true love is near.

"Tulips and crocus and hyacinth play,
All the day long in the merry month of May;
Hey bonny lass, your true love awaits.

"Yellow and purple and colours most gay,
The fairest of ladies dance merry in May;
Hey bonny lass, your true love does linger,
Under the starlight, a ring on your finger.
Hey bonny lass, true love, they will say,
Always, forever, in the merry month of May."

I drifted in and out of consciousness, only becoming fully awakened when yet another melody joined my sister's.

"Rosie!" I croaked, and swatted at her jaw to silence her.

"Yes, Meg?" she said, lowering her ear to hear me.

"That song —"

She paused to listen. "Someone has come to sing to you," she crooned. She turned her head and squinted into the light, then quickly drew a hand over her eyes. She smiled unsteadily. "I cannot see, but it is a bird on the sill of the grate, I am sure!"

"Soutache." I wheezed. "Help me —" and she did, assisting me to stand, leading me as close to the brightening grill as she dared. There on the ledge was my darling sparrow, one eye fixed on me while a sparkle of sunlight reflected on his glass bead. A song warbled in his throat and I laughed, though it sounded a dry rasping cough. I lifted a trembling finger onto which he could hop.

In my state, I felt as battered and left-for-dead as Soutache on the day he'd flown into the window at Hendry's. How much has happened since! Now, he was *my* saviour. From inside my corset I drew the note Rosie had left on the mantle, the paper yellowed and damp with sweat. I detached the graphite pencil on my châtelaine and wrote a simple message on the back of the note:

Carlisle, I am a prisoner at Blueford. Bring help.

I rolled the note and held it to Soutache's beak. Then he took to his wings and disappeared through the grill.

⚷

I remember my sisters talking. Talking about Lucy. About the books Rosie had read aloud to her. About a red bonnet, a bat called Flue, and a rather disappointing painting of an apple.

I remember my red-headed sisters entwined in one other's arms, dancing the length of the cellar. I remember their laughter as they disappeared into the wine closet, and each of Helen's exclamations as she unearthed the souvenirs contained within her trunks. I remember my sisters remembering.

I remember lying on the floor beside the door of the cellar, watching the moving patches of grey light as the day aged. Slipping in and out of sleep, I dreamt that I heard the lock open. Heard the swing of the door. Smelled fresh autumn air.

I remember strong arms lifting me. My father carrying me to bed after working late into the night, falling asleep at his workbench in a pile of velvet brocade. I remember a cloaked a figure in a brimmed hat that shielded not only his eyes, but also mine from the light. I remember the dry biting air, the smell of snow on the clouds. Winter had come, and summer I did not remember. I remember thanking God that the reverend had come.

⚷

My eyes flickered open. Steam writhed about me. I lay in a bathtub, stripped to my petticoats which clung to my skin, rendering them transparent. A blazing fire warmed my room. The flames raged hot: green and blue at their roots.

I rocked my head against the edge of the tub and something moved beside me. Through the steam, I saw him, sitting in the shadows beyond the bathtub.

He leaned forward, bringing his head into the circle of light cast by the fire. Deep folds lined his forehead. His mouth was set in a grim slash, outlined by the inky blue-black of his beard.

"I thought you were lost," he said, drawing close to the tub. He placed a cool palm against my cheek. "At last, your blood warms."

And so I was mistaken. My rescuer was not the reverend. And most likely not to be called my *'rescuer'* either. My cry for help — had Ford intercepted Soutache's message — had only entrenched me deeper into his power. I stiffened as Ford reached down to the floor, but he only lifted a chalice. I half expected it to be accompanied by a knife, poised to open and drain one of my veins.

"Water," he said, and held the cup against my lips. I craned my neck forward and drank heavily. Having drained the cup he refilled it from a pitcher and I drank again. Then he offered me a basket. Inside, buttered bread and boiled eggs.

I grabbed an egg and cracked its shell against the porcelain tub. With trembling fingers, I picked at the crumbling shell, pieces dropping into the tub, tearing the egg's delicate flesh as I struggled to complete the task.

Silently, Ford took the egg from my hands, and with a large steady thumb, whisked the remainder of shell away. He took a small wooden shaker from the basket and snowed salt over the egg's surface. "Salt will help with the dehydration. A sailor's trick," he said.

I devoured the egg, not meeting his eyes. He passed me the chalice again, and once more I drank. "I missed fresh eggs when I was sea," he said, shelling and salting another which he passed to me. "Do not be afraid for Rosamund. She'll be fine in the cellar, for now."

"Of course she will be. She's had her fill of *Chiroptera* blood," I spat venomously, quoting my academic sister when she'd wailed about the bat extinction.

Ford lifted an eyebrow. "So you know about Rosamund," he said, leaning back in the chair, falling into shadow. "And Lucy… you now know about Lucy?"

Lucy as well? Of course. I could now see Lucy was no different than my Rosie. But Lucy was the daughter of…this monster. Rosie ought to have never been touched. And what of Helen —

"You killed my sister!" I shouted, lunging forward in the tub, the bathwater sloshing over its edges. Droplets sprayed into the fire and hissed as they turned to steam.

Ford gripped the edge of the tub with a large fist. "I — yes…I took Rosamund's life, as she knew it. But she lives. She lives, of a sort. Forever…"

I shook my head with violence, tears streaming down my cheeks where they mingled with the steam from the bath. "Not Rosie, *Helen!*"

Ford froze and regarded me with thoughtful eyes. "You think I killed Helen? Helen I tried to protect. Helen I tried to save." He hung his head, and shook it from side to side. "If only I *had* killed her."

"You beast," I spat.

At that his face hardened and he rose and walked to the door. His hand on the doorknob, he turned to me with a dark expression. "Perhaps, but then I have never been a kind man."

Then he stepped out of the room, closed the door and the lock shot home. I was a prisoner once more.

16

I DREW MYSELF FROM THE TUB, petticoats clinging to my limbs as though I were Ophelia, drowned. I stripped by the fire, donning the last of my clean, unworn clothes: a delicate silk blouse and gabardine skirt. With its low, beaded neckline and bare arms, it was hardly the uniform for escape. How little I'd known when I'd packed my carpet bag of circumstances awaited me at Blueford Manor.

Having ate and drank, my mind was now sharp. I flew to the window, tore back the curtains, and pushed up the sash. A foot of snow dressed the grounds of Blueford and bleached out the blue hills in the distance. What month was it — November? How had I not noticed the season's passing days?

No matter. I had waited long enough. In this room, I had waited for Rosie. In the cellar, I had waited for death. I would wait no more.

The drop from the window was dangerously high. Even with two bed sheets tied together, I doubted the safety of such a descent. If I knew mooring knots, perhaps. But as it was, I knew no more about knots than tying off a thread. Besides, I did not even know whether I had the strength to break the thick glass in the window.

I was contemplating the drop when a familiar song greeted me. Soutache! My little friend lighted on the window sill and shook the snow from his feathered cap.

Given that Soutache was dusted with snow, I reckoned that

he had not been caught by Ford after all, and instead made the distance to Carlisle's cottage. If only my feathered familiar could speak! Hope alone would have to quench my thirsting quandary.

I welcomed in Soutache to warm on the mantelpiece and fed him crumbs from the bread basket. I myself ate again, taking advantage of as much nourishment as possible. Had Ford obtained the bread from the pantry where he had restrained Hester? And if so, had she tried to escape? Or been hurt? I prayed that she was well as I chewed on the last egg, and puzzled over my next step.

As before, I rattled the doorknob, but the lock held fast. The door was impassable and the window treacherous. There was, therefore, only one other exit.

The bed sheets proved useful after all; I tore them into strips which I wrapped like corpse dressings about my palms and arms, all the way up to the short sleeves of my blouse. I tore off several inches of my skirt's hem and split it up the middle so I could and knot the fabric about my knees, rather like a pair of pedal-pushers. My stocking calves I also bound in strips of linen. Thus prepared, I doused the fire with bathwater, waved the smoke out through the open window, and crawled into the fireplace.

Soutache joined my journey, his talons clasped to the shoulder of my blouse as I moved on hands and knees. I unfolded and stood in the dark tunnel of the chimney. My eyes could not adjust to the darkness for the chimney pots obscured any light from above; I looked straight ahead into complete blackness; I would have to proceed by touch alone.

I ran my fingers over the brick, feeling for the uneven edges that would provide a foothold. But the toes of my boots skidded over the bricks, unable to find purchase. I unlaced and kicked away my boots, and resolved to proceed in my stockings. The first few feet went easily enough, my legs splayed wide as I braced my thighs and palms against the chimney walls.

I counter-levered my way upward, Soutache warbling encouragement with each movement. I grew increasingly nervous and tired. I'd already climbed more than six feet and shuddered to think what would happen if I fell. And I dared not think what would happen if I became stuck. As no one knew where I was, no one would come for help. I reassured myself by remembering, Rosie traversed these tunnels without issue, and we were of similar size.

Blind as the bats that had once thrived at Blueford, I relied on Rosie's account of the chimney network and Soutache's voice to guide me. I approached where the chimney ought to change angle, sloping upward to connect with the wider stack ascending from the parlour. I hoped to God there was no fire downstairs.

When the tunnel changed course, I had to rotate my body if I were to continue. I shuffled my toes sideways over the bricks, sometimes slipping, but managed to catch hold of the bricks with my fingers and pull myself up into the new branch. I braced my feet against the corner I'd just rounded and lay across the bricks, pausing to slow my panicked breath.

The going would be more difficult from now as the stack rose at a forty five degree angle. I could easily slide back down into the vertical chute and drop to the stone hearth some nine feet below. My fingers stiffened with terror, but I had to go on. I resolved to stay on my belly, inching along the brick. I hadn't far to go; the stack would meet at a junction, where another sloped chute would carry me down to a tunnel, twin to the one I'd just ascended.

As I dragged myself forward and up, brick by brick, Soutache flew ahead, whistling cheerfully in the dark. His voice echoed and it sounded as though there were an entire flock encased within the chimney. Then his song disappeared; I'd made it to the junction!

In front of me gaped the enormous stack of the parlour's fireplace. The air here was fresher, and I paused a moment to breathe. Then, I refocused on the task of crossing the gap to reach the tunnel on the other side. It was at least two feet across. How did Rosie reach the other side? Would it be safer to go head or feet first?

Tired blood cramped my muscles, causing my arms to tremble. Holding steady where I was, I released one arm at a time, allowing them to hang over the edge into the chasm below, so that I might shake out the weary muscles. My legs were not as sore and so they would be my passage across. At the moment, I rested with them spread open, each braced on opposite sides of the tunnel. I decided to try this method to make the crossing.

I pulled my legs to my chest, careful to not tip my weight forward for fear that I would plummet into that dark opening. Once I was crouched on the edge of the gap, I stretched out my left leg, reaching across the empty space. My toes touched the opposite side.

In order to securely plant my foot on the far ledge, I needed a greater angle to bear down. I pushed my torso up into the space above my head, where the three foot wide stack rose to the rooftop. My arms shook as I moved one across the chasm to hold onto the far wall and kept one behind me to steady myself. I straightened my legs, now spread like the crossbar of a crucifix across the junction. If I fell now, I'd be as shattered as Lucy's doll. I shivered. As shattered as Helen.

I stayed where I was for a moment. My legs and arms fully extended, knee and elbow joints locked in a straight position, allowing my muscles to recover. I sucked in deep breaths, dusty with creosote.

There was no smoke, no heat, no sounds from above or below. The house was as silent as the snowy expanse outside. Except for Soutache. I heard a peppy chirp now, coming up the chute where my left leg rested. With a single movement, I heaved myself forward, falling head first into the downward sloping tunnel.

I lost my breath as my chest slammed against the bricks and felt a burning tear along my right forearm as it caught on a jagged lip of mortar. I slid forward and in a panic I hooked my toes on the ledge so that I would not slide. I hung for a moment, staring down the forty five degree grade, into blackness, my eyes searching for any speck of light. It was far too dangerous to descend head-first.

In one swift movement, I pushed up with my arms — my left doing most of the work — tucking my legs beneath me, rounding into a ball and shooting out my limbs to once again brace myself against the brick walls. There. I was righted correctly, feet now pointing downward. I slid slowly on my backside, inching towards the bend in the stack.

It came quickly, my heels slipping into an open space. I shot out my feet to catch on whatever uneven bricks I could find. Then I wriggled down into the straight section, sighing a prayer of gratitude. The worst was over, and I was nearly there. I lowered myself the remaining eight feet and dropped into the hearth of the studio.

Soutache praised me vociferously, alighting on my shoulder. I kissed his petite head. My forearm bled through the linen strips, which now hung in crimson shreds. I shook free the wrappings and examined the cut: long, deep, jagged. And continuing to hæmorrhage fresh blood. I grabbed a generous scrap of wedding dress silk and bore down on my right arm. Light-headed, I crouched on the floor while I waited for the bleeding to stop.

But no matter how hard I pressed, the bleeding did not slow. I did my best to fashion a tourniquet, but having to tie it with only one hand — and my left at that — was a futile process. There was no way I could wind the fabric tight enough to be effective. If only Soutache were the size of an albatross. Then he might be able to aid in my ministrations by pulling on one end of the silk to tighten the knot. As it was, he flew in dizzying circles about my head, screeching his concern.

My eyes spilled tears of frustration and I cursed to Heaven, feeling drowsier by the second. If I fainted, how would I rescue my sisters? Free my niece and Hester? No, this would not do. The wound needed closure. I threw the blood-soaked silk into the coal grate and set to work.

As I prepared, I moved about the studio as lightly as Soutache, fearful that Ford should hear my steps. In stockinged feet, I prayed my footsteps were inaudible. There was a little water left in the pitcher and wash basin which I used to scrub the soot and chimney grime from my hands. My nails were trickier to clean and remained as blackened as Rosie's. Using a pair of sewing scissors, I trimmed my nails down to the quick. They smarted, but I knew they were clean. Having thus prepared my hands, I proceeded to prepare for surgery.

I lit a candle and held a needle in its flame until it turned black. With my left hand, I awkwardly cut a swatch of muslin. All the while I worked, the wound continued to flow freely. Now it was time to address the cut. I lightly touched my finger to its ragged edges, determining its sensitivity and where it was deepest. As I prodded, blood bubbled up to the opening and spilled over my wrist. I could not delay.

Wincing, I washed the wound with what little water remained. Once done, I balled up a piece of fabric to shove between my teeth, and, having threaded the sterilised needle, pushed it into my throbbing arm.

Tears blurred my eyes, making each stitch difficult. I bit down hard on the gag as I tied and snapped off each length of thread, choking off the cries in my throat. Painstakingly, I closed up the flesh, the stitches uneven and widely spaced, unable to give myself more than a dozen. I'd stitched a haphazard seam that would surely scar. But imperfect as it was, it was enough; the bleeding staunched and I wound muslin around my arm to protect the wound.

Mended, I was now free to go. Free — *I was free!* — free to flee this dreadful house. But there were more birds in the cage and I could not release them alone. I needed help.

⚷

I don't know how long I pressed my ear to the studio door, but I knew I had to find the courage to leave this room or none of us would be safe. And so, with a pounding heart, I at last turned the knob and pulled open the door. I stood for a moment, listening, expecting to hear Ford's footsteps. But they did not come. I peered into the hallway. But for the carved rabbits and wrens looking as frightened as I, the corridor was empty.

Although it was only a short walk to the end of the hall and down the stairs to the front doors, it seemed as though the passage would take an eternity. I summoned a deep breath, gave yet another prayer, and held a finger to my lips, reminding Soutache to remain silent. Perched on the windowsill, he bobbed his head in acknowledgment. I had already informed him that he could not come; I would have to travel with haste and it was easier for me to go alone.

I could not stand in the shadows of the corridor for eternity. And so I was moving, my bare feet carrying me the length of the red carpet, down the staircase, across the entryway and to the front doors, which opened smoothly and quietly under my hands. Only when I was outside, did I realise I had held my breath the entire journey.

I stood outside the Manor, the cool air brushing my face, bare arms and feet. The snow dampened all sound. Nothing moved, but for a handful of snowflakes swirling in the steel grey sky.

And then I ran — around the back of the manor and to the bridge that crossed the dark waters. Snow settled upon my hair and skin like fallen stars from the heavens. I took the stone path that wound up the slope, and — despite wearing no shoes — I quickly summited the hill. My feet, turned numb by the ice underfoot, skidded over the sharp rocks as I ran down the other side of the slope. I could only hope they were not being torn into ribbons as I raced straight for Carlisle's cottage. Gasping with relief as I reached the door, I pounded my fists upon it.

It opened at once and I fell into Carlisle's arms, my fingers grasping hold of him, desperate for salvation. His arms tightened about me and he looked down into my face. Snowflakes tangled in my eyelashes and I blinked them away so that I might see more clearly.

"What is it?" he demanded. But a look in his eye told me he

knew why I'd fled, and he did not wait to hear my answer. He pressed two fingers to my throat, but there was little need to search for my pulse as he had once done. Now, my veins bulged in my neck as I gulped lungfuls of air.

And then his mouth was upon mine, warm and firm. Soft and tender. I was lost in the taste of him, lost in the feeling of his hot hands upon my cold skin, his rough fingers pulling through my dishevelled hair. I shivered, but not with cold. When we broke apart, breathless, his eyes darkened as he took in my bloodied appearance.

"Don't move," he commanded, disappearing into the little pantry of his cottage. But I could not have moved, had I wanted to; I collapsed on the floor. It was the first opportunity my muscles had to relax since my climb through the chimney stacks.

I saw that my feet bled from several cuts and the bandage around my wounded arm was newly soaked with blood. And I noticed I was still shivering — whether from the cold, exhaustion, fear or the kiss, I did not know.

Carlisle returned with a basin of steaming water, a bottle of rubbing alcohol and a white linen sheet. He deposited these before the fire, then returned to me, lifting me in his arms and carrying me to the chair I had occupied on my last visit. To think, only an hour ago, I had been terrified of fire as I clambered through the chimney stacks. Now, it was the most blessed thing I could imagine.

As I warmed my limbs, Carlisle disappeared again, this time returning with a bottle of whiskey. It was the same drink Ford had offered me mere days before. He poured a finger into a glass and ordered me to swallow.

I did as instructed and relaxed into the chair. Sleep beckoned to me, but I could not rest. I needed to tell Carlisle everything that had happened. That was *going* to happen, if we did not go now. But something in his manner told me he would not listen to a word I said until he had completed his task.

Kneeling at my feet, he tore away the last shreds of my

stockings. He gently bathed my feet, banishing the last of their frigid numbness, and restored circulation by massaging them with warm strong hands. Then he carefully inspected each sole, ensuring that any debris was removed. Once cleaned, he doused each in alcohol, squeezing my hand as I cried out in pain. He passed me the linen and instructed me to tear it. In these strips he wrapped each foot.

Once finished this task, he attended to my arm. He said nothing when he saw my inept attempt at stitching the wound, but his dark eyes met mine knowingly and his jaw tensed. This too, he cleaned and tightly rebound with ample compress to absorb the blood.

All the while, he continued to ply me with the whiskey, until my head sagged against the chair. I must have slept for when I next opened my eyes, the basin, bandages, and whiskey were gone. I could now feel each individual cut and bruise and my entire body throbbed. I straightened in the chair, trying to stand.

"Be still," said a voice, eerily familiar. I whirled about, thinking it Ford. But no, it was Carlisle, seated off to the side in the gloom, so that he might watch me. How strange I had confused them.

"I need to return," I said, struggling to my feet. "My sisters. Lucy. Hester."

"Tell me," he said, leaning forward, placing a hand upon my knee. I could smell whiskey on his breath. And with his face half hidden in shadows, I had to remind myself that he was not Ford, but Carlisle.

With a trembling voice, I told Carlisle all that had passed from the time we had last parted. I told him of Rosie's appearance, of finding Helen, of my journey through the chimneys. At last my voice broke — I had no idea if he would even believe my story. It certainly strained the boundaries of any truth I had ever known. Had I not witnessed these events myself, I may not have believed them real.

I held back my tears, awaiting his judgment.

"I'll fetch the Constable," he said, which caused my shoulders to collapse with relief. I shifted to rise, but he placed a hand on my knee, halting my progress.

"Stay," he said. "You are in no condition to walk to Harrowgate."

"I do not wish to be alone," I said in a shaking voice. "What if Ford were to find me?"

"He'll not come here," Carlisle said.

"Please," I pleaded.

"I promise you'll be safe," he said, drawing a loose strand of hair away from my mouth, "This is sacred ground. No one at Blueford has ever walked through this doorframe, nor ever shall. None save you, sweet Margaret."

At these words, my pulse quickened as a hummingbird pumps its wings. I felt as light as one, too, able to finally lay down the burden of all I'd discovered, knowing I could truly trust someone.

But his parting would leave me bereft. And what danger might come to *him*, should Ford guess to whom I'd run? "You will be quick?" I pleaded, finding his fingers with my own.

"As smoke on the wind," he agreed. Then his mouth was against mine once more, comforting me. My tooth caught on his lower lip and I could taste blood and whiskey on his tongue. And then he was gone in a whirlwind — crossing the room, snagging a cloak and lantern and disappearing out the door. A blast of cold air invaded the room as he left and I huddled beside the fire.

I closed my eyes and rested my head against the chair. But I did not wish to sleep. As much as Carlisle reassured my safety, I knew the nightmare was not yet at an end. I opened my eyes, determined to focus on something — anything! — that might keep my senses alert.

And how I did not see it before surprised me. There on the hearth, as though it had been tossed into the fire, but missed its mark by mere inches, was what appeared to be a small white thimble made of paper. But it was not a thimble. Rather, it was a small roll of paper once bound to a bird's leg.

I reached down and unfurled it, to be sure. There were my words, hastily scrawled:

Carlisle, I am a prisoner at Blueford. Bring help.

So Soutache had delivered the note, and Carlisle had read it and done nothing. No, not nothing — he had decided to destroy it. He made no mention of the note and had listened to my account as though it were news. And responded in kind. But why?

A sudden and most terrible thought seized my heart: help was not coming. In fact, I was now in more danger than before.

I would have to go to Harrowgate myself. I leapt from the chair but immediately collapsed in pain. My feet could not tolerate my standing weight. They would not be able to carry me the distance to town. The only one who could go in my stead was Hester. I would have to free her first and there was no time to waste. How long, in my condition, would it take to return to Blueford?

I tore through the wardrobe in Carlisle's room, searching for a wool cloak. As I clawed through his clothing, a leather satchel fell from a hook and spilled its contents upon the floor; it was stuffed with photographs.

The first showed two young boys, no more than ten, standing before a London home. They looked familiar to me, and so I examined another. A chill ran down my spine. This photograph was taken before the same house, only this time there was no disguising the young men. One was Ford. The other, Carlisle.

Family names marked the back of the portraits. Johnathan Ford, Carlisle Ford. They were brothers. They'd had a sister, called Lucille, but after the age of eight there was no more evidence of her. Their father was a sea captain, their mother, née Farrow, a dark beauty. The photographs fell from my hands like autumn leaves on the wind.

How foolish I had been not to recognise how similar their temperaments, their moods, their darkness. Together, they had concealed the secret of Helen's death. And when Carlisle returned, he would surely bring Ford.

By the door stood an old pair of galoshes. They were much too large and each sliding step might reopen my wounds, but at least my feet would not freeze in the snow. I wrapped the cloak about my shoulders, opened the door and stepped out into the black of the night.

I'M NOT SURE WHAT I EXPECTED as I approached Blueford Manor; that my disappearance had been discovered? That the manor would be lit like some great chandelier while a search party was underway? But the house looked as slumbering now as when I departed.

I ran to the cellar door and tested the knob, only to find it still locked. I wanted to call to my sisters that I was here, but a fear of alerting Ford — or Carlisle — stopped me. *Carlisle.* How easily I'd believed his lies. Had I trusted him implicitly because he'd said he was a man of God? Or did I trust him because he'd felt familiar? Until now, I had not realised that it was Ford he reminded me of. On first glance, Ford's beard obscured the resemblance. But now I saw in how many ways the brothers were alike, and not only in appearance: deceptive, duplicitous, dangerous.

I placed my palms against my warm cheeks and blinked away the tears; I would not allow Carlisle to cause me to cry. Especially now.

My sisters must wait until I could break down the door. I crept my way along the edge of the house to the back entrance. As usual, it was unlocked and so I slipped inside, divesting myself of Carlisle's boots. Though I knew Ford — and possibly Carlisle — to be here, the house felt crypt-like as always. I crouched low as I peered into the kitchen. The room was empty and the door to the pantry still closed. Joyously, I saw that the key was still in the lock where Ford had left it. I waited a moment, listening for footsteps.

When I heard none, I slipped across the room and turned the key.

I opened the door a crack and, not wanting to alarm Hester, and I whispered her name.

I heard a scrambling sound within and then Hester's voice: "Miss! Oh, Miss! You are alive! I feared the worst." A moment later I was inside the pantry and we clung to one another, each grateful to know the other lived. There were tears on her face and I wiped them away with my fingers.

"Ssh! He mustn't hear us," I warned.

She nodded and held out a bottle of wine.

"It's all I've drunk for days," she said, with a hiccup. I took a long swallow, relishing the warmth from the alcohol. We sat together for a moment in silence as I replenished myself. Then Hester opened a can of preserves for me and I greedily gulped back the fruit and juice. It was the last can; though caged in her miniature chapel, Hester seemed to have been fairly comfortable. She had arranged sacks of flour and barley for a mattress. Empty jars of preserves and the rind of cured meats showed me she had eaten well. Of the bread stores, only crusts remained.

"I've been meaning to tell you, Miss," she said, as I ate and drank, "Of something I learned from Mrs Abbot, the baker's wife. On my day off in Moorwood, I told Mrs Abbot about Reverend Farrow being so kind as to drive me into town. She says he ain't ever had a church here. In fact, she's never even seen him *inside* a church. She said he ain't even a man of cloth. She says he came face to face with the devil and it took away his faith."

"I know, Hester," I said. "And if you see him, you mustn't trust him. Promise me."

"I promise, Miss," she said, nodding fervently and clutching her rosary.

"Hester, I need you to do something for me," I said, taking both her hands in mine.

She nodded, desperate to help. "Of course, Miss."

"It will require great courage," I informed her, "so if you cannot do it, I understand."

Her face paled, but her words were firm. "Whatever you need, Miss. You have always been kind to me."

"I need you to walk to Harrowgate and fetch the local Constable. Tell him to gather men and come at once."

It hardly seemed possible, but Hester's face grew even more ashen. "Now, Miss? Go out into the night? With Master Ford about?"

"Yes," I said, nodding. "I know it's dangerous but —"

"I'll go," she said, jumping to her feet. Then she paused, "I have no boots."

"There is a pair you can use," I said, checking to ensure the kitchen was still empty before leading her out into the hall to the pair I had stolen from Carlisle. I removed his wool cloak from about my shoulders and placed it around hers. Lastly, I lit a lantern and handed it to her. Kissing her cheeks, I said, "God be with you."

"You as well, Miss," she replied, with a steely look in her eye that I'd never seen before. And out she went, the cloak flapping about her legs like a murder of angry crows.

Using Hester's set of keys, I returned to the locked bedchamber I had occupied, both as guest and captive. I was startled to see that — other than the tub of tepid bathwater beside the hearth — the room looked the same as it always had: my unfinished novel forgotten on the bed stand, my carpetbag beside the wardrobe, a single feather from Soutache that I had pinned to the drape. So much had changed since I had last been here, that I expected the room to be somehow transformed. That it had not was somewhat disconcerting.

I searched for Soutache, but did not see him. I said a prayer for my feathered companion as I shoved my feet into the boots which lay abandoned in the fireplace, grimacing as the cuts and bruises protested enclosure. But I ignored the smarting pain, retracing my

steps down the hall to the kitchen, out the rear entrance and to the cellar. The snow continued to fall and my breath came in quick, fast clouds. In a matter of moments, I'd pushed the key into the lock and turned it with a satisfying click. I shoved the door wide, for there was no sunlight to harm my sisters. I no longer even cared if I awakened Ford. Alone he could overpower me, but three sisters working together was another matter altogether.

I burst into the cellar and raced to the storage closet, shouting my sisters' names. There, I found them asleep, hand in hand, resting against the wardrobe doors. In the gloomy closet I could not at first distinguish between my sisters, their red hair and pale limbs and ravaged wedding gowns tangled together in a heap. But then the skeletal bat attached to Rosie's hair alerted me to their identities. As I drew close, Helen stirred. She opened one eye, and tracked me as I drew near. I stooped before her, and she opened the second.

"He took you from us," she said flatly, examining me. "But did he *take you* as he did Rosamund?" Helen gazed ravenously at my bare neck.

"I am fine," I said, but her eyes focused on my bound arm and she sniffed, catching the scent of my blood. Her hand shot out and grasped my forearm. I allowed her to press the wound to her nose and inhale, watching her closely all the while. "You are still fresh, little Margaret," she said, smiling at me with sharp teeth. Then she sighed and dropped my arm with defeat. The movement jostled Rosie's head and caused her to wake.

"Meg!" Rosie croaked, shaking her head clear of sleep. "You came for us!" She scrambled to her feet.

I laid a hand on hers, imploring her to remain still. "We shall be safest here, for the time being. Hester has gone to fetch the police."

But Rosie had no intention to sit. "He locked us in here," she snarled, "with nothing more to eat!"

I startled by her vehemence. "We've not long until help arrives," I consoled.

"Well, I do not intend to starve to death!" Rosie snapped.

"You are already dead," Helen said, her voice low and brittle. "No amount of blood will bring you back to life."

Rosie did not answer with words, but turned her head to glower at our older sister.

Helen laughed — a short, cruel sound. "Oh, you dear little rose thirsting in summer! A tiny drop a day will do. You must control the urge, or it will make you a monster." Helen's eyes fell to her lap, lost in a memory. "You must learn to live with the thirst."

Rosie shook her head violently, the bat made of bones clinging to the flying tendrils of her hair. "I won't stay here a moment longer. The sun has gone down, the door is open. I am going above ground! At the very least we cannot leave Lucy alone in the house!"

I said with haste, "Think, Rosie, I beg you! Let us wait until the police arrive before we fetch Lucy."

"Patience, Rosie. My daughter is not in any danger," Helen added.

"How can you say that?" Rosie demanded, bending over Helen. "He did this to me! To you! He killed you, Helen! Or have you forgotten?" Then, she spun on me. "I am going for Lucy now, with or without your help!" She turned and ran from the room, crushing the bat corpses under her bare feet as she went. The cellar door closed behind her with a bang.

I was alone with Helen.

Helen did not move, slumped against the wardrobe, looking after our youngest sister with a slight smile playing on her lips. She hardly seemed aware of my presence, and when she spoke, it was more to herself than to me.

"*He* didn't kill me."

"IT WAS THE FALL OF '94," Helen began, regarding me through half-lidded eyes. "Lucy fell ill with whooping cough. The prognosis was bleak." She swallowed hard, the stitches along her neck bulging as her throat moved. "The night this all began, the doctor left early to allow us privacy. Privacy to say our farewells. Instead, Ford held me at her bedside and confessed there was a way to save her life.

"Of course I could not refuse. How could any mother? But Ford warned me to consider carefully. He could save her life, indeed forever. *Life everlasting, but forever a child.*" Her voice broke off, lost in a dream. "Childhood was a precious time, was it not, Magpie?" she asked at last and I nodded my head.

"Still," she said, taking a breath, "he urged me to think. We would have to keep her indoors. She would never be able to leave Blueford Manor, unless under the cover of darkness. She could never have friends, for they would see that she did not age. And she would always cough, for her body would be locked in present time. The virus would indeed be halted — would harm her no more — but forever she would be wracked with the affliction.

"As he explained what would happen to Lucy, my husband's own strange habits began to make sense. Whatever magic he planned to work on our daughter, he had already worked upon himself. Or so I thought. Naively, I imagined he had brought some elixir of eternal life back from his last voyage at sea for he had changed on that last trip, and told me his days of being a captain had ceased due to some grievous miscalculation.

"I never thought that it was his very condition that had banished him from naval life. Rather, I'd thought his night-time meanderings, his lack of appetite, his reclusive habits, all to be symptoms of a destroyed reputation."

I inched closer to Helen, and stretched out my hand. She took it. Her fingers felt like marble, cold and hard.

"He urged me to be cautious in my thinking, for it was a magic I did not understand. But my daughter was sick and dying. Of course a life confined to Blueford Manor was preferable to the cold ground. It was *life!* And so I begged him to ease her suffering. If there was a way to save her, he must do it now. She was slipping away and there was no time to waste. He told me to wait outside her room and that he would call me in when it was done.

"At first I did not notice the changes in Lucy. Yes, she was suddenly bright and cheerful, the fever broken. And it was true she had no desire to play during the day, instead preferring to stay up at night, but I interpreted this as a desire to spend more time with her father, her saviour, who was inclined to keep night hours.

"But her nocturnal habits meant I saw her much less, and I began to feel separated from my family. Feeling like the sole occupant of the house, I was not even able to oversee our servants, and my husband suggested we reduce the staff. He convinced me we could make do with a single housekeeper who could cook, and suggested we hire a new one every three months to avoid questions about our unusual daughter.

"For a while, I took solace in the studio, painting flowers and fruit, but Johnathan and Lucy seemed to care little for my art.

"I decided to change my habits. If this were the cost of connecting to my daughter, it was a small one. Or so I thought. I started staying up at night to play with my daughter, and sleeping during the day. I abandoned the garden and my floral studies. Instead, I spent more time star-gazing with Johnathan, and began to make paintings of the constellations. For a while,

I was happier. But as winter closed in, I never saw the light. True, I had my daughter. But our games never changed, for she never grew. As a mother, what could I teach her, for her fingers never became more dexterous? What could I show her, for we never left the house? Night after night, I dragged myself through the house, repeating the motions of life without actually living. I longed for companionship, and thought often of you and Rosie. But I was frightened to invite you. What would you think?

"I could see Johnathan was concerned for me. He became increasingly attentive, sending Lucy to her room straight after dinner. She was free to stay up on her own, to play as she pleased, but he fiercely protected his time alone with me. He was amorous in his attentions, having flowers delivered each day as the ones I had planted on the estate had long since withered and died without my hands to care for them.

"But my heart did not meet his attentions; I fell out of love with my husband and I turned him away, night after night. Even though I would not share his bed, he desired my company beneath the stars, begging me to lie with him beneath the ballroom's glass cupola as we had used to do.

"One night, after Lucy had overheard us in disagreement, she knocked on my door. She was clearly upset, her eyes wild and black as I had never seen them before. I invited her into bed and pulled her into my arms to rock her. As she nestled against my breast, she suddenly bit my neck.

"As though she had become a baby again, I could not release her latch. I screamed for Johnathan, but was helpless to pry her free. I could only cry as she drank my blood. *Drained* my blood, it seemed. When I recovered my senses, everything was different. The room was dark, but I could see as clear as an owl. Lucy was perched on my chest, watching me like a gargoyle, but she did not feel heavy in the least.

"Then, I began to feel terrible urges. I craved meat — raw — and would steal into the kitchen at night, looking for remnants. One night in the kitchen, I startled a rat in the pantry. Before I knew what I had done, I'd broken its neck and sucked it dry.

"I confessed to Johnathan what I'd done. He flew into a rage — not over the rat — but by what Lucy had done. He reminded her, harshly, that she must never bite anyone — or anything — ever again. She was only to drink what he brought her each morning: fresh blood from a mouse he'd catch each night in the orchard.

"It was their ritual — one sip for little Lucy, one sip for her father. And now one sip for me, for I too was to partake in this beverage to stave off the cravings.

"It was a terrible way to live, if living it was. Once I became one of them, I suffered with the knowledge of what life was like for Lucy, ruled by a lust for blood. And I saw the pitifulness of her life, for she would remain forever in a child's body, reliant on her parents. At least I had seen London and Paris! I'd travelled my country. I had enjoyed a childhood with sisters I loved! Now, I could never give Lucy a sister or brother. Never take her to the continent. Never see her marry or bear children of her own. I could not go on like that. Every ounce of Lucy's suffering became my suffering, and I carried the weight of her curse on my own cursed shoulders.

"The next day — an hour before dawn — I went to the roof. I cannot say whether I was prepared to end my existence that morning, or if I only desired to freedom to make the choice. But I yearned to glimpse the earliest inkling of dawn and so I told Lucy that Venus was in the sky and would be visible just before light. As the sun rose, we would be able to see it, but if she wanted to come, she must come quickly. With our keen eyesight that tracked bats in the night sky, we would be able to see the planet the second it glimmered. *We will look for a little white pearl in a vast navy sea,* I had told her.

"She cried violently and railed against me, for she knew the sun was dangerous. She wanted me to stay in her room, to be there when her father returned from the orchard, to meet him like always as he brought us a warm mouse, wriggling and soft. For Lucy, this was the brightest moment of her day, when her mother and father came together and helped her tear apart a little mouse and gleefully share a thimble's worth of blood.

"To her, we were the perfect family and I saw that she was becoming more monstrous every day; the very instances that haunted me filled her with delight. While Johnathan and I determined the very least amount of blood that was required to satiate our beastly cravings, Lucy desired more. She seemed unable to control her animalistic urges.

"I knew Johnathan and I would live a century searching for a cure for our daughter — I studied plants and he the Zodiac — hoping for an antidote and yet never finding a solution. And all the while we would toil side by side as parents, hating each other for what'd we'd done to our daughter.

"And that same tortuous expanse of time — that living hell for Johnathan and I — would be Lucy's childhood. A time which ought to be tender and sweet. Instead, we had condemned our daughter to Purgatory.

"Often, I contemplated what life would have been like without Lucy, had she died of whooping cough. Such thoughts led me to think of new thoughts. Could I end it for Lucy? Drown her in holy water? Smash her perfect little head covered in satin curls, the very head that had come through my legs?"

Helen paused to cough, sounding eerily like her daughter. It had been some time since my sister had wet her throat. I shifted my position uneasily, curled up in the dark.

Helen continued, "She must have told Johnathan about Venus for in that hour before dawn, he found me on the roof. He hauled me into the shadows and begged me to reconsider taking my life. The only way to atone for what we had done was to remain a family, as happy as possible, for that was the reason we had made the terrible decision in the first place. And not just for Lucy, Johnathan said. A family life would be *our* salvation, too.

"Perhaps those little acts — a story before bed, a wriggling mouse, a sailor song at bath-time — could save her soul. Would save his. Who was I to doubt him? And I was glad he saw an ending to his penance. But still I could not see an ending to my own.

"I resolved to jump. And so I tore free of his arms and ran for the edge.

"Johnathan protested, saying the fall would not kill me. Eternal life could be ended in few ways, and this was not one of them. I ordered him to tell me how I might die, but he refused, tears upon his face.

"*Then I shall jump!* I had screamed, stepping upon the parapet. He ran for me and grabbed my arm, wrenching it from the socket. As I tumbled over the edge, I saw my daughter's face. She had come up to the roof unannounced and was watching from the shadow of a chimney stack. And then when Johnathan could no longer hold my weight, I slipped from his grasp. The last thing I heard was his cry of anguish as I floated, free as a bird, through the last hour of night.

"I hit the cobblestones below and pain exploded in my body, and then...nothing."

Helen paused and rubbed the stitches along her neck. "He was wrong, for I *did* die." She trailed her fingertips over the ridged seam encircling her neck and looked at me with sad eyes. "Or so I thought, but here I am."

I reached out and drew her hand to my mouth — the one belonging to the arm I'd repaired — and kissed it through my tears. "Forgive me," I said.

⚷

I do not know how long Helen and I sat together in the dark, awaiting the return of Rosie with Lucy, but they did not come. Soon it became clear that they would not.

"Come," I said to Helen, taking her by the hand. We left the cellar under cover of the night, all the while cursing Rosie's impatience. If my sister had been caught by Ford, she would need the both of us to rescue her.

This time, we entered through the front doors as they were closest to the staircase. We slipped inside, moving as quiet as the mice in the orchard. Up the stairs we went, direct to Lucy's room. Upon seeing her daughter's room once more, Helen collapsed onto the bed in tears, hugging Lucy's broken doll.

But I did not want to delay our search; I whispered for Helen to remain as she was, safely hidden, and I would continue alone. If Rosie and Lucy were to appear, she could alert them to remain until I returned.

The instant I was alone in the rabbit-lined corridor, a sense of dread gripped my heart. A quick check of the studio and my own bedchamber led me to believe they were nowhere upstairs. At least not in plain sight.

"Please, God, not in the chimneys!" I prayed, imagining Rosie coaxing our niece into the treacherous tunnels.

I stood in the entrance hall, wondering where to search, ignoring my aching feet when I heard it: laughter. It tinkled through the entrance hall like a pair of funeral bells. I crossed the hallway and slowly entered the kitchen.

The pantry door stood open. From within, I heard childish giggles and whispers. I stepped through the doorway and stopped at the sight.

Lucy hung by her feet from the top shelf of the pantry, the curls in her hair cascading like a waterfall. The locks were curiously powdered white, as though she were a miniature Marie Antoinette. Indeed, her face and arms were also dusted in the same white substance, giving her the appearance of a corpse having been dumped in a pit of quicklime.

Rosie crouched on the floor beside Hester, who was huddled in the corner clutching a crucifix made of two wooden spoons lashed together with butcher's twine. Her eyes implored me, wild as a lamb's, being led to slaughter. Rosie wielded a butcher knife.

I shrieked and threw myself between Hester and my sister.

"What in God's name are you doing? Who do you think you are?" I demanded.

"I know who I am!" Lucy chirped, from up above. "I'm a bat!"

"Indeed you are," I snapped, over my shoulder, "Get down at once, Lucy. This is not a game!" I spun around and used my ragged, knotted skirt to mop the tears from Hester's face.

"Oh, Miss," Hester cried, her fingers tightening on my arm, "I left the house as you said, only it was very difficult to see with the snow flying every which way, like a storm of falling stars. And suddenly, out of the darkness, came a figure in black, maybe Master Ford. Maybe that Mr Farrow! I didn't know, I just turned and ran, and I came straight back here to get a butcher knife. I wasn't going out to face him again without one!"

Brave, valiant Hester! She blew her nose into her sleeve and glowered at Rosie through her tears. "And I found them in here, making a mess of my chapel. Look what they did!"

All of Hester's prayer cards and wooden crosses were reduced to ashes, the pantry's wooden shelves charred where dozens of little fires had burned and gone out. Sacks of grain that had recently made up Hester's makeshift bed were split open, their contents spilled on the floor and used to absorb the saucers of Holy Water. Thick molasses smeared the prayer shawl.

Behind me, Lucy jumped to the floor, appearing proud of her vandalism. I did not give her the opportunity to boast, ordering her to the kitchen to fetch water for Hester. I pushed Rosie aside and pulled Hester into my embrace. The claret coloured rosary entwined around her neck dug into my breast as she clung to my body, wracked with sobs.

Neither Rosie nor I spoke until Lucy returned with the water. As Hester drank, Rosie finally found her voice.

"We only wanted a little sip," my sister sulked. She dropped the knife to the floor where it landed with a clatter.

Hester jumped as she drank, spilling water onto her lap.

"Don't be absurd, Rosie!" I scolded. "And Lucy, you should know better. What has your father told you about biting?"

Lucy stared at her toes, chastised, but Rosie defended, "It is a natural urge, and she cannot control it!"

"By God, she can!" I hurled in response. I thought of the times I had enjoyed Lucy's company in the studio, sewing while my niece played with Helen's paint-set or with Flue. I had never felt, in those hours, that I'd been in danger. It was Rosie who was losing control of her desires.

Rosie lunged forward, lowering her face to meet mine. "And what would you know, Magpie?" She roughly toed Hester. "Besides this mealy mouse, you're the only one at Blueford who hasn't experienced this...*need*." She drew back her lips and ran a pale lilac tongue over her teeth. "You used to know everything I felt. Now, you know nothing of me. I hate that you are different. I wish you were part of the family."

Her eyes raked over my neck. I put my hand under her chin and lifted her face so I could meet her eyes.

"Stop thinking this way, Rosie. Remember yourself. Remember London. Remember the Willis family. There is more to you than —" I searched for the words — "these desires." Rosie did not appear convinced. I said levelly, "If you harm me, Rosie, it will be an unforgivable act. And isn't that what you want? Forgiveness? Look how Ford is tortured by what he's done! And Lucy — how hard her life has become!"

"Don't bring her into it!" Rosie hissed, straightening up to grab Lucy's hand. "Lucy's done nothing for which to be ashamed!"

Hester moved quickly then, shooting out her foot and catching the knife blade with her heel. She pulled it forward and scooped it up. Rosie did not notice as she cuddled Lucy.

"I did not mean that Lucy ought to feel shame," I impressed upon my sister. "But one day she may feel remorse for what she's done to her mother."

Rosie's perfectly white brow crumpled like a piece of paper. "What did you do?" Rosie asked, staring at Lucy. Then the thought occurred to her and she dropped Lucy's hand and glanced at me. "Not Helen?"

"I didn't push her!" Lucy shrieked, and Hester flinched at the sound, dropping the knife.

I consoled my niece, taking the hand Rosie had released. "No, no, you did not." I said softly. "She jumped, I know...but the fall did not kill her."

Lucy shook her head in denial. "No, Aunt Margaret, Mother's dead." Lucy looked at me coldly. "Father said he buried her."

Rosie dropped to her knee and placed a hand on Lucy's shoulder. "But as you live and I live and your father lives, so, too, does your mother."

"No," Lucy said, shaking her head. "No. I saw her head. Saw it nearly come off." Hester whimpered and edged away from us.

"Remember Soutache. And Flue? Do you remember what we did for Flue?" I asked.

Lucy's eyes widened. "You gave Mother a new arm? A new head?"

I laughed and Hester's eyes bulged at me. "She's waiting for you now, Lucy."

My niece smiled with sharp teeth, "Under ground?"

I shook my head. "In your room."

Lucy's smile conveyed both excitement and apprehension as Rosie took her hand and ushered her out of the pantry. I sighed as they departed and looked at Hester. She sat motionless as a stone, watching me with horrified eyes.

"They'll not harm you now," I said, not knowing how to explain. And what could I tell her anyway, to dilute the details of our macabre story? To her, I was as hideous as Rosie or Lucy or Ford. I sighed and walked to the doorway. "You should leave here, Hester. I know the walk is difficult, especially in the snow, but take what you need from the house. Food. Blankets. Anything..." I moved towards the door, pausing to pick up the knife and hand it to her. "Write to me in London — at Hendry's Millinery. When I return — if I return — I will send you a month's wages."

Still she said nothing, and so I left her in a heap on the floor, clutching the wooden spoon cross.

I did not wish to follow Lucy and Rosie. The reunion between mother and daughter would need to be celebrated between the two of them alone, and it was not my place to interfere. I hoped Rosie as well would allow them their time together.

I was no longer afraid to be on my own at Blueford Manor. Perhaps it was because I had challenged Rosie and survived. Perhaps I had simply grown too weary to be afraid. Whatever, the reason, I no longer cared if Ford discovered me walking freely about the house.

I walked the length of the lower hall and heard arguing male voices emanate from the parlour. I shrank back against the banister railings, disappearing into the darkness as footsteps approached. It was Carlisle. As I suspected, he had not gone for reinforcement. His face was dark with emotion, his head lowered, his cloak flapping about him like the wings of an angry rook as he stalked out of Blueford. The slam of the door behind him echoed throughout the house.

I waited a few moments, then approached the parlour. Inside the room it was dark but for the fire. One leg slung over an armrest, Ford slumped in the blue velvet chair which was turned to face the fireplace. Orange light flickered over the hard planes of his face. He did not stir as I drew near, though his eyes never left my face.

I sat on the chair next to him, much to the relief of my aching feet and I looked at him. "You keep your beard because if you were to shave it would never grow back," I said.

"I keep it because it reminds me of life at sea. Reminds me of when the cold salt water used to sting my forehead and eyes, but my neck was always warm." He sighed, "Now, it is heat and dryness that shocks my skin."

"Then why sit by the fire as you do so often?" I questioned.

He smiled dimly. "It reminds me of the sun. Do you know

how enchanting red hair appears in sunlight?"

But he did not appear to expect me to answer. Indeed, he seemed hardly affected by my presence. But still I sat, saying nothing for a spell as I watched the fire beside him. "Why did you keep her in the wardrobe?" I asked at last.

He glanced at me, and then my bandaged arm, but did not comment on the injury. "I could not bury her, for I was unsure if she were truly dead, or if some life still pulsed in her brain. Beheading is one way our kind can die. But Helen's neck was not fully severed, and so how could I know for certain? Who can understand such a curse? Not I." He ran a frustrated hand through his hair.

"I would find a way, I vowed, to repair her. No matter how far I had to travel to find the cure. Stowaway to America — to New York — where the wretched curse befell me. I was packing bags for Lucy and I when you and Rosamund arrived, stopping me in my tracks. I had hoped to deter you both from coming for a funeral service if I wrote to you a concise and cold letter. After all, neither of you had ever come before." His hand tightened in his hair.

"But then I did to Rosamund what I told myself I'd never do to any creature ever again, no matter how strong the desire." He looked at me with a strange look, his eyes following the curve of my neck. I resisted the urge to pull my hair down to hide my throat from his view.

"And having done such a thing to Rosamund, she consumed my thoughts. I no longer thought about how to make things right with Helen, but anguished over whether I could make things right with Rosamund. Your sister believed marriage would save her soul. And I believed it might create some normalcy of family life again for Lucy." He shook his head, like a tree in winter shaking off its leaves.

"I misjudged you," I confessed.

He laughed suddenly, the reflected light of the fire dancing over the planes of his face. He looked like a jack-o-lantern on All

Hallows Eve. True, he had cast Lucy — and thus Helen — into a hell of sorts. But only because he loved them, and was uncertain he could survive the death of his daughter. I recalled my father's own grief when our mother died. Recalled how his strong form faded but to a shadow. As though he were a fine suit jacket, grief had pulled one thread from the weft each day, until he was no more than a threadbare rag, and a man I no longer recognised.

I would not see Ford fade in such a manner. Perhaps all might be mended.

"Johnathan," I said, "I can grant you salvation. Or at least a little joy." I took a deep breath and announced: "Your wife lives."

"Helen?" His eyes searched mine. "Your needle?" he demanded, leaping from the chair, and pulling me to my aching feet. "We must go down at once!" and he was already dragging me from the room.

"Wait!" I said, struggling to keep up. "She is not in the cellar. She's with Lucy."

He stopped, and I crashed into his back. But before I could right myself, he yanked me around to his front, and gripped my jaw, twisting my face to his. "What were you thinking? But of course, how could you know?"

"Know what?" I asked. But he was already running, dragging me behind.

Ford took the stairs two at a time, pulling me by my injured arm and I feared that it, like Helen's, might be wrenched from its socket. The wound throbbed and the bandage grew bloody once again, but I didn't protest; Ford was angered — *frightened* — beyond reason.

"You fool!" he raged at me, eyes black as coal. "You and your damned needle!"

"You yourself admit you'd revive her, if you could!" I countered, my throat tight with emotion.

"Only if I could find a cure! " he snarled, "I'd never dream of bringing her back as she was — *is!* She wanted nothing but to end the torturous long nights, the thirst for blood, always the blood…"

Ford released me and burst through the door of Lucy's room. He returned immediately, one arm flung across his face. "Please, Margaret, the light! Quickly!"

I ran into the room. Torn from the curtain rods, the heavy window drapes lay in a heap on the floor. Bright light reflected off the snow and washed the room with its brilliance. I ripped a velvet curtain down from the four poster bed and brought it out to Ford. He threw it over his head and raced back into the room.

"They're not here," I said, following him into the room. He paused, surveying his daughter's bedchamber from beneath the curtain that was wrapped about his head and shoulders like one of Millicent's turbans.

Indeed, the room was void of Helen and Rosie, of Lucy and her doll. Even Lucy's bookshelves stood empty of their contents, each volume thrown onto the fire which burned to a ferocious height. Shards of paper danced in the flames before shooting up into the dark tunnel of the chimney.

Helen's doing, or Rosie's? But why? Both had fond memories of reading to Lucy, but especially Rosie; it was the one occasion that lured her out of the chimneys and into the arms of our niece. The handiwork had to be Helen's. "Why would she burn Lucy's books?" I wondered, watching the flames eat the well-loved volumes.

"To burn down the house," Ford said sullenly. He shoved a boot in the fire and kicked apart the teepee of books.

Maybe. But if her intention was arson, why not light the bedclothes or curtains? And why tear the curtains down, for Helen posed as much risk to herself and daughter as to her nemesis, Ford. There was only one answer. Flooding the room with light meant it would be impossible for Ford or Rosie to come in through the door or come down from —

"The chimney! Rosie's in the chimney!" I screamed, lunging for the pitcher on the washstand. But the pitcher was empty, its contents poured out on the floor. Ford yanked away the velvet he wore and threw it on the fire, suffocating the flames.

Devoid of cover, sunlight hit his skin, cooking the flesh of his face. A spot high on his right cheekbone began to blister and blacken in front of my eye.

"Johnathan!" I cried, scrambling for more bedding, but he shooed me aside and, the fire now extinguished, ducked into the fireplace and climbed up into the chimney.

"Rosie," I called again, but she did not answer. I heard Ford grunting and watched his legs return to the hearth, bearing the weight of something above his head. A moment later, Rosie's legs, black with smoke, slid into view.

I crawled into the fireplace as far as I could to help Ford as he lowered Rosie. I grabbed her legs while he supported her upper body as we manoeuvred her out onto the hearth. Then we carried her into the corridor where the light did not travel.

As we lay her unconscious upon the hall runner, I saw that the lower part of her wedding dress was burned to ashes. The toes of her shoes had burned away at the tips. I quickly unlaced them and threw them aside. On both feet her toes had been burnt away, black stubs in their place. The stench was obscene. I gagged and rubbed my watering eyes, and vowed that I would repair them — somehow — with my needle.

Her hair also suffered; singed and blackened at the ends, it was now several inches shorter. And smelled sickeningly sweet. The skeleton of the bat clattered and clicked its bony wings as though crying for its keeper.

Ford crouched over my sister and drew his fingers down her jaw, "Rosamund? Rosamund!" he whispered. When she did not answer, I slapped her cheek. Ford glared at me, but Rosie's eyes fluttered open.

"Oh, Meg!" she moaned. "I went into the chimney to rest while they reunited, but I'd not been there five minutes when Helen lit a fire! And out of dear Lucy's books! I tried to climb higher. But it was so hot, I fainted. It was hot, so hot," her eyes rolled back and her head tilted.

"Stay awake, Rosie," I urged, shaking her shoulders.

Ford broke in, "Where did she take Lucy? The roof?"

"Why would she take Lucy to the roof?" I asked, before Rosie could respond.

"Do you not see?" Ford snapped. "She meant to kill Rosamund. She'll treat Lucy no different!"

A sick taste rose in my throat. Helen would destroy them all.

19

Rosie insisted she come on the search so I bound her feet in strips torn from a bed-sheet, and continued to wind the cotton up her thighs to cover her legs. I knotted a second bed sheet around her neck, pulling it over her head like a hood; now that her hair was burnt into a curly bob, the back of her neck would be easily exposed to sunlight.

I slipped an arm about her shoulders and helped her to stand on feet bereft of their toes. She winced and tears rolled down her cheeks, but she said nothing and I knew she swallowed her pain for Lucy's sake. There was not another moment to delay. Together we made our way to the stairs — she hobbling and leaning heavily upon me, and I half-dragging her cold, blackened body. Shrouded in the white bed sheets, she looked like an Egyptian mummy come to life.

Ford had fled Lucy's room as soon as he knew Helen was alone with Lucy, but when we came down the stairs he was no closer to them than the two of us. His fist pounded the ballroom door and he hollered for his daughter, his face purple with rage. He threw his shoulder against the heavy wood but it was no use; the doors were locked fast.

"Stop!" I cried, coming up to the door, with Rosie tucked at my side. "You'll harm yourself."

"The dead are surprisingly vital," he snapped, rubbing his shoulder. "And it is Helen who will do harm." He dropped to one knee and put his mouth to the keyhole. "Lucy," he bellowed, "stay in the shadows!" He prepared to lunge at the doors again.

"I have the keys," I interrupted, helping Rosie into Ford's arms so that I could retrieve Hester's keyring from my skirt pocket. Ford snatched the keys from my hand and set about unlocking the door, supporting Rosie in one arm. I heard muffled voices from within, but I was unable to tell if Lucy laughed or cried.

"Damnation," Ford snarled, for while the locked turned, the door did not open when pushed. "She has barricaded it. Wait here," he said, stalking off across the entrance hall to the front doors and disappearing outside.

Rosie was back in my arms, crying. I stroked her short hair through the bed sheet. In the tatters of her wedding gown she no longer appeared the beautiful sister I had rendered in my sketchbook.

"I am so sorry," I whispered into the folds of white. Tears slid onto my shoulder.

"Get away from the door," Ford demanded, reappearing once more, his feet treading heavily on the floorboards. His hair was laced with snow and the skin of his face, neck and forearms was blistered from the daylight. In his hands, swung an axe.

I backed away, taking Rosie with me, as Ford raised the axe and drove it into the carved wooden stags, first shattering the door handle, then delivering blow upon blow, tearing apart the structure of the door until, with a final kick, Ford smashed his way into the ballroom. Swinging the axe, he knocked aside the furnishings piled high on the other side. Through the opening in the door, I heard Helen shriek.

I left Rosie and climbed through into the other room, like a shadow following Ford.

"In God's name, Helen —" Ford gasped, as we drew up to my sister and niece. In the shadowed arcade along the far wall of the ballroom, Lucy sat in a rattan chair, her scarlet bonnet jauntily perched on her head. Helen stooped beside her daughter where she finished wrapping a ribbon from my sewing scraps around one of Lucy's ankles, binding her to the chair. Lucy's other ankle and two wrists were already bound with gay ribbons, as though the two of them were playing a game.

But there was no jest in Helen's expression.

"Stop at once," Ford commanded.

Helen cocked her head to the side and let an extra length of ribbon flutter to the floor. "I know you think me mad," she said, laughing at Ford. "But what wickedness you've done, convincing me that this —" and she flung a hand towards Lucy, knocking away the hat — "is an acceptable life for our daughter! You are no more fit to parent than I! " Lucy did not speak, but her eyes were dark and apprehensive.

"Then let us decide again," Ford roared, bearing down on Helen. "But not this way! Not now!" He grabbed her roughly and tried to pull her away from Lucy, but he suddenly shouted with pain, and released his hold. Helen laughed, twirling my fabric shears in the air like a toy.

I ran to Ford who clutched his arm, a deep gash to the bone leeching aubergine blood. My stomach curdled. I tried to tear a length of fabric from my skirt, but without scissors to snip the seam, the gabardine held fast. Panicked for time, I tore the delicate blouse from my torso and bound it tightly about his forearm, drawing close the gaping wound. The blood quickly soaked through the thin fabric, but I held my fist against the wound and the blood began to clot. I met his eye, despite being clad only in my corset, and smiled at our twin wounds. He gripped my hand to test his strength and I found his fingers to be feeble.

"She's cut tendons, I fear," he mumbled, but my shout cut him off: "Helen, no!"

The scissors were now placed at my niece's neck. Fear filled Lucy's eyes while delight danced in Helen's. "We are only moments away from freedom, my love," Helen cooed.

Ford pushed me aside and moved towards his daughter, dropping to one knee to look in her eye. "Stay strong, Lucy," he said and she nodded, though her lower lip trembled as she glanced at her mother.

Helen tossed a wicked look at Ford, then smiled sweetly at Lucy. With her free hand, she drew aside her long red hair to show Lucy the stitches round her neck. "Look, darling. My neck was cut, too. Nearly all the way around. I shall cut yours completely, and then we shall be the same."

I stared at Helen's wavering hand with dread; the shears that I had used to cut Lucy's hat, Rosie's dress, Hester's shawl, were about to become an instrument of death. I did not know whether to keep my eyes on Helen, or on Lucy. Or on the scissors themselves.

Ford rose from his knee, strength coiled in his arms and legs, poised for movement. And as he stood, Helen dug the tip of the scissors into the flesh of Lucy's neck. My niece cried out as a bead of black blood welled up like spilled ink. "Stay back, you monster!" Helen screeched at her husband. "You'll never hold your daughter again!"

Ford, however, did not reply for in that moment, the sun burned through the clouds of snow and struck the surface of the dome, a hard shaft that split the room into light and shadow. Lucy screamed as sunlight flooded the arcade, scorching her eyes. Ford kicked Lucy's chair out from under her, toppling it onto its side and knocking her into the shadows. Lucy screamed again as her face struck the floor and Rosie, who had painstakingly made her way into the ballroom, arrived at her side in this moment, her loving arms untying the ribbons that bound Lucy's hands and feet.

Helen lunged at Ford, bearing down with the scissors. I threw myself on her, clawing at her arms as she stabbed wildly, but her strength outmatched mine and she threw me to the floor with little effort. "Margaret, you forget your allegiance!"

"Stop this madness!" I beseeched her.

She whirled on me. "You think it ends here? If I let this man walk free, you will be next!" She lifted the scissors and pointed them at my heaving chest. My heart pounded and felt dangerously exposed in the corset. "Unless I save you now," she pondered, lightly tracing the cold tip of the scissors from my collarbone to the cleft of my breasts. I crawled backward through the shadows, unable to find my feet. But I could not lose her; Helen mirrored my movements, the scissors staying in contact with my flesh.

"Or —" she said, pressing the tips deeper until they drew blood, "perhaps you might like to know what you're missing. It is, after all, a family affair." She licked her lips and winked.

Behind her, Ford approached in the shadows, but Helen's senses were keen. She held up her empty hand as though reciting an oath. "Stop, husband. If you advance further, so will my scissors. And as much as I know you would like to possess Meg body and soul, I would rather it be my teeth that make the first cut in her virgin flesh!"

My eyes fixed on Helen's teeth, a row of white blades. "Please, Helen, no," I whispered.

"Goodbye, Meg," she smiled as the scissors cut into my breast —

— and then I heard a sound which reminded me of spring. It was a bird, singing a tune that was joyfully familiar. Soutache!

The little bird plunged through the hole in the glass dome overhead, more hawk than sparrow, diving at Helen. His claws tangled in her hair and his beak pecked her face. She shrieked and swatted at him with the shears. But he was too quick for her, careful to stay out of her reach. I turned to run, blood cascading like a river between my breasts, but Helen's hand locked on my wrist, stopping my flight. She pulled me against her side, her jaws craned for my neck, but Soutache was relentless, beating his wings between her eyes. Then Ford was behind me, trying to grab hold of Helen as well, but she lashed out with the shears, slicing his chest, driving him back.

Soutache began another assault and she snapped at him with her teeth, catching one wing. Trapped, Soutache screeched, and Helen's fist snatched him and squeezed. With a burst of vigour, I wrapped my free hand about Helen's wrist and spun her into the circle of sunlight beneath the cupola. Surprised, she released Soutache who flew up into the safety of the dome.

The sun had melted the snow that capped the solarium and Helen's skin began to smoulder.

Our hands were still locked together and I tugged on her to return to the shadows. But her eyes locked on the blistering flesh of her hand that held the scissors and she collapsed onto her knees, dropping the shears. "I never imagined it so painful…"

I fell to her side and pulled her into my arms, trying to block the sun with my back. "Please, Helen," I begged. "If it is painful, come away." I grew desperate for she did not seem to hear me. I looked into the shadows and dimly saw the huddled forms of Rosie and Lucy, with Ford bent over them. They looked so much like a family, I almost forgot our terrible circumstances. But they could not help me. Only I could be here with Helen, here in the sunshine. I shrugged out of my skirt and threw it over her hair, which had also started to smoke.

Helen spoke. "Not the light. The light is not painful. I mean the life I endured." She looked at me, and as the rays hit her face, her cheeks started to sear. "I never imagined the pain Lucy would know when I agreed to save her. Never imagined the pain I would know."

"Let me help you. There may be a way! Ford said — "

"No!" She exclaimed, shrugging off my skirt.

Then Ford was there, crying out her name. He threw his body on hers, fighting to smother the flames that were beginning to dance along her fingertips. But Helen resisted his rescue, clawing and biting at his face, desperate to remain in the sun. I called for Rosie to help me separate them, for her strength would be in my favour, but she cowered at the edge of the arcade, frightened of the burgeoning fire, her own trauma still fresh on her skin.

Then, in a burst of strength, Ford hauled Helen out of the light, but she fought back, digging her nails into the dance floor, as though fighting a wave that dragged her out to sea. White sparks snapped in her dry hair and then, in a single rush, she combusted into flame. Helen's scream split the air and was echoed by Rosie's, who buried her face in Lucy's flour-dusted hair.

Ford still clutched Helen's legs, fighting to save her, but her upper body was fully consumed. I grabbed at him, pulling with all my might, dragging him away from the inferno. I dropped him in the shadows, and returned for my sister.

Helen was now fully engulfed in flame, but her eyes were calm as the fire snapped each of the stitches in her neck. And even though her head tipped to the side, no longer supported, her eyes remained on me.

She opened her mouth to sing as her lips blackened and split, "*Hey bonny lass your true love does linger, Under the starlight, a ring on your finger —*" She coughed from the smoke and wheezed, "*Bloody roses all about—*" and the rest was lost to the flames. Then she fell forward onto the floor, resembling a heap of branches thrown upon a bonfire.

I screamed, crawling forward to clutch the hem of her wedding gown, burning my fingers. I did not leave her side until she was nothing more than a pile of grey ash.

When I finally stood, I saw Rosie watching me from the corner of the solarium. Her face was streaked with tears, the sheet drawn up to obscure her face like she was some sort of tragic Greek statue.

"Johnathan," she said, pointing to a figure on the floor.

I craned my neck to see that Ford remained where I had left him, his hands badly burned and his face blackened from the flames. Lucy was curled into his side, coughing in the smoky atmosphere.

I stooped over him, and called his name. But he did not respond, and his head lolled against the floor, his face devoid of expression.

"Help me," I said to Rosie, who had come to stand behind me. But I was wrong. For Rosie had not moved from her place in the shadows. I didn't say anything as Carlisle lifted his brother in his arms.

It had been a very long day.

My back ached from leaning over the dining room table on which Carlisle had placed Ford. I had worked by the light of a lantern, stitching together the tendons, muscles, veins and flesh of his injured arm. While I worked, Carlisle tended his brother's burns, washing and cleaning them, and binding them with linen. And as much as he tried to salvage Ford's right hand, the flesh was blackened and required amputation.

And so Carlisle and I locked the dining room doors, so that Rosie and Lucy could not enter, and only Hester with her key — having returned with Carlisle — could come in with clean, boiling water. Soutache, who was always welcome, did not sing from his perch on the mantelpiece.

Carlisle and I talked only of the task at hand, sharing no other comment. He knew quite a bit about bones, such as the way they fit together at the wrist, and this is where we would cut. He also knew what his brother required to live. As it was, Ford would not be able to manufacture enough blood to survive the procedure and would need a supply for replenishment. Hester he tasked to return as soon as possible with a half a dozen live chickens.

And so we toiled in lamplight, I his assistant as he cut. He my assistant as I sewed. Hester appeared ever so often to squeeze a spongeful of fresh blood into Ford's parched mouth. And when the work was done, the detritus of our surgery burning in the fireplace, I laid down my needle and sighed. There was nothing left to do but allow Ford to rest.

I said nothing to Carlisle as I left the dining room, pushing open the front doors of Blueford Manor and stepping out into the cold winter sunshine. I held my face to the light and breathed deep, rejoicing as the cold air filled my lungs. In London, the High Street lampposts would be dressed for Christmas.

"Miss Jaye," a voice said, and I turned to see that Carlisle had followed me outside. His face looked drawn and haggard. Soot stained his hands as though he too, had been through the fire.

His eyes tracked the front of my corset where bloodstains announced the wound made by Helen's shears. "You will not let me tend to you, but you are injured as well." His voice did not sound his own.

"I am not hurt," I said, but it was a lie as my heart felt newly broken by Helen's death. Even deeper than it had been the first time I'd lost her. How many springs would come and go, flowers blossom and wither, before my heart was healed of Helen's anguish?

He stepped close and brushed ashes from my nose. Then his fingers trailed down the side of my neck to my collarbone, and the expanse of skin between my breasts, crusted with blood. "You lie."

It was the only lie I had told Carlisle. He, on the other hand…

I recoiled from his touch.

"Please, Margaret, you misunderstand," he said.

"Do I?" I asked.

"Hear me speak."

I searched his eyes, which were lighter than I'd thought. In the clear daylight, I could see green flecks dapple the grey depths of his irises, and I nodded, too tired to resist.

"On the day I drove Hester to Moorwood I steered the conversation towards her employment, and did she enjoy living on the estate as much as I did.

"I expected she might be spooked by the bats, but quite another matter had frightened her. She said if you were not so kind to her, she would think you unnatural. For she told me about a rather curious bird you possessed, and Lucille's newest plaything, a bat with a glove for its wing.

"This news shocked me, dear Margaret. I returned at once to question my brother. He assured me that you were untouched — unchanged. We argued, and I was unable to discern the best steps to ensure your safety. And so I left in a rage.

251

"And my rage distilled into doubt, and by that night I'd succumbed to the belief you had become one of them. Naturally, I questioned the note delivered via Soutache (himself a startling harbinger), believing instead that you wished to ensnare me in a trap. The handwriting was shaky, and appeared very much like Rosie's since she'd turned and so my suspicions gained strength. But when you came to the cottage, I saw that indeed you were very much alive," — his voice cracked — "and very much injured." His fingers were gentle as they traced the bandages on my arm.

"I was on the Southern Cape when I received the letter." Carlisle took my hand firmly, not allowing me to pull away. "I believe it was the winter of '94. My brother had fallen out of touch, not responding to my letters. So naturally, I was delighted to hear word." He paused and I was reminded of how both Rosie and I had lost contact with Helen.

"But the words inside were not ones of salutation," he continued, "but full of torment and despair. He named himself a demon, not worthy of life. He wrote that he had left the fleet and sold his property in London, moving his family instead to the country. I immediately ceased my research of penguins." Carlisle glanced at me, his brow furrowed. "I am not ordained, Meg. I am — or was — a professor. Of ornithology," he added.

"Once I arrived at Blueford, I did not leave my brother's side for weeks. All the while he rampaged, but I did not believe his ravings, such mad words about the creature that bit him and the cravings he experienced. I thought him delusional, stricken by some foreign fever, and I pored over encyclopaedias of disease and illness. Helen thought he was lost to the bottle, as many seamen become, and so cloistered herself with Lucy, who was frightened by her father's temper.

"And then, some months later, I was out watching bats and I saw Lucy chasing mice in the orchard. Each mouse she caught, she bit into the flesh, and swallowed the blood. All the while, she peered over her shoulder to ensure she was alone. And not long after, I began to see all the oddities of my niece and brother. My mind wrestled with the knowledge. How could such a creature exist? One that had no heartbeat? That defiled Natural Law? That conformed to no taxonomic rank? Like a bat, the only mammal that flies, a creature that flouts the laws of its class.

"I abandoned my studies of bird evolution, and focused on the occult, paganism and nocturnal creatures.

"As I grew to accept my brother and niece — and eventually Helen — as they were, I took up permanent residence at Blueford. I knew I could never again teach the sciences, for their laws no longer applied to the world I knew. Johnathan had been my elder brother, but soon I became his senior.

"But more than losing faith in my career, I stayed because I could not leave his side. I am his keeper; I run the estate, manage the finances, help my brother and niece maintain appearances. I took our mother's name and fabricated a profession, that I might be a benign and nondescript tenant of the estate.

"I am sorry I have wronged you, Margaret, by the lies I have told, and the truths I've not spoken. Sometimes I am half-mad myself, for my mind still struggles with the truth of my brother's life."

He rubbed his thumb over the back of my hand, lost in thought for a moment. Then his eyes met mine, from a faraway place. "That day you saw me watching you by the river — I had to make sure Lucy didn't bite you. I wanted Ford to send you away, to keep you safe, but he would not hear of it. He seemed to think you could somehow save Rosie.

"When you asked me to speak to Rosie, it was an opportunity that Heaven sent. Ford coaxed Rosie from the chimney flue and arranged private counsel for she and I. I played the part of a clergyman and demanded your sister keep her distance. I explained to her that being wed would not lift the curse. In fact, darkening the door of a church would result only in her incineration, but she would not listen to such warnings.

"But being greatly troubled by her sins, I appealed to her guilt: I reminded her that the greatest of all her trespasses would be to expose you to her sickness. It is terrible theology," he admitted, with a weak smile, "but it was all she needed to hear. She agreed — comforted by your presence at Blueford — to remain in hiding and enjoy your company from afar.

"And you are stubborn, Margaret, my dear. I desperately hoped you would give up on your sister, pack your bags, and return to London. When you did not go, I pleaded with Ford to frighten you on your way. But he would not do it. I saw in his eyes what you did for him — the liveliness, the life, you had brought back into his home. He was the happiest I had seen in a long while."

Did I not make Carlisle happy in this way, I wondered? His hands on me told me he at one time had cared. But he had done everything in his power to drive me away, and I knew he could live without me. But in this moment, I was not sure I could live without him.

The pain of this realisation robbed me of words. As I stood silent, head bowed, Carlisle dropped my hand and stepped away. "I understand," he said, "my brother is very magnetic."

I responded, in a dull voice, "Only as a compass, for he was at the centre of everything — the one person in at Blueford who knew the truth about Rosie. About Helen and Lucy." I paused. "And the truth about me."

Yes, Ford was always able to see deep into my heart. He'd understood the love I felt for my sisters and niece, and even Soutache, better than I did myself. He probably even understood my feelings for Carlisle in a way that I did not.

I looked at Carlisle through a mist of tears. "And what of the truth about you?"

"The truth is I would not have allowed any harm to come to you. The truth is I was a shadow at Ford's back, watching his every step. The truth is, my heart had stopped beating the moment my brother's did." He came to me then and clasped my hands to his chest. "Until I met you."

My heart expanded — it felt as giant as the glass dome capping the ballroom — until it cracked open, and hope and happiness burst free. I wanted to tell him my heart beat to match his, that my lips, dry and cracked from the inferno, thirsted for his. But I did not have to say anything, for his mouth found mine and, blissfully, I drank in his breath.

⚷

Lucy was tucked into the bed in my room, while Flue nestled in her damp ringlets. Rosie lay next to her, a book in her hands. It was the first time I had known Lucy to sleep at night. Poor thing — how exhausted she was.

We'd bathed in succession by the fire, helping one another scrub away the soot and ash. Though Lucy had suffered the loss of her mother — again— she had laughed in the bathtub, though for only a moment, forgetting the tragedy while Rosie and I scrubbed her with bubbles.

I sat on the bed next to Rosie and began to comb her cropped red curls. The skeletal bat danced as I worked, careful to stay out of the path of the comb's teeth. From the bedpost, Soutache sang a lullaby, but his was the only cheerful voice in the house.

"You'll be in black no more," I said to Rosie. It was time the women of Blueford Manor wore all the colours of a garden. And I would be happy to make such dresses.

She smiled at me over her shoulder, "Does that include the chimneys?"

"Especially the chimneys," I said.

She sighed and stilled my hand. "What am I to do, Magpie?"

"You are to be married," I said.

"Oh, Meg," she said, with great tenderness as she touched my face. "I do not believe it is me that Johnathan loves."

I turned away to set aside the comb, though in fact it was to hide the colour in my cheeks. "It is only because you have not given him the opportunity to do so. Rest now. We'll talk in the morning." Then I placed my sister's book on the bed stand, kissed

255

her cheek and left the room.

I went to the kitchen, for I was desperately hungry. How long since I'd eaten? And during that time, how much we had all endured. I knew Hester was asleep and so I busied myself slicing bread and salted ham.

There was a noise at the door, and I lifted my head to see Ford standing there, watching me.

"You should be in bed," I said, though he looked alarmingly recovered having drank dry several more of the chickens.

"I cannot sleep," he replied, shuffling over to the kitchen and dropping into a chair. "For I am always awake at this time." He pushed aside one of the chairs, and motioned for me to sit next to him. I claimed my repast and a glass of water, and joined him.

"Would you like anything?" I asked, gesturing to my plate.

Ford shook his head. "Our kind do not require food."

"Not at all?" I queried.

"Taking meals was simply a way to bring us together, to remember the way we used to be. The things that used to bring us joy. And like calipers, to measure the length of a day. Please, eat," he said, "Do not mind my presence."

I looked at him and said, "I do not mind your presence at all," and took a mouthful of bread and chewed.

He examined his truncated right wrist, bound and bandaged, and lonely for its hand. "You know Margaret, for a man that will not age, I suddenly feel very old."

"You will learn to use your left hand, as you did your right," I said, taking a long swallow of water.

"Until then, a cripple," he frowned.

"Say you lost it at sea," I advised.

"The woes of a pirate?" he asked, raising his brow.

I laughed and ate the last of the meat.

"Thank you for trying to save Helen. And for saving Rosie," I said, setting aside my empty plate.

"But it was I who cursed your sisters to such an existence in the first place," he said, selecting a strand of my hair and twirling it between the fingers of his good hand.

There was a chasm of grief between us. Sins that could not be washed away. For every day that I saw Rosie I would be reminded of what had occurred to Helen. But every day, as well, I would remind myself of Ford's promise.

"You said you would care for my sister. For Rosie," I said, and I could feel my throat tighten. "Do you intend to keep that promise?" It was hard for me to talk, as the touch of his fingers on my hair set off shivers along my skin.

He sat silent for a long while, his fingers in my hair and I could not meet his eyes. "I do," he said at last, releasing my curl.

And for some reason, I wanted to cry.

His voice sounded rough. "She is good to Lucy. She is good to me. She will bring us some happiness." He paused, flexing his left hand as it rested on the table, watching the tendons tighten and release. Tighten and release. "Does that bother you, Margaret?" he asked. "That I will spend my years with Rosamund instead of you?"

"Not at all," I whispered, and even I did not know if I was lying.

"Look at me," he said, and I did. His eyes were bright with tears of his own. And although there was a smile on his face, he looked sad, as though something he very much desired had slipped from his grasp and fallen to the bottom of the sea. "Her life shall be joyful, I promise," he assured me, taking my hand and squeezing my fingers. "Until our last days."

I blinked away my tears and said the only words I could. "Thank you."

"And what of you, dearest Meg?" he asked, after a good long while. "What star will you follow?"

1923

Millicent Willis burst into the salon wearing a dress from last year's collection. Inspired by the discovery of King Tutankhamun's tomb, I had designed day suits and dresses that featured beaded lapels in peacock-coloured stripes. Upon seeing my designs, Millicent had eagerly replaced her penchant for Indian idioms in favour of Egyptian exoticism. As was the rage on the continent and in America, Millicent lined her eyes in black kohl and painted a scarlet pout upon her lips, the selfsame lips that proclaimed Carter one of our own, and if anyone had the right to Deco style, it was us Londoners.

But today's undertaking required more risk than new cosmetics or clothes. Millicent settled into the salon chair with a nervous giggle as the hairdresser loosened her chignon. She looked at me and winked.

Hester would never do such a thing as this. But then, old fashioned as it was, Hester's braid, coiled into a tidy bun, was entirely proper for the wife of Harrowgate's new vicar ('new' being relative as they had been wed and installed in the vicarage for more than fifteen years now). She was role model to not only the parish, but her own brood of five children.

Her eldest daughter, Maggie, lived at Blueford where she kept house and cared for my sister's family. And under her cheerful guidance, the house was not half as dreary as I once remembered it. Maggie and her siblings, being rather eager naturalists, had brightened every carved rabbit and raven with a lick of wood polish. Gay curtains replaced those that had hung heavy with dust, and colourful patchwork upholstered the threadbare furnishings. On the grounds, a riot of colour bloomed each spring, for Maggie and her siblings had planted flowers throughout the estate hoping to attract a multitude of insects, and thus restore Blueford's bat population to its former numbers.

Tomorrow, at dusk, I would be on the estate once more, and would join Maggie to watch for the bats returning to roost. And I was hoping to spy three oddities in the flock — one which flew with a glove for a wing, another that resembled a pile of matchsticks, and my own little Soutache — who long ago had joined his mystical brethren in the skies.

But more than the bats and my bird, I was eager to see my family for we were travelling to Blueford to celebrate my birthday. It had been a few months since our last visit and now, Lucy would be home from boarding school, which was always Rosie's favourite time of year. Each year, our niece travelled abroad to a new foreign school. Though forever age six in appearance, she boasted more than a decade of studies and spoke a half a dozen languages. Now no matter where she travelled, she was considered bright for her age.

As Lucy's disposition brightened by her ability to see the world, so brightened our memories of Helen. Now we all recalled only her sweetest aspects, and in particular her talent. Her flower paintings had become famous, purchased by elite in both England and abroad. Such funds kept Blueford's residents in a comfortable lifestyle. That is, when the Master and Mistress were at home, for as often as Lucy was installed on the continent, my sister and her husband cruised the seas, shuttered away in their stateroom, either relishing the romance of the rolling waves or burying their noses in the latest Agatha Christie pocketbook.

"Ready?" I smiled at my friend.

"Heave ho!" Millicent exclaimed, always a good sport.

I smiled at myself in the mirror, confident that the lady's short hairstyle was here to stay, much like automobiles and electricity. In past years, I'd learned to style Rosie's clipped locks in a myriad of ways, all which flattered her face. And hats, once so indispensable, were no longer the staple accessory of the day. No, a bob with a fringe would be the new brim over my eyes.

The hairdresser combed out my long hair. And I noticed that a few strands of grey now lined my chestnut curls.

"You'll never be the same," Carlisle said, with a smile in his voice.

I laughed and caught my husband's eye in the mirror. He was seated in a chair by the salon door, an issue of the *Evening Standard* in his lap, though his warm, loving eyes were not on the paper, but on our daughter Helena who crouched on the floor, her fingers seeking out the desiccated remains of a long-dead spider.

"Hurry, Mummy!" my twelve-year-old beauty sang, her fingers capturing her quarry, "I want to see!"

But before the hairdresser could begin, Helena danced to my side and cupped her hands so I might view her find. I peered into the nest of fingers to see a dry white spider unfold its legs and breathe new life. She smiled at me and laughed, and I kissed her forehead. I winked at Millicent as Helena ran to show her father — who always took great delight in her accomplishments — what she had done.

The hairdresser glanced at me and I nodded.

Yes, I was ready.

Then the hairdresser clipped a lock of my hair exposing my left ear. Lightened of its weight, the lock sprang up and curled under my jawbone. As the hairdresser continued to trim, more and more of my neck became visible — long, thin and white but for a single blue vein that travelled its length.

Acknowledgements

Thank you to our brilliant beta readers who saw the book in a much rougher form: Sam, Cynthia, Elizabeth, Joanne, Dana, Andrew and Jenny.

Thank you, Corene, for running your editorial eye over the pages prior to publication.

Thank you, Kate, for being a wellspring of encouragement and faith for both of us throughout this novel's journey.

To all of you — your input was invaluable.

Deepest and sincerest thanks to Kathryn for being my number one coach and helping me complete *Bluebeard's Bride* when my darling baby daughter distracted me from creative output. Many thanks to my husband Steven for supporting me in every dream. Your emotional and financial support made this book possible. And to my grandmother Ev, thank you for your generosity.

~ Roberta

Immense gratitude to Roberta for introducing me to the moody, suspenseful and utterly engaging world of *Bluebeard's Bride*. And for having the confidence to allow me to play within the pages of its gothic landscape.

Finally, and as always, thank you to my family. Especially to my beautiful boys — Nathan and Andrew — and my girl, the divine Analeigh. I do this for you. Know that your dreams can come true.

~ Kathryn

And thank you, dear readers, for choosing our story.

Roberta Cottam

Roberta's short fiction and poetry is published in several issues of *The Claremont Review* and been featured in the anthology, *Naming the Baby. Shakespearian Shopping Theatre,* co-written with her sister Kathryn Cottam, was short-listed for The Arts Club in Vancouver. She holds a BFA with distinction from the University of Victoria and was a faculty member of the Art Institute of Vancouver where she taught one of her favourite subjects, Costume History. Roberta has illustrated for several international brands, including Lululemon, and has collaborated on clothing designs with Nelly Furtado and Joe Jonas through the non-profit organization, Me to We. Find her online at **www.robertacottam.com**

Roberta believes a woman's most beautiful quality is her sense of adventure.

Kathryn Cottam

Kathryn Cottam holds a B.A. in English Literature from the University of Victoria and is a graduate of the Vancouver Film School Screenwriting Program. Kathryn has been both a story editor and screenwriting judge. Her script, *Bus Station Zombies*, was a semi-finalist at the Austin Film Festival Writing Competition and her first novel, *The Shoemaker: A Tale of Love, Magic & Unnatural Acts* was published last year by Fox Tale Press and was nominated for best Fantasy Novel of 2013 by *InD'Tale Magazine*. Visit her website at **www.kathrycottam.com**

A gothic novel, a cup of tea and a blustery storm is Kathryn's idea of a perfect evening.

Also by Kathryn Cottam

the
SHOEMAKER
A Tale of Love, Magic & Unnatural Acts

CHAPTER ONE

EDWARD CORDWAINER is the ordinary son of an extraordinary father. He was born and raised in the small village of Houndstooth, under the magnificent height of Utterly Peak, a mountain so high its top is always hidden by clouds, and the village itself is rarely touched by hot summer sun. Houndstooth owes its existence to its proximity to the King's Summer Palace. For when royalty is in residence, it is the citizens of Houndstooth that keep the King, Queen, Princess and their multitude of servants supplied with fresh crusty breads, deep fried pickles, sweet honey peaches and dry salt pork.

Edward's father, Thomas the Elder, loves Houndstooth because he can name every friend and foe that walks its cobblestone streets. He reminds Edward daily how fortunate they are to reside in a place where no one is a stranger. Little does he know, this is precisely why Edward dislikes the village. For in a place where you know everyone, and everyone knows you, it is difficult to hold secrets. Not that Edward has many, or any, secrets. T'is just that he wishes he could have at least one.

Edward's mother, Marianne, died when he was but seven years young and Thomas did his very best to ensure the boy was not without a mother's love. In fact, he enrolled various women of the village in helping to raise his son. Chicken casseroles, pork pot pies and lamb stews would arrive from the kitchen of the Grocer's wife, Cynthia Hardcastle, each week for Sunday supper. Thus ensuring Edward's belly was full for the week ahead. Jenny Juniper, the tailor's wife, would sew him a new school uniform each September and thus Edward was never teased for wearing pants with cuffs that were well above his ankles. And finally, Betsy Candlewick, the local baker, provided Edward and Thomas with leftover raisin biscuits each day thus ensuring the time honored Houndstooth tradition of afternoon tea-time was maintained in their household. But no matter the meat, bread or suit, Edward was convinced Marianne, had she lived, would have done better.

Local rumor swirled regarding his mother's death on Utterly Peak. The Grocer whispered that Marianne had discovered Thomas's many affairs and so she had climbed high above the clouds and snow and jumped to her death. While the Tailor was equally certain that Thomas had always been faithful, but was wed to a woman with a touch of the brain fever and who, while wandering about the mountain one fateful day, accidentally fell to her death. Regardless, whatever new version of the story reached Edward, he adamantly refused to believe the ones in which his mother took her own life.

Yes, t'was true she was unhappy in Houndstooth. For at night while he lay in bed, and his father was in the shop below cutting leather for tomorrow's shoes, he would hear his mother pace the creaking floorboards of her bedroom, muttering and wailing. He chose to blame her sorrow on his father and not any weakness inherited from her own mad mother. For, Marianne was from the city and coming to live in Houndstooth had broken her heart.

If only Thomas had packed their belongings and moved the lot of them back to Ferrybone, where Marianne was happy. Perhaps then she would not have climbed Utterly Peak, would not have accidentally fallen and would not have been dashed into pieces on sharp black rocks.

Edward knows her death was accidental for she would never have chosen to desert her son to his father's care, to the village of Houndstooth, to the meager life of the shoemaking trade. Marianne despised this life. She despaired at the calluses the hard wooden broom handle gave her soft palms as she swept up scrap shoe leather every afternoon in the shop. She hated crawling across the rough wooden floorboards on hand and knee, searching each crack and cranny for the hog hair bristles that fell from her husband's hand as he stitched the leather. And she especially loathed the ugly (yet sturdy) dirt brown boots Thomas made for the farmers who worked the field and the dull (yet supportive) sandals for the women who ran the local shops. The only reason Marianne stayed, the only reason she tolerated this life, was Edward. But she also decreed that he was to have an education and not a trade. And she made her husband agree that when old enough, Edward would be sent abroad for university so that he could become a man of great importance.

But then Marianne died and everything changed.

Edward, who had been praised by his grade school teachers for his cunning and logic, began to miss more and more of his schooling in order to help his father in the shop. For with Marianne dead, Edward was now required to assist Thomas in his labors. And the more school Edward missed, the more his grades fell and the less inclined he was to apply himself to make up his studies. And while, yes, the hog hair bristles seemed to fall more quickly to the floor than ever before, and his father's hands shook with the threading, and his eyes squinted with the cutting, all these things seemed deliberately acquired in order to sabotage Edward's future promise.

And then the morning of the day before Edward was to graduate, he rose to find the kitchen stove cold. This was unprecedented. All his life, Edward remembered rising to find a pot of lukewarm congealed porridge on the stove from his father's breakfast, eaten hours earlier, so he could take advantage of the morning sun that filtered in through the shop window. But that morning, there was no pot, no porridge. Moreover, his father was not to be found in the shop, the kitchen or in the water closet out back. Edward retraced his steps, upstairs to his father's bedroom above the shop, and knocked on the door. There, Thomas sat on the bed, his bare feet flat on the floor, his once muscular hands, now gnarled like tree roots, settled in his lap. He raised his head to look straight in Edward's eyes and said: "Who's there?"

Perhaps it was the way the morning sun lit his father's face, but for the first time, Edward saw how completely the milky white cataracts had drawn across the old man's eyes like curtains, shutting off all vision.

And with the loss of Thomas the Elder's sight, came the loss of Edward's dream to leave Houndstooth. For being a shoemaker who kept his prices reasonable, Thomas did not have the funds to employ someone to cook, clean or care for him. Moreover, there was no other Shoemaker in the village, and none willing to relocate to so northern a destination, and thus the shop could not be sold. In the end, Thomas refused to close his doors simply because he was blind. Edward became his eyes and hands, constructing shoes under his father's guidance (though they tended to look nothing like what Thomas used to make). At times, Edward doubted his father's blindness. After all, how could his sight be there one day, only to be gone the next?

Edward entertained daily thoughts of running away and leaving the old man to his misery. But his feet rebelled against such action and he would find himself paralyzed, and unable to move. For his mind could not stomach the cruel things the villagers would say about him behind his back should he choose this path.

So like his father, before him, Edward became Houndstooth's Shoemaker.

But the choice to stay was like a fish bone caught in his throat, always threatening to choke him.

Arriving Fall 2014 by K. M. Tremills,
Kathryn Cottam & Roberta Cottam

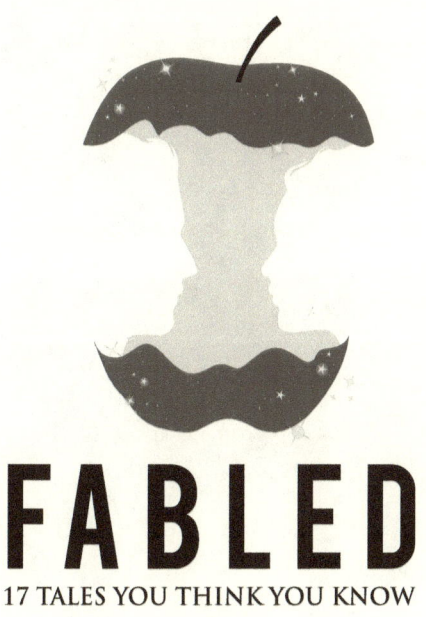

FABLED

17 TALES YOU THINK YOU KNOW

Twelve Dancing Princesses
Rumplestilskin
Pandora's Box
& other stories you thought you knew

A volume of seventeen contemporary stories inspired by fairy tales, myths and nursery rhymes.

From the bestselling authors of *Messenger*, *The Shoemaker: A Tale of Love, Magic & Unnatural Acts* and *Bluebeard's Bride*.

Fox Tale
PRESS